Desperate in DC

A multimedia novel of marriage,
motherhood and money,
set in the exurbs of the nation's capital.

Desperate in DC

BY CRYSTAL WALKER AND PHOEBE THOMPSON

Published by Desperate in DC
Washington DC, MMXIII

www.desperateindc.com

ISBN 978-0-9898532-0-0

Graphic art and book design: Kelly Anne Day

Back cover photography: Kerri Redding

Web support: Niki Van

Media strategist: Allen Media Strategies LLC, Burke Allen, Jessica Lloyd, Will Bowers and AJ Rice

Invaluable reading, editing and general life guidance: Christine Gordon

Printed in The United States

The relationship between real life events and people captured in this novel is purely coincidental.

Trust us, it's fiction.

Chapter 1

August, 2012 Vol. 41, Issue 8
Always FREE, but donations appreciated!

Please direct submissions and inquiries to:
whining@villagepress.com
P.O. Box 357 Village Town, MD

VILLAGE WHINER

Your trusty monthly newsletter of
the "Most Livable Village," 1989
Village Times Magazine

Village Whiner: August

The Board of Managers is delighted to announce that a brand new Holier than Thou Foods will be built right here in the Village on the vacant lot adjacent to the Episcopal church on Eastern Avenue. This follows months of spirited debate about the merits of building a common retail site versus a community playground, but plans for the latter were ultimately shelved when it was discovered there was no legal way to use public funds and still exclude children who lived outside the Village. It is a shame that so many residents who objected to the store just so happened to be out of town at the time the final vote was taken, but HTTF has assumed that they will take the needs of the community into consideration in their plans. In the meantime they encourage residents to contact them with any suggestions or concerns via email at
complaining@voiceless@wwelhavepermission.com

Welcome New Neighbors Gathering

Please join us at the Village Green on Sunday, August 24 for our annual gathering to welcome new families to the neighborhood. I am sure you are all aware how lucky we are to live where we do, within walking distance of the nation's capital, and yet tucked away across the Maryland border, where we can enjoy the safety and tranquility of our green and leafy hamlet, without having to think about homelessness, crime, or un-plowed streets. It is not for nothing that our Village motto is 'The best of all worlds.'

This year we have several new families in our midst, including Professor and Mr. Lieberman from Trenton, New Jersey, the Brown family from Boston, whose two boys are in their first and final years at Harvard and Yale, respectively, and the Walker family from Kansas City and their three charming children and brand new addition, a beautiful baby girl. It is between us the Village Green once again fills up with the joyful sound of children's laughter. (New neighbors, please note: loud games and talking are discouraged on the Village Green after 6pm). We hope you will join us for the Sunday ice cream social to welcome one and all.

At this time, the Village Country Club would like to extend an opportunity for new and existing residents to apply. New residents are generally not considered for membership until they have been residents for a full calendar year, to give other members a chance to get to know them. Until then, potential applicants are encouraged to sign themselves and their children up to our own dear Miss Gertrude Manner's social etiquette class in preparation. Miss Gertrude's Manners and More takes place the first Thursday of every month at the Village Hall from 6-9 pm (see below). Black tie (for boys) and ankle length gowns (for girls) are required.

Diversity Group

For those Village residents who are looking for an alternative to the Village Country Club, particularly those raised in foreign cultures or Takoma Park, Maryland (aka, San Francisco East), we offer the opportunity to join the Village Diversity Group, which reaches out to under-represented groups within our community. Our goal is to meet these people where they are and serve the global community in ways it may not even know it needs. New member meeting this Wednesday, August 6 at 7 pm. The dress code is casual, although organic, sustainable natural fibers are preferred. There will be no child, pet or elder care available at this meeting, so please make any appropriate arrangements before coming.

Tennis Team

The Village Tennis team is on hiatus through the end of this month, while the clay courts are re-surfaced. Play will resume in September, but we trust team members are continuing to practice in the interim. For those without access to private courts, there are some very pleasant public courts located across the DC line on Livingston and Grant St. NW. Please note: the Montgomery County Parks and Recreation Service has asked us to remind residents that no way to reserve these facilities, no matter how much you pay in property tax.

Miss Gertrude

Does your child know how to use a knife and fork, ask a lady to dance, or how to exit a limousine without flashing their undergarments for lack of them to the world? We may live in modern times, but these skills are still vitally important for getting ahead in life, particularly here in the nation's capital, where a person is judged by the strength of his or her handshake. Unfortunately, Miss Gertrude has noticed a precipitous decline in performance for all three children 5 and older, with classes scheduled for the third Thursday of the month, from 6-9 pm at the Village Hall. Classes are by invitation only, so look out for yours in the mail. For more information, please email
miss.classetiquette@villagevenue.com

Application to Join Village Country Club

Name:

Address:

Number of persons in your household: (including offspring, but excluding house hold help, unless number exceeds 6, in which case please list titles and duties):

1. _____   4. _____
2. _____   5. _____
3. _____   6. _____

Occupation:

Sponsors (please list at least 10.) Must be existing Club members, and not related either to applicant or each other:

1.
2.
3.
4.
5.
6.
7.
8.
9.
10.

Annual Income (rounding down but not up to nearest 50k is acceptable):

Which facilities are you most likely to use (check all that apply):

☐ Tennis
☐ Golf
☐ Pool
☐ Gym
☐ Ice-rink
☐ Bowling Alley
☐ Bridge Club
☐ Mahjong
☐ Men's steam room (new!)
☐ Gentleman's Lounge
☐ Childcare
☐ Ladies' Lounge (please note: this room is not due for renovation until 2014)

August, 2012 Vol. 41, Issue 8
Always FREE, but donations appreciated

Please direct submissions and inquiries to:
whining@villagepress.com
P.O. Box 357 Village Town, MD

Village Whiner: August

The Board of Managers is delighted to announce that a brand new Holier than Thou Foods will be built right here in the Village on the vacant lot adjacent to the Episcopal church on Eastern Avenue. This follows months of spirited debate about the merits of building a commercial retail site versus a community playground, but plans for the latter were ultimately shelved when it was discovered there was no legal way to use public funds and still exclude children who lived outside the Village. It is a shame that so many residents who objected to the store just so happened to be out of town at the time the final vote was taken, but HTTF has assured us that they will take the needs of the community into consideration in their plans. In the meantime, they encourage residents to contact them with any suggestions or concerns via email at info@complainingisuselessnowwehavepermission.com.

Architect sketch

Welcome New Neighbors Gathering

Please join us at the Village Green on Sunday, August 24 for our annual gathering to welcome new families to the neighborhood. I am sure you are all aware how lucky we are to live where we do - within walking distance of the nation's capital, and yet tucked away across the Maryland border, where we can enjoy the safety and tranquility of our green and leafy hamlet, without having to think about homelessness, crime, or unplowed streets. It's not for nothing that our Village motto is 'The best of all worlds'.

This year, we have several new families in our midst, including Professor and Mr. Lieberman from Trenton, New Jersey; the Brown family from Boston, whose two boys are in their first and final years at Harvard and Yale, respectively; and the Walker family from Kansas City and their three charming children and brand new addition, a beautiful baby girl. It is particularly refreshing to welcome so many youngsters into our midst, and to listen as the Village Green once again fills up with the joyful sound of children's laughter. (New neighbors, please note: loud games and talking are discouraged on the Village Green after 6pm). We hope you will join us for the Sunday ice-cream social to welcome one and all.

At this time, the Village Country Club would like to extend an opportunity for new and existing residents to apply. New residents are generally not considered for membership until they have been residents for a full calendar year, to give other members a chance to get to know them. Until then, potential applicants are encouraged to sign themselves and their children up for our own dear Miss Gertrude Manner's social etiquette class in preparation. Miss Gertrude's Manners and More takes place the first Thursday of every month at the Village Hall from 6-9 pm (see below). Black tie (for boys) and ankle-length gowns (for girls) are required.

Diversity Group

For those Village residents who are looking for an alternative to the Village Country Club, particularly those raised in foreign cultures or Takoma Park, Maryland (aka, San Francisco East), we offer the opportunity to join the Village Diversity Group, which reaches out to under-represented groups within our community. Our goal is to meet these people where they are and serve the global community in ways it may not even knows it needs. New member meeting this Wednesday, August 6 at 7 pm. The dress code is casual, although organic, sustainable natural fibers are preferred. There will be no child, pet or elder care available at this meeting, so please make any appropriate arrangements before coming.

Tennis Team

The Village Tennis team is on hiatus through the end of this month, while the club courts are resurfaced. Play will resume in September, but we trust team members are continuing to practice in the interim. For those without access to private courts, there are some very pleasant public courts located across the DC line on Livingston and Grant St., NW. Please note, the Montgomery County Parks and Recreation Service has asked us to remind residents there is no way to reserve these facilities, no matter how much you pay in property tax.

Miss Gertrude

Does your child know how to use a knife and fork, ask a lady to dance, or how exit a limousine without flashing their undergarments (or lack of them) to the world? We may live in modern times, but these skills are still vitally important for getting ahead in life, particularly here in the nation's capital, where a person is judged by the strength of his or her handshake. Unfortunately, Miss Gertrude has noticed a precipitous decline in performance for all three skills, so she is extending her Manners and More class to children 5 and older, with classes scheduled for the third Thursday of the month, from 6-9 pm at the Village Hall. Classes are by invitation only, so look out for yours in the mail. For more information, please email: msg@class4peoplewhohavenone.com.

Village Vendor of the Month
Perky Sparks

She worked for our first President Bush in the office of protocol, then stayed home to raise her two adorable children. Now, with both children at boarding school, she's ready to "do" for your house what you never knew you wanted. Perky's defiantly WASPish taste might be considered by some to be stuffy, but if you are looking to exude the whiff of old money, she's just the woman for the job. Serious email inquiries welcome at ishop4snobs@perkybydesign.com.

Application to Join Village Country Club

Name:

Address:

Number of persons in your household: (including offspring, but excluding household help, unless number exceeds 6, in which case please list titles and duties):

1. _____
2. _____
3. _____
4. _____
5. _____
6. _____

Annual Income (rounding down but not up to nearest 50k is acceptable): _____

Occupation:

Sponsors (please list at least 10.) Must be existing Club members, and not related either to applicant or each other:

1. _____
2. _____
3. _____
4. _____
5. _____
6. _____
7. _____
8. _____
9. _____
10. _____

Which facilities are you most likely to use (check all that apply):

- ☐ Tennis
- ☐ Golf
- ☐ Pool
- ☐ Gym
- ☐ Ice-rink
- ☐ Bowling Alley
- ☐ Bridge Club
- ☐ Mahjong
- ☐ Men's steam room (new!)
- ☐ Gentlemen's Lounge
- ☐ Childcare
- ☐ Ladies' Lounge (please note: this room is not due for renovation until 2014)

Wednesday, August 8

From: momof3law@hotmail.com
To: phoebegb@sahmsrule.net
Subject: Birth Announcement

Do you mind taking a quick look at Baby's birth announcement to make sure I've avoided any major faux pas before I send it to the printers?

Our friends and former neighbors in Kansas City are clamoring for news, so I need to get this out as soon as possible, even if I haven't slept a wink in the 48 hours since we left the hospital. Turns out, Baby clings to my boobs in the same intense way George did long b/f any of our cherubs arrived.

From: phoebegb@sahmsrule.net
To: momof3law@hotmail.com

I don't see any attachment. Can u resend? Btw, you might want to consider getting a new email address, now that you are a mom of 4!

From: momof3law@hotmail.com
To: phoebegb@sahmsrule.net

Generally don't like to use my work email for personal correspondence, but it seems like everyone else in DC does. Any idea why that is?

From: phoebegb@sahmsrule.net
To: momof3law@hotmail.com

They do it to prove how important they are – a practice I would encourage you to adopt, so long as you aren't engaged in a torrid workplace affair, or revealing something you wouldn't like the firm's email monitor to see.

From: crystalwalker@sterlingmorris.com
To: phoebegb@sahmsrule.net

Sterling Morris said it was OK for me to use my new work email, so long as I make sure to include the disclaimer at the bottom. Trust me, an affair is the last thing I need in my life right now, between unpacking the moving boxes and getting all four cherubs settled before I start my new job. Here's the birth announcement–I think I attached it this time!

CONFIDENTIALITY NOTICE: This e-mail communication and any attachments may contain confidential, privileged and titillating information for the use of the designated recipients named above. You are not authorized to forward this e-mail to anyone unless authorized, or for purposes of idle gossip. If you are not the intended recipient, you are hereby notified that you have received this communication in error (or possibly on purpose) and that any review, disclosure, dissemination, distribution or copying of it or its contents is prohibited, no matter how juicy it is. If you have received this communication in error, please destroy all copies of this email and any attachment. Do not, whatever you do, forward it onto all your friends first!

Skye Chat
crystalwalker
oops. Wasn't expecting you to be online at 4 a.m. Hope my email didn't wake you. Only time I get on computer is when Baby is nursing but rest of the world is asleep. If I prop her up on a pillow, I cAn even tYpe with tow hands!

phoebethompson
this is actually best time of day to reach me. May no longer have babies to juggle, but I've developed habit of waking up for several hours during middle of night ever since twins were born. Used to drive me crazy till realized it's actually most peaceful part of my day. I can catch up on email and shop online w/o being interrupted to service anyone else's needs.

crystalwalker
that's gr8, but aren't u exhausted?

phoebethompson
permanently, altho' find the occasional catnap at stop lights helps.

crystalwalker
btw, thank u for driving me to hospital the other day, after George was unable to leave work to take me. Hard to know what could be more important than the birth of one's last child, but speeding tix will be a glorious reminder of how fast u drove to get me there.

phoebethompson
It was honor to be present at the birth of yr 4th child – and what a beauty she is, too! Also a thrill to be caught up in an actual birth drama – the urgent phone call; the legitimate need to speed; the fact that no one else, including the putative father of your unborn child, could be there for you during yr hour of need.

crystalwalker
must confess, I was a little intimidated when u first stopped by with homemade beetroot and black bean muffins to welcome us to neighborhood a couple of weeks back. Not sure if it was the perfect blonde bob, the extra-short tennis dress or the devoted at-home mothering. But now that you've stared down my cervix w/o flinching, feel sure we'll be BFFLs.

phoebethompson
you and George caused quite a sensation round the Village when you first moved in, as I don't think anyone had seen quite so many children from just one marriage. Here in DC, only the very wealthy or those on their second or third families (the two usually go together) breed with such abandon. Also refreshing to see a family of brunettes in this enclave of natural and highlighted blonds (I will leave you to guess which I am). And delightful to be able to spend so much time with you during a month in which every other resident and their dog in the Village seems to be out of town. Glad my

words of support proved helpful during active labor, which you insisted on enduring, like so many DC super-mums, without any kind of narcotic relief. I made the mistake of giving birth to twins in my native London, where the midwife took it upon herself to let epidural wear off for pushing stage. I have an outstanding contract on the woman to this day.

crystalwalker
emailing announcement again now, and will make sure to actually attach it this time. BTW, don't know what to make of the various Village newsletter offerings. Can u pls advise if we should join the Country Club or Village Diversity Group?

phoebethompson
depends if you prefer hanging out with people who like alcohol or wheat grass in their smoothies.

crystalwalker
the former, of course.

phoebethompson
then it's Country Club all the way, my friend. Must invite you to Prospective Cocktails asap, so you can see for yourself.

crystalwalker
would love that, but don't you have to have a third generation drinking problem to get into such places here on the East Coast?

phoebethompson
trust me, the only family pedigrees you'll find at the Village Country Club belong to member dogs, not their owners, although they may like to pretend otherwise.

crystalwalker
guess it takes someone from the mother country to sort out the true WASPS from the wannabees. Fingers crossed they accept applications from people who hail from flyover country.

Thursday, August 9

Posting on Village Listserv
From: phoebegb@sahmsrule.net
Any idea why the pool at the Village Country Club is closed for TWO weeks this summer for renovations? What makes them think that every Village Resident can decamp to their beach house for the duration? Has it escaped the club's notice that it is currently 98 degrees and steaming like a tropical rainforest out there?

Posting on Village Listserv
From: phoebegb@sahmsrule.net

Hello? Anybody out there? Guess everyone IS out of town. Of course, some of us expressly chose not to go away, so our children can take algebra before 5th grade.

Lata,

Por Favor, can you take the twins to the piscina publica today? The aire acondicionado is broken and we can't afford to get it fixed right now.

Phoebe

From: phoebegb@sahmsrule.net
To: bradthompson@p_Nis_sytems.com

Can't believe we are ONLY people we know who are in town at the moment. The sacrifice for the sake of your hardware better be worth it. Thank God for the Walkers! They do seem to be a lovely family and quite sophisticated. But I do wish their eldest son, Kevin, would get rid of that ghastly haircut. He may have the twins all atwitter, but isn't it preferable to be able to see where one is going? I can only hope he will come to his senses before school starts.

Friday, August 10

From: crystalwalker@sterlingmorris.com
To: phoebegb@sahmsrule.net
Subject: Birth Announcement

Did you see the birth announcement? Here it is again as I'm sure the third time is the charm. Let me know what you think.

A wonderful gift, so precious and sweet
our hearts are full, our lives complete
Hubby and Crystal are delighted
to announce the surprise entrance
of a fourth cherub into a family
already overflowing with joy

darling girl
9 lbs. and 12 oz.
August 1st
Formal name and Announcement to follow

From: phoebegb@sahmsrule.net
To: crystalwalker@sterlingmorris.com
Re: Birth Announcement

Indeed it is, although I am a little puzzled by the lack of a name on the announcement. I can only assume you were anxious to get the card out to meet the expectations of your friends and family in Kansas City. I do hope the delay means you are affording this decision the weight it is due here on the East Coast. Far be it from me to suggest you might want to dispense with the double monikers you so delightfully employed with your first three cherubs, but I think you should know that such a practice may not help Baby's prospects here.

From: crystalwalker@sterlingmorris.com
To: phoebegb@sahmsrule.net
Re: Birth Announcement

Lack of name is result of fear at making the same hasty mistake my parents did with me, and thereby christening my youngest with something that may have sounded charming when conjured up after drinking one or two glasses of bubbly, only to condemn one's only child to a name that sounds like a stripper.

Any considered (and sober) advice you have to offer on this subject would be much appreciated.

From: phoebegb@sahmsrule.net
To: crystalwalker@sterlingmorris.com
Re: Birth Announcement

You may want to consider a more androgynous approach, as a way to help Baby avoid a glass ceiling in her future career. I have a good friend by the name of Mykal who clerked for the Supreme Court for three years before anyone realized she was a woman. Remember, no decision is too small to weigh carefully, especially when it comes to your child's future college applications. There are several baby name consultants I would be happy to recommend, if you are interested.

A couple of other minor suggestions:
Here in Washington, it is considered important to avoid any ornamentation, which detracts from the central message. Recycled paper also earns you brownie points. You can check out some examples at www.moretastefulthanyou.com.

Also, it's really not to your advantage to announce your reproductive capacities in a city where many people, including yours truly, have found the use of technology essential to produce offspring. Wouldn't want to seem like you are bragging about your natural ability to pop them out now would you? Otherwise, the announcement looks great.

P.S. Keep meaning to ask: What is it that brought your charming family to DC in the first place?

From: crystalwalker@sterlingmorris.com
To: phoebegb@sahmsrule.net
Re: Birth Announcement

If you like the idea of early morning coffee klatches before heading home to do one's domestic duties towards God and family, then Kansas City may be for you. If, like me, you happen to be a Women's Studies graduate, the place can be a challenge. So when George was given the opportunity to leave his law firm and join Plunder & Hogg's Environmental Affairs division, I told him to go for it – although not before I was able to secure a partnership with a law firm here in DC too. It seemed like the perfect way to show the cherubs more of the world, especially with what I hope will be the impending re-election of our first African American president! I could only be happier if he were a woman.

Unfortunately, George and I have not had a moment since to discuss Baby's name, or even whether or not we should sue the Ob/gyn who informed us we were having another boy, which has resulted in a costly repaint of the nursery we just had done.

What brought you to DC – aside from the love of a good man?

From: phoebegb@sahmsrule.net
To: crystalwalker@sterlingmorris.com
Re: Birth Announcement

That, and the naive belief that this was just one more pit-stop on a life of jet-set travel.

Actually, I moved to DC as a reporter for BBC America a decade ago, but quit working after I met Brad and had the twins. I simply couldn't imagine working and not being there for my little angels. Now, we can't afford the travel, let alone the jet, which just between ourselves is the reason we canceled our annual trip back to London this summer. Brad assures me all that will change just as soon as the patent on his technology comes through next month, however, so fingers crossed he is right.

While our political views could not be more different, it's been delightful to be able to spend so much time getting to know you and yours these past few weeks (and not just because everyone else is out of town). Who knew a transplanted Brit and a gal from the midwest could have so much in common? Still, I simply can't imagine having to go back to work so soon after giving birth. I don't know how you do it!

From: crystalwalker@sterlingmorris.com
To: phoebegb@sahmsrule.net
Re: Birth Announcement

The prospect of starting at Sterling Morris only six weeks from now does have me feeling overwhelmed, as I am not sure our new German Au pair is up to the job of getting the three older cherubs off to school and handling them for a few hours in the afternoon before I get home. Nina IS only eighteen, but I may need to rethink our childcare arrangements before I start work.

Back in Kansas City, George and I used to trade off leaving the office early to pick the elder three cherubs up from daycare, but as the only registered Democrat in a traditionally Republican lobbying shop, he is having to work flat out making contacts with the potential new administration before the election. Hopefully, it's a temporary situation, but something about the attitude of all the other cigar-smoking frat boys in his office makes me think they're not used to the concept of a man having to do his share of changing diapers and cleaning up baby barf. Hope I'm wrong about that.

Fortunately, the staff at Baby's new day care downtown seem more than competent. But why did they need to know her Apgar scores before agreeing to admit her, and why do they insist on thrusting flashcards in her face all day long?

Must sign off to call my new boss before she wakes up from her nap (Baby, not boss). Hope we can catch up properly in person sometime soon.

Saturday, August 11

From: Rich Simplicity
To: phoebegb@sahmsrule.net

Rich Simplicity: A monthly newsletter bringing you a life of ultimate simplicity, no matter how much money I have.

Volume 03, Issue 08

Blessings,
Thank you for subscribing to the Rich Simplicity newsletter. For only $19.99 a year, you will be privileged to read the deep, moving and ultimately transformative words of Vira Bliss - mother, muse and spiritual guide - as she shares her thoughts on motherhood, marriage and the Blessings of Living Simply*, no matter how much money you may have.

While Vira was raised in privilege and blessed by conventional standards with beauty and wealth beyond most people's wildest dreams, she soon learned that stunning physical attributes and a life of luxury were not the path to true happiness. This is why, at the age of 22, she left behind her family and modeling career to embark on a spiritual search for what is Truly Important*. Roaming the world with only a backpack (carried by her boyfriend), Vira began to seek out the secrets to inner peace from tribal peoples across the globe. Faced with a crisis in Lhasa, when she discovered the monks at the Tibetan monastery she was staying in didn't take American Express Black, Vira was forced to pay for her room and board by washing dishes in the monastery sink. For three weeks, she scrubbed, rinsed and dried, frequently weeping at the injustice (not to mention the damage to her nails), but it was from her fellow monks that she learned how to wash each plate, bowl and spoon with patience, reverence and even joy. In the process, she learned the True Secret of Happiness*, which lies in learning to appreciate whatever we are doing right at the present moment, in the Here and Now. Eventually, of course, Vira's father wired cash and she was able to move along in her journey, but she never forgot the lessons of her destitute three weeks.

Vira currently lives in a charming cottage in a Village just outside Washington DC with her five-year old son, Ravi, but her real home is Planet Earth and her family is the Global Village, where we all ultimately reside. So please join in and share Vira's journey, as she visits some of the most isolated (and beautiful) places on earth in a selfless but relentless quest to bring back the True Blessings of Rich Simplicity*.

Please note: there will be no personal note from Vira this month, as she is currently on retreat on a yacht anchored off Cap Ferrat in the south of France. She will resume writing in September.

From: phoebegb@sahmsrule.net
To: crystalwalker@sterlingmorris.com
FW:
Thought you might be interested in subscribing to this e-newsletter, which is penned by a neighbor, the recently divorced and distressingly attractive brunette who lives in the Victorian mansion on the corner of Church and Park.

The house has at least 8 bedrooms, so not sure what she means by calling it a 'cottage.' Then again, I used to think a village needed a corner shop and a pub before it could truly be called that, so maybe it's a cultural thing.

From: crystalwalker@sterlingmorris.com
To: phoebegb@sahmsrule.net
Just signed up, although I'm not sure I can ever be friends with someone who is both:
a) attractive
b) single and
c) claims to have all the answers, when half the time I can't even remember my own cherubs' names. Still, as someone who struggles on a daily basis with how to be content with less, it will be interesting to see how her little experiment in living the simple life works out.

Sunday, August 12

Note from Nina to Crystal:

Please refill my birth control pills. A.S.A.P. at Rodman's. Insurance issue, so call first.

Text from Crystal to Phoebe
George dining at Palm D'Or tonite (2nd nite in row.) Do you know anywhere that might deliver a prescription for Nina's Pill? I would run out, but Baby screaming.

Text from Phoebe to Crystal
I have samples from all major brands to deal with hormonal issues. Sending down with twins. Pls say they are nutritional supplements, in case they ask.

Text from Crystal to Phoebe
You = godsend!
BTW, blister pack arrived with a couple missing. Don't suppose they'll do twins any harm. Bless 'em for tking their supplements!

Text from Phoebe to Crystal
Girls reported back they tasted yuk, and have sworn only to consume pills in shape of teddy bears from now on. Trust they have learned important lesson, altho' have hidden all Mummy's little helpers, just in case.

PARKING VIOLATION

DMV ADJUNCTION SERVICES,
PO BOX 2014, WASHINGTON, DC 20013

☒ POLICE DEPT ☐ BUILDING CODE ☐ ZONING ☐ OTHER

02801

A MUNICIPALITY PLAINTIFF VS.

DEFENDANT

NAME **Mr. Walker, George** 202 444 6213
Last   First   Middle   Phone No.

ADDRESS **800 Pennsylvania Ave NE**
Street

CITY **Washington** State **DC** Zip Code **20013**

Eyes **Brn.** Ht. **6 2** Wt. **210** Sex **M** Race **W.** Date of Birth **05/21/65**

Driver's License Number **DC384723**

VEHICLE

Registration No. **V9881000234H8** State **DC** Year **2012**

Make **Mercedes** Year **2012** Color **blk.**

0. ☐ Pedestrian   1. ☒ Passenger Car   2. ☐ Recreational Van or Truck   3. ☐ Bus   4. ☐ Truck Tractor   5. ☐ Trailer or Semi-Trailer   6. ☐ Motorcycle or bicycle   7. ☐ Other   8. ☐ Commrl. Mot. Veh.   9. ☐ Platonized Haz. Mat.

THE UNDERSIGNED STATES THAT ON **08/10/12** AT **1:25** M
Mo. Day Yr. Time

Defendant did unlawfully commit
THE FOLLOWING OFFENSE:

(Describe)

COMPLAINT

In That

**Expired meter
too close to hydrant**

IN VIOLATION OF ORDINANCE NO. **6748393040**

AT _____
(Location of Offense)

FINE **125** .00

PARKING

TRAFFIC

VIOLATION

☐ No Lights When Required
☐ One Headlight
☐ No Registration Light
☐ No Front Plate
☐ One/No Taillights
☐ No Brake Lights
☐ No Turn Signal
☐ Illegal Window Tint
☐ Obstructed Windshield
☐ Loud Muffler
☐ Illegal Sound Amplification
☐ Other _____

☐ Any Prohibited Parking Zone
☐ In Any Crosswalk
☐ Within 20 Feet of Any Intersection
☐ Reducing Width of Roadway to Less Than 10 Feet
☒ Within 15 Feet of a Fire Hydrant
☐ Blocking Sidewalk/Alley/Driveway
☐ No Parking During Restricted Times
☐ Facing Wrong Direction
☐ Snow Route Restrictions
☐ Posted Handicapped Zone
☒ Other **exp. meter**

☐ Unlawful Possession of Tobacco
☐ Liquor Sales Hours
☐ Liquor Closing Hours
☐ Selling/Providing Liquor to Minors
☐ Possession/Consumption of Liquor by Minor
☐ Failure to Abate Nuisance
☐ Failure to Remove Abandoned Motor Vehicle
☐ Open Fires
☐ Dog Running at Large
☐ Assault
☐ Disorderly Conduct
☐ Drunkenness/Drinking on Public Street
☐ Trespass to Veteran's Memorial
☐ Fighting
☐ Other _____

You may pay your fine in person at the Police
Department or by mail. Fines will double if
not paid within ten days.

REORDER FROM P. F. PETTIBONE & CO.

Nina,

Please drive the minivan, NOT George's new Mercedes. Trust me, you don't want to be responsible for first ding.

Crystal

Wednesday, August 15

Phoebe Thompson

Dear Crystal,

How thoughtful of you to leave a box of donuts on my front steps earlier today, although it was quite unnecessary for you to thank me for my meager contribution to Nina's health and well-being. Unfortunately, we don't eat anything that isn't both sugar-free and organic, so I do hope you don't mind my sending the twins back down with them now. Nina looks like she could use a few to fill out that skinny body of hers, and I trust the cherubs will enjoy them as well.

Phoebe

Thursday, August 16

Text from Crystal to Phoebe
Got your charming note, but no donuts. Hope twins didn't discover Midwestern approach to nutrition on their way? :0

Text from Phoebe to Crystal
Hm. Must be time for another little talk about evils of refined sugar.

Text from Crystal to Phoebe
Speaking of sweet things, noticed shadowy male figure in bathrobe thru window while dropping off box around 11 am. Could this be your lover? My lips are sealed, but you know how other neighbors will talk.

Text from Phoebe to Crystal
Did I mention Brad works from home?

Text from Crystal to Phoebe
That explains it. Barely see George these days, as I'm usually asleep by time he gets in.

Text from Phoebe to Crystal
Have you tried instituting cocktail hour? My mother observed it w/o fail, and claims it encourages workaholic husbands to hurry home. Also makes the evening run smoother, even on days they can't make. Just say the word, and I will ask Lata to mix up an extra Pisco Sour (or two).

Text from Crystal to Phoebe
Wasn't sure what that was until I looked it up, but sounds just like what I might need.

Text from Phoebe to Crystal
Pisco = well worth the pump and dump. Thank you!

Friday, August 17

Text from Phoebe to Brad
Gone to gym. Please try and get out of bed before noon so Lata can change the sheets.

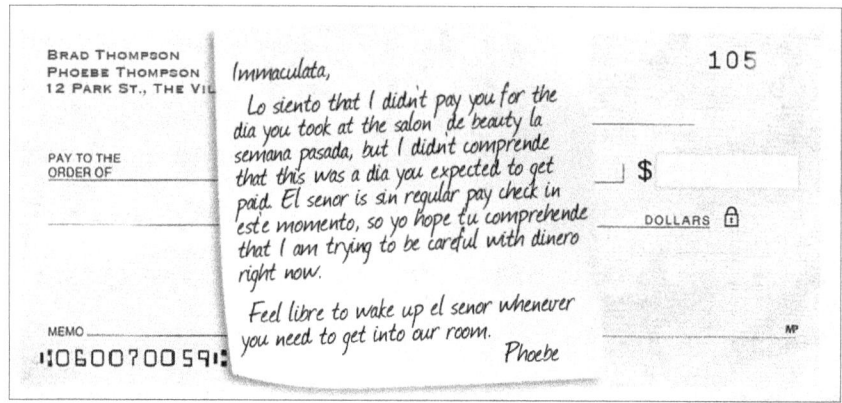

BRAD THOMPSON
PHOEBE THOMPSON
12 PARK ST., THE VIL
PAY TO THE
ORDER OF
MEMO
⑈0600700 59⑈

105

Immaculata,
Lo siento that I didn't pay you for the dia you took at the salon de beauty la semana pasada, but I didn't comprende that this was a dia you expected to get paid. El senor is sin regular pay check in este momento, so yo hope tu comprehende that I am trying to be careful with dinero right now.
Feel libre to wake up el senor whenever you need to get into our room.
Phoebe

$
DOLLARS

Saturday, August 18

Mebook Message From Phoebe to Crystal
P would like to add you as a friend on Mebook.
To confirm P as a friend, click Add or Ignore.

Mebook Message From Crystal to Phoebe
Just set up my Mebook account, and already have 59 friends, including old high school boyfriend. Apparently, it's no longer just for teens. Occurs to me this may be perfect way to keep up with family and friends in KC, and let them know when I've had a chance to update my blog. You can link to it at www.fascinatingifonlytomyself/dcdiary.com.
Information: Current City: Washington, DC
                Hometown: Kansas City
                Relationship Status: Married
                No. of days till start at new law firm: 49
                Motto: There's no place like home

Sunday, August 19

Posting on Village Listserv
Just a reminder about our New Neighbor Gathering and Frozen Yogurt/

Gelato Social at the Village Green today, from 2-5 pm. We know that many of you are just back from vacation, but we do cordially suggest you take a break from contacting your divorce lawyer and/or children's' tutors and join us in providing a warm welcome for our newest neighbors before all the fall craziness starts.

From: crystalwalker@sterlingmorris.com
To: phoebegb@sahmsrule.net
FW: Posting on Village Listserv
Are you going?

From: phoebegb@sahmsrule.net
To: crystalwalker@sterlingmorris.com
Wouldn't dream of it. Important not to appear too available until you've figured out if you actually want to be friends with these people first.

Text From Crystal to Phoebe
You were so right. Only people there were Liebermans and Browns, who insisted on dropping the H-bomb (Harvard) every 5 mins. Naturally, Kevin and Kimberly responded by getting into a fight and dropping the F-bomb, at which point we decided it was time to leave. See u soon, I hope!

Monday, August 27

Wall Post on C's Mebook Profile
First day of school! Kevin refused to let me accompany him and his two younger sibs to the bus-stop, so I ended up waving from the doorstep, feeling like the mama turtle watching her babies scrabble down the beach towards the open sea. Anyone know if the private schools have started back yet?

Response from P
You know what they say: the more you pay, the less they go. Twins don't start back until after Labor Day.

Response from C
Remind me again where your girls go to school? Seem to recall you giving me a name that sounded like something we were warned NEVER to try in college, but that can't be right.

Message from P
My girls attend the Center for Research and Creativity (or CRAC, for short). Not as well known as Seton, but don't let anyone tell you it's a school for children with special needs. We prefer the term specially gifted. Unfortunately, Brad's business is not bringing in the (admittedly astounding) amount of income required to keep the girls in CRAC and pay all our other bills, so we're currently applying for financial aid.

How was the cherubs' first day?

Message from C

Fine, but the absence of anyone playing on the street or the Village Green after school is deafening. Is there a child catcher on the loose, or are children simply being chauffeur driven from one activity to another once school lets out?

Message from P

A lot of people are still on vacay b/c the private schools haven't started yet, but I think you will find the situation doesn't change much once they do. As a matter of fact, you have just described the twins' after-school routine perfectly. How else can they expect to master Spanish, Mandarin and classical jazz by the time they reach middle school? Must seize the opportunity of a chink in their schedule to get them together with the cherubs for a play date soon.

Lata,

Mi vecinas four niños are coming for tea this afternoon. Por favor de no slip any worm medication into their bebidas, as they are unlikely to be carriers of the Candiru parasite or any other tropical disease.

Gracias

Tuesday, August 28

Wall Post on Crystal's Mebook Profile
Just been informed by Karson's preschool teacher that it's never acceptable to put your hands around another child's neck – even if the child in question snatched your basketball and is taunting you with it. Hard to believe anyone seriously feels threatened by a boy who has yet to break thirty-five pounds, particularly in a class where some kids appear suspiciously close to puberty, but I guess East-Coasters are made of softer stuff.

Mebook Message From Phoebe to Crystal
Welcome to DC, my dear, where children are held back whenever possible to give them an academic edge when it comes to applying for college. You'd think admissions officers might start to notice that the average DC child is mastering his ABC's around the same time he or she is also learning to shave, but I dare say it's never too early to start lying about one's age.

Speaking of school, only 168 hours (one more week) before the twins go back. Can't say they were happy about having to attend math camp this week, but they should have thought about that before they came home with Bs on their last report cards, shouldn't they?

BTW, you may not want to post QUITE so much personal information on your wall concerning Karson's troubles at school. Such candor is charming, but you never know when such information can be used against you round these parts. Whatever passes between us regarding personal and familial shortcomings, of course, goes in the vault. Remember, knowledge is power!

Mebook Message From Crystal to Phoebe
Thanks for the word of warning. No wonder my newest MeBook friends here in DC only seem to post what they had for breakfast.

Wednesday, August 29

From: phoebegb@sahmsrule.net
To: crystalwalker@sterlingmorris.com
Subject: Playdate
So glad we were able to get your cherubs together with my twins yesterday afternoon. Kimberly-Ann broke the ice nicely when she offered to show my youngest (by two minutes), Cecily her tattoo – temporary, I assume. And who knew Karson-James would prove to be my eldest twin's soul mate? He may be several years Emily's junior, but I wouldn't be surprised if a shared enthusiasm for World of Wizardry could one day translate into another kind of lifelong passion.

From: crystalwalker@sterlingmorris.com
To: phoebegb@sahmsrule.net
RE: Playdate
Thanks for the whispered word of warning about your housekeeper's fondness for homemade purgatives. I had the cherubs discreetly dump

27

Lata's 'Guava and Acai smoothies' she made for them in the bushes as soon as her back was turned. Pretty sure they have consumed worse things than an Amazonian laxative dressed up as a protein shake in their time, but I guess it's better to be safe than sorry.

Hope we can get together again soon!

From: crystalwalker@sterlingmorris.com
To: gwalker@plunderhogg.com
Can you PLEASE come home early for once to shoot some hoops with your oldest son? Kevin-John claims not to have been assigned any homework yet, so he's moping around the house and tormenting his younger brother. No wonder Karson feels obliged to resort to violence with his peers at pre-school.

From: crystalwalker@sterlingmorris.com
To: gwalker@plunderhogg.com
Fine. Just don't come crying to me when the cherubs start sending you their therapy bills.

From: phoebegb@sahmsrule.net
To: crystalwalker@sterlingmorris.com
Subject: Blood-curdling Screams
Heard what sounded like distant wails coming from the vicinity of your house last night, and briefly considered offering to help with Baby, until sanity in the form of one of Lata's pisco sours intervened.
Everything OK?

From: crystalwalker@sterlingmorris.com
To: phoebegb@sahmsrule.net
RE: Blood-curdling Screams
Cries of anguish were not Baby's but my own reaction to George's announcement that he's going fishing in Wyoming with a couple of clients next week. That leaves Nina and me behind to cope with all the cherubs. He claims the trip is strictly for work, but he did admit to feeling the need to get away from all the demands placed on him at home these days. Doesn't he realize that a maternity leave spent running a household with four demanding children is not exactly spring break in Daytona for me?

I know we both made the choice to move to here and have another baby. I just failed to anticipate I would be raising it as a single mother. Was this what the Sisters at my Catholic girls' school meant by having it all?

From: phoebegb@sahmsrule.net
To: crystalwalker@sterlingmorris.com
RE: Blood-curdling screams
If Brad so much as thought about taking a trip without me after I had just given birth, he'd be a hunting souvenir by now. As it is, your predicament is but a distant memory for those of us who feel our husbands don't travel enough.

In theory, Brad is responsible for bringing in all the household income, while

I do everything else. Since the most common alternative to this arrangement appears to be for a woman to bring in the income and still do everything else, I prefer to delegate at least one responsibility to my other half. To be fair, Brad does like to cook, but I'm not sure the occasional bowl of homemade pesto, delicious as it may be, is enough to make up for the fact that he has singularly failed to provide any significant earnings for a substantial period of time. And while I do believe in the man, I am also rather anxious about the dwindling size of our savings account. At this rate, we can barely afford to send one of the twins to community college.

If only I could remember which one promised to administer my sponge baths once I'm in the nursing home.

Text from Crystal to George
What time will you be home tonite? In case u forgot, it's Nina's night off. U can't possibly expect me to cook dinner AND handle homework/bedtime 4 all 4 cherubs alone. Can u?

Skye Chat
crystalwalker
do u happen to have some of Brad's pesto to spare? George just texted to say won't be home till 10, and cupboard is bare. Willing to pay top dollar!

phoebethompson
Will ask Brad asap.

Text From Crystal to Phoebe
Pesto = DELICIOUS. Please tell Brad he's a godsend!

Brad,
Can you spare time out of your busy gaming to whip up a batch of pesto for Crystal? I know you are inundated with Cuban commandos to kill, but maybe you can put down the controller for long enough to help a neighbor in need. Kisses.

Phoebe

Thursday, August 30

From: phoebegb@sahmsrule.net
To: crystalwalker@sterlingmorris.com
Subject: Domestic Bliss

What a charming picture you and Baby presented when I stopped by to drop off the pesto yesterday evening. There you were, snuggled up with this sleeping bundle of potential, while I was forced to return home to the same tedious old husband and rapidly aging children, whose personalities (and issues) were only too real. I know this is only part of the picture, and that babies are exhausting, but Brad has started pushing me to have another one of late – either that, or go back to work. Seeing as we are unlikely to conceive the old-fashioned way, I suppose I'll just have to step up my volunteering (important to look busy) and hope his patent comes through in time for us to adopt a child before some Hollywood celebrity gets to them first.

From: crystalwalker@sterlingmorris.com
To: phoebegb@sahmsrule.net
RE: Domestic Bliss

You have an amazing ability to filter out the rest of the story while you were visiting yesterday. Didn't you notice Kevin demanding I allow him to download slash metal music on his mePod, or Kimberly whining that her life was ruined by the arrival of another girl in the family? How could you miss Karson trying to turf Baby out of her bouncy chair when he thought no-one was looking?

Thank God, I had a bowl of Brad's pasta to look forward to after I had wrestled (almost) all of them into bed. That stuff is addictive. The last time I remember getting that excited about a bunch of green leaves was back in college.

Skye Chat

phoebethompson

Keep quiet about pesto and there'll be more where that came from. In meantime, do hope you get some sleep! Should help in these and so many other matters. Find weekly mani/pedis especially helpful for relaxation, and my last luxury (aside from Lata) to be discarded during tough times. Just so happens I have an appointment in half an hour. Care to join?

crystalwalker

Yes, but concerned au pair and George will judge me for being frivolous. Used to be so much easier to slip into salon on way home from work.

phoebethompson

Remind me where George is traveling next wk? As for Nina, just say u have an important meeting to attend, which is TRUE. Do you think Lata believes me when I walk out door dressed in power suit and return with fresh coat of OPI's Slutty As a Presidential Intern? A hard stare is usually all it takes to silence that mocking look in her eyes.

crystalwalker
George claims the fishing trip is essential both for work and his mental health, as he finds it hard to relax w/o some kind of rod in his hands. Guess I'm entitled to feel the same way about pampering.

phoebethompson
Lata just showed up wearing favorite pair of jeans again. Swear she only does it to prove she looks better in them at fifty than I do at…well, let's not go there. As soon as I wrestle 'em off her, I'll swing by and pick you up.

Friday, August 31

Text from Crystal to George
WTH is your travel itinerary? U promised to email it before u left! Can't BELIEVE how irresp. Ur with 4 chrbs at home. U cd be mauled by bear and dead for weeks before we found out!

Text from Crystal to George
Can't BELIEVE u wd go somewhere w/o cellphone coverage.

From: crystalwalker@sterlingmorris.com
To: jsmith@plunderhogg.com
Subject: Travel Schedule

Dear Jane,
Can you please forward my husband's travel itinerary for the next 7 days ASAP? He promised to get it to me before he left, but it must have slipped his mind. My children and I will sleep much better at night knowing where my husband is.

Thanks.
Crystal

GIGANTIC
World Travel Inc.
"WE'LL GET YOU THERE SOMEHOW"

2001 Frontier Drive
Washington, DC 2005
ph   (202) 888-6979
fx.   (202) 888-6980
www.giganticworld.com

Monday 03SEP 2012 9:57AM EST
Passengers: Walker, George and Myers, Taylor
ITINERARY / INVOICE 034829839 DATE 03Sept
AIR TICKET 2387834743 WALKER, GEORGE
AIR TICKET 2387834744 MYERS, TAYLOR

Agency Record Locator: KUSXZ03
Date Booked: 07JUL10
Electronic Billed to AMEX 8344 $1,299.41
SUB TOTAL $1,299.41
NET BILLING $1,299.41 TOTAL AMOUNT DUE: 0.00

| AIR | Monday, 10SEP 2012 |

Northworst Airlines
from: Washington, DC (IAD)
To: Denver, CO (DEN)
Stops: 01
Seats 03A, 03B
Equipment: Boeing 767 Jet

Flight Number: 1699
Depart: 03:28pm
Arrive: 05:18pm
Duration: 03hrs 12 min.
Time between flights 01hrs. 2 min.
STATUS: CONFIRMED
MEAL: brown bag avail for purchase
Class: H
Miles: 1537

- CONNECTION -

Northworst Airlines
from: Denver, CO (DEN)
To: Chyenne, WY (CYS)
Stops: 0
Seats 22D, 22E
Equipment: Boeing 767 Jet

Flight Number: 292
Depart: 06:20pm
Arrive: 06:55pm
Duration: 02hrs 15 min.
Time between flights 0 min.
STATUS: CONFIRMED
MEAL: brown bag avail for purchase
Class: H
Miles: 996

| ACTIVITY | Tuesday, 11SEP 2012 |

Gigantra Activity schedule for **Walker, George and Myers, Taylor:**

8:30pm   Dinner at Old Faithful Hunting Lodge and Spa, with Senator S. from Texas and reps from
           Gigantra Pharmaceutical. G. Walker to present client toast

| ACTIVITY | Wednesday, 12SEP 2012 |

6:00am   Luxury stretch Land Rover from Pimp Yo' Ridemobiles to pick up duck shooting party from front
           entrance of Lodge. Champagne breakfast to be served en route.
4:00pm   Hot Stone Massage with Vanessa L. back at Lodge
7:00pm   Dinner at Lodge

| ACTIVITY | Thursday, 13SEP 2012 |

0:00 (TBD) CAST AND BLAST Cookout overlooking Big Laramie River. Grill and supplemental picnic hamper
           to be provided by Gigantra Pharmaceuticals

| ACTIVITY | Friday, 14SEP 2012 |

2:00pm   Go-karting at the Senator Alan Simpson Drag Strip in nearby Laramie, WY
4:00pm   Deep pore-releasing facial with Michelle W. at Lodge

GIGANTIC
World Travel Inc.
"WE'LL GET YOU THERE SOMEHOW"

2001 Frontier Drive
Washington, DC 2005
ph   (202) 888-6979
fx   (202) 888-6980
www.giganticworld.com

ACTIVITY   Saturday, 15SEP 2012

10:00am   Limo to pick up party at lodge. Visit to Yellowstone Hot Springs.
           Swimsuits optional!

ACTIVITY   Sunday, 16SEP 2012

10:00am   Tee-off time - 18-hole Golf Game with Senator from Maryland at
           Fairmont Country Club

           Followed by Drinks and Dinner at the club.

           Baby shower for Senator's wife in ladies' grill room.

ACTIVITY   Monday, 17SEP 2012

           Free Day

AIR   Tuesday, 18SEP 2012

Northworst Airlines	**Flight Number:** 224
from: Chyenne, WY (CYS)	**Depart:** 01:15pm
To: Denver, CO (DEN)	**Arrive:** 01:50pm
Stops: 01	Duration: 35 min.
Seats 16A, 16B	Time between flights 02hrs. 1 min.
Equipment: Boeing 767 Jet	STATUS: CONFIRMED
	MEAL: brown bag avail for purchase
	Class: H
	Miles: 967

- CONNECTION -

Northworst Airlines	**Flight Number:** 1674
from: Denver, CO (DEN)	**Depart:** 03:15pm
To: Washington, DC (IAD)	**Arrive:** 09:11pm
Stops: 0	Duration: 03hrs 04 min.
Seats 02D, 02E	Time between flights 0 min.
Equipment: Boeing 767 Jet	STATUS: CONFIRMED
	MEAL: brown bag avail for purchase
	Class: H
	Miles: 1674

From: crystalwalker@sterlingmorris.com
To: phoebegb@sahmsrule.net
Subject: Help!

May need more than a fresh mani/pedi to get me through latest marital crisis. Just before he left, George told me that someone called 'Taylor' from the office would be accompanying him on this trip. Naturally, I assumed that Taylor was a man, but when I happened to call George's office about his travel itinerary this morning, I discovered that Taylor is in fact a twenty-nine year-old WOMAN. Turns out, your tip about gender-neutral names was right on the money.

I am currently leaning towards painful castration, but suspect my hormones may be messing with my judgment. I considered sending all the cherubs to him IMMEDIATELY, but then realized they may get an education for which they are not yet prepared. Any advice before I choose to exercise my second amendment rights?

From: phoebegb@sahmsrule.net
To: crystalwalker@sterlingmorris.com
RE: Help!

I'll be right over. Please resist the urge to do or say anything you might regret in the meantime. I'm sure there must be some innocent explanation, even if I can't for the life of me think of one right now.

From: crystalwalker@sterlingmorris.com
To: phoebegb@sahmsrule.net
RE: Help!

Just left a message for George at the lodge where he and Taylor are staying, saying there's been a family emergency. Didn't specify what. Thanks for coming over. Don't know what I would do without you, esp. now that I appear to be on the brink of becoming a single parent for real.

DC Diary

The Walkers Take on the Nation's Capital

BLOG ARCHIVE

Baby Kurtis, Obama Fever
    and Missing Friends in
    KC

Baby Kurtis, Obama Fever and Missing Friends in KC

It's been a whirlwind few weeks, but George and I are finally settled into our new home in DC, along with our three older cherubs, German Au Pair, dog, lizard, two hermit crabs and newest addition! Kurtis was born on Friday, August 1 weighing 6 lbs and 12 oz, and measuring 21 inches. She's absolutely perfect in every way, and her sibs all love her to death - in her younger brother, Karson's case almost literally.

Both Kevin and Kimberly miss their friends in KC, although they are starting to make friends at the local Village Public school, which started last Monday. So far, they seem to like it, but the best thing about it may be the fact it runs from pre-k through seventh grade, which means for the first and only time, all three older cherubs are in the same school.

DC is abuzz with excitement right now at the prospect of re-electing our first African American president. It's refreshing to be in a part of the country where being a liberal is actually considered a virtue sometimes, instead of a sin. Of course, George is working flat out raising money for the campaign, so we don't get to see him as much as we'd like. He seems to have business dinners most nights, plus golfing or other sporting activities he needs to attend at weekends - when he's not traveling, that is. At times, I feel like a single parent, but I'm hoping George will be able to scale back his hours and focus on the environmental issues he really came here to represent, once the election is over.

We have made lots of new friends, especially right here in the neighborhood, which is almost like a real English country village (in fact, my new neighbor, Phoebe is British), although Phoebe's petition for a Village pub has apparently fallen on deaf ears. Fortunately, there's no lack of drinking at the Village Country Club, which we are on the waiting list to join, so we should find some like-minded peeps once we get in.

Hope our friends and family from KC will pay us a visit here soon!

Posted by Jan at Walkers at ...

M⊙ ⚑ ⧉ ⊕

No comments:

Post a Comment

Comment as: Select profile ⋮

(Publish) (Preview)

DC Diary
Baby Kurtis, Obama Fever and Missing Friends in KC

It's been a whirlwind few weeks, but George and I are finally settled into our new home in DC, along with our three older cherubs, German Au Pair, dog, lizard, two hermit crabs and newest addition! Kurtis was born on Friday, August 1 weighing 6 lbs and 12 oz, and measuring 21 inches. She's absolutely perfect in every way, and her sibs all love her to death - in her younger brother, Karson's case almost literally.

Both Kevin and Kimberly miss their friends in KC, although they are starting to make friends at the local Village Public school, which started last Monday. So far, they seem to like it, but the best thing about it may be the fact it runs from pre-k through seventh grade, which means for the first and only time, all three older cherubs are in the same school.

DC is abuzz with excitement right now at the prospect of re-electing our first African American president. It's refreshing to be in a part of the country where being a liberal is actually considered a virtue sometimes, instead of a sin. Of course, George is working flat out raising money for the campaign, so we don't get to see him as much as we'd like. He seems to have business dinners most nights, plus golfing or other sporting activities he needs to attend at weekends - when he's not traveling, that is. At times, I feel like a single parent, but I'm hoping George will be able to scale back his hours and focus on the environmental issues he really came here to represent, once the election is over.

We have made lots of new friends, especially right here in the neighborhood, which is almost like a real English country village (in fact, my new neighbor, Phoebe is British), although Phoebe's petition for a Village pub has apparently fallen on deaf ears. Fortunately, there's no lack of drinking at the Village Country Club, which we are on the waiting list to join, so we should find some like-minded peeps once we get in.

Hope our friends and family from KC will pay us a visit here soon!

Chapter 2

September, 2012 Vol. 41, Issue 9
Always FREE, but donations appreciated

Please direct submissions and inquiries to:
whiner@villagepress.com
P.O. Box 387 Village Town, MD

VILLAGE WHINER

Your trusty monthly newsletter of the "Most Livable Village," 1989
Village Times Magazine

Board Approves Road Bumps

Following the tragic death of Tinklepaw, the beloved two-year old Chihuahua belonging to Miss Van Houtzen on Center Street in a traffic accident last week, the Board has voted unanimously to install speed bumps throughout the Village. It is hoped the bumps will ensure the future safety of children and pets, whose lives are endlessly put in danger by commuters cutting through our precious neighborhood on their way to and from downtown DC.

Comments Chief of Police, Archie Ambrose, "Even though we have yet to record a single case of anyone exceeding the 20 mph speed limit, we feel it is only a matter of time before another tragedy like this one occurs. Motorists are now on notice that anyone caught speeding will be dealt with severely by the Special Ops division of the Village police force, who are on standby to track down and punish violators to the full extent of the law."

Tinklepaw will be buried under the first speed bump, at the intersection of Spring and Georgia Streets on Sunday, September 12. Following a roadside memorial service to commemorate her short life.

Diversity Group

As some of you are no doubt aware, there has been some negative publicity about the Village in the letters section of The Post recently, following the ejection of a homeless man after he was found sleeping on a park bench on the Village Green earlier this summer. We want people to know that the Village is a welcoming place for one and all, which is why Miss Gertrude has offered to lead a free seminar on personal grooming for life on the streets at the Village Hall on Friday, September 5, from 5.30-7.30 p.m. Residents are encouraged to invite their homeless friends to attend. Cocktails and light hors d'oeuvres will be served.

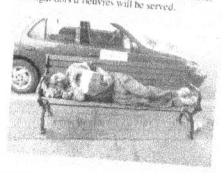

Club News

The Minxy Eels lost their last swim meet of the season against the DC Divers, finishing second from last in the I-League Inter-club rankings. Our performance was hampered by the lack of a practice pool, as a result of the Club Aquatic Center renovations. Many thanks to the local public rec. association, which graciously allowed us to use theirs during off hours, and did not object to our insistence on adding chlorine. Thanks also, to Tommy McVane's mother and aunt for organizing the post-season banquet, which featured their family's signature spaghetti and meatballs. Never before has so much pasta been prepared by so few, or consumed by so many. No wonder Tommy is known as "Da Bomb" for his ability to turn any body of water into a wave pool every time he jumps in.

Renovations on the Club Aquatic Center are now complete, but the outdoor pool is closed for the fall/winter season, and will re-open on Memorial Day next year.

We will be hosting Prospective New Member drinks in the main Club bar on Thursday, Sept 19th at 7 pm. Please submit your 1,500 word personal recommendations for potential new members to the Club office no later than 5 pm on Thursday, September 3, to give us time to conduct character reference and background checks before issuing invitations.

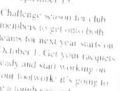

Tennis Team

The Ladies and Gentleman's Inter-club tennis league resumes its fall schedule on September 15.

Challenge season for club members to get onto both teams for next year starts on October 1. Get your racquets ready and start working on your footwork, it's going to be a tough season!

Miss Gertrude

Response to the Manners and Shoe class has been so overwhelming that Miss Gertrude has offered to write a column on etiquette in the Village Crier each month. Miss Gertrude is quite pleased this opportunity presents itself at a time when loved ones are beginning to hint that it is time for her to retire and move out of her beloved home to the Village, and into assisted living. She hopes the column will demonstrate to the world that just because one has the excessional run-in with a lamp post or forgets to turn off the oven does not mean one's mind is gone.

In that vein, Miss Gertrude's words of wisdom this month may come down to this: respect one's elders, especially when one's inheritance depends upon it.

Village Playgroup

The Village Playgroup will start its fall schedule on Friday, September 12. Interviews for slots will be held on Tuesday, September 2nd at 9 am in the reception room at the Village Hall. Please note, toddlers will be assessed for their developmental readiness to interact and play with others.

Evidence of high IQ, parental earning power or impressive personal connections is NOT considered sufficient grounds for admission. It is strongly recommended that parents, not caregivers, accompany the child for the intake meeting. Formal dress, for children, is not required.

CLASSIFIEDS

For Sale by Village:
six teak park benches, only slightly used.
$600 each OBO.
For more information, please email:
noriffraffallowed@ccvillage.org.

September, 2012 Vol. 41, Issue 9
Always FREE, but donations appreciated

Please direct submissions and inquiries to:
whining@villagepress.com
P.O. Box 357 Village Town, MD

Board Approves Road Humps

Following the tragic death of Tinklepaw, the beloved two-year old Chihuahua belonging to Mrs. Van Houzen on Center Street in a traffic accident last week, the Board has voted unanimously to install speed humps throughout the Village. It is hoped the humps will ensure the future safety of children and pets, whose lives are endlessly put in danger by commuters cutting through our precious neighborhood on their way to and from downtown DC.

CAUTION SPEED HUMPS

Comments Chief of Police, Archie Ambrose, "Even though we have yet to record a single case of anyone exceeding the 20 mph speed limit, we feel it is only a matter of time before another tragedy like this one occurs. Motorists are now on notice that anyone caught speeding will be dealt with severely by the Special Ops division of the Village police force, who are on standby to track down and pursue violators to the full extent of the law." Tinklepaw will be buried under the first speed hump, at the intersection of Spring and Georgia Streets on Sunday, September 12, following a roadside memorial service to commemorate her short life.

Club News

The Moray Eels lost their last swim meet of the season against the DC Divers, finishing second from last in the F League Interclub rankings. Our performance was hampered by the lack of a practice pool, as a result of the Club Aquatic Center renovations. Many thanks to the local public rec association, which graciously allowed us to use theirs during off hours, and did not object to our insistence on adding chlorine. Thanks, also, to Tommy McVane's mother and aunt for organizing the post-season banquet, which featured their family's signature spaghetti and meatballs. Never before has so much pasta been prepared by so few, or consumed by so many. No wonder Tommy is known as 'Da Bomb' for his ability to turn any body of water into a wave pool every time he jumps in.

Renovations on the Club Aquatic Center are now complete, but the outdoor pool is closed for the fall/winter season, and will re-open on Memorial Day next year.

We will be hosting Prospective New Member drinks in the main Club bar on Thursday, Sept. 19th at 7 pm. Please submit your 1,500 word personal recommendations for potential new members to the Club office no later than 3 pm on Thursday, September 4, to give us time to conduct character reference and background checks before issuing invitations.

Diversity Group

As some of you are no doubt aware, there has been some
negative publicity about the Village in the letters section
of The Post recently, following the ejection of a homeless
man after he was found sleeping on a park bench on the
Village Green earlier this summer. We want people to know
that the Village is a welcoming place for one and all, which
is why Miss Gertrude has offered to lead a free seminar on
personal grooming for life on the streets at the Village Hall
on Friday, September 5, from 5.30-7.30 p.m. Residents
are encouraged to invite their homeless friends to attend.
Cocktails and light hors d'oeuvres will be served.

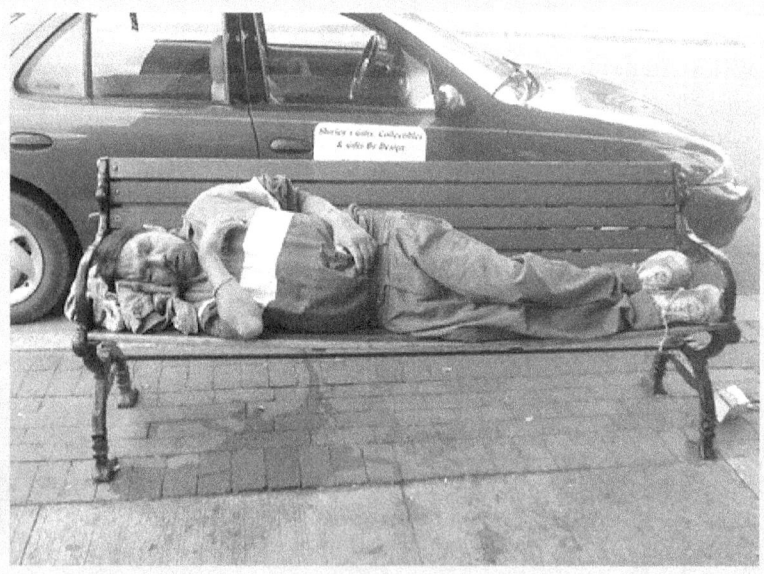

Tennis Team

The Ladies' and Gentlemen's Interclub Tennis League resumes its Fall schedule on September 15.

Challenge season for club members to get onto both teams for next year starts on October 1. Get your racquets ready and start working on your footwork: it's going to be a tough season!

Miss Gertrude

Response to the Manners and More class has been so overwhelming that Miss Gertrude has offered to write a column on etiquette in the Village Crier each month. Miss Gertrude is quite pleased this opportunity presents itself at a time when loved ones are beginning to hint that it is time for her to retire and move out of her beloved home in the Village, and into assisted living. She hopes the column will demonstrate to the world that just because one has the occasional run-in with a lamp post (or forgets to turn off the oven) does not mean one's mind is gone.

In that vein, Miss Gertrude's words of wisdom this month may come down to this: respect one's elders, especially when one's inheritance depends upon it.

Village Playgroup

The Village Playgroup will start its fall schedule on Friday, September 12. Interviews for slots will be held on Tuesday, September 2nd at 9 am in the reception room at the Village Hall. Please note, toddlers will be assessed for their developmental readiness to interact and play with others.

Evidence of high IQ, parental earning power or impressive personal connections is NOT considered sufficient grounds for admission. It is strongly recommended that parents, not caregivers, accompany the child for the intake meeting. Formal dress, for children, is not required.

CLASSIFIEDS

For Sale by Village:
six teak park benches, only slightly used.
$600 each OBO.
For more information, please email:
noriffraffallowed@ccvillage.org.

Sunday, September 2

From: crystalwalker@sterlingmorris.com
To: phoebegb@sahmsrule.net

Thank God for your superior forensic investigation skills. After 11 years of marriage, I know my husband isn't the world's best communicator (at least at home), but you'd think he might have mentioned the fact that one of his principal partners in the lobbying firm is a NUN. And yet, all it took for you to uncover this startling piece of information was a single phone call to your former BBC contact at the FBI. Clearly, your former career in journalism continues to serve you well, although remind me not to leave any more empty pesto bags in the trash. They could so easily be misconstrued.

I guess things could have been much worse. I was certainly relieved to discover that Taylor Myers is a sister in the semi-cloistered community of Our Lady of the Pines, which works to preserve natural habitats – one of Plunder & Hogg's specialties, principally because they provide a fat tax credit to the fabulously wealthy (including, apparently, these Texan clients). I would have felt better, however, if the photograph you found of her on the convent's Mebook page could have shown her looking less like Julie Andrews and more like the Sisters I remember from Catholic school.

I won't rest easy until I have physically removed George's penis after he gets back. In the meantime, I'm using my Catholic training to pray Sister T. did not choose to ditch the chastity belt along with the traditional black habit when she took her vows.

Monday, September 3

Lata,

Por favor de no put through any telefono calls from people asking for me or el senor by nuestros nombres familiales. Estos are telefono calls from people asking for dinero, and we don't have any right now. Por favor to tell them we are de vacaciones right now.

Gracias

Tuesday, September 4

Goggle Calendar Reminder
Phoebe: Walker family recommendation letter for Prospective new Club member application due.

From: phoebegb@sahmsrule.net
To: crystalwalker@sterlingmorris.com
Glad to hear you feel somewhat reassured of George's continued fidelity, although I fully support you in any decision to castrate upon his return. Even if he's not guilty yet, most men are, eventually, so I don't see the harm

in taking preventative measures.

No time for tea today alas, as I have to finish the prospective new member recommendation for your Club membership application. Researching the Walker family tree is taking longer than I thought. OK if I refer to Grandpa Walker's colorful bootlegging career as his pioneering work in micro-brewing?

From: crystalwalker@sterlingmorris.com
To: phoebegb@sahmsrule.net
Thx so much for taking care of this. Feel free to embellish as necessary!

Skye Chat
phoebethompson
Brad's patent came through this morning, but what he neglected to mention is that he and his partner still don't have any customers for his technology. If things don't look up soon, I may have to rethink my own career ambitions, beyond becoming good enough to play my way onto the Club Tennis Team, and being there for Cecily and Emily.

crystalwalker
Aren't those two mutually exclusive? :0

phoebethompson
Not if children are in school while you enjoy a private session with Xavier on grass.

crystalwalker
Don't mean to attack you at this difficult time, as no-one could question devoted nature of your mothering. But I get so tired of being judged for not being a stay at home mom. Most of the ones I've met so far here in the Village spend more time on themselves than they do with their kids. What's the difference between hiring a sitter so you can go for daily workout/ massage/lunch with friends, and hiring a nanny so you can actually go out and earn a living?

phoebethompson
None, except you have a less frazzled, more toned and hopefully much happier wife and mother at end of the day. If you'd seen Xavier, you'd understand.

Besides, the room rep responsibilities I've assumed at CRAC the last several years certainly require more time than I could offer a full-time job, although I dare say being named 'Parent Volunteer of the Year' is less of an honor and more of a recognition of time served.

crystalwalker
Frankly, I'm a little perturbed at how much parents are expected to do for their children here in DC. Just this morning, I found myself helping out in Karson's pre-k classroom as part of my 30 hours of our family's annual 'service obligation,' whatever that means. Tried sending Nina in my place,

but was informed by the school that substitutes were unacceptable, which is how I ended up sweeping up soggy Cheerios from the classroom floor while the kids went outside for recess. WTH?

Oops. Baby has woken up from her nap. TBC.

Wednesday, September 5

From: crystalwalker@sterlingmorris.com
To: phoebegb@sahmsrule.net
I know you genuinely cherish the time you spend with the twins, but I also think our girls benefit from having a strong career-woman role model in their lives. If there was anything good to come out of my parents' divorce when I was two, it was the realization that every woman needs to be able to stand on her own two feet, just in case hubby falls under a bus – accidentally or otherwise.

From: phoebegb@sahmsrule.net
To: crystalwalker@sterlingmorris.com
The trouble is, I was raised to believe a woman could do anything she wanted, but that never included anything practical, like fixing the roof or paying the mortgage. Instead, my parents encouraged me to find personal fulfillment, on the assumption that some husband or other would always be around to take care of the bills. Clearly, this was misguided, but at the time the twins were born, I simply couldn't imagine going back to twelve hour shifts at the BBC.

Now, of course, I find myself struggling with the urge to express my frustration with Brad for not being the nerd in shining armor I once took him for, however unreasonable that might sound. I'm the first to recognize it's hard to tell a loved one how much you resent them for not being more successful when you haven't earned a penny yourself in the last nine years. And as a working mother, I'm sure you feel there is no reason I shouldn't go out and support the family I helped create. But the thought of finding a job at my age, after almost a decade of not working, is daunting, to say the least. I seriously doubt I could land a job as an intern in television these days, let alone my old reporting gig.

From: crystalwalker@sterlingmorris.com
To: phoebegb@sahmsrule.net
Didn't anyone tell you that having a British accent automatically adds 20 points to your IQ?

From: phoebegb@sahmsrule.net
To: crystalwalker@sterlingmorris.com
Frankly, it would be better if it took twenty years off my face or added several cup sizes, which we all know is the only way a woman gets taken seriously in TV news.

From: crystalwalker@sterlingmorris.com
To: phoebegb@sahmsrule.net
Sorry to hear things are rocky between you and Brad right now. What exactly is his technology for, anyway? Happened to catch him in his bathrobe again this afternoon when I dropped off the latest Us Now – I mean, of course, US News and World Reportage.

From: phoebegb@sahmsrule.net
To: crystalwalker@sterlingmorris.com
You might well wonder what kind of gainful employment enables a man to start his day by lounging in bed reading the paper until 10 am, before springing into action and flinging on his bathrobe for the commute to the office upstairs. What kind of high-powered career involves having to juggle between online Poker and the submarine game on his computer, while simultaneously discussing world politics with his business partner in San Jose over the phone? Could it be that between the two of them, they are engineering a cure for AIDS and bringing about peace in the Middle East at the same time? No, dear Crystal, it turns out that the high-tech, cutting edge and let's-not-forget revolutionary technology upon which my family and I are pinning our financial futures is called a Pneumatic-Nano Injection System – or P-NIS for short. One day, I am assured, it will enable the oil industry to extract probe for deposits without having to drill large holes into the earth first – provided anyone can stop laughing long enough to buy it.

From: crystalwalker@sterlingmorris.com
To: phoebegb@sahmsrule.net
With a name like that, who can fail to take Brad's product line seriously?

Thursday, September 6

From: phoebegb@sahmsrule.net
To: crystalwalker@sterlingmorris.com
Are you on Witter yet? The twins are telling me it's de rigueur for everyone to be on it these days, although I can't imagine why the world would want to hear what I am doing right now in 140 characters or less. Still, I'm thinking of signing up, just to see if I can acquire my very own stalker. Personally, I am not that interested in my own life, let alone anyone else's right now, but I dare say we need to do these things to stay au courant.

From: crystalwalker@sterlingmorris.com
To: phoebegb@sahmsrule.net
Just signed up for an account, and already following my favorite movie star – the one who recently divorced his much older actress wife. I only hope she can relax into her stretchy pants from now on.

Witter from @femilawyermom
Cancelled cab and waiting for hubby at airport while au pair takes cherubs to diner. Can't wait to see him!

Witter from @femilawyermom
Flight from Denver just landed, but no sign of hubby. Beginning to get butterflies in my tummy. Just like old times!

Witter from @femilawyermom
No response from his cellphone and just spoke to the airlines. They have no record of him on the flight.

Witter from @femilawyermom
If hubby doesn't get his ass home soon, he's going to find 4 cherubs, 1 lizard, 2 hermit crabs, a cat and a dog waiting for him in the hunting lodge hot tub on Monday.

@hottublov is now following femilawyermom

Friday, September 7

Witter from @femilawyermom
Labor Day at home with 3 kids, baby, Au Pair and a zooful of pets. If anyone sees my husband, please ask him to call home. It's not an emergency, but his life does depend on it.

From: crystalwalker@sterlingmorris.com
To: phoebegb@sahmsrule.net
George finally called just now to say he'd been forced to hop straight on a plane to New Hampshire straight from Denver, to show congressional delegation impact fishing is having on local trout population – and presumably impact that population themselves. I've told him in no uncertain terms never to pull a stunt like that w/o talking to me first.

Meanwhile, au pair and the three eldest cherubs are all down for the count with strep. Nina's parents called from Hanover this morning at 5 am, demanding I serve her hot tea and cold compresses in bed. Apparently, they trust these more than the antibiotics I fetched for her from the pharmacy at 11 pm last night.

Oh, and did I mention that Baby is waking up on the hour every hour, demanding to be fed?

From: phoebegb@sahmsrule.net
To: crystalwalker@sterlingmorris.com
I know this may come as cold comfort, but organizing political and corporate junkets in remote corners of the country is often the best way to capture the attention of a busy Senator or network executive, precisely because no-one else can reach them and they've got nowhere else to go. But do not be alarmed at reports tracking the success of a lobby firm's practice proportionately with the likelihood of being eaten. That's complete nonsense, as the nearest most of them get to danger is slipping in the steam room or sauna. My advice to you would be to hunker down and spend some of hubby's

hard-earned cash. You might be surprised to find how much better this makes you feel.

From: crystalwalker@sterlingmorris.com
To: phoebegb@sahmsrule.net
Would love to seek revenge on George for leaving me in this plight by engaging in a little retail therapy, if it weren't for the fact that I can't find anything clean to wear.

From: phoebegb@sahmsrule.net
To: crystalwalker@sterlingmorris.com
I always thought running out of clean clothes was the perfect excuse to go shopping, but am sending Lata down to wash a couple of loads in the interim. Happy to accompany you in an assault on the Village Shoppes – just say the word and I'm there.

Saturday, September 8

From: crystalwalker@sterlingmorris.com
To: phoebegb@sahmsrule.net
Feeling MUCH better, thank you. So kind of you to act as my personal shopper this pm, and of Lata to do our laundry while I was gone. Slipped her a couple of twenties for her trouble.

Generally, I would feel guilty about spending money I haven't earned, but when the cat's away, the mice will play with his credit card, right? Besides, George assured me before he left that all the sacrifices we are making now, in terms of him being gone all the time, are paying off in terms of the new accounts he's bringing in. But why does that fill me with resentment, instead of making me feel better? I know we should be working together as a team, not competing with each other, but I can't help feeling jealous of the fact that HIS career is blossoming, while mine is on hold.

From: phoebegb@sahmsrule.net
To: crystalwalker@sterlingmorris.com
I don't think you need to feel guilty about a THING, dear C, especially given how frugal you were in your purchases.

I admired how you found one or two steals at TP Maxx, but glad I was also able to entice you into Saks, as you look FABULOUS in the DVF cocktail dress. Very kind of you to offer to lend me it for the Prospective New Member drinks at the Village Country Club next week. Hope I can return the favor soon, once finances permit and I can start buying new clothes again.

Lata,

Gracias for handling that nasty hombre from the collection agency el otro dia. I forget how good your ingles is, por que you always speak espanol to my girls. I would love you to be here for Cecily and Emily's birthday party at the end of the month, but I know your Medicos Sin Fronteras' trip to Peru is importante. I promise to collect donations of old clothes and dinero to take with you from all the senoras at the Club this week.

From: crystalwalker@sterlingmorris.com
To: phoebegb@sahmsrule.net

George just called me from New Hampshire to say that Sister Taylor was summarily ordered back to DC on convent business, which is just as well, as I'm pretty sure I could hear the hotel receptionist announce that happy hour was starting in the bar. Had no idea the lobbying business involved so much glad-handing, and so little actual 'work' – at least in any form I would recognize.

From: phoebegb@sahmsrule.net
To:crystalwalker@sterlingmorris.com

Trust me, I've learned over the years that it's all business, even if it takes place on a hunting trip, on the 9th hole or in the Gentlemen's Steam Room at the Club. George may never need to set foot in that swanky K street office of his, but it takes hard work to remember how the Senator from Vermont likes her whisky, or where her grandchildren go to school. And that stuff counts.

From: crystalwalker@sterlingmorris.com
To: phoebegb@sahmsrule.net

Trying to see the positive side of this development, especially at a time when so many others seem to be losing their jobs. But I can't help feeling insecure about the state of my marriage, especially when I look at the roll of post-partum fat above my work pants in the mirror. I have no idea how I'm ever going to juggle the demands of four cherubs, plus the house, dog, cat, lizard and hermit crabs after I start work at my new law firm next month.

Monday, September 10

The Committee for Village Youth would like to extend a cordial invitation to its 10th annual Back to School Bash

On Monday, September 24
at 3:30 p.m. at The Village Green
Please RSVP to the Village Office
by Friday, September 21

Note: this is an informal opportunity for new and existing Village moms and children to meet, mingle, and exchange child-rearing tips. It is NOT a guarantee of entrée into the Village Playgroup (see note in Village Newsletter for application information).

Tuesday, September 11

Album Posting on Crystal's Mebook Page
Featuring photo of George proudly displaying large trout he caught on trip. The conquering hero returns, a little stinkier and worse for wear, and with a Fedex cooler of frozen dead wildlife in tow. Torn between wanting to turn him into same, and feeling irrationally happy to have him home for more than 24 hours.

Response from P
Glad to hear George is back. Thanx for all the dead deer – Brad making venison ragu for dinner!

Posting on Crystal's Wall
Just found out George is leaving again on Monday for LA. Arrgh!

Comment from P
:(

Wednesday, September 12

Mebook Posting on Phoebe's Wall (accompanying photograph of scowling Cecily and Emily)
First full week back at school for twins next week! Hallelujah. If only Lata hadn't scheduled this week to go on her medical mercy mission, life would be (almost) perfect.

Text from Crystal to Phoebe
RU going to Back to School bash on Village Green this pm? Woken up by rap on door from woman introducing herself as 'resident block captain,' whatever that means, demanding to know if I plan on attending.

Text from Phoebe to Crystal
Must be Evelyn. Cecily and Emily and I will be there. Can u join?

Text from Crystal to Phoebe
Can't think of anything I'd rather do less, but feel I owe it to my 2 youngest to try and ensure they make the right Village connections. CU there.

Text from Phoebe to Crystal
Great. I'll bring refreshments.

Text from Crystal to Phoebe
Don't they supply?

Text from Phoebe to Crystal
Not kind we're looking for.

Thursday, September 13

From: crystalwalker@sterlingmorris.com
To: phoebegb@sahmsrule.net

Deliverance in a Starbucks mug! You really are a marvel. Always wondered how those other moms stayed at the playground long after I've started to contemplate the futility of my existence.

Using the light Cranberry juice is sheer genius. No sugar = no calories, right? Feel emboldened enough to ask Nina to crack open the vault and take over Baby's midnight feed using a bottle of precious frozen breast milk – one that's not laced with vodka.

Friday, September 14

Mebook posting on Crystal's wall
Help! According to everyone I spoke to at the party yesterday afternoon, my three older cherubs don't stand a chance of getting into their preferred Ivy League college if they continue to roam the Village streets after school lets out. I need to enroll them in extra-curriculars before it's too late. Any recommendations?

Mebook message, from Phoebe to Crystal
The cherubs have such a charming ability to scale all the trees at the Village Green, it would almost be a shame to interfere with their natural abilities. But if you really do insist on following the path of every other parent in the nation's capital, I have a professional after-school consultant I can recommend. Evelyn Braun happens to be our neighbor and the resident block captain to whom you referred in your earlier email. She is also the author of several bestselling books on childcare, and is regularly interviewed on public radio for advice on raising successful teens.

Skye Chat
crystalwalker
Are you awake?

phoebethompson
Yup. It's my witching hour, remember?

crystalwalker
Glad I'm not disturbing. I just wanted to get the skinny on Evelyn Braun, if you have time.

phoebethompson
It's pretty straightforward: For around two thousand dollars per child, Evelyn will give your child the entrée to the music, etiquette, language and sporting activities necessary to turn your children into Renaissance princelings.

crystalwalker
You're kidding. Two k per kid? My first car didn't cost that much.

phoebethompson
Trust me, they all charge that much, and Evelyn is the best.

crystalwalker
At this rate, we won't be able to afford to send the kids to any college, forget getting them into the Ivys! How do other parents around here afford all this stuff?

phoebethompson
Family money – do the math and you'll soon realize there's no way even your average lawyer can live in the Village and still afford to pay for the Club, the private schools, tutors, therapists and vacations their children seem to require, without considerable help from Mummy and Daddy.

crystalwalker
Seriously? That's insane. Do you have a contact number for this woman?

phoebethompson
Sure. By the way, did I mention that Evelyn's husband is the strapping construction man whose form you've probably admired as he toils over their house renovation?

crystalwalker
The one with the piercing blue eyes and all over tan? At least as far as I can tell, which is pretty far, given how low he likes to wear those jeans.

phoebethompson
That's right.

crystalwalker
So that's whose backside I've been staring at while blow-drying my hair. Is it wrong to lust after another woman's husband while you are still lactating?

phoebethompson
Who could blame you for admiring a man with such an impressive set of tools? But we need to focus here. Evelyn's extracurricular recommendations are too valuable to lose in favor of a man just because he happens to be competent with a screw. I'll email you her number in the morning.

crystalwalker
OK, thanks. Let me sleep on it. I'll talk to George in the meantime and see what he thinks.

Saturday, September 15

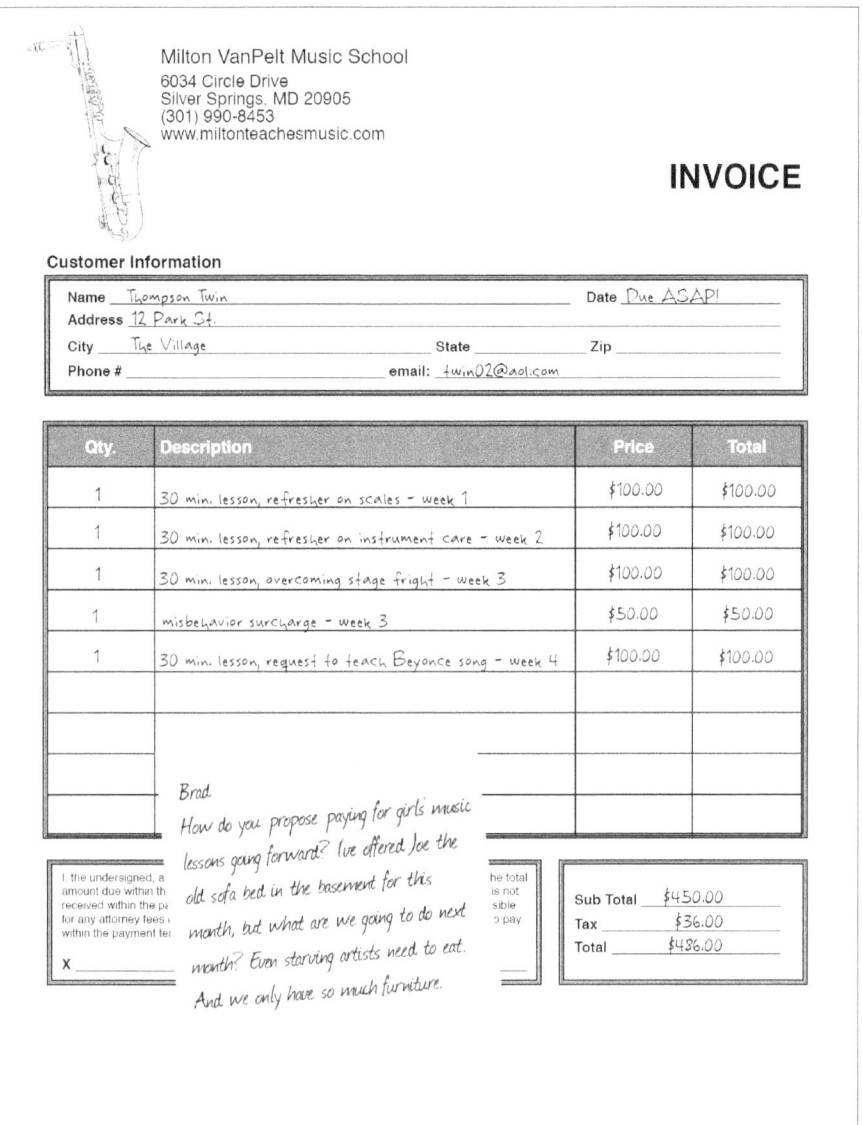

Milton VanPelt Music School
6034 Circle Drive
Silver Springs, MD 20905
(301) 990-8453
www.miltonteachesmusic.com

INVOICE

Customer Information

Name Thompson Twin   Date Due ASAP!
Address 12 Park St.
City The Village   State   Zip
Phone #   email: twin02@aol.com

Qty.	Description	Price	Total
1	30 min. lesson, refresher on scales - week 1	$100.00	$100.00
1	30 min. lesson, refresher on instrument care - week 2	$100.00	$100.00
1	30 min. lesson, overcoming stage fright - week 3	$100.00	$100.00
1	misbehavior surcharge - week 3	$50.00	$50.00
1	30 min. lesson, request to teach Beyonce song - week 4	$100.00	$100.00
	Brad.		

How do you propose paying for girls' music lessons going forward? I've offered Joe the old sofa bed in the basement for this month, but what are we going to do next month? Even starving artists need to eat. And we only have so much furniture.

I, the undersigned, a amount due within th received within the pa for any attorney fees within the payment ter

he total is not sible o pay

Sub Total $450.00
Tax $36.00
Total $486.00

X _____

Monday, September 17

Goggle Calendar Reminder
Back to School night, 6pm.

From: crystalwalker@sterlingmorris.com
To: phoebegb@sahmsrule.net
Turns out my own formal introduction to Evelyn took care of itself this afternoon, after Kevin inadvertently enraged Snuggles, her pet rottweiler, by repeatedly drumming a tennis ball against the side of her house.

Thankfully, Snuggles was inside at the time, but Evelyn offered to pay Kev to walk and feed him every day after-school, as a way to channel what she described as his 'kinetic adolescent energy' in a positive fashion, while she works on her latest book. Kevin was thrilled, of course, to be offered his first paid employment, but I'm freaked out by the idea of my sweet soon-to-be teenager taking his life into his hands every time he approaches the mutt with a bowl of Pedigree.

Evelyn has also offered to observe all the cherubs (Kurtis included) with a view to recommending suitable extra-curricular activities, as well. Given the current dire state of the economy, she's even offering us a 25% discount, which amounts to one cherub for free. She claims to be able to assess any child's cognitive, social and physical abilities within five minutes of meeting them, which is about how long it took for her to tell me she had a PhD from Stanford, and that her two books, 'Raising an Entitled Child' and 'Why It's Your Fault If Your Child Isn't Ivy League Material' are permanent bestsellers in the DC market.

Just out of curiosity, do you happen to know why she and Fred don't have children?

From: phoebegb@sahmsrule.net
To: crystalwalker@sterlingmorris.com
Not 100% sure, but in the same way that Catholic priests are considered sufficiently detached to advise couples on marriage, I imagine Evelyn's child-free status provides her with the perspective necessary to tell the rest of us what we are doing wrong with ours. As for Fred, I sometimes detect an element of frustrated fatherhood in the way he devotes himself to training Snuggles on the Village Green. But frankly, I'm occasionally envious of his child-free existence as well, so I guess that makes us even.

From: crystalwalker@sterlingmorris.com
To: phoebegb@sahmsrule.net
BTW, finally met Vira Bliss at the Back to School bash the other day. She is attractive, as you say, and her house is HUGE. Not sure how she squares this with her eco-friendly principles, but she did make a point of telling me the solar panels on the roof make it carbon neutral.

Her son, Ravi is the same age as Karson so I'm hoping the two of them will be friends. Remind me again how you know her?

From: phoebegb@sahmsrule.net
To: crystalwalker@sterlingmorris.com
Vira and I do a yoga class together twice a week, but she doesn't eat meat, drink alcohol or basically consume anything cooked, which makes me think the two of us can never really be close. How much raw carrot can a girl eat? Besides, I have a rule about not befriending attractive single women, esp. those rumored to have left their husband for another man (my Steamy Yoga Guru, Gunther Marshall, no less).

Text from Crystal to Kimberly
Where is my black mini-skirt? Need it ASAP!

Text from Crystal to Kimberly
I don't care if it looks better on you. I want to wear it tonight. And for the record, the zippers don't make me look like a wanna-be. Just vital and youthful.

Text from Crystal to Kimberly
hahahahahahaha not appropriate response. Find it in next 10 mins or lose sleepover privileges for rest of month.

Text from Crystal to Kimberly
Thanks, but accompanying note depicting skirt sobbing at its return is overwrought and unnecessary. I will wear proudly!

Text from Crystal to Phoebe, accompanying picture attachment
Would it be inappropriate to wear black mini-skirt to back to school night? Zippers involved. But so are tights. Kimberly says thought of me wearing in public makes her want to throw up.

Text from P to C
Generally, I would say we have to still wear this stuff while we still can, but not sure Back to School night is the occasion.

Tuesday, September 18

Skye Chat
crystalwalker
Should have taken your advice on miniskirt front. Had no idea the principal would limit the number of zippers allowed. Or that they enforce the fingertip rule when it comes to hemlines on adults.

crystalwalker
The worst part of the evening was stumbling home to find Kimberly waiting at the front door. She didn't say a word: just looked at me in horror before fleeing to your house. Aren't I supposed to the one giving knowing looks full of wisdom and experience?

phoebethompson
Kimberly was a delightful, if unexpected overnight guest, although I do wish she wouldn't let my twins use her MeBook page to connect with their public school peers. I know some parents allow it, but you are officially supposed to be 13, and I hate to encourage deception.

crystalwalker
Wish I could say a word with Kim is all that's required, but Lata Probed me this morning, and I happened to notice that she is friends with the twins too.

phoebethompson

I can't believe it! And to think I trusted Lata to tell me that kind of thing. I will demand they both take their pages down as soon as they get home from school.

crystalwalker

You may be missing a great opportunity for leverage. Why don't you commend their ingenuity, and make clear you now have another tool in your arsenal for important behavior modification purposes? Twins will be so thrilled to keep their MeBook page, they should behave impeccably for at least a week. And besides, gaining this kind of knowledge about what is really going on in your child's life is priceless.

phoebethompson

True. But can't they just de-Friend me when I'm not looking?

crystalwalker

Kim just regained MeBook privileges after attempting that little maneuver, so I don't think she will try that again. Of course, you will have to monitor MeBook more often yourself, but that's the fun part.

Mebook Friend Request from Phoebe to Twins

Phoebe Thompson would like to be friends with you on MeBook
'Darlings, if you don't 'Friend' me by midnight tonight, I am coming into your bedrooms and taking away your Powerbooks (Genius edition). Permanently.

Comment from Phoebe on Twins' Mebook Profile Pictures

You both look adorable, but I hardly recognized you in all that make-up. I really don't think it's appropriate at this age, especially on a public website, so I must insist you remove NOW.

Message from Phoebe to Twins

Alright, I will refrain from commenting on your profile pictures, if you refrain from commenting on mine. Your barb about my impending fortieth b/day was particularly cruel.

Wednesday, September 19

Skye Chat
crystalwalker

DVF wrap dress turned out to be perfect for prospective new member drinks at club last night, even if it did leave little to the imagination while nursing. Thanks for shopping advice!

phoebethompson

you looked stunning. And George cleaned up nicely from his lobbyist gone wild look while hunting, as well. What did you make of the other women there?

crystalwalker

well, there was the classic queen bee – Pookie Granger – surrounded by her acolytes. I'm thinking of Perky Sparks, who watches Pookie's every move, and won't do anything w/o her, although Bitsy Bottinger seemed pretty much glued to her side, as well.

phoebethompson

Pookie, Bitsy and Perky basically take over the best lounge chairs around the pool at the Village Country Club every day during the summer, issuing orders to the club waiters, husbands and passing children. I wouldn't mind, except that I'm not on the tennis team yet, so they have never ONCE invited me to join them! Hopefully, that should change once Xavier finds me a tennis partner for challenge season.

crystalwalker

Beginning to wonder why I've been so anxious to join the Club. I know George needs the connections for work, but I could personally do without women like Pookie and Perky, not to mention the deadly old white people food. Then there are the antiquated rules. Last night, I found myself hiding in the janitor's closet just to be able to use my cellphone on Club premises in order to speak to Nina about Karson's potentially dangerous fever spike.

phoebethompson

Tell me about it. They've only just allowed women to wear white after Labor Day – unless they're playing tennis that is, in which case everything they wear needs to be white, down to their underwear. And trust me, they're not shy about checking. Still, I appreciate the fact the Club doesn't stint on the liquor in their cocktails and the bartender will even fix me a Pisco in a pinch, so I wouldn't discount the place just yet.

crystalwalker

BTW. Ran into Pookie today at the grocery store, and she looked right through me, even after I waved and said hello. What gives?

phoebethompson

Pookie didn't acknowledge my existence for the first 5 years I lived in the Village. You basically have to be completely brazen about inserting yourself, and don't take no for an answer when she inevitably tries to shut you out. Why don't you come with me to club cocktails next Friday and I'll show you how it's done?

crystalwalker

Are you sure? Generally, I'm a very, very busy woman as you know, but it just so happens I might have a window next Fri. Are you sure it's OK if I tag along?

phoebethompson

Your natural Midwestern niceness in these matters does not serve you well. If anyone in DC waited to be asked for anything.........well–let's just say those people tend to live outside the Beltway.

crystalwalker

Speaking of pushy Americans, may I borrow your Tory Burke tunic with the buttons down the front? If you're not planning on wearing it, of course. I was thinking it's probably the only thing that will allow me to nurse baby without exposing myself the way I did with the DVF.

phoebethompson

It's the least I can do. BTW, I would encourage you to be discreet about nursing at the club. Members are just not used to seeing such voluptuous displays of motherhood.

crystalwalker

What about all the boob jobs?

phoebethompson

I'm afraid you really can't compare perfect lumps of silicone with a functioning set of mammary glands. One reminds the stuffier members of the new Village safety humps; the other of all the dark and dirty groping they were once forced to engage in with frat boys, in order to get their M.R.S. degree.

crystalwalker

Guess I could retire to the Ladies Lounge in order to nurse, but I have to say, it goes against every feminist fiber of my being. If it weren't for the fact that George's firm wants him to join the Club (and is willing to pay the dues) in order to schmooze some of the members, I would stage a public nurse-in.

phoebethompson

Trust me. It's much more fun to infiltrate the enemy, and destroy from within.

Thursday, September 20

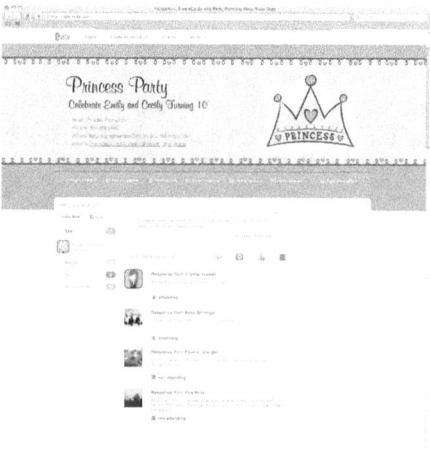

it to Facebook   Print Invitation   Export Guest List   Send a Message   Add to C

MESSAGE FROM HOST   Hide

Please join the Thompson Twins for High Tea with Princess Poppy to celebrate Emily and Cecily turning 10!

Phoebe Thompson

Event Conversation

Response from Crystal Walker

Kimberly and I would love to come!!

2 attending

Response from Bitsy Bottinger

Triplets will be there. OK to send the Nanny?

5 attending

Response from Pookie Granger

Unfortunately, Whookie and I have a prior engagement. Sorry to miss.

2 not attending

Response from Vira Bliss

Alas I will be on retreat that weekend and Ravi will be with his father. Will send Birthday Blessings® from my hammock under the palms.

2 not attending

From: phoebegb@sahmsrule.net
To: princesspoppy@partyhell.com
Sorry my deposit check for party bounced. Will drop off cash ASAP.

Craig's List Posting
For Sale: VBox 360, headphones and deluxe black leather La-Z-Man (barely used). $500 total (ONO). CASH ONLY. Transport to be arranged by buyer at a time when seller's spouse is not home.
For more information, email phoebegb@sahmsrule.net

Witter from @femilawyermom
First date night since Baby was born!

Witter from @femilawyermom
Dinner and movie = not best idea with 2 month old at home. Hubby and I both fell asleep during opening credits. Woken by usher at end. On plus side, best sleep I've had in years.

@insomniacmom is now following femilawyermom

Friday, September 21

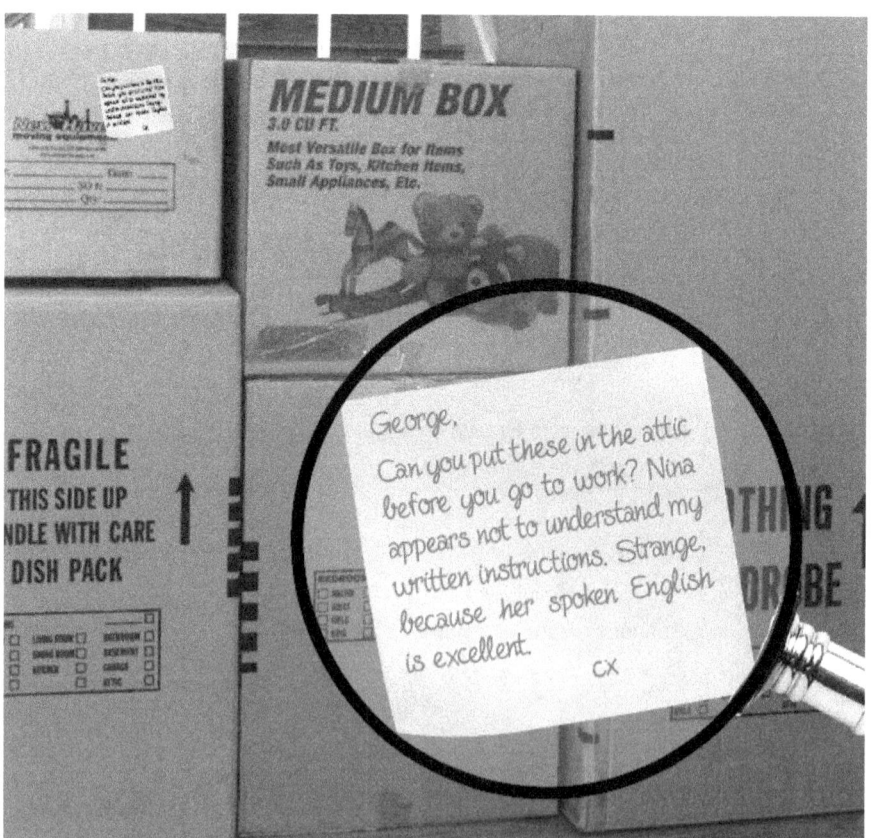

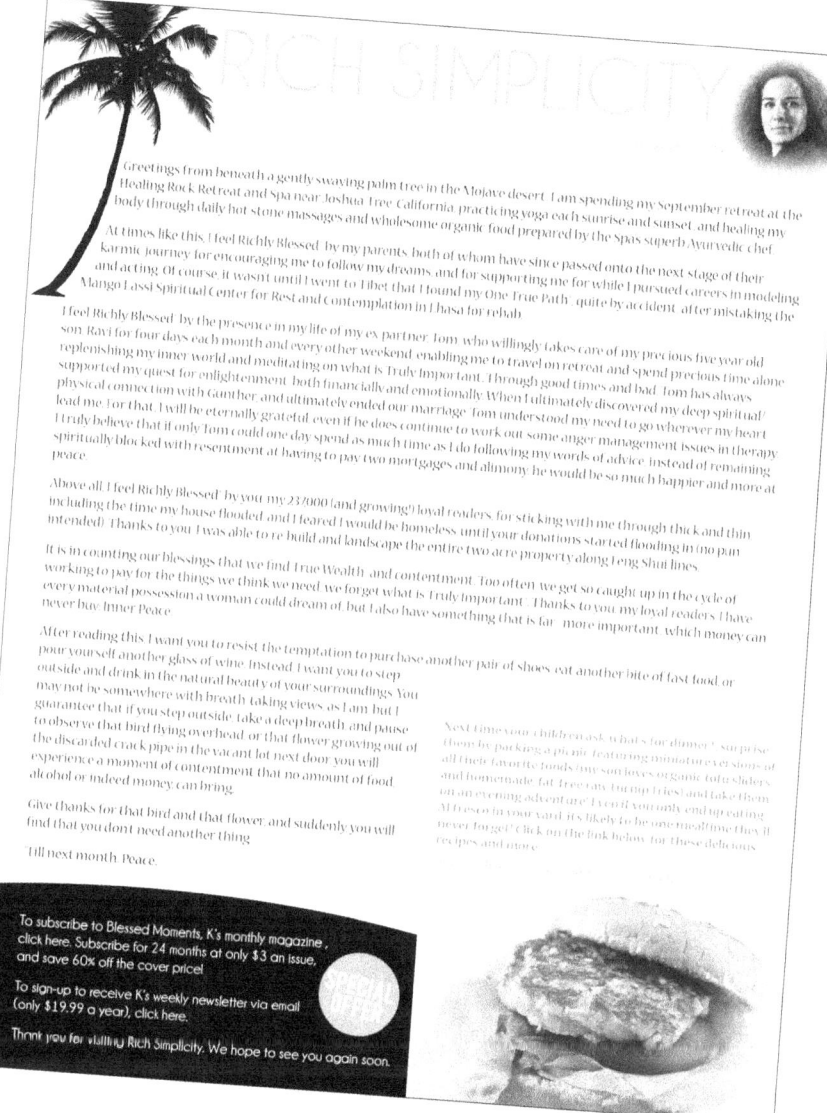

From: Rich Simplicity
To: phoebegb@sahmsrule.net

Rich Simplicity: A monthly newsletter bringing you a life of ultimate simplicity, no matter how much money I have.

Volume 03, Issue 09

Blessings,

Greetings from beneath a gently swaying palm tree in the Mojave desert. I am spending my September retreat at the Healing Rock Retreat and Spa near Joshua Tree, California, practicing yoga each sunrise and sunset, and healing my body through daily hot stone massages and wholesome organic food prepared by the Spa's superb Ayurvedic chef.

At times like this, I feel Richly Blessed® by my parents, both of whom have since passed onto the next stage of their karmic journey, for encouraging me to follow my dreams, and for supporting me for while I pursued careers in modeling and acting. Of course, it wasn't until I went to Tibet that I found my One True Path®, quite by accident, after mistaking the Mango Lassi Spiritual Center for Rest and Contemplation in Lhasa for rehab.

I feel Richly Blessed® by the presence in my life of my ex-partner, Tom, who willingly takes care of my precious five year old son, Ravi for four days each month and every other weekend, enabling me to travel on retreat and spend precious time alone, replenishing my inner world and meditating on what is Truly Important. Through good times and bad, Tom has always supported my quest for enlightenment, both financially and emotionally. When I ultimately discovered my deep spiritual/physical connection with Gunther, and ultimately ended our marriage, Tom understood my need to go wherever my heart lead me. For that, I will be eternally grateful, even if he does continue to work out some anger management issues in therapy. I truly believe that if only Tom could one day spend as much time as I do following my words of advice, instead of remaining spiritually blocked with resentment at having to pay two mortgages and alimony, he would be so much happier and more at peace.

Above all, I feel Richly Blessed® by you, my 237,000 (and growing!) loyal readers, for sticking with me through thick and thin, including the time my house flooded, and I feared I would be homeless, until your donations started flooding in (no pun intended). Thanks to you, I was able to rebuild and landscape the entire two acre property along Feng Shui lines.

It is in counting our blessings that we find True Wealth® and contentment. Too often, we get so caught up in the cycle of working to pay for the things we think we need, we forget what is Truly Important®. Thanks to you, my loyal readers, I have every material possession a woman could dream of, but I also have something that is far more important, which money can never buy: Inner Peace.

After reading this, I want you to resist the temptation to purchase another pair of shoes, eat another bite of fast food, or pour yourself another glass of wine. Instead, I want you to step outside and drink in the natural beauty of your surroundings. You may not be somewhere with breath-taking views, as I am, but I guarantee that if you step outside, take a deep breath, and pause to observe that bird flying overhead, or that flower growing out of the discarded crack pipe in the vacant lot next door, you will experience a moment of contentment that no amount of food, alcohol or indeed money, can bring. Give thanks for that bird and that flower, and suddenly, you will find that you don't need another thing.

'Till next month.

Peace.

From: phoebegb@sahmsrule.net
To: crystalwalker@sterlingmorris.com
FW: Rich Simplicity newsletter
Can't help feeling it's easier to go on a dinnertime adventure with your kids on a school night when you have a live-in chef to prepare the picnic, and a nanny to pick up the pieces.

From: crystalwalker@sterlingmorris.com
To: phoebegb@sahmsrule.net
Made the tofu sliders for cherubs and they reacted like I was trying to poison them. May take years to rebuild that kind of trust.

From: phoebegb@sahmsrule.net
To: crystalwalker@sterlingmorris.com
Somehow, I don't think Vira has ever had to deal with a true financial crisis. Or a husband quite as irate as Brad. Hell hath no fury like a man whose wife has just sold his favorite armchair.

From: crystalwalker@sterlingmorris.com
To: phoebegb@sahmsrule.net
Yikes. That would explain why I saw him chasing the Village Special Trash Pick-Up truck down the street dressed only in his (gaping) bathrobe just now. No wonder he seemed disappointed the truck only contained my empty moving boxes.

Any idea what Vira's ex does for a living?

From: phoebegb@sahmsrule.net
To: crystalwalker@sterlingmorris.com
A little birdie (Pookie) told me that Tom is a fund manager, who made and lost a fortune with a private equity group here in DC, which is why Vira started her blog. He has since returned to his original position as a partner in a law firm that specializes in defending big corporations for violating workers' civil rights, which is the perfect way to make big bucks AND hold onto your bleeding heart in this town.

Whenever Vira is not jet-setting around the world, she and Tom take turns home-schooling Ravi, because both the public and private schools around here are unable to cater to his extraordinary talents. Vira claims he is extremely gifted, although frankly, in the Village, whose child isn't?

Vira also claims she and Tom are still best friends, in spite of Gunther, so maybe it is possible to have an amicable divorce? Personally, I've always felt that it's conflict that keeps a marriage ticking (twins wouldn't exist if it didn't), but who am I to judge?

From: crystalwalker@sterlingmorris.com
To: phoebegb@sahmsrule.net
As the child of a broken home, I do feel qualified to reassure you that there is no such thing as a happy divorce. You and I may envy Vira's ability to walk

across the bedroom floor without hooking her toe on a discarded pair of tighty whities, but something about the way I keep finding my hands round my cherubs' tender young necks these past few days makes me think we were not meant to parent alone.

Tuesday, September 25

From: crystalwalker@sterlingmorris.com
To: phoebegb@sahmsrule.net
Subject: Birthday
Looking forward to twins' party this weekend. What would your girls like by way of a gift?

From: phoebegb@sahmsrule.net
To: crystalwalker@sterlingmorris.com
Re: Birthday
Gift card to 'Forever Dressing Too Young' for each would be GREAT.

Normally, we encourage Cecily and Emily to forego presents in favor of asking their friends and family to make a donation to charity, but I have decided to relax the 'no gifts' rule this year, and just not invite any of their friends from CRAC, who would be appalled by such rampant displays of materialism.

From: crystalwalker@sterlingmorris.com
To: phoebegb@sahmsrule.net
Re: Birthday
Forever Dressing Too Young = Kimberly's favorite store (and mine too, just between ourselves)! Consider it done.

Wednesday, September 26

Text from Phoebe to Brad
Don't forget twins' birthday tomorrow. Surely your daughters' happiness = more important than yr crappy old La-Z-Boy?

Thursday, September 27

Mebook Album Posting
with pictures from Cecily and Emily's birthday party
Can't believe my little darlings are ten years old. Here's to many more years of Double Trouble!

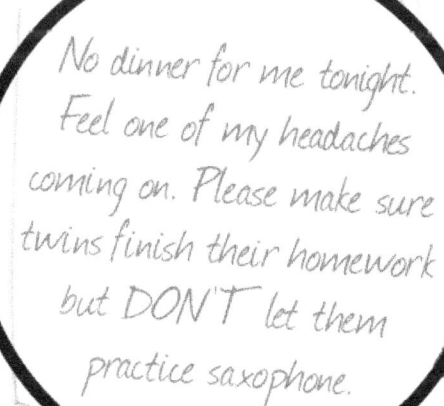

No dinner for me tonight.
Feel one of my headaches
coming on. Please make sure
twins finish their homework
but DON'T let them
practice saxophone.

Brad,

For the record, you and Lata do not do everything around here! And even if you did, you would both still need someone directing you. You have no idea the work involved in managing the help.

P.S. Changed my mind. We'd like a bowl of pesto after all.

xo

Sunday, September 30

DC Diary

The Walkers Take on the Nation's Capital

Snuggles, Country Club and Maternity Leave

Well, it's been another busy month, but Kevin, Kimberly and Karson are all settling in nicely at school and starting to make friends, even though most of our neighbors seem to send their kids to private school (the snobby kind, Dad, not the military academy you were forced to attend). Kev and Karson in particular miss their father, who's been traveling most of the month, and even when he's home doesn't have time right now to shoot hoops or throw a ball.

Still, Kevin did make it onto the under-fourteen rec baseball team, which practices at the local park on Tuesdays and Thursdays. He also has a job walking our neighbor's pet rottweiler, which should keep him busy, although I've already caught him paying Kimberly to do it for him - twice. Check out the cute picture of Snuggles below!

I've met some interesting women at the Village Country Club, which we are in the process of applying to join. There's the usual country club posse, who seem a little hostile to newcomers, but my friend, Phoebe assures me that if I persevere in being friendly, they will accept me in the end. They do seem to drink a lot, which bodes well for the future, although as I'm still nursing, I find I have to tip the contents of my cocktail into one of the Club lounge's potted ficuses more often than I'd like.

My maternity leave is flying by, but there's still so much to do in terms of unpacking the last of the moving boxes, getting the kids' after-school activites sorted out and generally coping with life that I don't know how I'm going to manage a new job, as well. At least it looks like I've found a wonderful creche (fancy DC word for daycare) for Kurtis right next to my office, so I will at least be able to nurse her during my lunch hour. Guess this craziness is what people mean by having it all, right? Apologies you are getting our September update in October! Promise to try to be more timely in the future.

'Till next month!

No comments:

Post a Comment

Comment as: Select profile   ⬦
Publish   Preview

DC Diary
Snuggles, Country Club and Maternity Leave

Well, it's been another busy month, but Kevin, Kimberly and Karson are all settling in nicely at school and starting to make friends, even though most of our neighbors seem to send their kids to private school (the snobby kind, Dad, not the military academy you were forced to attend). Kev and Karson in particular miss their father, who's been traveling most of the month, and even when he's home doesn't have time right now to shoot hoops or throw a ball.

Still, Kevin did make it onto the under-fourteen rec baseball team, which practices at the local park on Tuesdays and Thursdays. He also has a job walking our neighbor's pet rottweiler, which should keep him busy, although I've already caught him paying Kimberly to do it for him - twice. Check out the cute picture of Snuggles below!

I've met some interesting women at the Village Country Club, which we are in the process of applying to join. There's the usual country club posse, who seem a little hostile to newcomers, but my friend, Phoebe assures me that if I persevere in being friendly, they will accept me in the end. They do seem to drink a lot, which bodes well for the future, although as I'm still nursing, I find I have to tip the contents of my cocktail into one of the Club lounge's potted ficuses more often than I'd like.

My maternity leave is flying by, but there's still so much to do in terms of unpacking the last of the moving boxes, getting the kids' after-school activities sorted out and generally coping with life that I don't know how I'm going to manage a new job, as well. At least it looks like I've found a wonderful creche (fancy DC word for daycare) for Kurtis right next to my office, so I will at least be able to nurse her during my lunch hour. Guess this craziness is what people mean by having it all, right? 'Till next month!

Chapter 3

October, 2012 Vol. 41, Issue 10
Always FREE, but donations appreciated

Please direct submissions and inquiries to:
whining@villagepress.com
P.O. Box 357 Village Town, MD

VILLAGE WHINER

Your trusty monthly newsletter of the "Most Livable Village," 1989
Village Times Magazine

Reminder Re: Leaf Blowers

Happy Halloween! 'Tis the season of mists and mellow fruitfulness. Also the season of leaf removal and blocked gutters. Residents are reminded that leaf blowers are not permitted in the Village between the hours of 5pm and 10am. We know this is inconvenient for those of you who work outside the home, but the Board of Managers does keep a list of landscaping services that are approved to work here during daylight hours. Please contact Sue in the Village Office for more information.

Club News

The Village Halloween party will take place on Friday, October 30 at 5 pm. The party will kick-off with a Costume Parade around the Park, followed by refreshments and games in the Village Hall. Block captains are reminded of their responsibility to round-up Village citizens and encourage them to attend.

Please adhere to the following guidelines in doing so:

1. Knocking on doors is the preferred method of communication. [illegible]

[illegible]

Due to the Halloween festivities, there will be no Manners and More class this month. The Village Diversity Group is also on hiatus, in protest at the Village Board's refusal to ease its restrictions on cross-dressing for the party itself.

Board Member Resignation Letter

To the Board:

Effective immediately, I, Barbi Van Houzen (better known as the late Tinklepaw's owner), must announce my decision to resign from the Village Board of Managers, following the reckless decision to allow Holier Than Thou Foods to break ground on their so-called 'gourmet food emporium' this month. They did this in spite of the compelling arguments I presented about the danger of having a clean, well-lit grocery store competing with our independent neighborhood shoppes. I for one cherish the ability to buy over-priced, wilted produce from the surly staff at Megabers, which has miraculously stayed in business for over forty years. I feel sure others agree, but may be too intimidated by the outspoken HTTF supporters on the Village Board to take a firm stand.

My only regret is that I must leave the Village government so ill equipped to deal with the vast array of complex issues before them – including, but not limited to the numerous but unfounded claims for vehicular damage resulting from the recent installation of speed humps on Center Street. As I keep telling the people who complain, if they weren't speeding, the damage would not have occurred!

Still, I trust that I served Tinklepaw in death as I served her in life: never without more concern for my darling pug than for real live people. May she rest in peace, and may the remaining Board members find out sooner rather than later how very obvious my absence is from their numbers. Of course, they should feel free to commemorate my resignation by re-naming our meeting room in my honor. I will forward the petition list immediately upon request.

Sincerely,
BVH

Village Authors Update

The Village is pleased to announce its latest literary success: Vita Bliss, who lives in the charming villa with the Feng Shui gardens on Church Street, is publishing her first memoir entitled The Blessings of Motherhood: a Journey Through My Son's First Year of Life this month. Share Vita's frustration and joy as she learns to navigate the choppy waters of motherhood (Babies poop, pee and cry! Who knew?) and ultimately comes to appreciate the profound and timeless lessons of love, which women who have been having children for thousands of years without writing a book about it, have always known.

The book is dedicated to Vita's lactation consultant and mothering mentor Gaia Eterna (professional name), who has asked us to note that she advises women on the life-changing but ultimately rewarding transition from successful careers to professional motherhood, and not on how to raise your child.

A book party and organic baby food tasting will be held on Saturday, October 18 at 7 pm in the Village Hall. Yoga Guru Gunther Marshall, founder of Steamy Yoga in Georgetown, will read excerpts from the book (in character, where relevant).

Miss Gertrude

Although Miss Gertrude would love to limit her discussion points to high-minded endeavors, she understands that the delicate matter of how best to discard of one's dog doo has recently become a hotbed of Village controversy, with the poop hitting the porch fan at least literally, in one case. Rather than instituting DNA testing (for Village dogs, not owners) in order to definitively match deposits to culprits, Miss Gertrude urges a more neighborly approach before it's too late. To the new resident who screamed at her neighbors for letting their pooches do their business on the public median in front of her property, do not be surprised to find unwelcome gifts of same on your front lawn. Planting trees on said median is no excuse! And to anyone who likes to leave still warm baggies by the side of the road while they complete their walk-run, then forgets them, do not be surprised when said baggies re-appear through your mailbox later on. In both cases, a little more thoughtfulness and consideration for others' (not to mention collective property rights) goes a long way.

It should also be noted that it is really never permissible to allow one's toddler to go in public behind a bush on the Village Green, even when said child is 'desperate,' as is often claimed by moms who can't be bothered to run the kid home. Miss Gertrude would hate to encourage a practice that, while harmless enough during potty training, might result in a lifelong compulsion ending in multiple [illegible] and quite possibly a criminal record if the act occurs within 50' of a public school.

Tennis Team results

Our sterling Ladies A team, also known as the WASPS, battled valiantly against the formidable opponents fielded by our arch rivals from Beauview Country Club on Connecticut Avenue during the first match of the interclub season last Tuesday. Alas, following some long and contentious games, including one exchange in which our opponents accused team captain Pookie Granger of drawing her finger across her throat in a menacing fashion, we ultimately lost in a bruising battle that lasted well past midnight. Final results below:

Ladies Number 1 Doubles 0-6, 7-5, 0-1*
Ladies Number 2 Doubles 3-6, 1-3 Forfeited*
Ladies Number 3 Doubles 6-1, 2-4 Retired**

Meanwhile, the Gentleman's Doubles program continues to suffer from lack of a team coordinator since Biffy McTavish's secretary retired a year ago. Gentlemen, the age of the executive personal assistant is over, so please stop relying on your wives to wash your whites, schedule your matches and print out your scorecards. We look forward to seeing you on the courts.

Starting this month, prospective club tennis team members and their partners are permitted to challenge existing team players. Pairs are required to issue a written challenge (no email, please), and must agree to complete all matches before midnight on December 31. Challengers must win all three of their games in order to advance onto the team next summer. Current team members who lose any of said matches will forfeit their right to play on the team for 12 calendar months, unless they can present a valid reason for their poor performance.

Finally, we hope you will join us for the annual Club tournament on Sunday, October 12 at 5 pm. Remember to come with an opposite sex partner (random spot checks will be conducted!) and dressed to play tennis (whites only, please). Winners will be awarded His 'n' Hers matching tennis sweaters monogrammed with their initials and the title of "Club Champion, 2008". Look forward to seeing you there.

** Lost in 8-10 in tiebreak*
** Due to unfortunate hair-pulling incident*
*** After opponent faked foot injury to avoid losing second set, and therefore the match*

CLASSIFIEDS

ORGANIC PESTO FOR SALE
THE LAST HARVEST OF THE SEASON IS IN, SO GRAB IT WHILE YOU CAN!

Warning: Ours is an all-natural, artisanal product featuring organic, homegrown herb, so we cannot be held responsible for any adverse effects resulting from ingestion.
To arrange for pick-up email:
onebiteandyouarehooked@yahoo.com

October, 2012 Vol. 41, Issue 10
Always FREE, but donations appreciated

Please direct submissions and inquiries to:
whining@villagepress.com
P.O. Box 357 Village Town, MD

Reminder Re: Leaf Blowers

Happy Halloween! 'Tis the season of mists and mellow fruitfulness. Also the season of leaf removal and blocked gutters. Residents are reminded that leaf blowers are not permitted in the Village between the hours of 5pm and 10am. We know this is inconvenient for those of you who work outside the home, but the Board of Managers does keep a list of landscaping services that are approved to work here during daylight hours. Please contact Sue in the Village Office for more information.

Board Member
Resignation Letter

The
on
wit
by
cap
Vil

Du
Div
cro
• • • •

Club News

The Village Halloween party will take place on Wednesday, October 31 at 5 pm. The party will kick-off with a Costume Parade around the Park, followed by refreshments and games in the Village Hall. Block captains are reminded of their responsibility to round-up Village citizens and encourage them to attend.

Please adhere to the following guidelines in doing so:

1. Knocking on doors is the preferred method of communication. Any time after 6 am (7 am on weekends) is acceptable, and does not constitute harassment, per current village by-laws;

2. Villagers should be encouraged to attend the party in costume. Any resistance should be met with a pleasant reminder that residents have a duty to uphold the pledge to community support they took when they were granted permission to purchase (or, in the case of a select few, rent) their home;

3. Women over 40 wearing fishnet stockings will be asked to re-consider their wardrobe choice before admission. Claims that said hosiery forms part of a burlesque costume will not be accepted, unless accompanied by a picture on the box demonstrating same.

Due to the Halloween festivities, there will be no Manners and More class this month. The Village Diversity Group is also on hiatus, in protest at the Village Board's refusal to ease its restrictions on cross-dressing for the party itself.

Board Member
Resignation Letter

To the Board:

Effective immediately, I, Barbi Van Houzen (better known as the late Tinklepaw's owner), must announce my decision to resign from the Village Board of Managers, following the reckless decision to allow Holier Than Thou Foods to break ground on their so-called 'gourmet food emporium' this month. They did this in spite of the compelling arguments I presented about the danger of having a clean, well-lit grocery store competing with our independent neighborhood shoppes. I for one cherish the ability to buy over-priced, wilted produce from the surly staff at Mcgrubers, which has miraculously stayed in business for over forty years. I feel sure others agree, but may be too intimidated by the outspoken HTTF supporters on the Village Board to take a firm stand.

My only regret is that I must leave the Village government so ill-equipped to deal with the vast array of complex issues before them - including, but not limited to the numerous but unfounded claims for vehicular damage resulting from the recent installation of speed humps on Center Street. As I keep telling the people who complain, if they weren't speeding, the damage would not have occurred!

Still, I trust that I served Tinklepaw in death as I served her in life: never without more concern for my darling pug than for real live people. May she rest in peace, and may the remaining Board members find out sooner rather than later how very obvious my absence is from their numbers. Of course, they should feel free to commemorate my resignation by re-naming our meeting room in my honor. I will forward the petition list immediately upon request.

Sincerely,
BVH

Village Authors Update

The Village is pleased to announce its latest literary success. Vira Bliss, who lives in the charming villa with the Feng Shui gardens on Church Street, is publishing her first memoir, entitled The Blessings of Motherhood: a Journey Through My Son's First Year of Life this month. Share Vira's frustration and joy as she learns to navigate the choppy waters of motherhood (Babies poop, pee and cry! Who knew?) and ultimately comes to appreciate the profound and timeless lessons of love, which women who have been having children for thousands of years without writing a book about it, have always known.

The book is dedicated to Vira's lactation consultant and mothering mentor, Gaia Eterna (professional name), who has asked us to note that she advises women on the life-changing but ultimately rewarding transition from successful careers to professional motherhood, and not on how to raise your child.

A book party and organic baby food tasting will be held on Saturday, October 18 at 7 pm in the Village Hall. Yoga Guru, Gunther Marshall, founder of Steamy Yoga in Georgetown, will read excerpts from the book (in character, where relevant).

Miss Gertrude

Although Miss Gertrude would love to limit her discussion points to high-minded endeavors, she understands that the delicate matter of how best to discard of one's dog doo has recently become a hotbed of Village controversy, with the poop hitting the porch fan at least literally, in one case. Rather than instituting DNA testing (for Village dogs, not owners) in order to definitively match deposits to culprits, Miss Gertrude urges a more neighborly approach before it's too late. To the new resident who screamed at her neighbors for letting their pooches do their business on the public median in front of her property, do not be surprised to find unwelcome gifts of same on your front lawn. Planting trees on said median is no excuse! And to anyone who likes to leave still warm baggies by the side of the road while they complete their walk/run, only to forget them, do not be surprised when said baggies re-appear through your mailbox later on. In both cases, a little more thoughtfulness and consideration for others (not to mention collective property rights) goes a long way.

It should also be noted that it is really never permissible to allow one's toddler to go in public behind a bush on the Village Green, even when said child is 'desperate,' as is often claimed by moms who can't be bothered to run the kid home. Miss Gertrude would hate to encourage a practice that, while harmless enough during potty training, might result in a lifetime compulsion ending in multiple citations, and quite possibly a criminal record if the act occurs within 50' of a public school.

Tennis Team results

Our sterling Ladies' A team, also known as the WASPS, battled valiantly against the formidable opponents fielded by our arch rivals from Beauview Country Club on Connecticut Avenue during the first match of the interclub season last Tuesday. Alas, following some long and contentious games, including one exchange in which our opponents accused team captain Pookie Granger of drawing her finger across her throat in a menacing fashion, we ultimately lost in a bruising battle that lasted well past midnight. Final results below:

Ladies Number 1 Doubles 0-6, 7-5, 0-1+
Ladies Number 2 Doubles 3-6, 1-3 Forfeited*
Ladies Number 3 Doubles 6-1, 2-4 Retired**

Meanwhile, the Gentlemen's Doubles program continues to suffer from lack of a team coordinator since Buffy McTavish's secretary retired a year ago. Gentlemen, the age of the executive personal assistant is over, so please stop relying on your wives to wash your whites, schedule your matches and print out your scorecards. We look forward to seeing you on the courts.

Starting this month, prospective Club tennis team members and their partners are permitted to challenge existing team players. Pairs are required to issue a written challenge (no email, please), and must agree to complete all matches before midnight on December 31. Challengers must win all three of their games in order to advance onto the team next summer. Current team members who lose any of said matches will forfeit their right to play on the team for 12 calendar months, unless they can present a valid reason for their poor performance.

Finally, we hope you will join us for the annual Club tournament on Sunday, October 12 at 5 pm. Remember to come with an opposite sex partner (random spot checks will be conducted!) and dressed to play (tennis whites only, please). Winners will be awarded His 'n' Hers matching tennis sweaters monogrammed with their initials and the title of 'Club Champion, 2012'. Look forward to seeing you there.

+ Lost in 8-10 in tie break
* Due to unfortunate hair-pulling incident
** After opponent faked foot injury to avoid losing second set, and therefore the match

CLASSIFIEDS

ORGANIC PESTO FOR SALE
THE LAST HARVEST OF THE SEASON IS IN, SO GRAB IT WHILE YOU CAN!

Warning: Ours is an all-natural, artisanal product featuring organic, homegrown herb, so we cannot be held responsible for any adverse effects resulting from ingestion.
To arrange for pick-up email:
onebiteandyouarehooked@yahoo.com

* Please note, ads may only be placed by Village residents with home-based businesses.

Text from Crystal to Phoebe
Our internet down and George Go-Karting with National Association of Loggers and Truckers in West VA. Any chance Brad can come and investigate?

Text from Phoebe to Crystal
Not sure you realize the gravity of the La-Z-Boy incident. Brad not speaking to me until I track down and repurchase, but new owner proving equally attached to damn thing.

Text from Crystal to Phoebe
Give me buyer's number, and I'll work on him.

Text from Crystal to George
Forced to sext a complete stranger in return for right to buy back Brad Thompson's favorite recliner. Does that trouble/turn u on?

Text from Phoebe to Crystal
Brad THRILLED to be reunited with his beloved. Thank you! How did you persuade the boy (actually, 40 year old man) to sell it back?

Text from Crystal to Phoebe
Let me just say, it wasn't pretty. What was it Vira was saying about material things not being important to happiness and Inner Peace? Or was it world peace? So hard to keep it all straight.

Text from Phoebe to Crystal
Just remember, Vira claims not to own a TV, but her nanny and son have been at our house all morning, watching ours.

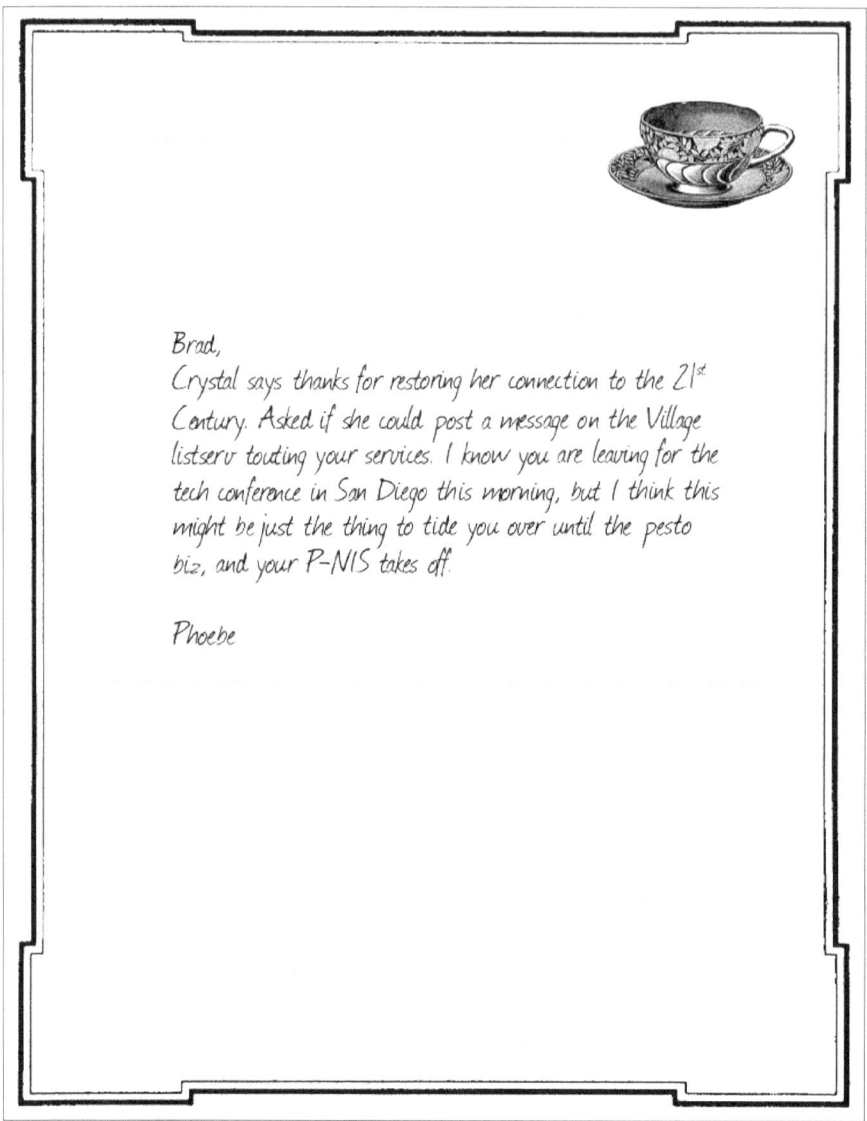

Brad,

Crystal says thanks for restoring her connection to the 21ˢᵗ Century. Asked if she could post a message on the Village listserv touting your services. I know you are leaving for the tech conference in San Diego this morning, but I think this might be just the thing to tide you over until the pesto biz, and your P-NIS takes off.

Phoebe

Posting on Village listerv
From: crystalwalker@sterlingmorris.com
Re: Fabulous Find

Has your hard drive crashed, your firewall crumbled; your printer died just when you needed it most? I recently confronted a future devoid of meaning, after my internet connection went down. Then I called Computer Guy. Five minutes later, my connection was restored, and with it, my sense of purpose. Best of all, he lives just around the corner! Call 301 961 X0X0 or email ineverleavethehouseotherwise@hotmail.com for service.

From: crystalwalker@sterlingmorris.com
To: phoebegb@sahmsrule.net
Re: Fabulous Find

Vira just saw my post on the Village listserv singing Brad's praises and asked if he might be available to help her set up an online payment system for Rich Simplicity merchandise. I gave her Brad's cell – hope that's OK. I trust it doesn't bother you to have him fiddling with the connection on another woman's USB port.

From: pheobegb@sahmsrule.net
To: crystalwalker@sterlingmorris.com
Re: Fabulous Find

Happy to let Brad tinker with any other woman's system in the entire Village right now, as I'm frankly too mad about our financial situation to let him anywhere near mine.

From: crystalwalker@sterlingmorris.com
To: phoebegb@sahmsrule.net

At the risk of sounding old-fashioned, I am troubled by your willingness to ignore your wifely duty. Having witnessed the philandering behavior of my own father over the years, I'm convinced it's the best shot we have at keeping hearth and home together- particularly when times are tough, as they sound like they are for you guys right now. No doubt my comrades from St. Stevens Women's Studies Class would be up in arms at the idea of sublimating our own sexual needs (or lack of them) to pander to the patriarchy, but then again, I also doubt they would concern themselves with the petty details involved in raising children.

I'm sure you're feeling tense waiting for one or other of Brad's ventures to take off, but my advice to you in the meantime is to lie back and think of Mother England as often as possible– or at the very least, what color to paint the bedroom ceiling.

From: phoebegb@sahmsrule.net
To: crystalwalker@sterlingmorris.com

Point taken. As it happens, Brad leaves for San Diego tomorrow a.m. to attend ConDom (Conference on Drilling for Oil and Mining). I'm delighted he's showing initiative on the work front, but we all know what that means: Five minutes talking shop, followed by hours of drinking surrounded by twenty-something hostesses who don't know any better than to act impressed with a man's hard drive.

By way of precaution, I've taken to bed, called Brad to join me and am flicking through the latest Architectural Digest for stimulation. Shouldn't take long...Talk soon.

Wednesday, October 3

Text from Phoebe to Crystal
Would it be wrong of me to take Xavier as my date to Prospective New Member cocktails at Club tonight in place of Brad?

Text from Crystal to Phoebe
Not if you take me with you.

Text from Phoebe to Crystal
Sounds like the perfect plan. Pick you up at 7.15.

Text from Crystal to Phoebe
CU then.

Thursday, October 4

Posting on Village Listserv
Please note that it is entirely unacceptable for members of the Club staff (including tennis pros) to perform lap dances on Club property at any time, including Club Cocktail Hour. Members caught with the tennis pro or any other individual draped across their personage will have their Club privileges suspended immediately, pending an investigation. Intoxication is NOT an excuse.

On a related note, could the member who leapt into the pool fully-clothed at midnight please retrieve her purse and shoes from Club offices. She may otherwise miss her British passport.

From: crystalwalker@sterlingmorris.com
To: phoebegb@sahmsrule.net
Congratulations on making your mark, last night! You certainly left Pookie in no doubt that you are a force to be reckoned with, esp. after you challenged her to an impromptu set of singles.

From: phoebegb@sahmsrule.net
To: crystalwalker@sterlingmorris.com
Please refrain from using exclamation points right now. Did we really play in heels?

From: crystalwalker@sterlingmorris.com
To: phoebegb@sahmsrule.net
writing in small print to avoid jarring your already sensitive nerves. you took heels off, from what I recall, then quickly abandoned play in favor of 'christening' the new pool.

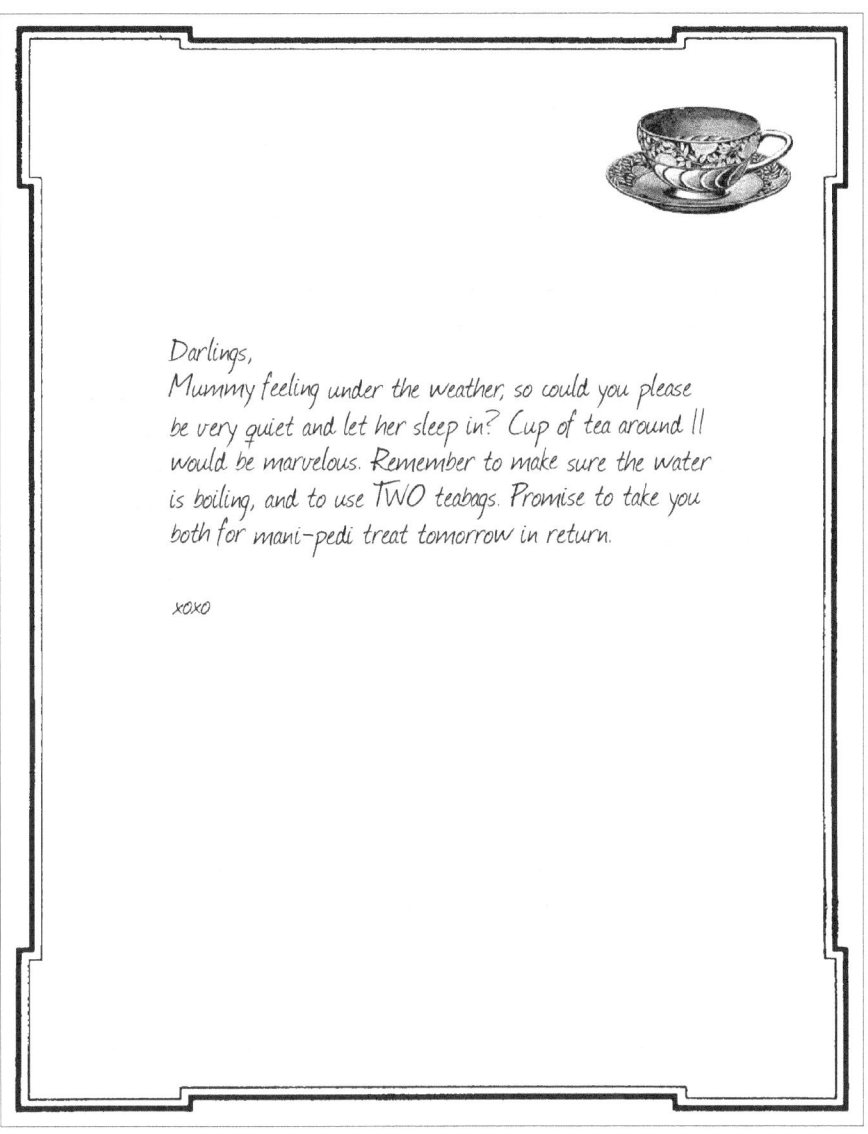

Darlings,
Mummy feeling under the weather, so could you please be very quiet and let her sleep in? Cup of tea around 11 would be marvelous. Remember to make sure the water is boiling, and to use TWO teabags. Promise to take you both for mani-pedi treat tomorrow in return.

xoxo

From: phoebegb@sahmsrulet.net
To: crystalwalker@sterlingmorris.com
OMG. Going back to bed in hopes this will all turn out to be a bad dream.

Mebook Posting on Phoebe's wall:
Thank God Lata's back! Detox drinks at my place at 5.

Bienvenidas back, Lata!
Lo siento I was not at el aeropuerto to greet you personalmente, but feeling rather under the tiempo this morning. Sorry the Shuttlebus was so crowded. They really need to ban people from bringing back all that Peruvian chicken in their suitcases. (Don't forget to leave el mio in el frigo).

I know you haven't had much sleep, but could you please change all the sheets, make appetizers for ten and buy flores? I have some senoras coming over for a fiesta this evening. Some bebidas would also go down wonderfully well if you have an extra momento.

Phoebe

Skye Chat
crystalwalker
great turnout for your neighborhood gathering tonite. Feeling any better about things after our friends from the Club heroically showed up for second night in a row?

phoebethompson
i think they misunderstood what I meant by detox drinks, but hopefully Lata's purgatives did them as much good as they did me. My spirits feel completely restored. Helps that Bitsy agreed to be my tennis partner for challenge season, so all's well that ends well, I suppose.

crystalwalker

fingers crossed Bitsy remembers her commitment in the morning.

phoebethompson

Sure she won't, but good breeding won't allow her to renege on her offer, esp. after I send her a reminder tomorrow.

Friday, October 5

From: phoebegb@sahmsrule.net
To: crystalwalker@sterlingmorris.com

Glad to learn you just fell asleep the other night while we were on-line chatting and weren't bored by the tedious details of my scheming to join the Club tennis team. How bizarre that you ended up nose first on the 'z' key!

From: crystalwalker@sterlingmorris.com
To: phoebegb@sahmsrule.net

Sorry. Just replaced the keyboard. Back in biz now.

Rest assured, you could never be boring. I might even be able to help you with your tennis team ambitions, based on an incident that happened today. Basically, I managed to endear myself to Bitsy by picking up her triplets from the bus stop along with my cherubs, after she forgot to collect them. I had never seen them there before and simply assumed she sent her kids to private school, like everyone else in the hood. Turns out, her triplets are in pre-K with Karson!

Judging by the state of her usually perfectly coiffed hair, the weekend's festivities had taken their toll. She seemed anxious I not breathe a word about her parenting lapse to anyone else, especially Pookie, with whom she is apparently not on speaking terms after Pookie wrestled the last bag of pesto out of Brad's hands the other day.

But why would Bitsy choose to forego private school for her brood in favor of paying Club dues?

From: phoebegb@sahmsrule.net
To: crystalwalker@sterlingmorris.com

The Bottingers have a legacy Club membership through Bitsy's mother, Barbi Van Houzen, who was Captain of the Ladies' tennis team for many years. Bitsy's husband is also in real estate, so while they've had some good years (hence the six bedroom showhouse), they are apparently suffering in the current economy, which is why they chose not to opt for private school for the triplets' pre-k year.

The reason you haven't seen Bitsy's brood at the bus stop before is probably because many such parents choose to assuage their guilt over sending their offspring to public school by chauffeuring their precious charges to and from, rather than have them ride the school bus.

From what I could tell at the club the other night, Pookie is proving less than sympathetic about Bitsy's money troubles, most likely because she grew up on the wrong side of the Village, and remembers how Mrs. V.H. opposed her family's Club membership way back when. I often wonder how the two of them ever got to be BFFs, given the amount of time they seem to spend fighting.

From: crystalwalker@sterlingmorris.com
To: phoebegb@sahmsrule.net
That explains it.

I promised the bus stop incident would remain between the two of us (which includes you, btw), but I suspect this knowledge could provide us with the necessary extra leverage to get you onto the team and me into the Club one day.

From: phoebegb@sahmsrule.net
To: crystalwalker@sterlingmorris.com
Mum's the word. For now.

Saturday, October 6

From: phoebegb@sahmsrule.net
To: crystalwalker@sterlingmorris.com
My turn to feel insecure about my husband's whereabouts. Not a peep from Brad or his business partner since he left for the conference. Meanwhile, the phone is ringing off the hook with Village residents desperate for him to come and fix their internet connections, not to mention order his precious pasta sauce. Do you think I should be concerned?

From: crystalwalker@sterlingmorris.com
To: phoebegb@sahmsrule.net
Charming as Brad undoubtedly is, I think you over-estimate his willingness to engage with the outside world. I can barely get the man to tear his attention away from the screen long enough to look me in the eye, let alone engage in conversation. Assuming said 22-year olds are even impressed with his P-NIS (a big if), I highly doubt they have the gaming skills or patience to engage him in the kind of virtual combat game guaranteed to win his heart. He probably just can't hear his cellphone ring over the cacophony in the video arcade.

Text from Phoebe to Brad
WTF RU? Pls call immediately!

Sunday, October 7

Text from Crystal to Phoebe
Any news?

Text from Phoebe to Crystal
Yes – he arrived home on the red eye this morning. Claims not to have heard phone over noise of conference the other night. We just have to trust them, right?

Text from Crystal to Phoebe
Trust, but verify.

Text from Phoebe to Crystal
Offering to do all laundry today instead of Lata, just to be on the lookout for anything suspicious. Right now, only troubling sign is that he seems to have worn the same pair of underpants 3 days in a row.

Note to Lata
Gracias por fixing the fan in our bedroom. Lo siento for turning it on while you were still working on it. Donde es el jabon por la washing machine, y how do I put it in?

Monday, October 8

From: crystalwalker@sterlingmorris.com
To: georgew@plunderhogg.com
What do you mean you won't be home for dinner? Again?

From: crystalwalker@sterlingmorris.com
To: georgew@plunderhogg.com
OK, I guess a pick-up game with the Prez does trump family dinner. Make sure you get autographs for cherubs. xxx

Text from Crystal to Coach Geoff
Can u do me huge favor and give Kevin ride home from baseball practice? Hubby has important meeting and I have to take Baby to urgent care for possible ear infection.

Text from Crystal to Coach Geoff
Sorry – didn't realize practice ended early. Will be there asap.

Text from Crystal to Nina
Know ur officially off the clock, but any chance you can pick up Kevin from baseball practice?

Text from Crystal to Nina
Fine. Enjoy the movie. I will go after get meds.

Text from Crystal to George
u o me BIG time.

Darling,

I'm so sorry Dad and I were late to pick you up from practice yesterday. Of course, if you hadn't lost your cellphone, you might have been able to reach us to let us know about the time change, but I agree, it's probably time we replaced it now, especially as I'm about to go back to work.

I hope you didn't mean all those things you said about hating me and Dad, and how we've ruined your life by taking you away from all your friends in KC. It's true, we have been very busy and distracted of late, but we promise to do better going forward.

If you come out of your room before lunch, Dad has offered to take you to the Apple store to check out the me-phone. I know you have a big birthday coming up soon.....

xo, mom

Tuesday, October 9

Goggle Calendar Reminder from Phoebe to Brad
What: Round Robin
Where: Club
When: Noon-5pm

Note: Remember, it's important to lose against Club Prez & Wife, to improve my chances of getting onto Ladies Tennis Team!

Wednesday, October 10

Skye Chat

crystalwalker

thinking of giving Kevin the me-phone for his 13th birthday next week, as I need to be able to reach him once I go back to work. But I'm worried such an extravagant gift might be frowned upon around these parts. Can u plz advise?

phoebethompson

CRAC has an official no cellphone, no screen policy until my girls graduate, which is why I like to think they can actually spell and write full sentences, unlike so many of their contemporaries.

Tennis Ladder Results

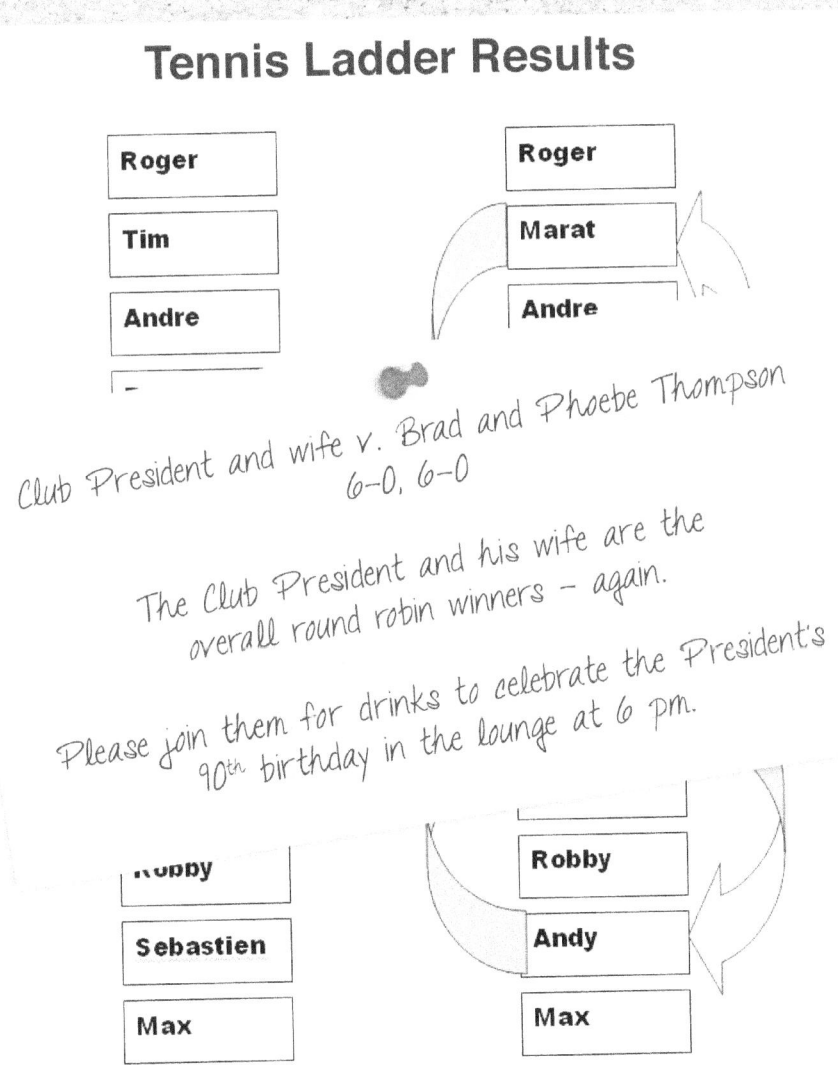

Roger

Tim

Andre

Roger

Marat

Andre

Club President and wife v. Brad and Phoebe Thompson
6-0, 6-0

The Club President and his wife are the overall round robin winners – again.

Please join them for drinks to celebrate the President's 90th birthday in the lounge at 6 pm.

Robby

Sebastien

Max

Robby

Andy

Max

crystalwalker

I've always raised my cherubs to be comfortable with technology, since they will have to live in the real world sooner or later. Then again, as your girls so charmingly demonstrate every time they miss a cultural reference, not everyone does.

Besides, Kevin opted not to have a party this year because he's bummed about not being able to invite any of his old KC buddies over to celebrate, so I feel the need to make it up to him somehow. Guess I will sleep on it and decide tomorrow.

Thursday, October 11

Text from Phoebe to Brad
So much for faking our loss. Who knew greatest generation could also be most ruthless?

Text from Phoebe to Bitsy
Pookie just hurt big toe in freak pedicure accident. She's refusing to rest it, per doctor's orders, so think we have excellent chance of beating her this season. Semi-private with Xavier tomorrow at noon?

Friday, October 12

Text From Crystal to Kevin
Happy Birthday, sweetie! Hope it didn't take you long to find this under your pillow. xo Mom

Text from Crystal to Kevin
OK, kiddo. If UR not up in next 10 secs, me-Phone is going to become MY phone.

Text from Crystal to Kevin
Love ya!

Text from Phoebe to Bitsy
Feeling utterly spent. Isn't Xavi a marvel? Issuing challenge to Club Prez's wife and partner as soon as I can muster energy to put pen to paper. Amazing how the old biddies can master the backhand lob, but not email, apparently.

Phoebe Thompson and Bitsy Bottinger challenge Nancy Hart and Gertrude Fine to a tennis match at a time and place of their choosing.

The courtesy of a response is requested by return mail, and no later than October 15th

Sunday, October 14

Text from Phoebe to Bitsy
Gertrude and Nancy want to play TODAY at noon. Does that work?

Text from Phoebe to Bitsy Bottinger
Great! Let's show 'em how it's done. See you on court.

From: phoebegb@sahmsrule.net
To: bitsybottinger@yahoo.com
You looked FABULOUS in those shorts today, before our opponents cited Club rules against mannish tennis attire and insisted you change. Way to channel your resentment at being forced to wear the spare circa 1970 tennis dress into some smashing overheads (literally), even if you did expose the matching frilly granny panties in the process.

1 down, 2 to go!

Monday, October 15

Mebook Post on Crystal's Wall
Anyone happen to have an accurate set of scales? There seems to be something seriously wrong with mine. A full-grown bull moose can't weigh this much.

Response from Phoebe

Not sure it's such a good idea to worry about your weight so soon after giving birth. After all, your boobs alone must count for at least a full third of your current girth. If you insist, however, I can lend you my 'good' scales, which I swear melt away the pounds without you having to lift a finger!

Response from Crystal

On yours, I weigh a full 2.8 pounds more than I did on my own. How soon can I return them?

Response from Phoebe

Are you quite sure you read the instructions before alighting? If you look closely at the fine print, you will learn upon no account ever to weigh yourself without first carrying out a purification ritual involving at least two days of fasting, evacuation and liposuction, not to mention the ritual sacrifice of a chicken. To do anything less is the rookie weigh-in equivalent of stepping on a landmine.

Skye Chat

crystalwalker

Desperate enough about my heft to return to exercise—beyond the usual bending over I do for George and cherubs all day long. Vira claims that two 5am morning sessions a week of yoga are all she needs to maintain her size zero figure, and recommends Steamy Yoga in Georgetown. Isn't that where you go?

phoebethompson

Steamy Yoga is the BEST. I was skeptical at first, but Gunther's uninhibited massages of student behinds are to die for. He's just agreed to let me take classes for free, in return for sweeping the studio floor and putting away props, so I'm committed to going to the Early Bird class twice a week from now on. Would love if you could join!

crystalwalker

Just signed up for tomorrow's class. Back in Kansas City, I would NEVER have considered exercising before dawn, but it may be the only time I have to work out after I start work next month, so guess I might as well get into the habit now. May wear my Slap'n'Tickle thong beneath my yoga pants, just in case it inspires more touching.

phoebethompson

You do realize the yoga class is full of twenty-something nymphs whose creamy complexions make ours look like death by comparison? My advice is to spend as much time in Corpse pose as possible.

Tuesday, October 16

From: phoebegb@sahmsrule.net
To: crystalwalker@sterlingmorris.com
What did you make of Gunther? He's a little long in the tooth, to be sure, but the combination of chiseled bod, bristling chest hair and touchy, feely manner is just a little too good to be true, which of course makes me think he must be a sexual predator. At my age, however, one learns to be grateful for such attention.

Hope it was as good for you as it is for me!

From: crystalwalker@sterlingmorris.com
To: phoebegb@sahmsrule.net
Not sure if I'm experiencing the enlightenment that comes from reaching Nirvana, or just enjoying the fact George has to handle the cherubs' morning routine while I'm gone, but I think I can honestly say the effects last longer than any mere orgasm.

Between Baby and three elders clinging to various parts of my body, often simultaneously, having another human being touch me generally results in a swift kick to the groin – but then again, I had no idea having my sacrum adjusted during Doggie pose (or whatever that was called) could feel so good.

I'm beginning to understand what Vira means by Finding your Bliss®.

Wednesday, October 17

From: phoebegb@sahmsrule.net
To: crystalwalker@sterlingmorris.com
FW:
Have you checked out Vira's video? Brad claims she likes to work in bed, hence the need for him to spend time on his hands and knees adjusting the wi-fi reception in her boudoir.

Hmm.

From: crystalwalker@sterlingmorris.com
To: phoebegb@sahmsrule.net
Was that a uniformed chef I spotted bringing her a snack? Hardly seems worth hiring one, for a couple of lettuce leaves and no dressing. Are you going to her book party tonite?

From: phoebegb@sahmsrule.net
To: crystalwalker@sterlingmorris.com
Wouldn't miss, although I fear the only drinks she's serving are organic, sustainable and fair trade, which would be fine except I hear they are also NON-ALCOHOLIC.

From: crystalwalker@sterlingmorris.com
To: phoebegb@sahmsrule.net
Would it be wrong to bring something stronger?

From: phoebegb@sahmsrule.net
To: crystalwalker@sterlingmorris.com
Not if we explain that we never imbibe anything that hasn't been fermented first. Better for the digestion, of course.

See you there.

Thursday, October 18

Skye Chat
crystalwalker
Did u spot Nina hovering around Gunther at the book party? I'm troubled.

phoebethompson
Overheard her telling him she wants to study yoga next year at college back in Hanover, and he has apparently offered to give her private lessons.

crystalwalker
No wonder Nina found the old coot so compelling! Surprised Vira didn't notice, but then again, she claims jealousy is just a delusion of the ego. According to her, we are all inter-connected, so how can we possibly mind when our significant other threatens to sleep with someone else?

phoebethompson
Must convince my own daughters not to fall under the sway of such nonsense.

crystalwalker
Will try and do same for Nina, altho' it's hard to impart life wisdom via text, and she has uncanny ability to ignore my verbal directives.

Friday, October 19

Witter Posting from femilawyermom
Just cancelled laser hair removal appointment to attend meeting with principal at son's preschool. Does God want me to start my new job looking like a European intellectual? And why do I feel like the one in trouble?

ilikeemhairy is now following femilawyermom
hairypitsrok is now following femilawyermom
underarmsniffer is now following femilawyermom

From: crystalwalker@sterlingmorris.com
To: virginia_williams@vps.com
cc: gwalker@plunderhogg.com

I understand my preschooler appeared in the nurse's office this morning with a bloody nose. I apologize for missing the call from the school nurse about this, but surely you don't require FATHERS to explain what they were doing every time they are unable to take a call?

Also, is it really also necessary to suspend my son from school tomorrow for a fight he claims he did not start? I trust the other boy involved has been suspended too, or does verbal provocation (calling my son a crybaby after he fell off the monkey bars) somehow not count?

From: crystalwalker@sterlingmorris.com
To: gwalker@plunderhogg.com

I know you are busy making the vast sums of money we apparently need to live in DC, but I just got back from meeting with principal at VPS, and I'm very concerned about Karson.

The school counselor says he's manifesting behavior typical of boys whose parents are going through bereavement or a divorce, or whose mother or father has been sent for a second or third tour of duty in Iraq. Thank God my lawyer training came back to me, so they've agreed NOT to suspend Karson for fight we both know he started, provided both he and other kid involved sign a contract for good behavior. This means no physical contact, and no teasing, taunting or verbal abuse for the rest of the semester.

I had to fight hard for inclusion of this last. Call if you want more details.

Out of Office Reply from gwalker@plunderhogg.com
I am away from my desk until Tuesday, October 20. If you have any urgent inquiries, please contact my assistant, Jane Smith.

George Walker
Plunder & Hogg Public Affairs
www.plunder&hogg.com

CONFIDENTIAL
This electronic transmission and any attachments are for the sole use of the individual or entity to whom it is addressed. It is confidential and may be subject to lobbyist/client privilege. Any further distribution or copying or other use of this message is strictly prohibited. If you received this message in error, please notify me, and destroy the attached message and any attached documents immediately after reading and forwarding it to all your friends.

Reply
AAGHHHHHHHHH!

Out of Office Reply from gwalker@plunderhogg.com
I am away from my desk until Tuesday, October 20. If you have any urgent inquiries, please contact my assistant, Jane Smith.

George Walker

Voicemail transcript from Crystal to George
It's six o'clock and I have no idea who you are or when you'll be in me. I haven't even seen you this week, let alone been able to dread what to do about Carleton, or how we are going to manage as a family after I start wok next week. We need to talk and, if we can't do that civilly, arrange a consultation with the couples' terrapin the Senator from Fairyland told you about after his wife faced the drunk driving conviction last year. I'm sure you remember HER well– you certainly gazed long enough at her moobs long enough the night we had dinner with them at the Palm D'Or.

Transcribed using Goggle Voice technology (and not edited using reason or good judgment)

Skye Chat
phoebethompson
Do u know where I can find a Warrior Princess outfit before Halloween?

crystalwalker
Look no further. Eldest daughter happens to have kept hers from last year. But won't twins want matching outfits?

phoebethompson
Warrior Princess is for me, not girls!

crystalwalker
Try www.anyexcusetodresslikeaslut.com. If you order right now, they might be able to express it overnight. I'm sending Kim down with hers too, just in case. It's a size 0, but with yr girlish figure, I'm sure it will fit.

phoebethompson
Wow, that was efficient! Please thank Kim for helping to remove costume after I got trapped in the leather bustier and couldn't breathe. Pretty sure they didn't have zips in ancient Greece. Of course, it doesn't help that I clearly no longer have body of pre-pubescent girl. Hope she wasn't too traumatized by the experience. Brad heard my cries for help and suggested I dress up as Steffi Graff, which is much easier, since I already have the tennis skirt and loose fitting polo. Not sure my legs quite measure up to Steffi's at her ball-crushing best, but it will have to do.

crystalwalker
George wants us to dress up as The Von Trapps. Wonder why?

Realize getting Sister Taylor in trouble with her order may have been mistake, as rumor has apparently gone round George's office that she's thinking of quitting (the convent, not firm). Need to work on getting her to recommit to being bride of Christ before she becomes one more attractive young woman determined to become someone's trophy wife.

From: aconcernedcitizen@yahoo.com
To: info@ourladyofthepines.org
I would like to commend the work of Sister Taylor, a non-cloistered member of your order, for her tremendous work saving our planet from the scourge of deforestation. I recently had a chance to meet her at a corporate retreat in Wyoming, where Sister Taylor passionately invoked our responsibility as descendants of Noah to preserve trees for the sake of all God's creatures.

I agree that her conclusion, 'We are all naked before God' was a little off-topic, and did not need to be accompanied by a dramatic representation of this point, but rest assured, she was forcibly restrained from carrying out this threat by the more sober (female) members of the party. I hope you will forgive this temporary lapse in her judgment, and reinstate her as a valued member of your order.

Sincerely,
A Concerned Citizen

Saturday, October 20

From: crystalwalker@sterlingmorris.com
To: phoebegb@sahmsrule.net
Counting down the hours until I start work on Monday, even if Kurtis did curl her lip in a lopsided smile today at something I said, in a manner I found irresistible. I will miss spending time with the her and the cherubs terribly, although it looks like the three olders will be so busy with their own extra-curricular activities from now on that I wouldn't see much of them anyway.

Evelyn Braun has recommended twice weekly sessions with reading and math tutors for Kevin, which only leaves him one day a week for therapy and baseball. Karson will attend math tutoring for gifted and talented pre-k kids, and group therapy to deal with his anger management issues. As for Kurtis, Evelyn thankfully saw no need to start enrichment activities just yet, although we are now on the waiting list for Baby & Me Musical Theory class at the Village Hall. She has also encouraged me to breastfeed until Kurtis goes to kindergarten. Apparently, that's how scientists think Mozart was able to compose his first scherzo before he turned five.

Of all the cherubs, Evelyn seems to find Kimberly the best adjusted, and has encouraged me to indulge her dreams of becoming an Olympic gymnast. When I dared suggest the four hour practices three times a week plus

Sundays might interfere with her ability to pursue other activities (not to mention mine), she actually rebuked me for not taking my daughter's athletic ambitions seriously enough!

I just hope all this frenetic activity (not to mention vast expense) at least pays off when it comes to applying to college.

From: phoebegb@sahmsrule.net
To: crystalwalker@sterlingmorris.com
The cherubs sound as busy as the twins these days! As a matter of fact, I'm planning to cut back. Latest research seems to suggest that exposure to loud music before the age of eighteen can actually harm a child's hearing (not to mention their parents'), which is why we have forbidden the twins from taking any more saxophone.

From: phoebegb@sahmsrule.net
To: margaretmcvitie@crac.edu
Dear Principal McVitie,
I know that you generally require half the year's tuition to be paid by October 25, and the remainder by January 1 of the following year, but my husband and I are currently experiencing a teensy cash flow problem, due to the economic downturn, and I am wondering if you might be willing to extend the deadline until the end of the month?

As longtime CRAC parents, I hope you will take our hitherto impeccable track record on timely tuition payments into consideration, and extend us the courtesy of a few extra days this one time. I do acknowledge that I might have addressed the issue sooner, but I've been hoping our financial situation would improve by now.

I hope you will also take into consideration my many years of service as a room parent and auction volunteer at a time when so few others were willing to step up.

Sincerely,
Phoebe Thompson
CPA President, CRAC Parent Volunteer of the Year 2006, 2007, 2008

From: phoebegb@sahmsrule.net
To: crystalwalker@sterlingmorris.com
Just liquidated last of my UK savings in order to pay for twins' tuition through the remainder of this year. How did it come to this?!

From: crystalwalker@sterlingmorris.com
To: phoebegb@sahmsrule.net
Sorry to hear things are still tight on the financial front. Did the conference in CA yield any results?

From: phoebegb@sahmsrule.net
To: crystalwalker@sterlingmorris.com
No, but Brad did get approached about some consulting work near the Arctic Circle, which I am encouraging (all right, forcing) him to take. May require

he spends up to one week a month in sub-zero temperatures, but frankly, given the way I feel about him these days, I'm looking forward to it.

From: crystalwalker@sterlingmorris.com
To: phoebegb@sahmsrule.net
Have you changed your mind about going back to work? It might help your stress levels to be less dependent on just the one (uncertain) income.

From: phoebegb@sahmsrule.net
To: crystalwalker@sterlingmorris.com
To be honest, between chairing the school auction (my penance for being late with the tuition), organizing the mother-daughter book group and doing all it takes to look half as good as I did at twenty, not sure how any mother in the Village finds time to work. According to Evelyn, my girls are also entering their most impressionable age, when the absence of a strong role model in the home after the girls get home from school can lead to obesity, drug abuse and even unregulated TV-watching.

Having said that, I'm beginning to wonder if staying home is even a choice these days, given how dire the entire world economy is looking.

From: crystalwalker@sterlingmorris.com
To: phoebegb@sahmsrule.net
No matter how much I might sometimes wish I had the luxury of not working, witnessing the divorce of my parents at the tender age of two has left its lasting scars. Chief among them is my resolution never to be financially dependent on a man. Who knows when they might decide to run off with a stripper, like dear old Dad, before finding God, or take a job in the Church and a salary which basically precludes the payment of any kind of child support?

Hence my decision to start my new job on Monday. The firm has offered to hold the position open for another month, but as the new girl in the office here in DC, I feel it's important to show that I'm as keen as the fresh-faced young Harvard Law School grad I'll be working with. Something about her willingness to sacrifice all personal relationships in a bid to make partner before she hits thirty reminds me of myself before I had the cherubs in a way I find unnerving.

As an added incentive, the daycare opposite my office has offered to feed, clothe and amuse Baby between the hours of 8am and 6pm – a triple feat I haven't been able to achieve since she was born. This leaves Nina free to deal with the three older cherubs' after-school driving schedule, which is turning out to be more complicated to organize than the average military campaign.

Fingers crossed it all works out!

Monday, October 22

From: crystalwalker@sterlingmorris.com
To: phoebegb@sahmsrule.net
My own office! My own computer – not a sticky keypad in sight! No time to write more now – partner meeting in five minutes – but suffice to say, it's good to be back. Hope all is well on the home front.

From: phoebegb@sahmsrule.net
To: crystalwalker@sterlingmorris.com
You'll be glad to hear that the cherubs appear to have held up fine in your absence. As a matter of fact, I just spotted Nina in George's Merc leaving to drop your daughter at the gym, albeit with a mePhone clamped permanently to her ear.

Do let me know if she needs any guidance on driving safely.

Text from Crystal to George
Can u pick Baby up from daycare? Have a legal brief to file b/f 6 pm.

Text from Crystal to George
I'm sure drinks with the Mayor seems more important, but in case u hadn't noticed, I am at work also!

Text from Crystal to Nina
Can you please pick Kurtis up from daycare today? Sorry for short notice – George and I both in meetings.

Text from Crystal to Nina
Hello?

Text from Crystal to Nina
WTH DID I JUST GET U A ME-PHONE IF YOU NEVER HAVE IT SWITCHED ON?! On my way to pick up Kurtis.

Tuesday, October 23

From: crystalwalker@sterlingmorris.com
To: phoebegb@sahmsrule.net
Sorry for not getting back to you sooner about Lata – no time to think, let alone write. Writing this left-handed while attempting to surrrrrrrrrreptitiously attach breast pump under jacket.

Offices are all glass cubicles, which makes it impossible to express milk anywhere other than the bathroom, supply closet or boardroom, all of which are invariably occupied by weeping or sleeping colleagues. Convinced there's a potential lawsuit right there.

I agree Nina seems a little immature. Put it down to the fact she led a very sheltered existence in Germany until now, and that her parents were relatively young when they had her (I believe you and Nina's mother even share a birth year.) However, this is clearly not working out, so give me a couple more days to get settled, and let's talk.

Must go: Helen Wheels (Harvard Law Grad) is heading my way clutching a pile of briefs so thick it could stop bullets. May be the only way I can get rid of her.

Wednesday, October 24

Text from Crystal to Phoebe
Have u seen Nina or Karson? They didn't show up for K's 1st anger management group therapy just now. Would leave work to look for them, but it's only my second day back. Can u do me BIG favor and ring doorbell to see if they are home?

Text from Phoebe to Crystal
Tracked Nina by ring tone and found her sunbathing TOPLESS around Evelyn's pool while Karson and Fred hid in bushes.

Text from Crystal to Phoebe
OMG. I may have to kill her. Any chance Lata might be able to pick Baby up from daycare B4 6 pm? Stuck at office and need someone with her driving skills to make it on-time.

Text from Phoebe to Crystal
Lata on her way, but no time to take evasive measures around speed humps, so trust George won't mind wear and tear on the Merc's suspension.

Text from Crystal to Phoebe
Whatever it takes! Will pay Lata double for her time.

Skye Chat
crystalwalker
Can't tell you how much I appreciate you and Lata for coming to my aid in my hour of need. Thank God Karson took to his room as soon as he got home from therapy, as I really didn't know what to say. It was an unseasonably warm fall day, but I can't believe 'Must keep clothes on' has to be added to the list of childcare requirements.

phoebethompson
What possessed you to hire such a walking, talking cliché in the first place?

crystalwalker
Let's just say, the photograph Nina sent did NOT do her justice. She appears to have ditched the braces, acne and prominently displayed religious symbolism since then. I would fire her, but I desperately need the help, and

have no time to look for someone new.

phoebethompson

I know it's not my place, but I really don't think Nina is up to job of looking after the cherubs. I had Lata 24/7 from time twins were born, and I wasn't even working. Brad's technology has yet to make any sales, so I would be willing to share her, so long as Lata can stop by to give me a neck massage whenever one of my tension headaches threatens. Sleep on it and let me know.

Skye Chat Between Nina's Parents and Crystal
crystalwalker

Do you realize it's 3 o'clock in the morning here in Washington, and that you woke me up? I'm sorry I yelled at your daughter, but she behaved in a very inappropriate way around my son. Karson is not used to public displays of nudity, unless it's his own. Plus she forgot to take him to an important medical appointment, for which I will now be charged $230.

crystalwalker

No, this kind of appointment is not covered by the State, as it would be in Germany, nor is it covered by our insurance.

crystalwalker

I'm sorry living with our family has not been the kind of cultural experience your daughter was looking for. It's true we have not taken Nina to any Broadway shows or museums, but I have frequently suggested she go by herself during her time off. As I keep reminding her, she is an adult, and I already have four children of my own to look after, plus I have just started back working full-time. In Germany, this probably still means you get to knock-off at 3, but here it means I have to leave before 7 am each morning, and I don't get home until 5.30 or 6. So forgive me if I am not always up to parenting your child also, after I get home.

C is offline.

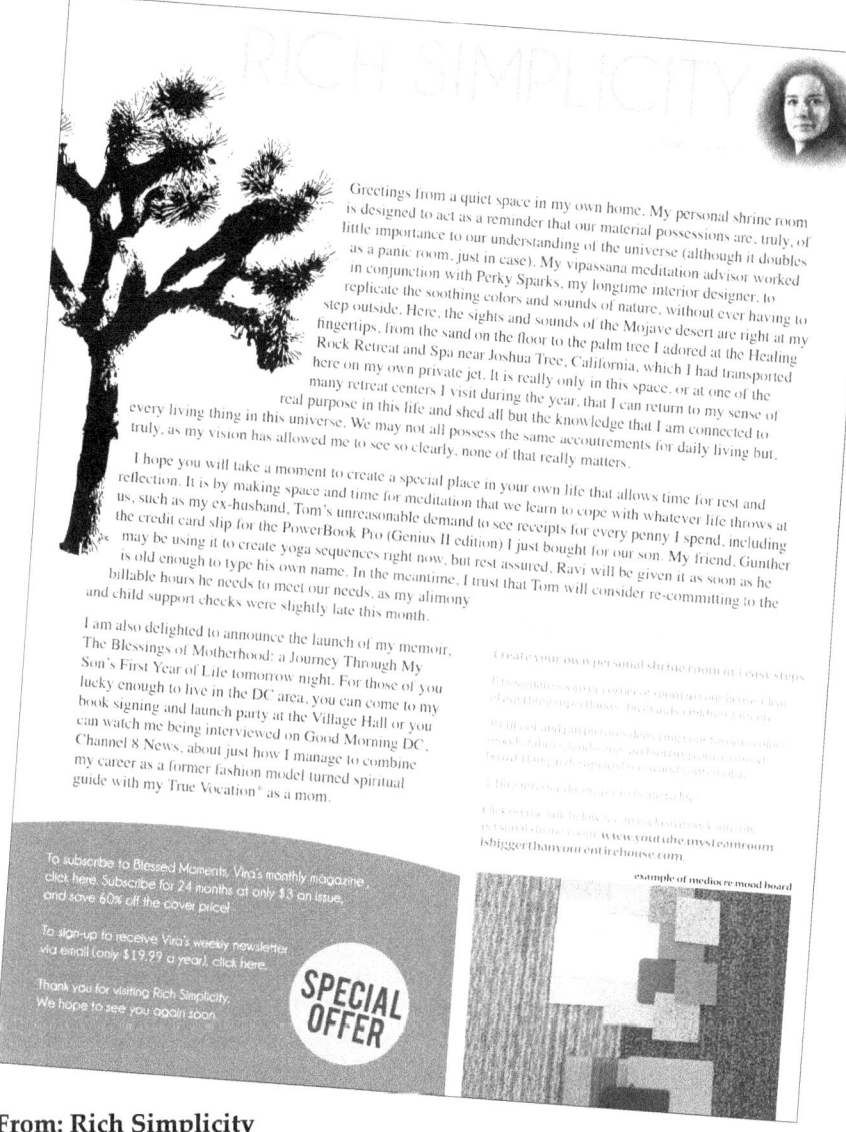

From: Rich Simplicity
To: phoebegb@sahmsrule.net

Rich Simplicity: A monthly newsletter bringing you a life of ultimate simplicity, no matter how much money I have.

Volume 03, Issue 10

Blessings,

Greetings from a quiet space in my own home. My personal shrine room is designed to act as a reminder that our material possessions are, truly, of little importance to our understanding of the universe (although it doubles as a panic room, just in case). My vipassana meditation advisor worked in conjunction with Perky Sparks, my longtime interior designer, to replicate the soothing colors and sounds of nature, without ever having to step outside. Here, the sights and sounds of the Mojave desert are right at my fingertips, from the sand on the floor to the palm tree I adored at the Healing Rock Retreat and Spa near Joshua Tree, California, which I had transported here on my own private jet. It is really only in this space, or at one of the many retreat centers I visit during the year, that I can return to my sense of real purpose in this life and shed all but the knowledge that I am connected to every living thing in this universe. We may not all possess the same accoutrements for daily living but, truly, as my vision has allowed me to see so clearly, none of that really matters.

I hope you will take a moment to create a special place in your own life that allows time for rest and reflection. It is by making space and time for meditation that we learn to cope with whatever life throws at us, such as my ex-husband, Tom's unreasonable demand to see receipts for every penny I spend, including the credit card slip for the PowerBook Pro (Genius II edition) I just bought for our son. My friend, Gunther may be using it to create yoga sequences right now, but rest assured, Ravi will be given it as soon as he is old enough to type his own name. In the meantime, I trust that Tom will consider recommitting to the billable hours he needs to meet our needs, as my alimony and child support checks were slightly late this month.

I am also delighted to announce the launch of my memoir, The Blessings of Motherhood: a Journey Through My Son's First Year of Life tomorrow night. For those of you lucky enough to live in the DC area, you can come to my book signing and launch party at the Village Hall or you can watch me being interviewed on Good Morning DC, Channel 8 News, about just how I manage to combine my career as a former fashion model turned spiritual guide with my True Vocation* as a mom.

Friday, October 26

From: crystalwalker@sterlingmorris.com
To: phoebegb@sahmsrule.net
Can't believe I'm already having to work from home today, following a nasty incident in daycare this morning, during which the executive director accused me of trying to send Kurtis in with a 101 fever and some infant Tylenol because I knew Nina couldn't manage a sick baby. Maybe I did, but I'm pretty sure she's just teething and I was desperate!

Upshot is they have refused to take her back until I have a doctor's note giving her a clean bill of health. I know George has taken the three older cherubs to school with a temperature before now, but young, impressionable female teachers are all too eager to give handsome, seemingly hands-on fathers the benefit of the doubt, aren't they?

From: phoebegb@sahmsrule.net
To: crystalwalker@sterlingmorris.com
So sorry to hear Kurtis is under the weather. Let me know if there is anything Lata can do to help.

From: crystalwalker@sterlingmorris.com
To: phoebegb@sahmsrule.net
Will do. Thank you.

Tuesday, October 30

From: crystalwalker@sterlingmorris.com
To: phoebegb@sahmsrule.net
Unfortunately, since I last wrote, Nina appears to have come down with some kind of stomach bug, which her parents are trying to blame on a case of worms. Not up to the rectal exam required to confirm, although a couple more days of watching her moan in bed may encourage me to give it a try. How did I ever manage to pump milk, advise clients over the phone and fax over a takeout order for dinner at one and the same time?

From: phoebegb@sahmsrule.net
To: crystalwalker@sterlingmorris.com
I really have no idea how you do all that you do, as my entire day has been absorbed with just tracking down Jane Austen costumes for the twins to wear to the Village Halloween festivities tomorrow night. Fortunately, the Club President's wife has offered me some of her own pieces from her attic, many of which may actually date from the 19th century. Feel terribly lucky, as I know the twins would have been humiliated if they couldn't recite their favorite passage from Lady Susan as they do the rounds trick-or-treating.

From: crystalwalker@sterlingmorris.com
To: phoebegb@sahmsrule.net
Secretly relieved NOT to be at work again today, as it means I can expedite an order for Halloween costumes online w/o Helen breathing over my shoulder.

Thank God, George has abandoned his plan to have us all dress in lederhosen. I suspect the cherubs' impromptu a capella performance at the bus stop the other day did the trick, as several of the other children immediately began referring to us as the Von Crapps. Just praying Kimberly won't balk at wearing one of the recycled outfits from the costume basket. I told her she would look darling as a linebacker, but frankly, that may be because it's her only other option.

Any chance I will bump into you at the Village Halloween party tomorrow night? Now that I'm back at work, it may be our only chance to see each other in person before the holidays.

From: phoebegb@sahmsrule.net
To: crystalwalker@sterlingmorris.com
Alas, I have a prior commitment.

The ancient society of Wiccans (re-chartered circa 1998) is claiming the tennis courts at the Club as sacred ground, and their annual Witchfest, complete with orgiastic dancing round the bonfire, is planned for tomorrow night.

The Club President is outraged and has determined to make the space unavailable by sponsoring a 24 hour tennis-a-thon in order to secure the courts. It was made clear to Bitsy and I, as aspiring team members, that the Board would look more favorably upon our chances if we volunteered to take the seven to eleven shift, along with a crack member of the Ladies' First Team.

Hoping the Wiccans will give up their efforts to take over the courts after a few swift volleys land within striking range, but in the meantime, Brad will accompany the twins to the Village Hall party in my place.

Wednesday, October 31

Text from Phoebe to Bitsy
Wiccans and I r at Club courts, waiting 4 witches to show. :0 Where ru?

Text from Phoebe to Bitsy
BTW, it's freezing out here. Can u bring sweatpants when u come?

Text from Phoebe to Bitsy
Still waiting.......

From: crystalwalker@sterlingmorris.com
To: phoebegb@sahmsrule.net
Couldn't resist sharing the details of my encounter with the Village People en masse with you before I collapse into bed.

Evelyn caused the first drama of the evening by attempting to smuggle Snuggles to the Village Hall disguised in a bonnet. When confronted by Barbi Van Houzen, however, she claimed the dog was better behaved than most Village children and shouldn't face discrimination. I am prepared to concede that his drooling is no worse than any teething baby's, but I did take a certain pleasure in the way she was ultimately compelled to spend the rest of the evening tending to the mutt outside.

Things then went rapidly downhill after Bitsy demanded I send the eldest three cherubs to the back of the line to enter the haunted house, claiming said attraction was for children aged five and under (conveniently including her triplets in the cut-off). Wasn't she supposed to be playing tennis with you this evening?

For once, George stepped in to save the day, by innocently inquiring the ages of her beautiful grandchildren. The man spends so little time with his Village peers, how was he supposed to know that the average age for first-time DC parents is now converging with the date they can start collecting social security? Naturally, Bitsy was too shocked to do anything other than order her husband to take her triplets home, before downing several plastic tumblers of Pinot G., leaving the haunted house to us.

My own family dramas aside, it took me a while to recognize Brad under all that English Cavalry officer gear. Some residents insisted on heckling him as a red coat, but your intention was clearly to have him play officer and a gentleman to your girls in their muslin dresses.

I managed to rescue him from the Club Prez, who appeared to have him confused with Benedict Arnold, and fobbed him off on Vira, who apparently didn't recognize him out of his usual work clothes either. She seemed quite smitten with his dashing attire, but you'll be glad to hear, I did manage to jog her memory by painting a rather more realistic picture of his daily appearance. 'Think unwashed Hugh Hefner' were my exact words, so pretty sure I left her with a more balanced view of your mate.

From: phoebegb@sahmsrule.net
To: crystalwalker@sterlingmorris.com
Bitsy was supposed to be playing tennis tonight, but made a unilateral decision that her children's well-being was more important. Ditto with Pookie and Perky, who for once must have actually decided to attend the Halloween party, rather than send the kids with their husbands or the nanny.

This does not bode well for our future tennis relationship, but not sure I have other options. As it was, the Wiccans and I ended up enjoying quite a feisty game of Canadian doubles, after which we exchanged emails and agreed to meet up at the same time next year.

Thanks for setting Vira straight on some of Brad's shortcomings. I had forgotten how well he scrubs up sometimes, so it's a good thing that he doesn't always dress to advantage. I don't think Vira is Brad's type, as he generally prefers a more outdoorsy, rugged kind of woman (hence the Steffi Graff skirt I am sporting, again). But I suppose it's helpful to be reminded every once in a while that one's spouse is considered a 'catch'. Maybe I'll take the opportunity to remind myself now, while he's still wearing the tight breeches and ruffled white shirt…..

Talk soon.

From: crystalwalker@sterlingmorris.com
To: phoebegb@sahmsrule.net
Sorry to be emailing you again into the wee hours, but just discovered a note on my pillow from Nina as I was climbing into bed, announcing that she has decamped for Evelyn's house, along with all her belongings. She actually has the temerity to claim our family is just too demanding!

Apparently, Evelyn has offered her a part-time job as her personal assistant, and she is planning to help out at Steamy Yoga, in return for free yoga teacher training from Gunther. I can only imagine how much touching that is going to involve.

Naturally, George has scheduled a booze cruise with a potential new client at their headquarters near Annapolis tomorrow, so once again it's up to me to sort this mess out. Sometimes I think I'd be better off putting my career on hold and becoming one of those housewives I disdained while in college. As you always remind me, however, being a stay at home mom in DC is almost as stressful as the job I'm considering quitting. But at least I wouldn't have to worry about making childcare arrangements at 2 am.

Please tell me your kind offer to let me share Lata is still open, that she is available to start first thing on Monday.

DC Diary

The Walkers Take on the Nation's Capital

BLOG ARCHIVE

Kevin is 13, Sterling Morris and Halloween

Where to begin? So much has happened this past month, it's hard to know where to start. First, Kevin turned thirteen on October 13. I can't believe I'm the mother of a teenager!

The cherubs are all busy with their new extra-curricular activities, thanks to our new after-school consultant, who thinks Kimberly could one day be a world class gymnast. She is also encouraging about Kevin's enthusiasm for baseball, especially after reading the writing sample he submitted, and says Karson is definitely Ivy league material, if only he can get his temper under control.

I just finished my first week at Sterling Morris. The other partners in the firm all seem nice enough, although they are very focused on maximizing their billable hours. I wish they would at least say hello whenever I pass them in the hallway, but I guess this would require them to engage in actual conversation - something I'm not sure many of them are capable of. But I can't say I have much time to chit-chat myself these days, so it's probably just as well they never seem to take a bathroom or lunch break, or even eat, for that matter.

The cherubs and I just got back from the Village Halloween party, which was fun. This year, we skipped the family theme, so Kevin dressed up as a Mummy (which reminds me, we are out of toilet paper), while Kimberly borrowed her older brother's old football kit and Kurtis made an adorable bumble bee. Karson was forced to go as I Dream of Genie, because Kimberly's costume from last year was the only one that fit, but we managed to persuade him he was Aladdin - I think. George and I went as ourselves - harrassed, tired and over-worked, which might explain why no-one had any trouble recognizing us.

Kevin the Mummy

No time to write more now, as I have a teensy little family crisis to sort out. Nina, our German au pair, has decamped to a neighbor's house, and I need to find a replacement asap - someone who can handle four cherubs without being one. :0

Can't wait for the holidays!

Posted by Crysta Walker at 11:01 AM

No comments:

Post a Comment

Comment as: Select profile...

Publish   Preview

DC Diary
Kevin is 13, Sterling Morris and Halloween

Where to begin? So much has happened this past month, it's hard to know where to start. First, Kevin turned thirteen on October 13. I can't believe I'm the mother of a teenager!

The cherubs are all busy with their new extra-curricular activities, thanks to our new after-school consultant, who thinks Kimberly could one day be a world class gymnast. She is also encouraging about Kevin's enthusiasm for baseball, especially after reading the writing sample he submitted, and says Karson is definitely Ivy league material, if only he can get his temper under control.

I just finished my first week at Sterling Morris. The other partners in the firm all seem nice enough, although they are very focused on maximizing their billable hours. I wish they would at least say hello whenever I pass them in the hallway, but I guess this would require them to engage in actual conversation - something I'm not sure many of them are capable of. But I can't say I have much time to chit-chat myself these days, so it's probably just as well they never seem to take a bathroom or lunch break, or even eat, for that matter.

The cherubs and I just got back from the Village Halloween party, which was fun. This year, we skipped the family theme, so Kevin dressed up as a Mummy (which reminds me, we are out of toilet paper), while Kimberly borrowed her older brother's old football kit and Kurtis made an adorable bumble bee. Karson was forced to go as I Dream of Genie, because Kimberly's costume from last year was the only one that fit, but we managed to persuade him he was Aladdin - I think. George and I went as ourselves - harassed, tired and over-worked, which might explain why no one had any trouble recognizing us.

No time to write more now, as I have a teensy little family crisis to sort out. Nina, our German au pair, has decamped to a neighbor's house, and I need to find a replacement asap - someone who can handle four cherubs without being one. :0

Can't wait for the holidays!

Chapter 4

November, 2012 Vol. 41, Issue 11
Always FREE, but donations appreciated.

Please direct submissions and inquiries to:
whiner@villagepress.com
P.O. Box 357 Village Town, MD

VILLAGE WHINER

Your trusty monthly newsletter of
the "Most Livable Village," 1989
Village Times Magazine

Board of Managers Meeting

Following the resignation of Mrs. Van Houten, known to many of you as the late Tinklepaws's owner, from the Village Board last month, it has come to our attention that an anonymous petition is in circulation to rename the Village Hall in her honor. However, while it is theoretically, constitutionally, to enact such a measure according to Village By-laws, such measures are generally reserved for residents who are either acclaimed to have provided selfless service to the Village over the course of many decades, by popular or ordeal. A perfect example of a resident who qualifies on all three counts is the Village Club President, whose years of toil on the tennis courts and golf green, not to mention the Club bar, have recently resulted in a unanimous vote to dedicate the Gentleman's Lounge after him in recognition of his selfless service. We hope Village residents will consider these criteria carefully before signing any new such petition.

In completely unrelated news, we are excited to report that Holier Than Thou Foods has broken ground on its new gourmet supermarket, and the store is on schedule to open on May 1 next year.

Investigation into strange smell detected round Village

Several residents have complained of an unpleasant odor around the Village. The smell, which some have likened to that of a decaying corpse, is most noticeable on unseasonably warm fall days, and appears to emanate from the corner of Center St. and Kirkside Avenue, where the late Tinklepaws was laid to rest. The Village is taking the precaution of digging up the speed bump under which she is entombed, in order to exhume and re-bury the body in a sealed vault. In the meantime, we have distributed the Village's supply of gas masks for residents on the affected streets. As an additional precaution, the wearing of said masks at all times while outdoors will be strictly enforced by block captains until re-burial is complete.

Diversity Group

The Village Diversity Group would like to congratulate the chairwoman of the women's group subcommittee on his successful gender reassignment surgery, and will host a tree planting ceremony outside the Village Hall on Sunday, November 7, at 2pm, to thank him for her years of devoted service.

Miss Gertrude

Judging by the overwhelming response to last month's column, Miss Gertrude suspects she has merely begun to pick at the hoary scab of etiquette infractions in our seemingly powerful community. Many of the issues raised in the letters, emails and verbal tirades Miss Gertrude has received involve situations that might have easily been resolved by a courteous visit or phone call to a neighbor—to politely ask them not to park in front of your house, say, or to inquire if they really need to mow their lawn at 6am. Instead, as is so often the case, the first inkling these neighbors had that they were being inconsiderate comes in the form of a tap on the door by officers from the Village's Special Ops, and the shining of flashlights into their home, which I am sure you will agree can so easily be misconstrued.

Miss Gertrude is forced to conclude that there is a small minority of Villagers who assume their family connections or positions in the current administration or prestigious private profession mean they deserve special treatment in every area of their lives, not just their sleep, but requiring a zone of silence for one square mile round one's property at all times supports an outsize sense of self-importance, as does copying an entire group upon an email response where a simple reply to the sender would have sufficed. Hard as it may be to believe, not everyone will be devastated to learn that you are unable to attend the annual Back to School Fall picnic, even if you do happen to run your own family foundation.

Similarly, it is important to remember that pretty much every adult who moves to the Village was also valedictorian of their high school class, graduated Summa Cum Laude from college and is now busy running the world. Thus, whenever you find yourself feeling tempted to boast about your extraordinary achievements, please remember that others may have done the same, and that neighborly relations might be better served by keeping your mouth shut.

CLASSIFIEDS

Looking for a few good Village children between the ages of 5 and 15 to participate in a study on the effect of eliminating all wheat, rice, sugar, caffeine, soda and dairy products from their diet for a period of one year (yes, kids, that includes chocolate and Diet Coke).

This study is expected to show dramatic improvements in the subjects' cognitive abilities and study habits, and will form the basis for resident child expert, Evelyn Braun's latest book *How to Raise a Genius (and what to do with children who aren't).*

Those interested should contact Evelyn via email at ivyleagueorbust@aol.com for evaluation and contract signing.

Tennis Team results

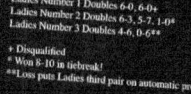

The Ladies A team has been temporarily suspended from the Inter-club league following allegations of cheating against our number one doubles pair by the Capitol Country Club in Spring Vale.

Loathe as we are to repeat baseless allegations, suffice it to say, the wearing of mirrored sunglasses indoors technically contradicts the USTF Code of Player Conduct, as it could be construed as an attempt to blind one's opponents using the reflection from the tennis bubble's overhead lights. We are not disputing the fact that our No. 1 pair, Pookie and Perky were wearing the eyewear in question, and that their opponents are apparently still recovering from 3rd degree burns to their retinas as a result. But we are disputing their contention that such injuries were inflicted on purpose. By way of proof, we hope to submit evidence to the USTF central council of Pookie and Perky wearing reflective sunglasses indoors during a PTA meeting that same evening at Delicate Flower pre-school. We hope the team's position in the league will be re-instated before the end of the year. Final results are as follows:

Ladies Number 1 Doubles 6-0, 6-0+
Ladies Number 2 Doubles 6-3, 5-7, 1-0*
Ladies Number 3 Doubles 4-6, 0-6**

+ Disqualified
* Won 8-10 in tiebreak!
**Loss puts Ladies third pair on automatic probation.

Gentlemen? We assume you are playing tennis, as we see with our very own eyes that you are taking up most of the club courts. Please report the results of those matches for publication by the Crier deadline next month. And no, it is not beneath your dignity for one of you to be designated as Secretary of the team.

Board of Managers Meeting

Following the resignation of Mrs. Van Houzen, known to many of you as the late Tinklepaw's owner, from the Village Board last month, it has come to our attention that an anonymous petition is in circulation to rename the Village Hall in her honor (owner, not dog). While it is theoretically constitutional to enact such a measure according to Village by-laws, such measures are generally reserved for residents who are either a) deemed to have provided selfless service to the Village over the course of many decades; b) popular or c) dead. A perfect example of a resident who qualifies on (almost!) all three counts is the Village Club President, whose years of toil on the tennis courts and golf green, not to mention the Club bar, have recently resulted in a unanimous vote to dedicate the Gentlemen's Lounge to him, in recognition of his selfless service. We hope Village residents will consider these criteria carefully before signing any new such petition.

In completely unrelated news, we are excited to report that Holier Than Thou Foods has broken ground on its new gourmet supermarket, and the store is on schedule to open on May 1 next year.

Investigation into strange smell detected round Village

Several residents have complained of an unpleasant odor around the Village. The smell, which some have likened to that of a decaying corpse, is most noticeable on unseasonably warm fall days, and appears to emanate from the corner of Church St. and Kirkside Avenue, where the late Tinklepaw was laid to rest. The Village is taking the precaution of digging up the speed hump under which she is entombed, in order to exhume and re-bury the body in a sealed vault. In the meantime, we have distributed the Village's supply of gas masks for residents on the affected streets. As an additional precaution, the wearing of said masks at all times while outdoors will be strictly enforced by block captains until re-burial is complete.

Miss Gertrude

Judging by the overwhelming response to last month's column, Miss Gertrude suspects she has merely begun to pick at the hoary scab of etiquette infractions in our seemingly peaceful community. Many of the issues raised in the letters, emails and verbal tirades Miss Gertrude has received involve situations that might have easily been resolved by a courteous visit or phone call to a neighbor - to politely ask them not to park in front of your house, say, or to inquire if they really need to mow their lawn at 6am. Instead, as is so often the case, the first inkling these neighbors had that they were being inconsiderate comes in the form of a rap on the door by officers from the Village's Special Ops, and the shining of flashlights into their home, which I am sure you will agree can so easily be misconstrued.

Miss Gertrude is forced to conclude that there is a small minority of Villagers who assume their family connections, or positions in the current administration or prestigious private profession mean they deserve special treatment in every area of their lives, not just at work. Yes, emergency room doctors need their sleep, but requiring a zone of silence for one square mile round one's property at all times suggests an outsize sense of self-importance, as does copying an entire group upon an email response where a simple reply to the sender would have sufficed. Hard as it may be to believe, not everyone will be devastated to learn that you are unable to attend the annual Back to School Fall picnic, even if you do happen to run your own family foundation.

Similarly, it is important to remember that pretty much every adult who moves to the Village was also valedictorian of their high school class, graduated Summa Cum Laude from college and is now busy running the world. Thus, whenever you find yourself feeling tempted to boast about your extraordinary achievements, please remember that others may have done the same, and that neighborly relations might be better served by keeping your mouth shut.

Diversity Group

The Village Diversity Group would like to congratulate the chairwoman of the women's group subcommittee on his successful gender realignment surgery, and will host a tree planting ceremony outside the Village Hall on Sunday, November 2 at 2pm, to thank him for her years of devoted service.

Tennis Team results

The Ladies' A team has been temporarily suspended from the Inter-club league following allegations of cheating against our number one doubles pair by the Capitol Country Club in Spring Vale.

Loathe as we are to repeat baseless allegations, suffice it to say, the wearing of mirrored sunglasses indoors technically contradicts the USTF Code of Player Conduct, as it could be construed as an attempt to blind one's opponents using the reflection from the tennis bubble's overhead lights. We are not disputing the fact that our No. 1 pair, Pookie and Perky were wearing the eyewear in question, and that their opponents are apparently still recovering from 3rd degree burns to their retinas as a result. But we are disputing their contention that such injuries were inflicted on purpose. By way of proof, we hope to submit evidence to the USTF central council of Pookie and Perky wearing reflective sunglasses indoors during a PTA meeting that same evening at Delicate Flower pre-school. We hope the team's position in the league will be reinstated before the end of the year. Final results are as follows:

> Ladies' Number 1 Doubles 6-0, 6-0+
> Ladies' Number 2 Doubles 6-3, 5-7. 1-0*
> Ladies' Number 3 Doubles 4-6, 0-6**
>
> + Disqualified
> * Won 8-10 in tie break!
> **Loss puts Ladies' third

pair on automatic probation.

Gentlemen? We assume you are playing tennis, as we see with our very own eyes that you are taking up most of the club courts. Please report the results of those matches for publication by the Whiner deadline next month. And no, it is not beneath your dignity for one of you to be designated as Secretary of the team.

CLASSIFIEDS

Looking for a few good Village children between the ages of 5 and 15 to participate in a study on the effect of eliminating all wheat, rice, sugar, caffeine, soda and dairy products from their diet for a period of one year (yes, kids, that includes chocolate and Diet Coke).

This study is expected to show dramatic improvements in the subjects' cognitive abilities and study habits, and will form the basis for resident child expert, Evelyn Braun's, latest book: *How to Raise a Genius (and what to do with children who aren't).*

Those interested should contact Evelyn via email at:
ivyleagueorbust@aol.com
for evaluation and contract signing.

From: sopcithurts@smithalumnus.edu

The Village Diversity Group women's subcommittee will hold an emergency meeting at the Village Hall at 8pm tonight to vote on whether or not our current chairwoman, who recently underwent gender realignment surgery, can continue on in his current position. While I think we can agree that all of us are supportive of a person's right to choose their own sex, some of us feel strongly that the chair position of the Women's Group Subcommittee should be reserved for someone who is actually, or at least currently, a woman. Others on the committee feel that 'gender' is a patriarchal construct anyway – one to which we should not yield in our organizational structure – so a straight up or down vote to decide the issue will occur at the meeting tonight.

The Committee trusts this can be conducted in a civil and respectful fashion, and looks forward to the participation of interested citizens of the Village.

From: crystalwalker@sterlingmorris.com
To: phoebegb@sahmsrule.net
Are you guys up yet?

Hoping the cherubs would sleep in with a sugar hangover, but no such luck. They've been gorging on candy since 6. Between cleaning up wrappers, stacking the dishwasher, running two loads of laundry and unblocking the toilet, this is the first time I've made it to my computer all morning, and it's almost 11. Helen Wheels probably has her Manolos up on my desk as I type. She certainly couldn't wait to broadcast the fact that I am sans husband and childcare yet AGAIN, and the cherubs don't have school, which is why I'm working from home. Bet she's never had to lock herself in the bathroom to take business calls.

Two quick things:

1) Did you get my email about Lata? Will put in a call to The English Nanny agency ASAP but any assistance she can give me today would be much appreciated, as I have a brief I need to edit for Helen by 5pm. Apparently, the woman does not need a social life.

2) What should I do about the cherubs' behavior outside Evelyn's house last night? They obviously heard me shrieking to George after discovering Nina's letter on my pillow, and proceeded to act out on the 'trick' aspect of trick or treating in a way that I am sure someone w/o children would never understand. I've calmed down (somewhat) since then, and now recognize that losing Nina may actually turn out to be a blessing.

From: phoebegb@sahmsrule.net
To: crystalwalker@sterlingmorris.com
Good questions, both. To answer:

1) Pelting Evelyn's house with eggs and feeding the prune leathers she offered by way of a Halloween treat to Snuggles certainly pales in comparison to appropriating one's au pair. The cherubs were understandably enraged on your behalf. Indeed, there are women in the Village who would judge

stealing one's husband less harshly. But I agree it may also not be wise to burn bridges with Evelyn just yet. You never know when you might need her. Given this, I suggest the cherubs deliver a hand-written note of apology (dictated by you, of course), along with an offer to wash her car and clean up Snuggles' resultant purge all over the front lawn.

2) More than happy to offer Lata's services to watch the cherubs today, but Brad leaves for the consulting job in Alaska tomorrow morning, and I haven't fully considered who will tend to my needs while he is gone. Then there's the teensy matter of consulting Lata. OK if I get back to you about all this?

From: crystalwalker@sterlingmorris.com
To: phoebegb@sahmsrule.net
I completely understand your oh-so-British attachment to Nanny, and will take any offers of help I can get today with the cherubs while you consider the matter. When and if you do decide to ask Lata whether she would be willing to work for my brood, do please let her know that we will double whatever you pay her (only fair, for double the number of children).

FAX

To: _FAQ: Immaculata Gracia_   C/O _Iglesia de la Blessed Loincloth_
Fax: _301-845-4555_

From: _Phoebe Thompson_
At: _la casa_
Phone: _1 (uno)_

PERSONAL

Sorry to bother you in church.

I know how importante el dia de dios is to usted, pero mi neighbor has a childcare emergencia, and has asked if you can work for her today. She will pay you doble for looking after her 4 kids plus the twins.

I told her no problema. Hope that's OK.

She also wants to hire you part-time before and after school every weekday starting on Monday. I told her how fidel you were to us, and that you would probablemente say non, no matter how much she is offering to pagar, pero I recommend you take the job, since we cannot pay you full-time any more.

Lo siento mucho,
Sra. Phoebe

FAX

To: _FAQ: Immaculata Gracia_   C/O: _Iglesia de la Blessed Loincloth_
Fax: _301-845-4555_

From: _Phoebe Thompson_
At: _la casa_
Phone: _1 (uno)_

PERSONAL

No need for you to commit just yet. Why don't you try it out for a week and see how it goes? Besides, even if you do work for Sra. Crystal part-time, I am hoping that you can still take una hora or dos of your dia for you to fix me my evening bebida and give me my neck massaje. Besides. Mujeres Maduras, Chicos Jovenes is just getting interesante, pero how will I understand que pasa without you there to translate?

From: phoebegb@sahmsrule.net
To: crystalwalker@sterlingmorris.com

Lata has agreed to work for you before and after school next week, but I hope you will continue to look for a more permanent solution, in case she changes her mind. After nearly a decade with us, I expected tears, at least, at the prospect of not working for us exclusively, but she is displaying surprising resilience – at least for now. I can't bear to break news to Cecily and Emily just yet, so have sent her off with them to their favorite Peruvian chicken restaurant for old times' sake.

Thinking of asking Brad to don tight breeches and flowing white shirt again while they are gone, so we can reprise another scene from Jane Austen before he leaves tomorrow for the Great North. Feeling unfamiliar and yet not entirely unpleasant sense of urgency about getting our mutual needs met before he goes. Almost like old times.

Monday, November 5

From: phoebegb@sahmsrule.net
To: crystalwalker@sterlingmorris.com
Just dropped Brad off at the airport to catch his flight to Anchorage, and surprised to find myself feeling sadder than I was expecting.

Of course, Cecily and Emily and I will miss him, but between cell-phones, email and Skye, we have all too many ways to communicate. And between you and me, it's something of a revelation to have the house to myself. This morning, I was able to exercise, shower and dress by 10am! With a husband who works at home, you never know when they are going to spring the kind of demand that requires you to do all those things all over again.

Any chance you can keep me company and watch the election predictions together on CNNBC tonight? I will probably need more than one of Lata's pick-me-ups to make it through as it will be a long night, I think.

From: crystalwalker@sterlingmorris.com
To: phoebegb@sahmsrule.net
Subject: Attachment: Excel Spreadsheet
Do wish I could join you for a little election-night nip, but no sooner did Brad leave than George finally returned from his weekend in Annapolis to make his presence felt in hearth and home. Seems he has finally got the message about needing to be involved in the cherubs' lives, and has declared that Mondays shall be 'Family Fun Night' from now on.

Forced Family Fun might more accurate. Wish me luck as I endeavor to rip the pacifier out of Baby's mouth, the mePhone out of Kevin's sight, the mePod out of Kimberly's ears and the video game out of Karson's cold dead hands long enough for us to all enjoy an old-fashioned bored game (sic).

BTW, I've taken the liberty of creating a schedule for Lata's hours this week. Feel free to amend as necessary. I'm hoping we can also trade off Friday/Saturday nights for date nights. Sound good?

Tuesday, November 6

Lata's Weekly Schedule

☐ = Thompson Household   ☐ = Walker Household

HOURS	SUNDAY	MONDAY	TUESDAY	WEDNESDAY	THURSDAY	FRIDAY	SATURDAY
BEFORE 07:00							
07:00 - 08:00	**FREE DAY**						
08:00 - 09:00		Help get cherubs to school and tidy house	Help get cherubs to school and tidy house	Help get cherubs to school and tidy house	Help get cherubs to school and tidy house	Help get cherubs to school and tidy house	
09:00 - 10:00	Lata in church all day.						
10:00 - 11:00	Call only for emergencies						
11:00 - 12:00	involving search						
12:00 - 13:00	and rescue	Housekeeping, Provide technical assistance to Brad as needed	Housekeeping, Provide technical assistance to Brad as needed	Housekeeping, Provide technical assistance to Brad as needed	Housekeeping, Provide technical assistance to Brad as needed	Housekeeping, Provide technical assistance to Brad as needed	
13:00 - 14:00	and/or						
14:00 - 15:00	welding skills						
15:00 - 16:00							
16:00 - 17:00		Cocktail duty	Cocktail duty	Cocktail duty	Cocktail duty	Cocktail duty	
17:00 - 18:00		Cocktail duty	Cocktail duty	Cocktail duty	Cocktail duty	Cocktail duty	Baby sitting (assuming they aren't asleep)
18:00 - 19:00		Bathtime and bedtime for two youngest cherubs	Bathtime and bedtime for two youngest cherubs	Bathtime and bedtime for two youngest cherubs	Bathtime and bedtime for two youngest cherubs	Bathtime and bedtime for two youngest cherubs	
19:00 - 20:00							Baby sitting until ?

From: phoebegb@sahmsrule.net
To: crystalwalker@sterlingmorris.com

Schedule looks great. Have you ever considered a career in the military? Pretty sure the war in Iraq would have gone differently if you'd been in charge.

ELECTION DAY RULES

VILLAGE RESIDENTS ARE ASKED TO CONDUCT THEMSELVES IN A CIVIL AND ORDERLY FASHION, AND TO RESPECT THEIR NEIGHBORS' RIGHT TO VOTE, EVEN IF YOU DON'T AGREE WITH THEIR CHOICE OF CANDIDATE.

PLEASE OBSERVE THE FOLLOWING RULES WHILE AT THE POLLING STATION:

- NO PUSHING, SHOVING OR SWEARING IN LINE.

- REGISTERED DEMOCRATS TO LINE UP TO THE LEFT OF THE VILLAGE HALL ENTRANCE. PLEASE FOLLOW THE ROPE LINE ROUND THE CORNER AT PEAK TIMES.

- REGISTERED REPUBLICANS TO LINE UP TO THE RIGHT OF THE VILLAGE HALL ENTRANCE. DARK GLASSES AND HATS WILL BE PROVIDED TO PROTECT YOUR IDENTITY.

- ELECTION OFFICERS ARE FORBIDDEN TO OFFER NECKLACES, BANGLES AND LOLLIPOPS IN THEIR PARTY'S COLORS TO ANYONE ENTERING THE POLLING STATION. OFFERING SUCH ITEMS UPON EXIT AS A REWARD FOR VOTING IS FINE.

- VOTING IS BY TOUCHSCREEN IN THIS COUNTY. PLEASE SEE A POLLING OFFICER FOR ASSISTANCE USING THIS EQUIPMENT, OR BRING A SMALL CHILD.

- POLLING OFFICERS TO RESPECT THE SECRET BALLOT. REMEMBER, IT IS A FELONY TO DIVULGE YOUR FELLOW CITIZENS' VOTE. IT IS, HOWEVER, PERFECTLY ACCEPTABLE TO ASK IF THEY ARE A REGISTERED REPUBLICAN OR DEMOCRAT IN FRONT OF EVERYONE AS THEY ENTER THE POLLING STATION TO PICK UP THEIR BALLOT.

 MAY THE BEST CANDIDATE WIN. GOD BLESS AMERICA!

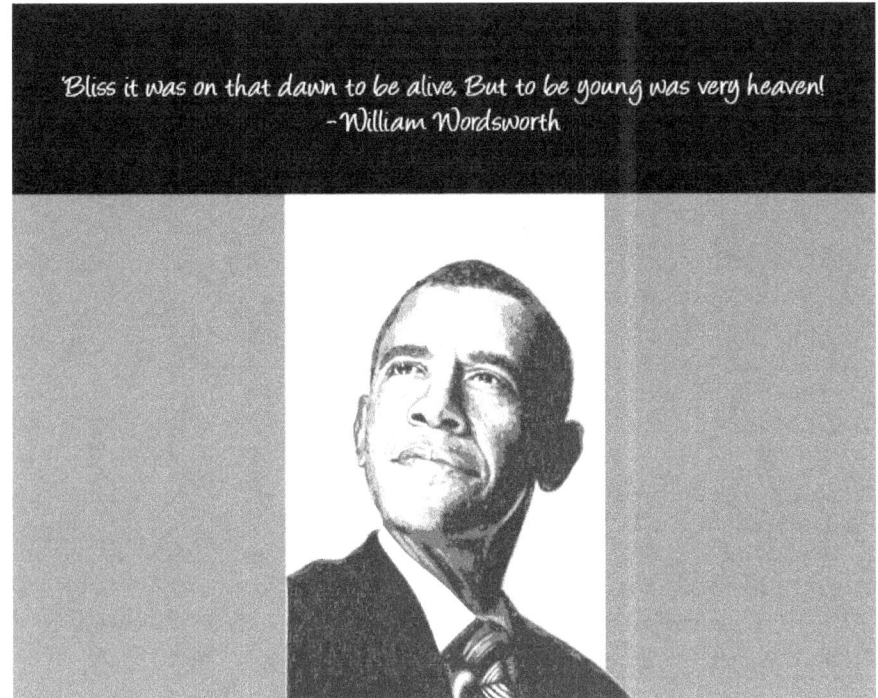

'Bliss it was on that dawn to be alive, But to be young was very heaven!
– William Wordsworth

PLEASE JOIN US FOR A COCKTAIL
PARTY TO CELEBRATE THE
RE-ELECTION OF OUR NATION'S FIRST
AFRICAN-AMERICAN PRESIDENT

Pookie and Buddy Granger
2020 Kirkside Drive

Wednesday, November 7th
7-9 pm

R.S.V.P. Regrets

Dress: Cocktail Attire

From: crystalwalker@sterlingmorris.com
To: phoebegb@sahmsrule.net
What are you planning on wearing to Grangers' tomorrow? Impressive how quickly they were able to pull this together. And to think, I assumed they were Republicans!

From: phoebegb@sahmsrule.net
To: crystalwalker@sterlingmorris.com
They were Republicans, at least until recently, but Pookie is nothing if not fashionable.

Still recovering from the trauma of having Pookie pay for a Nanette Lepere dress after my credit card was declined. Have a horrible feeling she will never let me live this down at the Club, unless I come up with a counter-strategy soon.

Can you pick me up on your way?

From: crystalwalker@sterlingmorris.com
To: phoebegb@sahmsrule.net
Will do.

From: phoebegb@sahmsrule.net
To: pookiegranger@hotmail.com
So kind of you to pay cash for my dress this afternoon. I simply have no idea why the assistant in Deja Vue would so rudely insist on cutting up my card. You'd think the woman worked at Neiman Marcus, not a consignment store, no matter how much they try and avoid using the word 'secondhand' in favor of 'vintage.'

I'm on the phone to the card company to sort it all out as I write, and will look forward to seeing you (and paying you back) tomorrow.

Cecily and Emily,
IOU $150.

Promise to pay you
back as soon as
Daddy gets paid.
xo

From: phoebegb@sahmsrule.net
To: crystalwalker@sterlingmorris.com
Oops. Slight change of plans.

Pookie needs a capable adult to help set up for the cocktail party. Any chance Lata can come to you at 3, then head down to Pookie's house by 4 to help supervise? I believe Vira also needs an extra set of hands, literally, for her in-home Reiki session on Thursday morning. You could send Lata there between 9-10, then keep her until noon, if that works. Just a suggestion.

Let me know if this is all too complicated. Promise to sort out all billing issues by end of week and give you a summary of your hours and mine.

Text from Crystal To Phoebe
Fine to spare Lata earlier in day, but were hoping she could watch cherubs while we're at Grangers' party.

Text from Phoebe To Crystal
Oops. Already asked her to sleep over, so we can attend.

Text from Crystal To Phoebe
George jumped at opp not to go to party, so problem solved. Claims he'll be exhausted after a hard few days rounding up last last minute votes for the candidate, but wait till he's had to handle bedtime for cherubs. CU at 7.

Thursday, November 8

Text from Phoebe to Crystal
thx for ride home last night. Good to see the Grangers still drink like Republicans.

Text from Crystal to Phoebe
yeshh.

Skye Chat
phoebethompson
Last night still a bit of a haze, but did Pookie manage to insult both of us in that rambling speech she gave during her toast to the President and First Family?

crystalwalker
So it wasn't just my imagination? I was beginning to think I had dreamt it, but it's starting to come back. She started by saluting the First Family's humble origins, then moved on to suggest that no middle class white family from the Midwest stood a chance in hell of making it into the Village Country Club, let alone any of the DC private schools, right?

phoebethompson
not in so many words, but rather by suggesting that you were a 'breath

of fresh air', and she hoped the stuffed shirts on the Club board would overlook your lack of illustrious ancestors in the interests of socio-economic diversity.

crystalwalker
and did she really say it was unfortunate the cherubs went to public school, because she feared they were being exposed to gangs, judging by the way they dressed and acted?

phoebethompson
in a word, yes, even though the Village Public School is about as gangsta as the average Florida nursing home. How about the fact that Pookie chose to advertise the fact that she had taken pity on me at Deja Vu yesterday and paid for the dress I was wearing – even though it was one she had donated earlier to Goodwill because it was far too big for her around the waist and hips?

crystalwalker
OMG, yes! Shall we kill her now, or wait until we can get away with it undetected?

phoebethompson
too incensed to think right now, but trust me, I will. I'll let you know.

crystalwalker
OK – I'm counting on you!

From: phoebegb@sahmsrule.net
To: crystalwalker@sterlingmorris.com
Still fuming about Pookie, but not sure how best to exact revenge on behalf of us both, although I may have suggested she might be responsible for a fungal foot infection that's spreading like wildfire through the Club's Ladies showers. I think part of what has me so upset is the fact that Brad and I ARE struggling financially right now, so for Pookie to poke fun at me for it hits a little close to the bone. Not all of us can be lucky (or cynical) enough to marry for money.

Spent afternoon ferrying girls between Latin and classical jazz, followed by discovery that we are out of pesto. It's enough to make me reconsider my offer to share Lata, especially now that Brad is actually in gainful employment again.

Any luck with the English Nanny agency yet?

From: crystalwalker@sterlingmorris.com
To: phoebegb@sahmsrule.net
Interviewed three nanny candidates during my lunch hour, but they clearly draw on a different gene pool than yours, dear P. One young lady arrived wearing a top that revealed almost as much bosom as I do while nursing. Another inquired where the nearest bars and nightclubs were. The third informed me that she insisted upon a 7:30pm bedtime for all her charges

(including, she implied, parents) and ordered me to tidy my desk before she left. I have three more lined up for tomorrow, although all of them seem to insist on no more than a 2:1 ratio when it comes to their precious charges, which means I would actually have to hire TWO full-time attendants to deal with my brood.

In the meantime, I hate to ask, but is there any chance Lata might be able to watch the cherubs tomorrow night instead of Saturday? George has promised to keep Fridays free for Date Night from now on, in honor of our re-elected President and his lovely missus, who apparently have pledged not to break their weekly dinner date for anything short of a national emergency. If the leader of the free world can take time off for romance, surely my husband can too?

From: phoebegb@sahmsrule.net
To: crystalwalker@sterlingmorris.com
Fridays are usually reserved for Lata and I to watch telenovellas (in the interest of improving my Spanish, you understand). But as I am actually rather low on funds this month until Brad gets paid (not that I would EVER admit this to Pookie), I do suppose it would be better if you can pay her for those hours.

From: crystalwalker@sterlingmorris.com
To: phoebegb@sahmsrule.net
God Bless for being willing to spare her, and God Bless Lata for being willing to deal with any number of my needy offspring! Her special forces training has served her well.

Friday, November 9

From: crystalwalker@sterlingmorris.com
To: jsmith@plunderhogg.com
Subject: George's Travel Schedule
So sorry to bother you again about my husband's whereabouts but a family emergency has arisen and I need to track him down. He left home early this morning to meet with the CEO of Blackbeard Systems, but is there some way I can reach him?

From: crystalwalker@sterlingmorris.com
To: jsmith@plunderhogg.com
Re: George's Travel Schedule
What do you mean my husband is on manoeuvres and can't get satellite reception from inside his tank? This is West Virginia we are talking about, not some godforsaken cave in Peshwar. Although, frankly it might be easier to reach him on a donkey trail up the Khyber Pass.

From: crystalwalker@sterlingmorris.com
To: jsmith@plunderhogg.com
Re: George's Travel Schedule

If the only way to reach him is via an airdrop from a drone, so be it. I'm guessing Blackbeard Systems can absorb the expense.

Message from Crystal to George, delivered inside a metal tube via parachute

Can u plz get yr ass home asap and focus on being a father first, and commando, second? Kevin has just been caught in the bushes outside Evelyn Braun's house by Fred, spying on Nina in the shower.

Satellite Phone Text between Crystal and George

WTF do you mean, boys will be boys? Village Special Ops are on the way over to interview him.

Satellite Text between Crystal and George

I am not overreacting, and it is most certainly not funny. May have escaped yr attn, but I am managing all 4 cherubs here alone. You had better be home w/in the next couple of hours, or there will be consequences.

Text from Crystal to Kevin

WTH were u thinking? U do realize I brought u into this world and I can take u out. U had better go to yr rm and stay there until death or dinner, whichever comes 1st. BTW, u have lost all phone/texting privileges 4 LIFE!!

Satellite Text between Crystal and George

Can't take call right now. On Bluetooth call to mom who gave Kimberly ride to gym meet. K apparently started her 1st period, and did not go prepared. My fault too, apparently. Why isn't it ever yours?

Text from Crystal to Kevin

Congratulations on becoming a woman, darling! Hang in there and I will have all supplies u need after u get home.

Text from Crystal to Kevin

Oops. Meant to send to your sister. Be kind after she gets home. Yr life depends on it, in so many ways.

Satellite Text from Crystal to George

Kev let off with warning. But cherubs need a father, and I need a husband who's more than an SMS presence in my life. I can't do this alone!

Text from Phoebe To Crystal

Everything OK? Just spotted local bobby leaving your house.

Text from Crystal To Phoebe

Too exhausted to explain. Will call/email in the am. Sweet dreams!

Saturday, November 10

From: crystalwalker@sterlingmorris.com
To: phoebegb@sahmsrule.net
Fred caught Kevin spying on Nina as she showered in the bathroom of Evelyn's basement nanny annex yesterday morning, after I reminded him to walk Snuggles. Had I known he would use the opportunity to turn into the Village stalker, however, I would certainly have kept him safely under lock and key. So much for turning the other cheek. Of course, Fred insisted on calling the police to 'teach the boy a lesson,' as he clearly believed poor parenting, not pubescent male hormones are to blame.

Naturally, I assured both Fred and the officer in charge that we would be adopting Evelyn's suggested regime of daily cold showers IMMEDIATELY, accompanied by a wheat, sugar and dairy-free diet and weekly visits to the local holistic apothecary for acupuncture and Chinese herbs. Officer Gonzalez let Kevin off with a warning after I sobbed into his shirt, and Evelyn has offered to include him in her upcoming study – the very one Vira and all the other mothers in the Village have been clamoring to have their kids join. Ironic, huh?

The Midwesterner in me is skeptical that this new dietary regime will accomplish anything other than making Kev miserable (a goal I shall relish), but I sense that it's important to be seen to be adopting the latest parenting techniques around these parts. And besides, I'm looking forward to eating the rest of his Halloween candy in bed tonight, after feeding him rice cakes for dinner. It's about the only pleasure I have left these days, besides calling the coordinator at Au Pair International to report that Evelyn's basement bathroom does not meet their stringent privacy standards. I guess it's too much to hope that Nina is immediately deported.

From: phoebegb@sahmsrule.net
To: crystalwalker@sterlingmorris.com
Congratulations on getting Kevin into Evelyn's study! Cecily and Emily are in also, which is a relief, as I was beginning to think my lifetime ban on high fructose corn syrup was for naught. I would save the call to the Au Pair coordinator for another moment when you again need leverage with Evelyn – perhaps in the unlikely event Kevin accidentally eats an M&M, and the results show up in his blood sugar tests. Otherwise, as you well know, Evelyn's report on any alleged transgressions may follow Kevin onto his college application.

Any chance you can join Vira and I for drinks at the Village Lounge tonight? Even though I wouldn't describe us as friends, exactly, she seems anxious to talk.

From: crystalwalker@sterlingmorris.com
To: phoebegb@sahmsrule.net
George and I have an emergency breakfast meeting to discuss how to handle Kev's behavior tomorrow at 6am, so I need an early night.

Have fun!

Lata,

Gone to work early, so can answer emails b4 weekly staff meeting.

Please DO NOT touch Kimberly's room. have ordered her to clean up b4 breakfast. or she is GROUNDED, indefinitely.

Karson has playdate today with Ravi at our house @ 3. so no screen time until after R. leaves, no matter how much the two of them whine. Kar knows that any infraction of this rule will result in the severest of sanctions (I leave you to decide what).

It's too late for the two bigs, so relying on you to help us avoid making same mistakes with our younger offspring.

Thank you.
Crystal

Monday, November 12

From: crystalwalker@sterlingmorris.com
To: phoebegb@sahmsrule.net
How was last night? Did you and Vira meet anyone interesting?

From: phoebegb@sahmsrule.net
To: crystalwalker@sterlingmorris.com
If by interesting you mean every middle-aged divorced man who likes to hit the local bars in his sweatpants, flip-flops and let's not forget athletic socks, then you are right. To make matters worse, Flip-flops even had the temerity to ask if I was Vira's big sister! No wonder I was forced to drown

my sorrows. I'd forgotten how excruciating the whole singles scene could be.

V. definitely seemed a little down last night. She let slip that Gunther was refusing to give her the second baby she's apparently desperate to have before it's too late, as he thinks the world is already over-populated (including, presumably, his own 3 children by two former wives). She wanted my advice about whether to break up with him and go it alone, or do nothing and hope the desire for a second child passes. Hard to know what to say, but I did try and offer her reassurance that there are plenty of available men who would love to have children with her, even if I couldn't think of any at that particular moment.

All very sobering. Doesn't help that I never seem to sleep well without Brad by my side. Xavier might know how to tire a girl out, but in the end, I find it's only my husband who can really put me to sleep.

From: crystalwalker@sterlingmorris.com
To: phoebegb@sahmsrule.net
Understandable that V. is feeling the ticking of her biological clock. A little birdie told me that she turns 42 next month, even though she looks at least a decade younger. Convinced the reason she looks so fresh is the result of much early cosmetic intervention and not merely superior insight. That, and not having four cherubs plus full-time career to contend with. What was I thinking?

George and I did a lot of soul-searching at Le Pain Q this morning, and have decided the cherubs would be better off going to private school. Given Kevin and Karson's recent behavioral issues, plus Kimberly's increasingly surly pre-teen behavior, we think they would do better in smaller classes, like those at the parochial Catholic school Kevin and Kimberly used to attend in Kansas City.

Given the recent uptick in George's business at the firm, we can just about afford it – although perhaps not, after spending fifty bucks on a couple of boiled eggs, a piece of sourdough bread (untoasted) and a couple of cappuccinos. :0

Can you offer some advice about which private schools may be most appropriate?

From: phoebegb@sahmsrule.net
To: crystalwalker@sterlingmorris.com
Ironic that you should be applying to private school just when Brad and I are thinking of withdrawing our girls from CRAC.

You do realize that statistically speaking, it's harder to get into the most prestigious private schools in DC than it is to get into Harvard? The $30k post-tax tuition is just the beginning. Don't forget the donation to the endowment and the annual school scholarship auction, plus the membership in Jetsets to fly schoolfriends and family around for vacations, just to keep up.

I often wonder if Brad and I would have made the same decision to send the girls, had we known things would one day be so tough. CRAC is an exceptional educational establishment, but paying the fees in post tax dollars has become an overwhelming source of anxiety of late. If I have to hear Brad's mother tell me one more time what a genius her son is, I may have to show her our latest bank statement.

Besides, I must confess my jealousy whenever I see the bus arrive to whisk your three eldest off to VPS each morning. Lata did take an evasive driving course back in Lima, but a couple of nasty run-ins with the new speed humps (she was caught flipping the bird at the camera, twice) have resulted in a temporary ban on her driving in the Village for three months, which means it's yours truly on chauffeur duty twice a day (and frequently more) while Brad is away.

From: crystalwalker@sterlingmorris.com
To: phoebegb@sahmsrule.net
Aside from joining the Village Country Club, which we are already pursuing, I understand that private schools are also the best way to gain entrée into DC's innermost circles, which should help George advance his career, as well as the cherubs' social prospects. Rather than spending years climbing the greasy pole, you can apparently circumvent the whole messy business by having your children play with the offspring of the great and the good, and faster than your little darlings can say 'My Mom/Dad is more important than yours,' hey presto, you're in!

Between you and me, Pookie's comments the other night were also a factor in our decision – or at least mine. I never want my cherubs to feel like second class citizens, the way I did growing up in Kansas City. As the only scholarship kid, and child of divorce at St. Stephens, I was often singled out for special (read, patronizing) treatment by the nuns, who loved to point out my single working mother's lack of attentiveness to my nails, the state of my uniform or my shoes.

Can't wait to see Pookie's face when I tell her the cherubs have just been accepted at Seton Academy.

From: phoebegb@sahmsrule.net
To: crystalwalker@sterlingmorris.com
Good God, woman. Do you realize how many DC parents would literally kill to have even one child at the same school as the daughters of the First Family? While I have no idea how you plan to accomplish this goal, rest assured, I will support you in every way possible. I too want to see the look on Pookie's face when I tell her that Brad has sold his business, and you casually mention that Kimberly has a sleepover at the White House.

Would you like me to set up a meeting with the Head Mistress to start with? She happens to be an alum from my alma mater, the LSE, albeit MANY years ahead of yours truly.

From: crystalwalker@sterlingmorris.com
To: phoebegb@sahmsrule.net
That would be AWESOME. I knew I could count on you!

Tuesday, November 13

Skye Chat between Phoebe and Brad
phoebethompson
I miss you so much, darling, I've taken to wearing your bathrobe in bed – with nothing underneath. Why don't you Skye me tonight after the twins are asleep, and I can show you what I mean?

phoebethompson
Forgot about the time difference. I'll probably be asleep by the time you get back to the hotel, but we can keep chatting while u work. Turns me on to think of you at the office. Are you actually wearing a suit and tie?

phoebethompson
OK. Switching on video camera now. Are you sure no one is looking?

phoebethompson
Yikes. Just caught glimpse of myself on-screen. They need to improve the video quality. Either that, or make it MUCH worse. Turning camera off, but let's keep chatting. BTW, who was that hussy in the miniskirt I spotted walking past your desk just now? Thought they were bundled up all the time up north?

phoebethompson
Goodness, the boss' wife is certainly young. BTW, Cecily and Emily just got back from evening with Lata down at C's, so I need to go and tuck them into bed. This single parent business is exhausting! xo

Wednesday, November 14

Goggle Calendar Reminder
Tennis Challenge Match against Sibby & Libby, 1pm

Text from Phoebe to Bitsy
Forgot about today's challenge match. Be there ASAP!

From: phoebegb@sahmsrule.net
To: bitsybottinger@yahoo.com
Thank you so much for keeping S&L talking while I raced over to the courts earlier.

Good thing they're both so young. I'm not sure they are even aware about Club rules about docking games for tardiness. Of course, what they lacked in experience, they made up for in speed and agility (not to mention youthful beauty), so I'm glad we were able to teach them a thing or two about ball control. Two down, one to go!

Thursday, November 15

Skye Chat
phoebethompson
Are you there darling? Sorry to wake you at the crack of dawn, but the mail just arrived, and I think there's been a mistake with your paycheck. They seem to have left off a zero or something. Can you contact the accounting department about their error?

phoebethompson
Yes, I do understand that a high hourly rate does not necessarily translate into a generous bi-monthly salary, but how am I supposed to pay for CRAC? Cecily and Emily's jazz teacher, not to mention therapy bills and Lata's (SEVERELY) reduced hours?

phoebethompson
Hello? Are you still there?

phoebethompson
Typical. Just don't expect me to cover for you when your mother asks what happened to all the birthday money she gave the twins.

Text from Phoebe to Xavier
Lo siento mucho, pero I have strained back and need to cancel next 4 lessons. Hope u will keep my spot open. I know Pookie = waiting to pounce, but up close, she's not nearly as young as she looks from 2 courts away.

Text from Phoebe to Xavier
UR v. sweet, but don't think one of yr special massages wd help with this problem. Will call as soon as I feel better. Un beso. xo

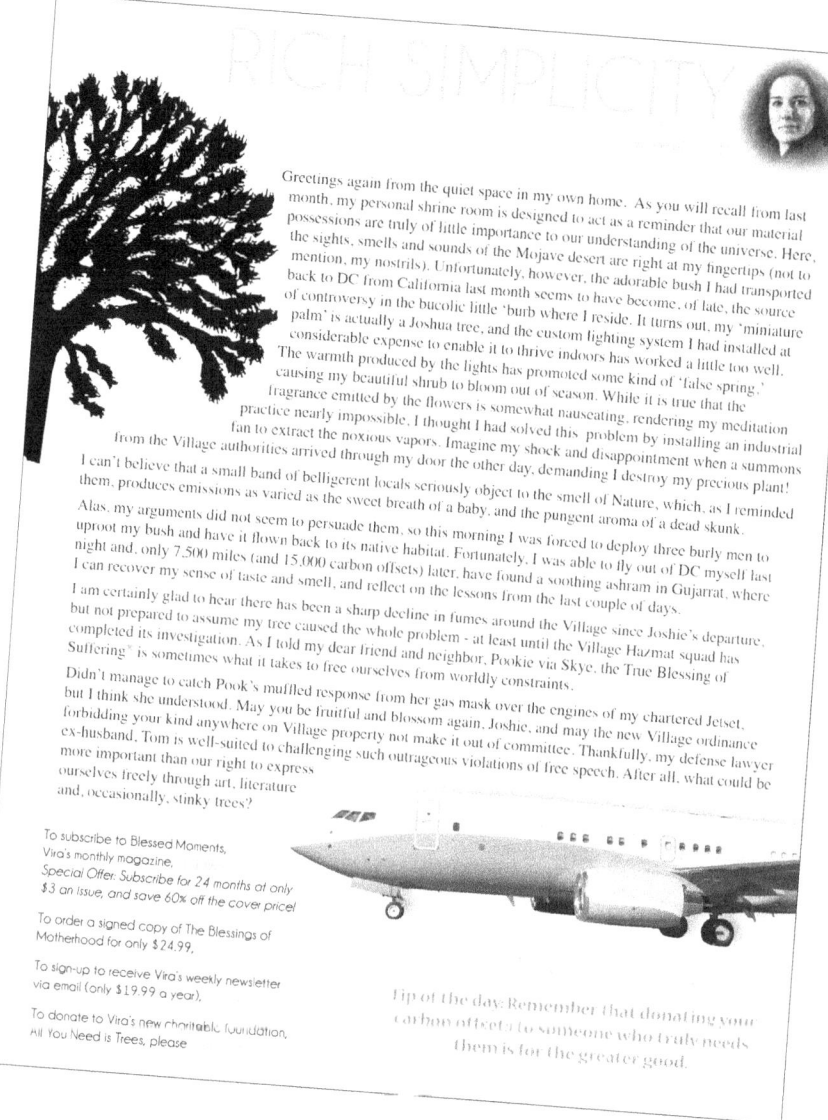

RICH SIMPLICITY

Greetings again from the quiet space in my own home. As you will recall from last month, my personal shrine room is designed to act as a reminder that our material possessions are truly of little importance to our understanding of the universe. Here, the sights, smells and sounds of the Mojave desert are right at my fingertips (not to mention, my nostrils). Unfortunately, however, the adorable bush I had transported back to DC from California last month seems to have become, of late, the source of controversy in the bucolic little 'burb where I reside. It turns out, my 'miniature palm' is actually a Joshua tree, and the custom lighting system I had installed at considerable expense to enable it to thrive indoors has worked a little too well. The warmth produced by the lights has promoted some kind of 'false spring,' causing my beautiful shrub to bloom out of season. While it is true that the fragrance emitted by the flowers is somewhat nauseating, rendering my meditation practice nearly impossible, I thought I had solved this problem by installing an industrial fan to extract the noxious vapors. Imagine my shock and disappointment when a summons from the Village authorities arrived through my door the other day, demanding I destroy my precious plant! I can't believe that a small band of belligerent locals seriously object to the smell of Nature, which, as I reminded them, produces emissions as varied as the sweet breath of a baby, and the pungent aroma of a dead skunk. Alas, my arguments did not seem to persuade them, so this morning I was forced to deploy three burly men to uproot my bush and have it flown back to its native habitat. Fortunately, I was able to fly out of DC myself last night and, only 7,500 miles (and 15,000 carbon offsets) later, have found a soothing ashram in Gujarrat, where I can recover my sense of taste and smell, and reflect on the lessons from the last couple of days. I am certainly glad to hear there has been a sharp decline in fumes around the Village since Joshie's departure, but not prepared to assume my tree caused the whole problem - at least until the Village Hazmat squad has completed its investigation. As I told my dear friend and neighbor, Pookie via Skye, the True Blessing of Suffering" is sometimes what it takes to free ourselves from worldly constraints. Didn't manage to catch Pook's muffled response from her gas mask over the engines of my chartered Jetset, but I think she understood. May you be fruitful and blossom again, Joshie, and may the new Village ordinance forbidding your kind anywhere on Village property not make it out of committee. Thankfully, my defense lawyer ex-husband, Tom is well-suited to challenging such outrageous violations of free speech. After all, what could be more important than our right to express ourselves freely through art, literature and, occasionally, stinky trees?

To subscribe to Blessed Moments,
Vira's monthly magazine,
Special Offer: Subscribe for 24 months at only
$3 an issue, and save 60% off the cover price!

To order a signed copy of The Blessings of
Motherhood for only $24.99,

To sign-up to receive Vira's weekly newsletter
via email (only $19.99 a year),

To donate to Vira's new charitable foundation,
All You Need is Trees, please

Tip of the day: Remember that donating your
carbon offsets to someone who truly needs
them is for the greater good.

From: Rich Simplicity
To: phoebegb@sahmsrule.net

*Rich Simplicity: A monthly newsletter bringing you a life of ultimate simplicity,
no matter how much money I have.*

Volume 03, Issue 11

Blessings,

Greetings again from the quiet space in my own home. As you will recall from last month, my personal shrine room is designed to act as a reminder that our material possessions are truly of little importance to our understanding of the universe. Here, the sights, smells and sounds of the Mojave desert are right at my fingertips (not to mention, my nostrils). Unfortunately, however, the adorable bush I had transported back to DC from California last month seems to have become, of late, the source of controversy in the bucolic little 'burb where I reside. It turns out, my 'miniature palm' is actually a Joshua tree, and the custom lighting system I had installed at considerable expense to enable it to thrive indoors has worked a little too well. The warmth produced by the lights has promoted some kind of 'false spring,' causing my beautiful shrub to bloom out of season. While it is true that the fragrance emitted by the flowers is somewhat nauseating, rendering my meditation practice nearly impossible, I thought I had solved this problem by installing an industrial fan to extract the noxious vapors. Imagine my shock and disappointment when a summons from the Village authorities arrived through my door the other day, demanding I destroy my precious plant!

I can't believe that a small band of belligerent locals seriously object to the smell of Nature, which, as I reminded them, produces emissions as varied as the sweet breath of a baby, and the pungent aroma of a dead skunk.

Alas, my arguments did not seem to persuade them, so this morning I was forced to deploy three burly men to uproot my bush and have it flown back to its native habitat. Fortunately, I was able to fly out of DC myself last night and, only 7,500 miles (and 15,000 carbon offsets) later, have found a soothing ashram in Gujarrat, where I can recover my sense of taste and smell, and reflect on the lessons from the last couple of days.

I am certainly glad to hear there has been a sharp decline in fumes around the Village since Joshie's departure, but not prepared to assume my tree caused the whole problem - at least until the Village Hazmat squad has completed its investigation. As I told my dear friend and neighbor, Pookie via Skye, the True Blessing of Suffering' is sometimes what it takes to free ourselves from worldly constraints.

Didn't manage to catch Pook's muffled response from her gas mask over the engines of my chartered Jetset, but I think she understood. May you be fruitful and blossom again, Joshie, and may the new Village ordinance forbidding your kind anywhere on Village property not make it out of committee. Thankfully, my defense lawyer ex-husband, Tom is well-suited to challenging such outrageous violations of free speech. After all, what could be more important than our right to express ourselves freely through art, literature and, occasionally, stinky trees?

From: crystalwalker@sterlingmorris.com
To: phoebegb@sahmsrule.net
Thank you SO much for setting up the meeting with Hilary Manning at Seton today.

Not sure whether to wear my regular work suit, or go looking like the most devoted soccer mom. If I can slip out early without Helen noticing, I might even manage a quick visit to the Village Shoppes first. Any chance you can join? I could certainly use your advice.

From: phoebegb@sahmsrule.net
To: crystalwalker@sterlingmorris.com
Must admit, I was a tad skeptical watching you dig through the Lowmans'

sales rack, until you stumbled across that magnificent Chica dress, which was perfect for your meeting with Hilary. Still, although DC isn't as fashion-forward as New York or London, I fear there are some discriminating people here who will recognize a piece from last season when they see it, so I'm glad I extracted a promise from you to try my favorite designer boutique as soon just as my store cards are re-instated.

How did the meeting go?

From: crystalwalker@sterlingmorris.com
To: phoebegb@sahmsrule.net
Meeting with Hilary was a pleasant surprise. Worried her frumpy appearance was an indicator she channeled the nuns I feared in high school, but I was relieved to discover it's actually a persona she projects in order to make parents and students feel more comfortable. You wouldn't believe all the wonderful ammunition she is able to gather in her dowdy state. Apparently, fund-raising is much easier when a cheating spouse has just confessed his latest conquest and doesn't want the current wife to end up with his brand new Porsche or the vineyard in Napa.

Of course you know that the President's daughters attend Seton, right? Naturally, Hilary claims the girls' applications were judged on merit, like everyone else's, but who actually believes that? Coincidentally, several current students who are not measuring up will be encouraged to pursue alternative educational opportunities to make space for more suitable incoming candidates. None of this is done overtly, of course, but the school will suggest numerous tutoring and outside support systems that make it impossible for the parents of the children in question to manage, even taking in to consideration generous trust funds. A month ago, I would have been outraged by this kind of behavior, but I'm beginning to understand how DC works.

Hilary and I have a dinner scheduled for Monday to discuss how to best prepare the cherubs for the extensive round of testing and interviews required. Hilary even offered to bring her two precious Shia-tzus to amuse the cherubs while we step out! Amazing that she's so generous with her time, especially since I happen to know she's going through a nasty divorce herself right now (no kids, thankfully). At least I was able to offer sympathy on the absent spouse front, as George is gone so much these days.

I think this may be the beginning of a beautiful friendship.

Monday, November 19

From: crystalwalker@sterlingmorris.com
To: phoebegb@sahmsrule.net
What did you make of Vira's revelation at yoga this morning about splitting up with Gunther? No wonder he refused to touch her in class. Or about Tom, her too good to be true ex-husband, getting a girlfriend?

From: phoebegb@sahmsrule.net
To: crystalwalker@sterlingmorris.com
Surprising on both fronts. I simply assumed Tom must still be in love with V, since he and she have been divorced for over two years, and he hasn't dated since – at least, until now. Couldn't catch most of your conversation as I was too busy trying not to collapse in sideways starfish pose, but do please elaborate.

From: crystalwalker@sterlingmorris.com
To: phoebegb@sahmsrule.net
Tom claims it was love at first sight, and the girlfriend has apparently already moved in after only three weeks. The plan is for them to get married by the end of the year.

From: phoebegb@sahmsrule.net
To: crystalwalker@sterlingmorris.com
Guess we can safely assume the new girlfriend is 22 and gorgeous?

From: crystalwalker@sterlingmorris.com
To: phoebegb@sahmsrule.net
Tiffany is 25 and a retired runway model. Also a Buddhist therapist who believes in reincarnation, so she thinks she and Tom were already married in a past life. Meaning: there's no need to bother with silly notions like 'getting to know one another,' since it's simply a matter of recovering those unconscious memories.

Poor Vira has had a rough month, between breaking things off with Gunther, losing her precious 'Joshie,' and now this. I do find her views on the Blessings of Having Nothing a little hard to swallow, coming from someone whose favorite charity is planting trees to compensate for all the Jetsets she is 'forced' to charter to overcome her crippling claustrophobia whenever she flys commercial. But still, I guess we're all just doing the best we can, right?

From: phoebegb@sahmsrule.net
To: crystalwalker@sterlingmorris.com
Amen. Calling her now to commiserate.

Tuesday, November 20

From: crystalwalker@sterlingmorris.com
To: gwalker@plunderhogg.com
Kurtis' Christening is set for the Sunday after Thanksgiving at the Village Episcopal church on the corner of Church and Center. Had to promise we would faithfully attend every Sunday from now on until the Second Coming, but we'll cross that bridge when we come to it.

Can you ask Sister Taylor if she will officiate? The church has a very liberal policy towards visiting clergy, and it would be a nice way to welcome her into the bosom of our family, now that the firm has decided to make her a senior partner. We also need to agree on godparents. Your sister is definitely OUT, after the last time she forgot Kimberly's name. Besides, she already told me she can't make the ceremony.

This is very important, so please clear your calendar to discuss over working lunch today.

From: phoebegb@sahmsrule.net
To: crystalwalker@sterlingmorris.com
Are you looking forward to impromptu lunch date with George? Let me know how it goes!

From: crystalwalker@sterlingmorris.com
To: phoebegb@sahmsrule.net
I would really have preferred to collapse into bed, not been forced to make conversation with a man who generally likes to think of himself as someone who would take a bullet without a peep. But George did manage to tell me he will present me with a lovely bauble to commemorate Kurtis' birth, so I really can't complain. There are perks to being married for thirteen years to the strong but mostly silent type.

Speaking of Kurtis, would you and Brad do us the honor of agreeing to become her godparents? I know religion is not Brad's thing, but I am confident that you are both more than capable of providing her with the requisite guidance when it comes to what truly matters – or at least, how to look good while faking it.

From: phoebegb@sahmsrule.net
To: crystalwalker@sterlingmorris.com
Touched that you would consider us to be worthy guardians of Baby's immortal soul, but pray, what is the etiquette governing extra-familial trust funds? Are we obligated to your youngest, in the (unlikely) event that our own friendship does not survive?

I ask only because it was touch and go there for a few days, when I wasn't sure if you would choose us or two of your former Midwestern friends as godparents. Now that you have asked us, dear C, rest assured that I have nixed all plans to spread rumors about your drinking. Oh, and of course we'll take care of Kurtis' spiritual development. Yoga does seem to be my religion du jour, but I always fancied finding out more about Scientology. Just say the Word and I'm there.

From: crystalwalker@sterlingmorris.com
To: phoebegb@sahmsrule.net
Any religion is really fine with me, so long as it doesn't interfere with Kurtis' chances of obtaining legacy family membership at the Club. So glad you've both agreed!

Text from Crystal to Kimberly
No, you do NOT have permission to skip gym tonight. Or homework.

Text from Crystal to Kimberly

I don't care if your stomach hurts. Drink one of Lata's energy drinks, then we'll talk.

Text from Crystal to Kimberly

Leaving office in 10, but have dinner with Head Mistress of Seton @ 7. One day, you'll thank me for providing u with role model of working mom. Until then, ask Lata to help you with homework. She has Phd in math and u can practice yr Spanish at same time.

From: crystalwalker@sterlingmorris.com
To: jsmith@plunderhogg.com
Subject: Urgent message for George

Can you please tell my husband that he needs to be home by 8.30pm, to pick our daughter up from gym? I will have my phone off for the next couple of hours, so please let him know that it is useless to protest.

Wednesday, November 21

Skye Chat
phoebethompson
How was dinner w/Hilary?

crystalwalker
Great! She seemed genuinely interested in the cherubs' potty-training experience, and practically begged me to send in their Apgar scores. Not even George listens to me drone on about them that way. When I told her about Karson's issues with competitive sports, she was very sympathetic, and actually recommended one of Evelyn Braun's books: Self-Esteem and the Importance of Nurturing Your Child's Belief That He (or She) Is Number One. If I hadn't had one of Lata's pisco sours clouding my judgment, I'd almost swear she was flirting. Almost tempted to go for it, too given the fact I basically never see George these days.

phoebethompson
careful. Lata's pisco sours are stronger than you think!

crystalwalker
I swear I had just the one, and nothing else with dinner, so I looked positively virtuous to HM. May have to pre-drink like this more often.

phoebethompson
Afraid that's a slippery slope. I've tried same with eating.

crystalwalker
speaking of eating, can you spare Lata for a couple of hours this evening? No way I'll be ready for the holiday weekend (not to mention the Christening) if I don't work late.

fine with me, if she doesn't mind helping Cecily and Emily with their Thanksgiving family art project first. Lata really has so much more patience for these things than me. BTW, let me know if you need any recipes for fat-free pumpkin pie or pickeled walnut and onion stuffing – both work well for a large crowd, especially in sense that nobody eats them, esp. after the holiday.

From: crystalwalker@sterlingmorris.com
To: phoebegb@sahmsrule.net
After witnessing Vira's little meltdown during weeping willow pose yesterday, I think her needs may actually be greater than either of ours these days.

Can't believe Tiffany has already started claiming Ravi's clinginess is due to bad karma and requires professional intervention to create some necessary separation from his mother. Or that she is three months pregnant with Tom's child, and Vira has only just found out. So much for only knowing each other 3 weeks right?

From: phoebegb@sahmsrule.net
To: crystalwalker@sterlingmorris.com
Quite. Didn't I say there was no such thing as a perfect divorce? BTW, keep meaning to ask what you guys are doing for holiday weekend?

From: crystalwalker@sterlingmorris.com
To: phoebegb@sahmsrule.net
My parents are arriving (together!) from KC this evening and staying through the Christening. George's mom also coming up from Boca. Thank God for Lata. I know they will disapprove of the amount of help I seem to need these days, but I have no idea how I would manage without her. But I'm in a total panic on the food front.

Can you remind me of the name of the fancy deli that cooks your holiday dinner but lets you warm it up on the day itself, so no one needs to know you didn't cook? It's probably too late, but I'm desperate!

From: phoebegb@sahmsrule.net
To: crystalwalker@sterlingmorris.com
Just dropped off the card for Delicious by Design. They're not cheap, of course, but I happen to know from experience that you can order at short notice and they are discrete—you can even pile all the dirty dishes in a crate behind the bushes for them to pick up after the long weekend. Unless your mom likes to snoop, she'll never even know.

My own mother-in-law insists I do nothing for dinner on holidays. May have something to do with the mince pies I brought to last year's meal, which MIL insisted on serving covered in gravy before discovering her mistake.

Good Luck!

Text from Phoebe to Brad

Welcome back, darling! Check out www.utube/you'lldashoutyoureyesafterwatching.com for a little peek of what's in store for you under my raincoat when I come and pick you up at the airport this morning. Tchuss! xo Steffi

Friday, November 23

From: phoebegb@sahmsrule.net
To: crystalwalker@sterlingmorris.com

Hope your Thanksgiving was more enjoyable, or at least less eventful than ours, which basically consisted of my mother-in-law making pointed comments about Brad looking 'tired and drained' from working too hard. Cecily and Emily also insisted on performing the Thanksgiving ditty taught to them by your cherubs. It starts out charmingly with wiggly hands used to represent turkey feathers, and ends with everyone being given the middle finger. Do hope my MIL bought their explanation that this is a traditional Native American welcome gesture.

Did I mention that Brad decided to invite Vira at the last minute? I dropped him off on the way home from the airport to fix a glitch in her payment system, and apparently he took pity on her after he found her sobbing into the satin pillows in her bedroom, saying that Tom had taken Ravi to Tiffany's parents' sweat lodge in Beaver Creek for the long weekend, so she was all alone for the holiday. I dare say, Brad did the right thing in the circumstances, but I could certainly have done without MIL's comments about Vira's cooking abilities after she brought a suspiciously perfect vegan pecan pie to dinner.

Can't wait to hold my new goddaughter in my arms on Sunday!

From: crystalwalker@sterlingmorris.com
To: phoebegb@sahmsrule.net

I guess it IS part of the American Thanksgiving tradition to invite people who might otherwise be alone.

I mention this only by way of explaining why I chose to invite Hilary Manning to our family feast at the last minute. Dinner was a triumph, thanks to your recommendation, and to Lata's superlative mixing abilities, which meant my parents and George's mother were unusually restrained in their conversation (always a blessing). I think they were intimidated by Hilary, in part, but also because they were having trouble articulating.

Saturday, November 24

Text from Phoebe To Crystal
What time do we need to be at church tomorrow?

Text from Crystal To Phoebe
Photographer coming at 8. Sorry! Service starts at 9. Planning early night in preparation.

Text from Phoebe To Crystal
Any dress code?

Text from Crystal To Phoebe
Yes, but not sure it applies to lactating mothers. Or English godmothers. Counting on you to wear something at least vaguely inappropriate.

Text from Phoebe To Crystal
That's my forte. CU tomorrow!

Text from Crystal To Phoebe
Sweet dreams! xc

Friday, November 30

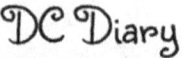

DC Diary

The Walkers Take on the Nation's Capital

Kurtis' Christening, Sister Taylor and Hilary Manning

Check out the photos from Baby's Christening!

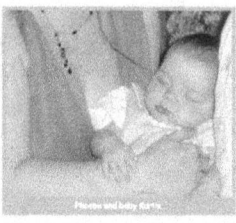

Phoebe and baby Kurtis

The bosom of the lady holding Kurtis in the rather low-cut dress belongs to my British friend, Phoebe. We've only known each other a couple of months, but have already become firm friends. What you can't see is Gramps staring down her cleavage.

George's senior partner, Sister Taylor

The lady in the habit is George's new senior partner, Sister Taylor. She doesn't wear it to work, except on Halloween, but she is as passionate about saving the planet as she is about Jesus. We asked her to officiate at Baby's ceremony today, and she did a beautiful job, even if she did give Phoebe and me a hard-time about what she described as our 'unnecessary' display of flesh. (George says she has become WAY more prudish since recently reaffirming her vows). At least I have the excuse that I am nursing.

Hilary Manning, Head Mistress

Seems the apple doesn't fall far from the tree, however, since Grandma spent the entire day lecturing our preteen, Kimberly, about her inappropriately short skirt. As you might expect, asking Kim why she didn't choose a pretty floral dress and sandals like Hilary Manning didn't go down well, which is too bad, as I'm hoping Hilary will soon be the cherubs' Head Mistress at Seton Academy.

Fingers crossed the cherubs will soon be attending the same school as the President's daughters!

Posted by Crystal Walker at Tuesday No comments:

⌂ ⓘ 🔗 ⓘ ⓘ

162

DC Diary
Kurtis' Christening, Sister Taylor and Hilary Manning

Check out the photos from Baby's Christening!

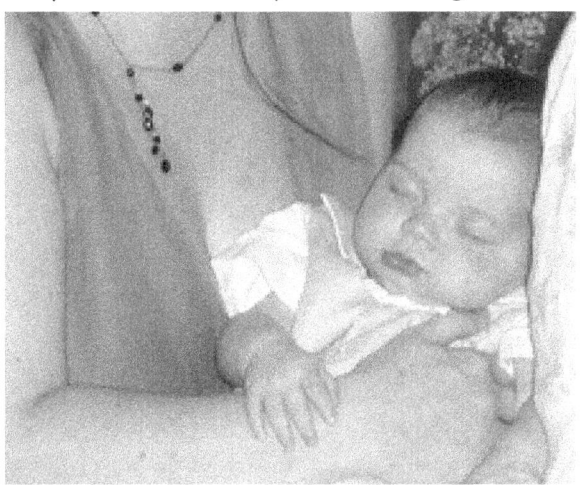

The bosom of the lady holding Kurtis in the rather low-cut dress belongs to my British friend, Phoebe. We've only known each other a couple of months, but have already become firm friends. What you can't see is Gramps staring down her cleavage.
The lady in the habit is George's new senior partner, Sister

Taylor. She doesn't wear it to work, except on Halloween, but she is as passionate about saving the planet as she is about Jesus. We asked her to officiate at Baby's ceremony today, and she did a beautiful job, even if she did give Phoebe and me a hard-time about what she described as our 'unnecessary' display of flesh. (George says she has become WAY more prudish since recently reaffirming her vows). At least I have the excuse that I am nursing.

Seems the apple doesn't fall far from the tree, however, since Grandma spent the entire day lecturing our preteen, Kimberly, about her inappropriately short skirt. As you might expect, asking Kim why she didn't choose a pretty floral dress and sandals like Hilary Manning (see above) didn't go down well, which is too bad, as I'm hoping Hilary will soon be the cherubs' Head Mistress at Seton Academy.

Fingers crossed the cherubs will soon be attending the same school as the President's daughters!

Chapter 5

December, 2012 Vol. 41, Issue 12
Always FREE, but donations appreciated

Please direct submissions and inquiries to:
whining@villagepress.com
P.O. Box 357 Village Town, MD

VILLAGE WHINER

Your trusty monthly newsletter of
the "Most Livable Village," 1989
Village Town Magazine

Village Reviews

Don't forget to join the Village Revelers on Sunday, December 11, from 5-7pm for carols and caroling in celebration of the holiday season. We'll start out at the Village Hall with cookies and cocoa at 5pm, then make our way round the Village, knocking on doors and thrilling our neighbors with rousing renditions of holiday classics. Remember that some residents may be initially hesitant to open their door to a bunch of warbling strangers, but persistence is often rewarded in a charitable contribution. (Please note: we have been advised by our legal team that refusing to leave until a contribution has been made may result in a public disorder charge, so no direct threats should be made. Just keep singing till they pay you to go away!) All donations will be put towards funding A Capella singing group programs in DC public schools.

Source of Toxic Odor Determined

Following an extensive investigation into the foul smell that pervaded much of the west side of our Village until late last month, the Special Ops unit climbed entirely by its own traffic cones has determined that the source of the offending odor came from a Joshua tree that was recently transplanted to a Village resident's home. Typically, Joshua trees blossom in the spring, but tropical heat in the Japanese-style mansion resulted in an early flowering. The tree owner has requested anonymity, claiming the impact to their "tube-pourri" is global warming, but one of our special investigators was able to determine that the shrub's early blooming was simply caused by the homeowner cranking up the heat in his spa room.

Village residents will be relieved to hear that the Joshua tree has now been permanently removed from the premises, so they may remove their gas masks and resume normal life - at least for now.

Village Diversity Group

In keeping with our Village's mission statement to become a self-sustaining and spiritually enriching environment, the Village Diversity Group has voted in favor of constructing a communal yurt on the grounds of the Village Hall. Originally used by nomadic Mongol and Turkic people of central Asia, the yurt is a portable, inexpensive alternative to Western-style housing, and can be used for multiple purposes, including playgroups, parties and even emergency shelter, should the need arise. We hope the yurt will be a model of sustainability and forward planning for our community and beyond as we begin to think globally rather than locally about our housing and spiritual concerns.

In other Diversity Group news, the women's subcommittee voted unanimously to retain their current head, who should be addressed henceforth not as "Madam Chairwoman" but simply as "Chair." Membership of the women's subcommittee will now be restricted to persons who choose to identify themselves as female, unless such gender identification is determined to be for the malicious purpose of disrupting the committee's work. In such cases, we reserve the right to expel the offending member, pending the results of an official inquiry.

Between the yurt and the debate in the women's subcommittee, the Diversity Group fell very behind on our plans to cook and serve a Thanksgiving meal to the homeless. Since we have already bought 20 frozen turkeys, 100lbs organic potatoes and all the trimmings, we plan to serve the dinner as part of our Kwanukkmas celebrations in the Village Yurt on December 26. To this end, we are looking for a few good volunteers to prep, cook and serve that not easy the meal itself. Help with clean-up and dishes would also be appreciated.

For more information or to volunteer, please contact Vita Bliss.

Miss Gertrude

Far be it from me to condemn the tradition of sending holiday cards featuring pictures of one's charming offspring at this time of year, but please do remember to include your first and last name somewhere in the missive, on the off chance that your recipient doesn't track your family's every birth or diaper change. And please keep the staging of such photos tasteful, to avoid any suggestion your progeny should be compared in any way to the Son of God. You may consider your beloved son or daughter to be the Second Coming, but it's doubtful that your friends, neighbors or even your extended family feel the same way. Ditto when it comes to Santa hats or gangster-themed septuplets. Your toddler may bear a striking resemblance to Al Capone, but the holidays are hardly the occasion to advertise this fact.

Finally, remember to send your photo to everyone who may have influence over your inheritance as most likely they are the only ones who will truly treasure that photo anyway. And don't forget to include these same dear ones in whatever holiday celebrations you have planned, as it is uncomfortable to drop by one's son's home, only to realize a party to which you have not been invited is in full swing.

Tennis Team Results

A stellar win by the Ladies Doubles Team on all three courts against Sensational Country Club last week, marred only by a Tisset incident involving the Village Special Ops unit. Our acting Ladies' Team Captain Nancy H. was the recipient of an untimely shock as her system on the number 1 court following a dispute over a line call, which rapidly deteriorated from verbal abuse to a cheating to pushing, shoving and ultimately an all out knock on the court.

While we so feel Special Ops over reacted, particularly by choosing to put the blame squarely on our blameless team mate, the pill laid the felicitous effort of electrifying her play and stunning her opponents who crumbled in the face of her renewed assault.

Meanwhile, courts 2 and 3 won without incident - a first in the team's history. Final results below.

The Gentleman's A and B Teams were forced to default on all their matches this month as they continue to languish without a team coordinator. It's a brave new world out there, boys! Time to wake up and made the coffee.

The temporary ban on the Ladies' A Doubles Team First pair from playing on the inter-club league will be lifted at the end of the year.

Ladies Number 1 Doubles 6-4, 6-0
Ladies Number 2 Doubles 6-3, 6-1
Ladies Number 3 Doubles 7-5, 6-4

Village Revelers

Don't forget to join the Village Revelers on Sunday, December 14, from 5-7pm for carols and carousing in celebration of the holiday season. We'll start out at the Village Hall with cookies and cocoa at 5pm, then make our way round the Village, knocking on doors and thrilling our neighbors with rousing renditions of holiday classics. Remember that some residents may be initially hesitant to open their door to a bunch of warbling strangers, but persistence can often result in a charitable contribution. (Please note: we have been advised by our legal team that refusing to leave until a contribution has been made may result in a public disorder charge, so no direct threats should be made. Just keep singing till they pay you to go away!) All donations will be put towards funding A Capella singing group programs in DC public schools.

Source of Toxic Odor Determined

Following an extensive investigation into the foul smell that pervaded much of the west side of our Village until late last month, the Special Ops unit (funded entirely by the generous contributions of speeding motorists caught by our traffic cams) has determined that the source of the offending odor came from a Joshua tree that was recently transplanted to a Village resident's home. Typically, Joshua trees blossom in the spring, but tropical heat in the Japanese style mansion resulted in an early flowering.

The tree owner has requested anonymity, claiming the trigger for this 'false growth' is global warming, but one of our special investigators was able to determine that the shrub's early blooming was simply caused by the homeowner cranking up the heat in her spa room.

Village residents will be relieved to hear that the Joshua tree has now been permanently removed from the premises, so they may remove their gas masks and resume normal life - at least for now.

Village Diversity Group

In keeping with our Village's mission statement to be a self-sustaining and spiritually enriching environment, the Village Diversity Group has voted in favor of constructing a communal yurt on the grounds of the Village Hall. Originally used by nomadic Mongol and Turkic people of central Asia, the yurt is a portable, inexpensive alternative to Western style housing, and can be used for multiple purposes, including playgroups, parties and even emergency shelter, should the need arise. We hope the yurt will be a model of sustainability and forward planning for our community and beyond, as we begin to think globally rather than locally about our housing and spiritual concerns.

In other Diversity Group news, the women's subcommittee voted unanimously to retain their current head, who should be addressed henceforth not as 'Madam Chairwoman' but simply as 'Chair.' Membership of the women's subcommittee will now be restricted to persons who choose to identify themselves as female, unless such gender identification is determined to be for the malicious purpose of disrupting the committee's work. In such cases, we reserve the right to expel the offending member, pending the results of an official inquiry.

Between the yurt and the debate in the women's subcommittee, the Diversity Group fell very behind on our plans to cook and serve a Thanksgiving meal to the homeless. Since we have already bought 20 frozen tofurkeys, 100lbs organic potatoes and all the trimmings, we plan to serve the dinner as part of our Kwannukmas celebrations in the Village Yurt on December 26. To this end, we are looking for a few good volunteers to prep, cook and serve (but not eat) the meal itself. Help with clean-up and dishes would also be appreciated.

For more information or to volunteer, please contact Vira Bliss.

Miss Gertrude

Far be it from me to condemn the tradition of sending holiday cards featuring pictures of one's charming offspring at this time of year, but please do remember to include your first and last name somewhere in the missive, on the off-chance that your recipient doesn't track your family's every birth or diaper change. And please keep the staging of such photos tasteful, to avoid any suggestion your progeny should be compared in any way to the Son of God. You may consider your beloved son or daughter to be the Second Coming, but  it's doubtful that your friends, neighbors or even your extended family feel the same way. Ditto when it comes to Santa hats or gangster-themed sepia prints. Your toddler may bear a striking resemblance to Al Capone, but the holidays are hardly the occasion to advertise this fact.

Finally, remember to send your photo to everyone who may have influence over your inheritance as, most likely, they are the only ones who will truly treasure that photo anyway. And don't forget to include these same dear ones in whatever holiday celebrations you have planned, as it is uncomfortable to drop by one's son's home, only to realize a party to which you have not been invited is in full swing.

Tennis Team Results

A stellar win by the Ladies' Doubles Team on all three courts against Senatorial Country Club last week, marred only by a Taser incident involving the Village Special Ops unit. Our acting Ladies' Team Captain, Nancy H. was the recipient of an untimely shock to her system on the number 1 court following a dispute over a line call, which rapidly deteriorated from accusations of cheating to pushing, shoving, and ultimately, an all-out tussle on the court.

While we do feel Special Ops over-reacted, particularly by choosing to pin the blame squarely on our blameless team-mate, the jolt had the felicitous effect of electrifying her play and stunning her opponents, who crumbled in the face of her renewed assault.

Meanwhile, courts 2 and 3 won without incident - a first in the team's history. Final results below.

The Gentlemen's A and B Teams were forced to default on all their matches this month as they continue to languish without a team coordinator. It's a brave new world out there, boys! Time you woke up and made the coffee.

The temporary ban on the Ladies' A Doubles Team First pair from playing on the inter-club league will be lifted at the end of the year.

Ladies' Number 1 Doubles 6-4, 6-0
Ladies' Number 2 Doubles 6-3, 6-1
Ladies' Number 3 Doubles 7-5, 6-4

Posting on Village listserv
From: pookiegranger@hotmail.com
Could the Board of Village Managers please arrange for extra trash and recycling pick up service over the holidays? I had my extended family staying over Thanksgiving, then hosted a cocktail party for 100 of my closest friends and neighbors to celebrate their departure. It's embarrassing to have the empty wine bottles and catering boxes still littering our driveway almost a week later. Even more embarrassing was finding the Special Ops team pounding on our front door on the night of the party, shining their high-beams into the grand room where my guests were milling and demanding we wrap things up (at 9pm!) because our neighbors had complained about the noise.

I find it strange that the Village is willing to pay these officers overtime to investigate the petty complaints of an excluded neighbor, but not, apparently, to pay its sanitation workers to remove a few extra bags of trash, which are still outside and attracting the attention of vermin as I write. If I wanted to live like this, I'd just move to DC proper.

From: tinklepaw4ever@aol.com
For the record, I was NOT going through Pookie's trash just now. I was retrieving a tennis ball I had thrown for my new puppy, Tinklepaw II, which had inadvertently rolled into her driveway. Nor did I snitch on Pookie's party (quite unnecessary, since you could hear the pulsating music from halfway down the block), although I may have alerted the authorities to a couple of guest parking violations. Tinklepaw II was quite disturbed by all the kerfuffle, and hasn't been herself since, which is why I have been forced to invest in a doggy diaper service to cope with the accompanying mess.

Reply: villageboard@thevillage.co.org
The Board of Village Managers takes any and all complaints about its services very seriously, and will report back on its investigation into the incident above within seven days.

Please note: the Board has received several complaints recently about dog owners letting their dogs off the leash. We have deputized block captains to remind dog owners about the Village's requirement that dogs be kept on the leash at all times, or face a $350 fine.

The Board is also considering separate fines for defamation of character, as when a dog owner states that the block captain's appearance and deportment are obviously not those of a trophy wife.

From: crystalwalker@sterlingmorris.com
To: phoebegb@sahmsrule.net
FW:
Trophy wife comment came from my dad, who claims he was yelled at by some interfering old biddy (his words, not mine) while walking ours off-leash. Just hope it wasn't Evelyn, as I'm counting on her to write letters of recommendation for the three eldest cherubs for Seton.

From: phoebegb@sahmsrule.net
To: crystalwalker@sterlingmorris.com
Actually, I believe it was Evelyn, as I overheard her telling your dad that her trophy husband would say same thing, if he weren't busy re-tiling her roof. Seems to me she handled your old man just fine, don't you think?

From: crystalwalker@sterlingmorris.com
To: phoebegb@sahmsrule.net
I admire the woman for having a thick skin. Must go and threaten to put the misogynistic old SOB in assisted living for putting my cherubs' future at risk. Thank God he and my mom are leaving tomorrow.

The Board of Village Managers
Cordially Invites You to Attend

The Annual Village Holiday Party

With Live Cabaret Performance of
'A Little Weinachte Musik'
debuting the singing, dancing and
acro-yoga talents of Ms. Nina Scheiner,
accompanied by Gunther Marshall on the sitar

Thursday, December 20, 6.30-9.30pm
RSVP: Regrets Only

This year's party will be held in the new Village Yurt,
but all other details remain the same.
Please note: the yurt is not heated, so dress warmly!

Santa will be available for family portraits from 6pm.
Remember, each family is restricted to 5 minutes only,
no matter how many times you have reproduced,
or how darling your offspring.

Sunday, December 2

From: phoebegb@sahmsrule.net
To: crystalwalker@sterlingmorris.com

Still trying to absorb the news that Brad has somehow managed to get himself fired from his consulting gig in Alaska. He arrived home unexpectedly on the red eye yesterday morning, and walked through the front door just as I was getting back from dropping the twins at school. Seems the woman who hired him didn't take kindly to being told, repeatedly, that her approach to their project was dumb. She apparently accused him of being 'aggressive, arrogant and incompetent' – epithets I would dearly love to use right now, if it weren't for the fact that for once, Brad looks quite shaken by this turn of events. He's lying on the sofa at home, licking his wounds like the proverbial wounded animal before the pack moves in for the kill.

From: crystalwalker@sterlingmorris.com
To: phoebegb@sahmsrule.net

So sorry to hear the bad news. Anything I can do to help?

From: phoebegb@sahmsrule.net
To: crystalwalker@sterlingmorris.com

Perhaps you can advise me on bus stop etiquette, as it looks like Cecily and Emily will be attending the Village Public School starting in the new year. The Co-Leader in Chief (aka the principal) at CRAC took offense at my suggestion that our family might qualify for financial aid, claiming this fund is reserved for poor, inner city kids, not the suburban 'nouveau pauvre', as she described us.

I realize we may LOOK less deserving than some, but doesn't she understand how expensive it is to keep up with one's neighbors here in the Village?

From: crystalwalker@sterlingmorris.com
To: phoebegb@sahmsrule.net

I want you to know that George and I are there for you during this difficult time. I'm sure the cherubs will be more than happy to show Cecily and Emily the ropes when it comes to VPS (tell them to avoid eye contact with anyone they don't know and they'll be fine). If there's anything else we can do, please let us know.

If it's any comfort, I think you will find the dress code at the bus stop quite refreshing after CRAC. Gone is the requirement to dress in some kind of chic work suit in the morning, even if you are just going to the gym. When it comes to VPS, pajamas are just fine. Anything fancier is actually frowned upon, unless you happen to be Bitsy, who appears to wear only La Perla slips to bed. Her nipples are used by all the VPS fathers to determine the temperature for the day, which makes her very popular with the moms also, since Dads are only too happy to do bus stop duty, especially in winter.

From: phoebegb@sahmsrule.net
To: crystalwalker@sterlingmorris.com
Strangely enough, I feel a certain sense of relief at this turn of events. Maybe this is the rude awakening we both needed to realize that Brad's business may not work out, and I need to think about going back to work?

From: crystalwalker@sterlingmorris.com
To: phoebegb@sahmsrule.net
Have you considered approaching your former colleagues at the BBC?

From: phoebegb@sahmsrule.net
To: crystalwalker@sterlingmorris.com
I think any prospect of getting my former position back is long gone. In my profession, looks matter, and there are women half my age lining up to do my old job – and they actually know how to use things like MeBook and Witter.

It might be time for me to consider a career change. Always fancied myself as an event planner, especially after organizing the CRAC Auction and Summer Fete for the past three years. Think I might just put out an ad on the Village listserv, to see if there is any demand for that kind of thing. Would appreciate if you can help spread the word.

Posting on Village Listserv
From: phoebegb@sahmsrule.net
Expert Event-planner available for parties/bar/bat mitzvahs, weddings, anniversaries and wakes

No party too small

For more information, email info@partyprincess.com

From: crystalwalker@sterlingmorris.com
To: info@partyprincess.com
Organizing a kid's birthday party is my idea of hell, but I am sure you will be amazing at it, dear P. We are counting on you for Kurtis' first birthday party next summer!

From: info@partyprincess.com
To: bitsybottinger@yahoo.com
I would be delighted to organize the triplets' sixth birthday party next Friday. Did you have something specific in mind? If not, I would be happy to come up with some ideas. Let me know what you were thinking, and we can go from there.

From: info@partyprincess.com
To: bitsybottinger@yahoo.com
A bouncy castle is always popular, and I would be happy to dress up as Princess Diana to hand out favors at the end.

I have a blue silk dress left over from my last May ball at Cambridge that will be perfect for the occasion, unless you prefer the 'divorced Di' look in the slutty black sheath. I also have some darling English parlor games that I have been dying to try out on Emily and Cecily, if only they would sit still long enough to learn the rules.

From: info@partyprincess.com
To: bitsybottinger@yahoo.com
Of course I can make a cake and a few nibbles to go with. No problem if the triplets won't eat anything store bought, or anything with artificial colors or flavors – my girls won't touch those either.

My mother-in-law just sent me the Countess Who Cooks' latest cookery bible, which has a recipe for a Castle cake featuring upturned ice-cream cones for towers. Will this do?

From: info@partyprincess.com
To: bitsybottinger@yahoo.com
Great! Can't wait to get started and will start uploading the email contacts for the party evites asap.

Monday, December 3

From: crystalwalker@sterlingmorris.com
To: exrev@hotmail.com
Dad,
I'm delighted you've discovered the internet, but it's not really appropriate for you to email me from the computer in Kevin's bedroom to request scrambled eggs for breakfast. I'm at work, in case you'd forgotten, which is why we said our goodbyes last night.

Sorry you and Mom are fighting again, but if you are very nice to Lata, she might whip you up something to eat before you go.

xo C

Text from Crystal to Lata
Thank you for making Dad breakfast and giving mom neck massage before they left this morning. Glad you like your new mePhone!

Text from Crystal to her father
Dad, there is no point in having a cell phone if you never TURN IT ON. Have a safe trip. Love you!

Text from Crystal to George
Coast is clear. I've asked Lata to take cherubs to McD's for dinner so we can celebrate. Fingers crossed we don't run into Evelyn. :0 xo

Tuesday, December 4

From: crystalwalker@sterlingmorris.com
To: phoebegb@sahmsrule.net
Missed both you and Vira at yoga this morning. Much as I enjoy having Gunther all to myself, I'm not sure attention is quite the word, given that he spent the entire class absorbed in his own personal Dying Cow pose. I know Vira doesn't want to see him right now, but what's your excuse?

From: phoebegb@sahmsrule.net
To: crystalwalker@sterlingmorris.com
I was up all last night baking a cake for Bitsy's Triple Threat birthday party. WTH was I thinking? BTW, with everything that's happened to our finances recently, I can no longer really justify employing Lata even part-time. Any chance you might be willing to pick up the slack? I think she may prove just the partner you need in hearth and home.

From: crystalwalker@sterlingmorris.com
To: phoebegb@sahmsrule.net
We would be THRILLED to have Lata full-time, and truly appreciate the sacrifice involved. Do let me know how the party goes tonight. And good luck!

Wednesday, December 5

From: phoebegb@sahmsrule.net
To: crystalwalker@sterlingmorris.com
I had forgotten that parties at the triplets' age are not drop-off affairs – at least here in the Village. In most cases, not one but two parents felt obliged to attend, along with the occasional birth parent, grandparent or babysitter, so that in total we had over 60 adults crammed into Bitsy's sitting room, all stuffing their faces with seaweed jello and carob-dipped rice cakes. The cake looked impressive enough, but half the kids refused to touch it after the first bite, claiming it tasted funny – probably because they've never tasted anything homemade before. The other half turned out to have allergies to eggs, dairy, gluten or anything prepared with extract of cochineal beetle, which is what I used to make the pink icing.

Then the bouncy castle developed a slow leak, which rendered it unusable after for the remainder of the afternoon, but neither the kids nor the parents in question had a clue about how to play pass the parcel or dead soldiers. This meant things quickly degenerated into a Lord of the Flies free-for-all among the kids, which the adults studiously ignored while finishing their drinks.

To add insult to injury, Bitsy paid me a grand total of $200 (including, apparently a 'tip') to cover my time. This works out to about $2/hour, based on how much time I've spent organizing, baking and working the damn thing. All in all, it has been the most financially unrewarding, not to mention exhausting week I've ever had, work wise, which is why I have begged Bitsy NOT to recommend my services to anyone else.

From: crystalwalker@sterlingmorris.com
To: phoebegb@sahmsrule.net
Sorry to hear the Party Princess biz did not work out. If it's any comfort, my hourly rate isn't that great either, when you factor in the number of hours I'm at work.

From: crystalwalker@sterlingmorris.com
To: gwalker@plunderhogg.com
Please come home EARLY tonite to help with Seton applications. We each need to write a 1500 word essay on what makes us worthy as parents to have our offspring attend. Bringing my resume and college transcripts home as supporting material, and suggest u do same.

Essays are due by noon on Monday. I know that seems like plenty of time, but remember we have 4 cherubs, and the weekend is looking packed (see attachment).

Text from Crystal to George
NOT enough to show your billable hours. Some of wealthiest families in DC fail to get into ANY private school – yes, even in this economy!

Text from Crystal to George
For record, don't c y I shd suppress my perfect grade point average to make yr own look better.

Sunday, December 9

Hon,

Not sure why you are stuffing
Santa's legs down chimney right
now, when you are due to take Karson to indoor
soccer at 10 and Kev to basketball at 3.

Taking Kim to her gym meet in Seneca Falls.
Lasts all day, so have Kurtis w/me, but trust
you will have dinner ready by the time I get
back. Will call on way. Oh, and essay for Seton
is due on Monday.

C.

Monday, December 10

Text Message from Crystal to George
Seton Applications not my idea of fun, but promise to make it up to u tonite if you get the applications completed. You will have to choose betw. dinner and sex, however. No way I can manage both.

Text Message from Crystal to George
What do you mean you have a holiday party at the Swedish Embassy? Why didn't you put this on the family calendar?

Text Message from Crystal to George
What do you mean you have a party every night between now and Christmas Eve? Am I invited to any of them?

Text Message from Crystal to George
Well, that's something, altho' have no desire whatsoever to attend.

Skye Chat between Crystal and Phoebe
(giving panoramic view of fridge where George's party invites hang)

crystalwalker
Check out all George's holiday party invitations.
Can you believe this stuff?

> SNAFUH Holiday Soiree
> 6-10pm
> Monkey house, National Zoo
> Dress: Tarzan or Jane (no real fur thongs, please!)

Please swing by and join the fun as the Safari Nature Alliance For Unlimited Hunting celebrates the holidays this month. Live monkeys will spice up the atmosphere on real potted vines as we thank our constituents for keeping SNAFUH alive (even if all the animals are not).

> ORGY (Organization of Really Great Youth)
> from 8-late
> 1100 South Capitol St., NE, DC 20001
> Dress: Togas required

Join us on Capitol Hill at Senator Ted Robbins' rowhouse for a slideshow and whatever happens next as our terrific new batch of eager young interns let their hair down. Their dedication to serving our nation's lawmakers for no pay needs to be recognized, which is why we developed this marvelous organization two years ago. We try to provide monthly outlets for this talented bunch of young people to relax and unwind. Undergarments optional but must, in no circumstances, be left on the street or hanging from trees.

Green NOW!
Annual holiday party,
Location: The Village Yurt, 5900 Connecticut Ave., The Village, MD
Dress: Warmly

Please celebrate the construction of DC's first yurt, which may well be the best model for the future of home building in this country – at least once occupants get used to the cold. So bundle up and get ready to raise a toast with organic chai as we celebrate the ways in which our model of sustainability (mostly) meets function!

phoebethompson
It's pretty impressive, I agree!

crystalwalker
Naturally, I'm taking ORGY off the list as no sex-deprived husband and father of four can be trusted around today's Capitol Hill staff. By comparison, other two gatherings seem fine.

From: crystalwalker@sterlingmorris.com:
To: helenweels@harvard.edu
I will be working from home this morning, reachable via email, cell, SMS and Skype. If any of the other partners asks where I am, tell them I am in an all-day mediation.

From: crystalwalker@sterlingmorris.com
To: helenweels@harvard.edu
Not that it's any of your business, but yes, I am dealing with a few personal issues. My childrens' applications to private school are due by midday, and the weekend was just too crazy to work on them. Other partners at the firm may have stay-at-home wives who deal with this kind of s@#*, but in my house, it's me. If you have any problem with that, please go ahead and talk to human resources. I simply don't have time. But rest assured, there is a little corner of Hell reserved for career women who don't support their sisters in time of need.

Text from Crystal to George
Applications = in. On-site assessments next (for us, as well as cherubs), followed by letters of recommendation. Don't forget to ask POTUS to write one!

From: crystalwalker@sterlingmorris.com
To. phoebegb@sahmsrule.net
Thank you so much for agreeing to write letters of recommendation for cherubs. Evelyn on board also. She has suggested I clean-up the family MeBook profiles in case Seton checks, which it seems is almost certain these days. According to Evelyn, it's actually important to demonstrate a positive, vibrant presence on social media, while studiously deleting any image or comment that might imply any member of the Walker family is poorly educated or behaved. May have to erase the best parts of our family history

but, surely, it's worth it, right?

Now that I've looked, I'm not sure what's more troubling: the fact that a) under 'Family', Kimberly has listed her sibs, her Dad and all her girlfriends, but not, apparently her mom; or b) that George does not acknowledge me as his life partner anywhere on his profile.

From: crystalwalker@sterlingmorris.com
To: phoebegb@sahmsrule.net
FW: Kevin Morris has confirmed your request to list him as family on MeBook.
Eldest son apparently prepared to acknowledge our relationship, but George continues to deny any such connection. Think I should be concerned?

From: phoebegb@sahmsrule.net
To: crystalwalker@sterlingmorris.com
If George is anything like Brad, he's probably forgotten you set up his account. Let me try friending him now, to see if he responds.

MeBook Message from Phoebe Thompson to George Walker
Phoebe Thompson has requested you become her friend on MeBook. To confirm you are friends, click on the Add link below. To reject, hide or otherwise ignore, click on Pretend They Don't Exist below.

Brad darling,

I know it's been a rough time, but do you think you might be able to rouse yourself before noon today? Several neighbors have been clamoring for some more of your pesto.

I have a tennis match this pm, but I've drawn up a schedule for us to share cleaning chores, now that we no longer have Lata. Please note, Monday is laundry day, and it's your turn to strip the bed. And no, staying in it all day— doesn't negate the obligation.

Today's tasks:

- 3:00 School pick-up: please ensure girls brush their hair using the brushes you will find in the glove compartment.

- 3:30pm Emily saxophone lesson: Feel free to listen a moment outside after dropping her, but be aware of the physical damage this may do to one's hearing.

- 4:00pm (30 mins): Free play before therapy. I like to set the kitchen timer for when it's time to leave, so the timer becomes "the bad guy" when it dings. The twins can occasionally balk at the idea of another activity at day's end, but it is critically important they see Dr. Pressapoint — especially now that we've cut back to shared sessions.

I know this may all seem a bit overwhelming, as you probably won't have a moment to yourself all afternoon, so I encourage you to try to get dinner ready while the girls are still at Dr. P's. Some kind of green vegetable would be appreciated. Ta Ta for now, darling. See you @ 6:00.

px

Posting on Village listserv
From: evelyn@ivyleagueorbust.com
Does anyone know where I can get more of that pesto that was for sale in the Village newsletter a couple of months ago? I've just finished my last baggie and am already craving more.

Response from bitsybottinger@yahoo.com:
Me too. My kids keep asking. I swear there is something addictive about it.

Response from pookiegranger@hotmail.com:
Almost fired my sitter after discovering she gave my kids the last batch. Where can I get more?

Response from Vira Bliss
Would pesto man be willing to cater my annual holiday gathering at the Village Yurt on Friday? My vegan caterer just quit after re-discovering bacon, so I need to find a replacement FAST.

Wednesday, December 12

From: phoebegb@sahmsrule.net
To: crystalwalker@sterlingmorris.com
Any chance twins can come to yours after CRAC, so that Lata can watch them until Brad and I get home from organizing Vira's annual holiday lunch? We have to make and serve enough pesto pasta to feed the five hundred (give or take). Probably won't be home until after 4.

From: crystalwalker@sterlingmorris.com
To: phoebegb@sahmsrule.net
Of course! It's the least I can do in return for the favor of you letting me have her full-time.

From: phoebegb@sahmsrule.net
To: crystalwalker@sterlingmorris.com
Thanks.

Skye Chat with Twins
phoebethompson
Mummy very busy logging names and addresses for Vira Bliss's party, but that was nice of Kim to let you use her computer. How was school?

phoebethompson
It is spelled 'Winnie the Pooh,' not 'Poo,' you are right. I will speak to the English teacher about refreshing her knowledge of English literature.

Did she give you a lollipop again today in class?

phoebethompson
I don't care if it was because you concentrated so well today. Remember, Santa doesn't bring presents to naughty girls who eat high fructose corn syrup before Christmas. Nor will grandmama and grandpapa, when they visit from London next week.

phoebethompson
All right – just this once. But don't let Evelyn Braun see it. Will fix you some lovely organic, apple slices with sugar free almond butter as soon as I get home xo

Text from Phoebe to Crystal
Can't thank you enough for loaning me Lata this pm. I am exhausted. Event planning biz definitely not 4 me.

Thursday, December 13

From: phoebegb@sahmsrule.net
To: crystalwalker@sterlingmorris.com
I've been so distracted of late that I've completely failed to ask about the cherubs' applications to Seton. Any news yet?

From: crystalwalker@sterlingmorris.com
To: phoebegb@sahmsrule.net
Applications have been sent, but still need to do on-site assessments and letters of recommendation from the great and the good. Thank you for being one of them.

Official word on whether or not cherubs get in will come in March. In the meantime, I'm happy to report, a little birdie (HM) told me that Kevin's test scores were sufficiently impressive for her to suggest we should be optimistic about a spot. Wait till they realize there is no correlation between IQ and willingness to do homework.

Kimberly is also likely to sail through the selection process. I'd like to say it was because of her test scores, but I suspect in her case they were more impressed by her ability to tackle and bring down her big brother during the individual leadership portion of the assessment. Karson will likely be wait listed for kindergarten, with many diplomatic assurances that his behavioral issues are most likely the result of immaturity, not character. If he doesn't get in this year, he almost certainly will next.

Since these comments are combined with vague mutterings about the school's expansion plans being stymied due to a lack of clasroom space, I'm thinking a timely donation from George's bonus check this year may seal the deal sooner, rather than later. What do you think?

From: phoebegb@sahmsrule.net
To: crystalwalker@sterlingmorris.com
I am sure you are right.

Speaking of charitable causes, my mother-in-law has asked me to write and deliver the keynote speech at a gala awards ceremony to honor her philanthropic work with Apart But Not Forgotten, a non-profit devoted to helping the children left behind when parents move to the US to find work. Brad is refusing to attend, but my MIL has been good to us over the years, so I do feel an obligation to return the favor.

Any chance you and Hilary might like to join? Tix are $250 each, but they are tax-deductible, and it's a good opportunity to rub shoulders with the great and the good. You can purchase them and make a donation at www.drinkforacause.com

From: crystalwalker@sterlingmorris.com
To: phoebegb@sahmsrule.net

Hilary and I are on board, and Lata has agreed to watch the cherubs. Ironic to think half the women in the audience probably wouldn't be able to attend the event, if their own nannies and housekeepers hadn't left their own offpsring behind in order to service their needs. :O

BTW, been meaning to thank you for bringing Lata into my life. She has really transformed it. I know you especially love the way she kneads a sore shoulder, but for me the piece de resistance is her ability to silence a child with an icy stare. Must admit it's worked on me a few times since then as well. Only hope it doesn't keep Kurtis from learning to talk. Again, may still be worth it.

One tiny gripe: What's with the insistence on praying before bedtime? The cherubs look angelic on their knees in their pajamas after their bath, but does she really have to introduce Hell into the equation? Although if it does keep Kevin on the straight and narrow when it comes to thoughts of Au Pair, I dare say that's no bad thing.

From: phoebegb@sahmsrule.net
To: crystalwalker@sterlingmorris.com

I suggest you invest in a rosary and reap the rewards in the afterlife.

From: crystalwalker@sterlingmorris.com
To: phoebegb@sahmsrule.net

Amen.

Saturday, December 15

Skye Chat
crystalwalker
Thank you for a delightful evening. Your in-laws seem lovely, although sitting through two hours of speeches about all your MIL's good works has given me insight into how the families of celebrities must feel when asked what it's like to be related to someone so gosh-darn fabulous.

phoebethompson
No comment. Glad you enjoyed the evening, but what was up with Hilary?

crystalwalker
What do you mean?

phoebethompson
You didn't notice? She was positively hostile towards me all evening. At first, I thought it was because I told her the twins used to attend CRAC, but she actually went on to ask me so many questions about YOU, dear C, that I concluded she was jealous of our friendship.

crystalwalker
Seriously?

phoebethompson
Yes. I've met this type in DC before. They are very driven, to be sure, but have trouble making social connections, so whenever they do, they can't bear to share. Rest assured, I spoke of you in the most glowing terms, including the fact that you are so open and generous with your affections that you had more than enough room in your heart for us both.

crystalwalker
Thank you. Fingers crossed it helps with the Seton parent assessments next week. George is outraged they seem to feel the need to interview us, as well as cherubs, but I'd submit to any amount of probing these days for the pleasure of telling Pookie where my cherubs go to school.

Sunday, December 16

From: crystalwalker@sterlingmorris.com
To: phoebegb@sahmsrule.net
Are you guys participating in the Village Revels tonight?

According to Bitsy, there are many housebound residents in the Village who anticipate this night all year. Apparently, the look on their faces after they fumble open their security locks to find a posse of their neighbors regaling them with a rousing rendition of 'Ding Dong Merrily on High' is……well, priceless. I'm told many of them break down in tears and reach for their meds at the sight.

George doesn't understand my crankiness as Christmas Day approaches, as he was raised in a home where holidays were celebrated full throttle. Some women might appreciate such enthusiasm, but I find his insistence on whistling holiday tunes and wearing a Santa hat in bed a little disturbing.

Text from Crystal to Kevin
Proud of your performance tonight. I know u wish Dad saved his opera voice for family birthdays, but he loves it, and u were a trooper to the end. Next year, suggest feigning laryngitis if you don't want to join in.

Monday, December 17

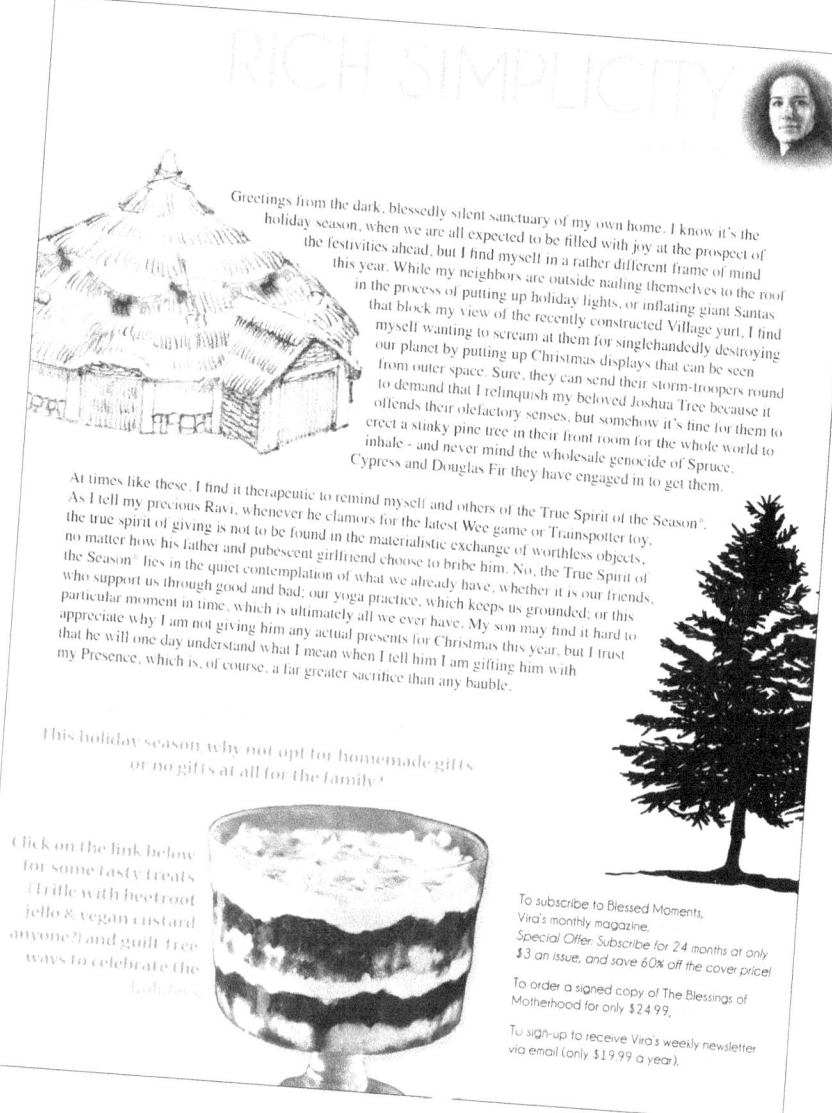

RICH SIMPLICITY

Greetings from the dark, blessedly silent sanctuary of my own home. I know it's the holiday season, when we are all expected to be filled with joy at the prospect of the festivities ahead, but I find myself in a rather different frame of mind this year. While my neighbors are outside nailing themselves to the roof in the process of putting up holiday lights, or inflating giant Santas that block my view of the recently constructed Village yurt, I find myself wanting to scream at them for singlehandedly destroying our planet by putting up Christmas displays that can be seen from outer space. Sure, they can send their storm-troopers round to demand that I relinquish my beloved Joshua Tree because it offends their olefactory senses, but somehow it's fine for them to erect a stinky pine tree in their front room for the whole world to inhale - and never mind the wholesale genocide of Spruce, Cypress and Douglas Fir they have engaged in to get them.

At times like these, I find it therapeutic to remind myself and others of the True Spirit of the Season". As I tell my precious Ravi, whenever he clamors for the latest Wee game or Trainspotter toy, the true spirit of giving is not to be found in the materialistic exchange of worthless objects, no matter how his father and pubescent girlfriend choose to bribe him. No, the True Spirit of the Season" lies in the quiet contemplation of what we already have, whether it is our friends, who support us through good and bad; our yoga practice, which keeps us grounded; or this particular moment in time, which is ultimately all we ever have. My son may find it hard to appreciate why I am not giving him any actual presents for Christmas this year, but I trust that he will one day understand what I mean when I tell him I am gifting him with my Presence, which is, of course, a far greater sacrifice than any bauble.

This holiday season, why not opt for homemade gifts or no gifts at all for the family?

Click on the link below for some tasty treats (Trifle with beetroot jello & vegan custard anyone?) and guilt-free ways to celebrate the holidays.

To subscribe to Blessed Moments, Vira's monthly magazine, *Special Offer: Subscribe for 24 months at only $3 an issue, and save 60% off the cover price!*

To order a signed copy of The Blessings of Motherhood for only $24.99,

To sign-up to receive Vira's weekly newsletter via email (only $19.99 a year),

From: Rich Simplicity
To: phoebegb@sahmsrule.net

Rich Simplicity: A monthly newsletter bringing you a life of ultimate simplicity, no matter how much money I have.

Volume 03, Issue 12

Blessings,

Greetings from the dark, blessedly silent sanctuary of my own home. I know it's the holiday season, when we are all expected to be filled with joy at the prospect of the festivities ahead, but I find myself in a rather different frame of mind this year. While my neighbors are outside nailing themselves to the roof in the process of putting up holiday lights, or inflating giant Santas that block my view of the recently constructed Village yurt, I find myself wanting to scream at them for singlehandedly destroying our planet by putting up Christmas displays that can be seen from outer space. Sure, they can send their storm-troopers round to demand that I relinquish my beloved Joshua Tree because it offends their olefactory senses, but somehow it's fine for them to erect a stinky pine tree in their front room for the whole world to inhale - and never mind the wholesale genocide of Spruce, Cypress and Douglas Fir they have engaged in to get them.

At times like these, I find it therapeutic to remind myself and others of the True Spirit of the Season'. As I tell my precious Ravi, whenever he clamors for the latest Wee game or Trainspotter toy, the true spirit of giving is not to be found in the materialistic exchange of worthless objects, no matter how his father and pubescent girlfriend choose to bribe him. No, the True Spirit of of the Season' lies in the quiet contemplation of what we already have, whether it is our friends, who support us through good and bad or our yoga practice, which keeps us grounded; or this particular moment in time, which is ultimately all we ever have. My son may find it hard to appreciate why I am not giving him any actual presents for Christmas this year, but I trust that he will one day understand what I mean when I tell him I am gifting him with my Presence, which is, of course, a far greater sacrifice than any bauble.

Skye Chat
phoebethompson
Glad we managed to get some holiday shopping done yesterday. Feels wrong to be spending money on anything except essentials right now, but at the same time, normal life can't just grind to a halt. And besides, I fear the whole 'my Presence is your present' idea would go down about as well as the Iraq war with the twins.

crystalwalker
Hope George's mom likes the reindeer plates, per our annual tradition of exchanging useless holiday-themed tokens that neither of us have space to store. Your MIL should be thrilled with the Vita-Pulse blender you bought her. That thing could shred a small tree!

phoebethompson
Not even a double shot of vodka could improve flavor of those organic kale, strawberry and yak's milk smoothies Vira likes to whizz up for breakfast. Still, MIL does like to pulverize stuff (her husband's ego, mostly), so I trust she will approve.

crystalwalker
Speaking of which, what did you make of Vira's newsletter just now? Could just be the usual holiday stress, of course, but I'm concerned the situation with Tom is getting to her. Not to mention the fact that Nina and Gunther seem to be spending an awful lot of time together. Did you know she's now taking privates?

phoebethompson

Really? Brad did report sounds of weeping coming from Vira's master bedroom when he was working on her server this morning, but frankly, I'm finding it hard to dredge up much sympathy for anyone else's situation right now, especially for someone whose ex unfailingly pays the bills.

crystalwalker

I understand, but are you sure you want your husband anywhere near her in this vulnerable state? You know how men can't resist a damsel in distress.

phoebethompson

Pretty sure most women can resist a full-grown man dressed in a Huggie and down booties, which is what Brad has taken to wearing at home ever since he got fired. But point taken. I will make a note to watch the relationship between them more closely from now on.

Tuesday, December 18

Posting on Village Listserv
From: villagepeople@thevillage.org
So far, we've had NO offers of help so far with the Kwannukmas dinner for the homeless in the Village Yurt on December 26.

We know it's a very busy time of year, but this is a great way to model caring and compassion to your kids (or an excuse to get away from them, if all that holiday togetherness proves too much). Please consider giving up just a few hours of your time, and remember, school-age children can earn Service Learning and Volunteer Enhancement (SLaVE) hours in the process!

From: phoebegb@sahmsrule.net
To: crystalwalker@sterlingmorris.com
FW:
I look forward to the prospect of spending Boxing Day in an overheated house stuffed with toys, children, parents and unemployed husband with about as much joy as my annual mammogram, so I'm signing up. Care to join?

From: crystalwalker@sterlingmorris.com
To: phoebegb@sahmsrule.net
God Bless you woman. Since I subscribe firmly to the philosophy that No good deed goes unpunished, I'll take a pass on the tofurkey, but let me know how it goes.

Wednesday, December 19

Darling,

Thank you so much for picking up my parents at the airport last night, and for making dinner. Can't believe my mother had the temerity to criticize you for NOT polishing the silver. Appreciate your restraint in not stabbing her with a salad fork.

Don't forget we have the Village Holiday party tomorrow night. A shirt and tie are required. Hugglet and slippers are definitely NOT an option.

xo Phoebe

Thursday, December 20

Skye Chat
crystalwalker
Nice to meet your parents at the party tonight. I can't believe you didn't mention the fact that your mother bears a striking resemblance to Margaret Thatcher! Too bad she didn't have Maggie's voice, as I could barely hear her over Nina's performance. Still, your mom couldn't have been more gracious. She even went so far as to compliment me on the length of my legs – or maybe that was just her oh-so-British way of telling me my skirt was too short?

phoebethompson
Glad Vira wasn't there to see it, even though that's because she was still at home, working late on her website with Brad.

crystalwalker
I would definitely keep an eye on that, if I were you. You know how spending time together at work can so easily lead to other things. Would hate for you to miss the warning signs because you are so caught up in re-kindling your career. Would it bother you if the connection with the Brad were merely intellectual in nature?

phoebethompson
Engaging women in intellectual discussion IS Brad's way of flirting. Thinking of deploying the nanny cam I bought to train on Lata when she first started working for us to figure out what's really going on. Just not sure I'm ready to watch the footage.

Text from Phoebe to Bitsy
Finally heard back from Pookie about 3rd and final challenge match, but only after I sent a registered letter. She suggests 10pm on Christmas Eve. Are you game?

Text from Phoebe to Bitsy
I know 10pm on Christmas Eve is terrible timing, but Pookie will respect us more if we put her in her rightful place. Think about it.

From: crystalwalker@sterlingmorris.com
To: phoebegb@sahmsrule.net
FW: Weather
Hoping you can help me decipher the following email from George to his staff and tell me whether he is likely to be home with me and the cherubs tomorrow. Wouldn't it be wonderful if we had a white Christmas?!

Staff:
The Weather Service has issued a Severe Weather Advisory for the entire DC Area for Friday, December. 21.

Heavy snowfall is currently forecast to begin mid-morning with total accumulations of 18-24 inches. The office will be closed tomorrow due to the anticipated precipitation, unless there is an accumulation of 2" or less, in which case we will remain open. If the snow is between 2-4" and you live within 12 miles walking, driving or metro distance from the office, you are expected to come in, unless the Federal Government declares a snow emergency, in which case we will be closed.

If you live outside the Beltway or more than 12 miles from the office, you are permitted to work from home. If the expected snowfall does not start until after the workday begins, the office will remain open until the accumulation is 2" or until the Federal Government shuts down, whichever comes first.

We hope this makes everything clear.

From: phoebegb@sahmsrule.net
To: crystalwalker@sterlingmorris.com
Re: Weather
I'm afraid I'm too brain-damaged by motherhood for me to follow George's no doubt marvelous logic. Trust your brilliant legal mind can figure it out.

Posting on Village Listserv
From: pookiegranger@hotmail.com
Re: LICE
It has come to my attention that there have been THREE cases of nits detected in the same pre-k class at Delicate Flower, and that all of the (related) children in question sat on Santa's lap at the Christmas Party at the Village Hall recently.

This means that your children too have most likely been exposed, and that we are facing an outbreak of epidemic proportions right here in the Village.

I have already been in touch with the Village authorities about the best way to contain and destroy the vermin before they spread further.

Unfortunately, the employee in question did not appear to take my concerns seriously, in spite of my reminder about who pays his salary. In fact, he actually laughed at my suggestion that we quarantine the infected family, even though that's what would have happened in the past. Frankly, what's a little red X on one's door compared to the health and safety of our children?

From: villagepeople@thevillage.org
Re: LICE
The Village Board has no authority to identify, quarantine or otherwise harass residents with contagious diseases, unless they threaten to spread those diseases in a public setting. As a precautionary measure, the Village Playgroup has been canceled for the remainder of the year.

From: pookiegranger@hotmail.com
Re: LICE
This cavalier attitude towards our children's health has forced me to call in the professional nit-picker (aka 'The Lice Lady') to investigate my own childrens' scalps for lice, and I would urge you to do likewise (202.666.4544/ ifleeceyou4fleas@yahoo.com).

While she did not find ANY lice or nits on my childrens' heads, most likely because I get my sitter to wash and blow dry their hair every day, I have already taken the additional precaution of having my rugs, sofas, comforters and curtains professionally dry-cleaned. I have also incinerated all my children's cuddly toys.

I hope whoever has brought this scourge into our lives appreciates how traumatic this was for my five-year old, Skipp, in particular, as he has slept with his precious bwankie wrapped around his left thumb every single night since birth. Skipp's therapist has congratulated me for encouraging him to throw bwankie onto the flames himself, thereby enabling him to feel a sense of ownership over the situation, but we have had to up my son's sessions to three times a week for the foreseeable future, at considerable expense.

From: anonimouse@yahoo.com
Re: LICE
Maybe if Pookie focused less on her dry cleaning/therapy bills and more on her marriage, she might realize that she has more important things to worry about.

From: pookiegranger@hotmail.com
Re: LICE
Just what, exactly, is that supposed to mean?

From: anonimouse@yahoo.com
Re: LICE
Just that you might want to figure out what kind of contagious diseases your

husband is spreading around. A little birdie told me they saw him knocking back tequila shots with Miss Banderburg, the pre-k teacher from Delicate Flower at the Village Lounge the other day.

From: pookiegranger@hotmail.com
Re: LICE
For the record, Ms. So-called anonymous, that was Miss. B. with my husband, but they were discussing Skippy's habit of playing with himself in class. His therapist says it's a legitimate form of self-expression, and must not be discouraged, or his creative spirit will be forever quashed. My husband says Ms. B. was very understanding, once he explained the situation, and she has promised to provide Skippy with the private corner and box of tissues he needs in order to express himself whenever he wishes.

Oh, and BTW, I just contacted the Village authorities to have you banned from the listserv, and they went one further and offered to extract your IP address and send Special Ops round to investigate. Can't say I was surprised to discover who was behind 'anonimouse' when I saw the squad car pull up outside your door just now. Given that your own husband practically forces himself on me under the mistletoe at every New Year's Eve party at the Club, perhaps it's time you focused on your own marriage, instead of mine?

From: bitsybottinger@yahoo.com
Re: LICE
Please ignore and DELETE the previous two exchanges from 'anonimouse,' which were in actual fact complete fabrications on the part of my fifteen year old niece, who infiltrated my computer while she was supposed to be watching the triplets this afternoon. She is obviously a deeply troubled young woman, who will never be allowed near my children again. I apologize for any offense caused, particularly to my nearest and dearest friend, whose husband was only acting as any responsible father would in choosing to engage with his son's twenty-five year old educator on an important matter in a pubic setting.

From: bitsybottinger@yahoo.com
Re: LICE
Last line should read 'public,' of course.

From: pookiegranger@hotmail.com
Re: LICE
Apology accepted. For the record, I'm pretty sure your husband was drunk and mistook me for you after you got your hair highlighted like mine that one time he tried to stick his tongue down my throat on New Year's Eve.

Skye Chat
phoebethompson
I trust you have been following the latest on the Village listserv. You just can't make this stuff up!

crystalwalker
Agreed. Hard to focus on work in the excitement.

phoebethompson
I am sure. Best part is that in spite of Pookie's public apology, Bitsy is still seething, and so fully on board for taking Pookie and Perkie down during our third and final challenge match on Christmas Eve. If she can channel her rage effectively, I think we're actually in with a shot at the number one spot!

crystalwalker
Admire your ability to care so much about a mere game, not to mention your willingness to play on Christmas Eve. I will be rooting for you all the way!

phoebethompson
Thx.

Friday, December 21

From: crystalwalker@sterlingmorris.com
To: phoebegb@sahmsrule.net
What is it about clients and their magical ability to time their urgent legal questions for the moment when you have just picked up Baby from day care and are desperately trying to beat the holiday traffic? Giving sound legal advice from your cell phone while Baby is screaming to be fed is hardly a winning proposition, let alone while your boobs are spurting milk. Of course, were George ever to find himself in this position, he would be viewed either as a desirable New Man (by female clients) or a good ol' boy doing his wife a favor (male), while I am clearly regarded as an incompetent ninny with the wrong sense of priorities when it comes to my work/life balance.

Meanwhile, Helen has pulled two all-nighters this week already on the discrimination suit my firm has filed against a chain of topless restaurants for refusing to hire women over the age of 30, and she's threatening to work through the holidays. I want to still have the same passion for injustice she has, but I just don't. And what's even better is the fact I no longer care.

From: phoebegb@sahmsrule.net
To: crystalwalker@sterlingmorris.com
So sorry to hear you had a rough day, but I wanted to let you know that your suggestion that I reach out to my former colleagues at BBC America seems to have yielded results.

Having drinks Monday night with my old boss, who thinks there may be an opening coming up on his new local afternoon news show on Channel 8, which happens to be located just across the city line, in northwest DC. I fear the skills of an aging former anchor are by now well past their sell-by-date, but I'm using the excuse to spend the day getting fully detailed at the M Street salon. Seeing as it's work-related, I'm going for the full works: acid peel and seaweed wrap followed by an hour of hot stone massage. For a week's worth of my daughters' tuition at CRAC, I figure I should come out looking as fresh as a daisy – albeit one chemically rejuvenated in DC's finest lab.

Monday, December 24

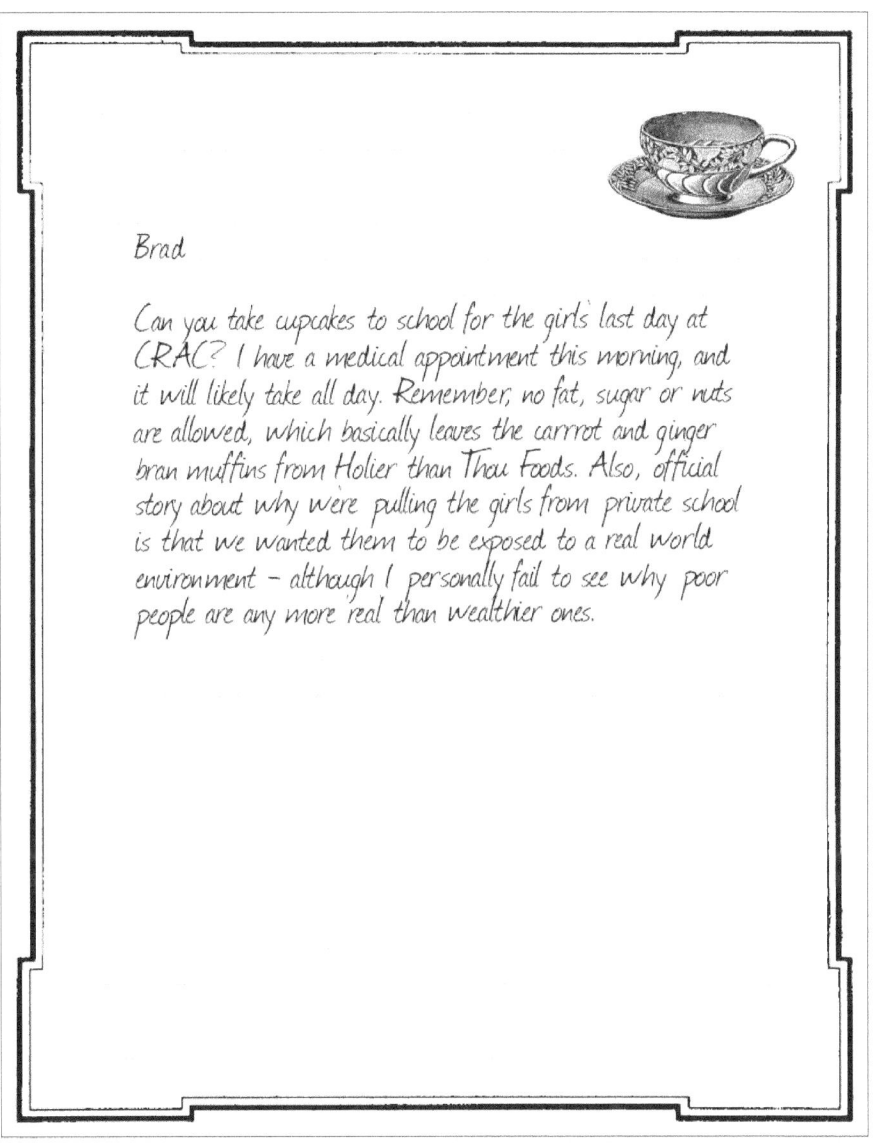

Brad

Can you take cupcakes to school for the girls' last day at CRAC? I have a medical appointment this morning, and it will likely take all day. Remember, no fat, sugar or nuts are allowed, which basically leaves the carrot and ginger bran muffins from Holier than Thou Foods. Also, official story about why we're pulling the girls from private school is that we wanted them to be exposed to a real world environment – although I personally fail to see why poor people are any more real than wealthier ones.

Text from Crystal to George
Can't believe Seton would schedule our parent interviews for Christmas Eve, but so be it. At least they agreed to do it b/f work. Meet you at the front entrance in 5.

Text message from Crystal to Helen Wheels
Running late, but shd be there by 10. Can u tell them I can't make partner mtg?

Text message from Crystal to Helen Wheels
What do you mean they refuse to start w/o me? Can't anyone do anything around here w/o requiring me to wipe their behind?

Text message from Crystal to Helen Wheels
Mtg is about me? Sounds ominous. B there in 5.

Skye Chat
crystalwalker
RU online? I have some big news.

phoebethompson
You're pregnant. Again.

crystalwalker
No, thank God. I quit my job.

phoebethompson
OMG. What happened?

crystalwalker
Turns out, you were right. I can't do it all.

phoebethompson
I can't believe that I, of all people, should be asking this, but what about your feminist principles? I thought you were determined never to be financially dependent upon a man?

crystalwalker
Me too, but apparently, the other (equity) partners feel I am not pulling my weight in billable hours. Final straw came when the partners actually convened a meeting to demand I not store breast milk in the office refrigerator, because the associates kept inadvertently using it for their afternoon coffee. Personally, I don't think there was anything accidental about it, but I took it as a Sign.

phoebethompson
Switching to email so can hit return without sending. This is too important!

From: phoebegb@sahmsrule.net
To: crystalwalker@sterlingmorris.com
Forgive me for being less than thrilled on your behalf, but the traumatic events of the last few weeks have shaken my fundamental belief in the importance of being a stay at home mum. Are you sure the economic crisis of the century is the best time to give up a steady income? I quit working at

the height of the dot-com boom, and look what happened.

What does George think about this latest development?

From: crystalwalker@sterlingmorris.com
To: phoebegb@sahmsrule.net
As a matter of fact, he is being strangely supportive, I suspect because he thinks having me at home will let him off the hook when it comes to dealing with the cherubs. I can't tell you how liberating it was just to walk away. HM was also very supportive when I told her, and seemed quite thrilled when I offered to volunteer one day a week in class for each cherub at Seton – assuming they get in, of course.

BTW, almost forgot. How did drinks with your ex-colleague go? Hope the post-op recovery from your treatments at the spa didn't force you to cancel.

From: phoebegb@sahmsrule.net
To: crystalwalker@sterlingmorris.com
I can't be seen in daylight after my skin treatment, which has left me looking and feeling as raw as a piece of bruised fruit. Exposure to sun is not recommended either, until the skin has had a chance to heal, so I retreated to my coffin until after sunset. Fortunately, I managed to apply enough foundation to ensure my former colleague did not shrink at the sight of me. Helped that we met in the Village Lounge, which is especially dark. Not even the bartender recognized me, which I'm taking as a good sign.

However, as I quickly discovered, the problem with taking a career break is that you continue to get older while the world you leave behind doesn't. Meaning that when my colleague took me to meet everyone in the Channel 8 newsroom afterward, there wasn't a single person over the age of twenty-five. Ironically, it's only now that I feel qualified to do what I did back then, but it's clear I have officially passed the age at which a woman can expect to be noticed, let alone taken seriously.

Still, I did manage to wrangle an interview with the female producer next week, so fingers crossed she has an enlightened attitude towards stay-at-home mothers re-entering the workplace.

From: crystalwalker@sterlingmorris.com
To: phoebegb@sahmsrule.net
Luck is the last thing you need, dear P. Did I ever tell you that you remind me of that British BBC correspondent, Kate Kay? The blonde with the killer cut glass accent and attitude to match. You two could be dopplegangers. The way that woman pops up everywhere, from NPR to the Sunday talk shows assures me, dear P, that you will do just fine.

From: phoebegb@sahmsrule.net
To: crystalwalker@sterlingmorris.com
I have been informed of the resemblance once or twice in the past. Always found her rather prim-looking, myself, although rumor has it, the woman has the kind of open marriage favored by the English upper-classes, which might explain her popularity with DC politicos. You'd never guess, would

you, from all the glowing profiles you read about her doting husband and four perfect children?

From: crystalwalker@sterlingmorris.com
To: phoebegb@sahmsrule.net
How does the woman have the energy to do anything else with a full-time career and children to raise?

From: phoebegb@sahmsrule.net
To: crystalwalker@sterlingmorris.com
Two words: 'Nanny' and 'boarding school'. Simple!

From: crystalwalker@sterlingmorris.com
To: phoebegb@sahmsrule.net
Must keep in mind for Kevin. Do you know that Evelyn threatened to eject him from her study after his blood-sugar levels tested suspiciously high last Monday?

Managed to forestall her by claiming Type II diabetes runs in the family, but need to keep a watchful eye on him until after she has mailed all her letters of recommendation to Seton. Deadline is January, so fingers crossed I can keep him off the hard candy until then.

Tuesday, December 25

MeBook Posting from Phoebe
Well, it looks like the Village Country Club Ladies' Tennis Team is about to acquire two new members. This is the best Christmas present I could wish for, short of a million dollars or a lifetime membership to my favorite day spa. Happy Christmas everyone!

DC Diary

The Walkers Take on the Nation's Capital

George's Pies: Stay at Home Mom

Merry Christmas to all our friends and family in KC, and to our new friends here in DC.

Right now, I am surrounded in a sea of wrapping paper after putting Kurtis down for her morning nap. The cherubs seemed thrilled with their presents, all of which seemed to require a wire cutter and electric chain saw to extract from their packaging. Kev, Kim and Karson are now helping George in the kitchen with his annual holiday pie-making. It's the only time he cooks all year, but when he does, he likes to get creative. This year, he's making apple, pecan- and his very own, original concoction, chocolate rhubarb!

George's amazing pies

The big news is that I have decided to quit work. I know I am the least likely person to become a stay at home mom, especially as a card-carrying, bra-burning member of the feminist movement. My sisters at St. Stephens will be horrified. But parenting four cherubs is SO much more intense than I ever imagined, not to mention the fact that kids in DC are expected to do so much more after school than they were in KC. Kimberly alone has around 20 hours of extra-curricular activities each week, not counting homework. All this is not to say that I've abandoned my principles. I just need a little breathing space to get back on form before getting stuck back in.

The bra has been liberated

Merry Christmas and all that. Look forward to seeing you on the other side.

No comments:

Post a Comment

Comment as: Select profile... ⬦

(Publish) Preview

DC Diary
George's Pies, Stay at Home Mom

Merry Christmas to all our friends and family in KC, and to our new friends here in DC.

Right now, I am surrounded in a sea of wrapping paper after putting Kurtis down for her morning nap. The cherubs seemed thrilled with their presents, all of which seemed to require a wire cutter and electric chain saw to extract from their packaging. Kev, Kim and Karson are now helping George in the kitchen with his annual holiday pie-making. It's the only time he cooks all year, but when he does, he likes to get creative. This year, he's making apple, pecan- and his very own, original concoction, chocolate rhubarb!

The big news is that I have decided to quit work. I know I am the least likely person to become a stay at home mom, especially as a card-carrying, bra-burning member of the feminist movement. My sisters at St. Stephens will be horrified. But parenting four cherubs is SO much more intense than I ever imagined, not to mention the fact that kids in DC are expected to do so much more after school than they were in KC. Kimberly alone has around 20 hours of extra-curricular activities each week, not counting homework. All this is not to say that I've abandoned my principles. I just need a little breathing space to get back on form before getting stuck back in.

Merry Christmas and all that. Look forward to seeing you on the other side.

Chapter 6

Janurary, 2013 Vol. 42, Issue 1
Always FREE, but donations appreciated

Please direct submissions and inquiries to:
whiner@villagepress.com
P.O. Box 357 Village Town, MD

VILLAGE WHINER

Your trusty monthly newsletter of
the "Most Livable Village," 1989
Village Times Magazine

Special OPS Update

Following a regrettable incident with the Tasers involving the captain of the Ladies tennis team at the Village Country Club last month, and a few awkward incursions into private homes, which brought some unflattering attention from the local DC chapter of the ACLU, the Board of Village Managers has issued new guidelines on the use of the Special Ops unit.

From now on, Special Ops will desist from using full riot gear until it is determined that the incident in question is of a serious nature. Complaining about a neighbor hosting a gathering to which you personally were not invited does not count. While we strive to keep our neighborhood safe and free from unwanted noise and people, we must attend, at least in theory, to the idea that a resident's private property is just that. Please feel free to direct any concerns you may have about this revised policy to the Village Managers, who is now required to file monthly reports about Special Ops activities with the local magistrate until further notice.

The recent snow has hampered construction at the new Holier Than Thou Foods, but work is expected to resume soon. In the meantime, residents are politely asked to stop emailing the Village office with any questions about the delay in construction, and to direct their inquiries instead to info@wellpaidpservwebsitethatsall.com.

Miss Gertrude

During the course of a lingering holiday visit to my son and daughter-in-law's home recently, Miss Gertrude was reminded that many children these days do not know how to eat at a table, having been raised on a diet of finger food in front of the television, or these days, computer screen.

To nip this crisis in the bud, Miss Gertrude will lead a class on how to train your toddler to hold a knife and fork correctly, how to sit at the table for more than two minutes without falling off your chair, pulling the tablecloth off the table or ending up with food in your hair, face, clothing or your parents, and how to eat at least one green vegetable without throwing up or choking to death on the spot.

Miss Gertrude's Table Manners for Tots workshop will take place directly after playgroup in the Village Hall on Thursday, January 8th at 12pm. Cost $57 per child. A five course lunch featuring soup, fish, some kind of boiled meat and at least three different kinds of vegetable including mushrooms will be served. Dessert will be contingent on good behavior.

Tennis Team Results

The Ladies Team has been on hiatus in order to cope with the inevitable onslaught of domestic responsibilities brought on by the holidays. They are looking forward to getting back to the business of pounding Xavier's balls as soon as the children are back in school.

Meanwhile, the Gentleman's Team finally managed to find time in December to take several rather lively meetings in the Gentleman's lounge. No decision about joining the USTA league has yet been announced, despite the mountain of empty bottles found in the Club recycling bins, but we trust the meetings were not merely a ruse to avoid spending time with wives nearest and dearest during the holiday season, and hope to report progress on this front soon.

Village Diversity Group

A big thank you to Phoebe Thompson, who managed to rope her husband, parents, brother and children into helping cook, serve and clean up after our Kwanzukkmas dinner for the homeless in the Village Yurt on December 26th.

Phoebe herself couldn't be there as she had a migraine, but dinner was delicious. In particular, we highly recommend the bread sauce our British helpers so kindly introduced to us. It may resemble a pot of congealed oatmeal, but the taste is absolutely divine.

We still have a lot of tofunkey and vegan plum pudding (also very tasty, especially jelley we set fire to it) left over, so if anyone would like a doggie bag, please contact Vita Bliss to collect before it all gets added to the Village compost pile.

WANTED

Five bedroom house for rent to
VIP guests during Inauguration week.

Willing to pay $10k or more for house in excellent
condition; more for house with live-in staff.

For more information, contact
valdrashandrun@aol.com

Special Ops Update

Following a regrettable incident with the Taser involving the captain of the Ladies' Tennis Team at the Village Country Club last month, and a few awkward incursions into private homes, which brought some unflattering attention from the local DC chapter of the ACLU, the Board of Village Managers has issued new guidelines on the use of the Special Ops unit.

From now on, Special Ops will desist from using full riot gear until it is determined that the incident in question is of a serious nature. Complaining about a neighbor hosting a gathering to which you personally were not invited does not count. While we strive to keep our neighborhood safe and free from unwanted noise and people, we must attend, at least in theory, to the idea that a resident's private property is just that. Please feel free to direct any concerns you may have about this revised policy to the Village Manager, who is now required to file monthly reports about Special Ops activities with the local magistrate until further notice.

The recent snow has hampered construction at the new Holier Than Thou Foods, but work is expected to resume soon. In the meantime, residents are politely asked to stop emailing the Village office with any questions about the delay in construction, and to direct their inquiries instead to info@ wellpaylipservicebutthatsall.com.

Miss Gertrude

During the course of a lingering holiday visit to my son and daughter-in-law's home recently, Miss Gertrude was reminded that many children these days do not know how to eat at a table, having been raised on a diet of finger food in front of the television - or these days, computer screen.

To nip this crisis in the bud, Miss Gertrude will lead a class on how to train your toddler to hold a knife and fork correctly; how to sit at the table for more than five minutes without falling off your chair, pulling the tablecloth off the table or ending up with food in your hair, face, clothing or your parents; and how to eat at least one green vegetable without throwing up or choking to death on the spot.

Miss Gertrude's Table Manners for Tots workshop will take place directly after playgroup in the Village Hall on Thursday, January 8th, at 12 pm. Cost: $57 per child. A five course lunch featuring soup, fish, some kind of boiled meat and at least three different kinds of vegetable (including mushrooms) will be served. Dessert will be contingent on good behavior.

Tennis Team Results

The Ladies' Team has been on hiatus in order to cope with the inevitable onslaught of domestic responsibilities brought on by the holidays. They are looking forward to getting back to the business of pounding Xavier's balls as soon as the children are back in school.

Meanwhile, the Gentlemen's Team finally managed to find time in December to take several rather lively meetings in the Gentlemen's lounge. No decision about joining the USTF league has yet been announced, despite the mountain of empty bottles found in the Club recycling bins, but we trust the meetings were not merely a ruse to avoid spending time with one's nearest and dearest during the holiday season, and hope to report progress on this front soon.

Village Diversity Group

A big thank you to Phoebe Thompson, who managed to rope her husband, parents, brother and children into helping cook, serve and clean up after our Kwannukmas dinner for the homeless in the Village Yurt on December 26th.

Phoebe herself couldn't be there, as she had a migraine, but dinner was delicious. In particular, we highly recommend the bread sauce our British helpers so kindly introduced to us. It may resemble a pot of congealed vomit, but the taste is absolutely divine!

We still have a lot of tofurkey and vegan plum pudding (also very tasty, especially after you set fire to it) left over, if anyone would like a doggie bag. Please contact Vira Bliss to collect before it all gets added to the Village compost pile.

WANTED

Five bedroom house for rent to VIP guests during Inauguration week.

Willing to pay $10k or more for house in excellent condition; more for house with live-in staff.

For more information, contact willtrashandrun@aol.com

From: phoebegb@sahmsrule.net
To: willtrashandrun@aol.com

I am contacting you with an offer of a house to rent in the Village, per your ad in the Village Whiner.

Our charming redbrick colonial is available for the entire week of the Inauguration. It has 4 bedrooms, not 5, but each is generously-sized and decorated in gracious, lived-in English country manor style. The house comes with a live-in cook/butler, who specializes in delicious homemade pasta sauces. We are only 5 minutes from the Village Shoppes, including the soon to be opened Holier Than Thou Foods, plans for which were featured in yesterday's Style section of The Washington Post.

I am attaching some pictures to this email. Let me know if you are interested.

From: phoebegb@sahmsrule.net
To: willtrashandrun@aol.com

I am frankly a little surprised to hear you were inundated with offers, but do suppose it's a sign of the harsh economic times, even here in the Village.

I am also sorry and a little shocked to hear you did not find our decor up to your standards (although calling it 'shabby' suggests you fail to understand genteel English taste altogether), and that you are unwilling to divulge the name of the family whose house you have ultimately decided to rent. I would strongly urge you to visit the abode in question, if you haven't already done so, as online photographs can be so misleading. Some of the newer houses in the Village are poorly constructed, so homeowners are known to disguise the odd crack or hole in the paper thin drywall with a strategically placed pot plant.

Please do not hesitate to contact me again, if you find the place you have chosen is not up to standards.

Voicemail Transcript from Crystal mePhone
Thanks for the invitation to join us for Cocktails at the Club for New Ear's Peeve. Wasn't it tweet of the boys to get us matching mePhone 5 for Christ What a Mess? I LOVE the apple that transcribes my vicemail massages and forwards them to email, don't you?

Transcribed using Yaktechnology@yakapp.com

Voicemail Transcript From Phoebe mePhone
So sorry Chad insisted on singing Old Long Sign as the cock stuck midnight. Thank you for NOT bringing Virtual Bliss. Not sure I could BARE the sight of her warbling a duet with my husband, especially since i've gained TREE pounds over the holidays, while she appears to have lost WAIT. Yogurt is the best. See you there.

Transcribed using Yaktechnology@yakapp.com

Text from Crystal to Phoebe
Actually did invite Vira for NYE last night, but she claimed to be spending evening menstruating.

Text from Crystal to Phoebe
Meditating. Autocorrect on mePhone a little too jealous.

Text from Crystal to Phoebe
ZEALOUS!

Wednesday, January 2

Posting on Village Listserv
From: exaupair@ivyleagueorbust.com
Would all teens and preteens participating in Evelyn Braun's study on the effect of sugar on the development of adolescent brains please report to the Village Hall tomorrow morning for urine testing? Evelyn's assistant, Nina Scheiner will be on hand to supervise.

Remember to drink a big glass of water before you come, so we can test you on the spot, to avoid the risk of teens substituting their pee for that of their younger sibling or pet. Water will be provided to anyone who forgets.

From: crystalmomof4exlaw@yahoo.com
To: phoebegb@sahmsrule.net
FW: Ve have ways of making you pee!
Would your girls mind picking up Kev and Kim on their way? Convinced my two will fail, but hopefully Evelyn will have submitted her recommendations for Seton by then, so shouldn't make any difference.

BTW, what do you think of my new email address? Hoping it conveys my priorities while reminding people of my professional background. I've learned over the past few months in DC that despite all the lip service paid to motherhood, it's really only one's professional title that commands respect. Also hoping that I can worry less about all that as I pursue a more yogic path through the suburban jungle.

From: phoebegb@sahmsrule.net
To: crystalmomof4exlaw@yahoo.com
New email = perfect.
Looking forward to changing mine in similar fashion, now that it looks like I will be rejoining the working world next Monday as the Senior Affairs correspondent for Channel 8 News. And by Senior, I mean ancient, as opposed to important. Turns out, the producer my former colleague, Brian introduced to me at drinks was very taken with my British accent and resemblance to Kate Kay, which he seems to think will go down particularly well with the old folk.

Given my complete absence from the workplace for almost a decade, I dare say it would be a mistake to point out fact that Brian's toupee started its career in broadcasting a good fifteen years before I did, yet no one considers him the go-to guy to report on the latest trends in low-rider Depends. You'll catch glimpses of me somewhere between the ads for Viagra and gentle, overnight relief from now on.

Hours are officially 8 to 4, unofficially more like 8 to 8, with weekends off for good behavior. The pay will just about cover the mortgage and utilities, but not food or Emily and Cecily's extracurricular activities, let alone therapy. I realize this may severely hamper their ability to master Latin before they graduate, but am hoping colleges will recognize the limited nature of their educational opportunities at public school, and evaluate them accordingly – even if we do have to move to West Virginia to drive home the point.

From: crystalmomof4exlaw@yahoo.com
To: phoebegb@sahmsrule.net
Congrats on the new position! Must celebrate soon – assuming I can manage to stay up past 8 o'clock. A big if, these days. And don't worry about the twins. Convinced the reason my two oldest are so well-adjusted (the Village Chief of Police's words, not mine) is because I had them in day care from six weeks on.

Feels weird but wonderful not be going back to work myself, now that the holidays are over.

I keep waking up in a panic, thinking there's something I've forgotten, followed by a flood of relief when I realize that I don't have to be anywhere except the bus-stop on Monday morning. Why didn't I do this years ago?

P.S. just told Kevin to take down pic of him being kissed by two teenage girls on MeBook. Don't want him being labeled a playboy just yet. It's exactly this kind of misstep that could derail his application to Seton. If you happen to spot any other inappropriate postings, please let me know.

From: phoebegb@sahmsrule.net
To: crystalmomof4exlaw@yahoo.com
My mother disapproves of me going back to work and is making pointed comments about absentee mothering as I write, even though I can't recall a single instance of her engaging with me and my brother beyond telling us to run along while the adults enjoyed their cocktails. Dare say, if I can survive almost two weeks with the woman in my house, Cecily and Emily can survive their pre-teen years with a mother who (god forbid) works.

P.S. Still no response from George to my request to friend him on MeBook, although I notice his profile picture has changed. Can't tell if it's a fish or a semi-automatic in his latest incarnation, but I am sure his lobbying partners will approve either way.

Thursday, January 3

Thank you for writing letters of recommendation to Seton for all three of my older cherubs. George and I so appreciate your help. If there is any way you could cc us when you send them in (deadline is Monday), that would be great. – Crystal

Friday, January 4

From: crystalmomof4exlaw@yahoo.com
To: ebraun@ivyleagueorbust.com

So sorry to hear Nina put a dent your brand new Mini Cooper and destroyed part of the rockwall Fred put in around your new driveway yesterday. You were very kind to let her borrow the car on New Year's Eve. I just hope the Village Special Ops will be equally understanding if she tests positive for alcohol, drugs or dare I say, sugar. :0

Didn't realize the cherubs' letters of recommendation were confidential, but I know you have a reputation to maintain. I trust you completely when you say you have written only the unvarnished truth, following your observation of the cherubs and the test results from your food study. I know that a woman in your position would never consciously sabotage a child's educational prospects based on one or two examples of misguided behavior, especially now that you are working with all four of my cherubs (at considerable expense) to maximise their potential.

Speaking of which, I will drop off the check for this month's payment today. Please consider the little extra in the total our way of thanking you for all your hard work last month.

Happy New Year!

Sunday, January 6

From: crystalmomof4exlaw@yahoo.com
To: phoebegb@channel8news.com

Below you will find an outline of the main areas you need to cover in writing the cherub's recommendations for Seton. Letters are due tomorrow. Apologies for the short notice. I truly appreciate your willingness to step up. There are three main areas to be addressed:

1) Evidence of extraordinary genius or leadership, as demonstrated by cherubs under your supervision (the time Karson talked Cecily and Emily into stripping naked with him behind the playhouse need not count)

2) Evidence of extraordinary acts of heroism or self-sacrifice, as when Kevin saved Nina from drowning in Evelyn's pool this past summer, going so far as to pump her chest and perform five sets of rescue breaths before she threw up on him

3) Evidence of modesty as befitting a student of a school founded on Buddhist principles, I doubt they care what the kids wear – at least I hope not, or Kimberly doesn't stand a chance. What they are looking for is more along the lines of George Washington refusing the offer of a kingship after the revolution. Nothing comparable immediately springs to mind when it comes to the cherubs, but I'm sure you'll think of something.

The letter should not read as though I or anyone else had primed you with information about what to say, and should be printed on letterhead announcing your credentials to act a person of standing here in DC. Ideally, I am told, such recommendations are written by the Great and the Good (understand Vira may have snagged the President himself for her son), but in your case, dear P, I am sure your new position as Senior Affairs reporter for the second most watched news channel in the nation's capital will seal the deal.

Thank you.

Crystal,

Mother insisted I bring you an example of my native cuisine, home-cooked, naturally by my father. While I am more than happy to oblige when it comes to writing glowing reports for the cherubs, are you quite sure you want to go through with the whole gruesome process? I ask only because I am rather looking forward to NOT hearing from Cecily and Emily's teachers on a daily basis about whether or not they ate all their sun-dried zucchini and eggplant pizza at lunch, or the fact that once again, they chose to communicate with each other in their own exclusive language at recess.

Then there's the whole delicate subject of diversity to consider. Your cherubs may ironically be a rarer breed at most DC private schools than the sons and daughters of international jet-setters, who attend for a year or two while their parents work at The World Bank or IMF. But now that the First Daughters are attending, you may need more than money and connections to get in. I suggest you start embellishing the family tree now, unless you are prepared to adopt an alternative lifestyle pronto.

Of course, I would be delighted to write the cherubs a letter of recommendation. Rest assured, I will NOT mention Kimberly's recent request to get her tongue pierced for Christmas.

-Phoebe

Phoebe,

My people are descended from the great mall-roaming tribes of the Midwest, so we do have a recipe for twice-cooked fried chicken that's been passed down from generation to generation in the oral tradition. Does that count?

Thank you for doing this, and please thank your father for feeding my family this evening. I trust he will approve of this particular brand of his favorite tipple.

Crystal

223

Monday, January 7

From: phoebegb@sahmsrule.net
To: bthompson@p_Nisdesigns.com
Re: Chore Chart while I'm at work

1. Wake twins
2. Make breakfast and lunches for Cecily and Emily. Remember, one doesn't like peanut butter, the other will eat nothing but. NO JUNK!
3. Drive Cecily and Emily to VPS for first day (they can ride bus after that)
4. Make beds, folding bottom sheet the way my mother told you. Contrary to your opinion, and the girls', it is simply NOT more comfortable to get into an unmade bed
5. EMPTY DISHWASHER AND PUT AWAY DISHES. (You may not see the point, but I do)
6. Wipe down kitchen counters and sweep floor
7. Fluff living room pillows. Root around under cushions for loose change, candy wrappers, and inevitably, the TV remote. Return to cradle for charging
8. Run at least 2 loads of laundry, before it starts to pile up. Don't forget to fluff, fold and put away!
9. Call plumber about leak in the living room ceiling
10. Take Mother shopping at Undergarments 'R' Us. Remind her she is a US size 14, not 10, as she always claims. Trust me, you don't want to have to bring this stuff back!
11. Take parents to lunch
12. Sort mail by category of bill, catalog or correspondence in baskets Lata wove specially for each
13. Pick girls up from bus-stop and take to therapy (don't forget to pack snack!)
14. Take girls to sax lesson. After today, you can decide who continues with instrument and who will take Latin. Can always switch later, if necessary
15. Help with homework. Remember: strictly no TV or screen time on weekdays.
16. Sort girls' backpacks, tossing uneaten leftovers and recycling completed art/homework projects when girls aren't looking
17. Complete any and all school medical, dental and emergency forms in triplicate by hand, along with permission slips and checks for upcoming field trips. Twins' medical files can be located in upstairs office, but I suggest you get dates of their latest tetanus shots tattooed somewhere discreet for future reference
18. Start dinner (pesto fine)

Will call if I think of anything else. Love you!

Text from Crystal to Phoebe
Planning to celebrate first day home from work by hosting a neighborhood

tea at 3. I realize it's also your first day at work, but feel free to stop by on your way home.

Text from Phoebe to Crystal
Cecily and Emily would love to come, and I will be there asap, altho' may not be 'till after 6. Hope you will have something stronger than tea available then. I'll need it.

Note from Crystal to Lata
Sorry about mess in kitchen. Baking with cherubs harder than I thought. Hopefully won't need to re-paint ceiling, as we should be able to scrape most of the mess with spatula.

Text Message from Crystal to Kevin and Kimberly
The 2 of u WILL apologize to Lata for flour fight and help her clean up b/f guests arrive, or there will be NO organic bran scones for you.

Text Message from Crystal to Kevin and Kimberly
Lata doesn't care if your brother was involved. And if u so much as think of using scone as missile, you can kiss mePhone, mePod and MeBook goodbye.

Skye Chat
phoebethompson
Cocktail was just what the doctor ordered, thank you. Sorry I had to dash, but I was exhausted and twins still needed to do their homework. Brad clearly has a lot to learn about time management.

crystalwalker
Sweet of Brad to drive Cecily and Emily on their first day at VPS. Glad you could make tea, although it felt like we barely had a chance to talk, once Pookie and Perky arrived. How was first day at work?

phoebethompson
Like one of those nightmares where you dream you went to work in your underwear. Only in this case, I didn't get to wake up. They have all this newfangled terminology I'm supposed to use, including something called a thumb drive, whatever that is. Find myself wishing I actually paid attention when Brad engages in tech talk.

crystalwalker
In my experience, it's best just to nod and pretend u know what people are talking about, then look up anything you don't understand. Thank God for Goggle!

phoebethompson
That's exactly what I did, although I'm still not sure if a thumb drive is a piece of technology, or some kind of fundraiser for people missing digits. How was your first day as a stay at home mom?

crystalwalker
Went by so fast, I ended up running out of time to shower, which is why I was forced to serve tea wearing the same grubby T-shirt and sweatpants I wore to bed last night. Thank you for not following Pookie's example and pointing out the trickle of baby spit-up running down my back. Of course, she was still dressed in tennis whites and 'glowing' from her game, but that's different somehow, isn't it?

BTW, is that really all these women do all day long? I know today simply flew by, but feel sure I will have to take up some kind of activity once I have the SAHM routine down. Just not sure I'm ready to join the professional USTF circuit.

phoebethompson
Haven't seen Pookie and Perky on the courts since Bitsy and I took them down, which may be the last time I ever get to play tennis again, now that I've started work. Heard a rumor that P&P have gone into business together – doing what, I have no idea. But to answer your question more generally, when I was a SAHM, I found there was usually just enough time to exercise, put the house in order and shower before one's children came home each day. Attempting to do anything more than that is an exercise in frustration, but no doubt your superior competence in all matters will find a way. Must turn in, as well. I'm exhausted. Sleep well!

crystalwalker
Sweet dreams.

Tuesday, January 8

Text from Crystal to Phoebe
Good to see you at bus stop this am. Scarf, lipstick and dark glasses not necessary, as no paparazzi in these parts. Plus you may be resented for raising bar for everyone else (except Bitsy).

Text from Phoebe to Crystal
Sorry. Nervous about being spotted by passing CRAC mom, till realized no private school parent up at such ungodly hour. Wish driver hadn't ejected twins from front seat, ignoring their protests about motion sickness. Trust experience hasn't traumatized them too much.

Text from Crystal to Phoebe
Front seats reserved for kindergartners, who = upset at having to stand. Driver may relent tomorrow, after cleaning Cecily's parting gift off floor. Might have helped if girls had not expressed their concerns in pigeon Spanish. FYI, Dave hails from New Jersey, not Honduras, and his English = just fine.

Wednesday, January 9

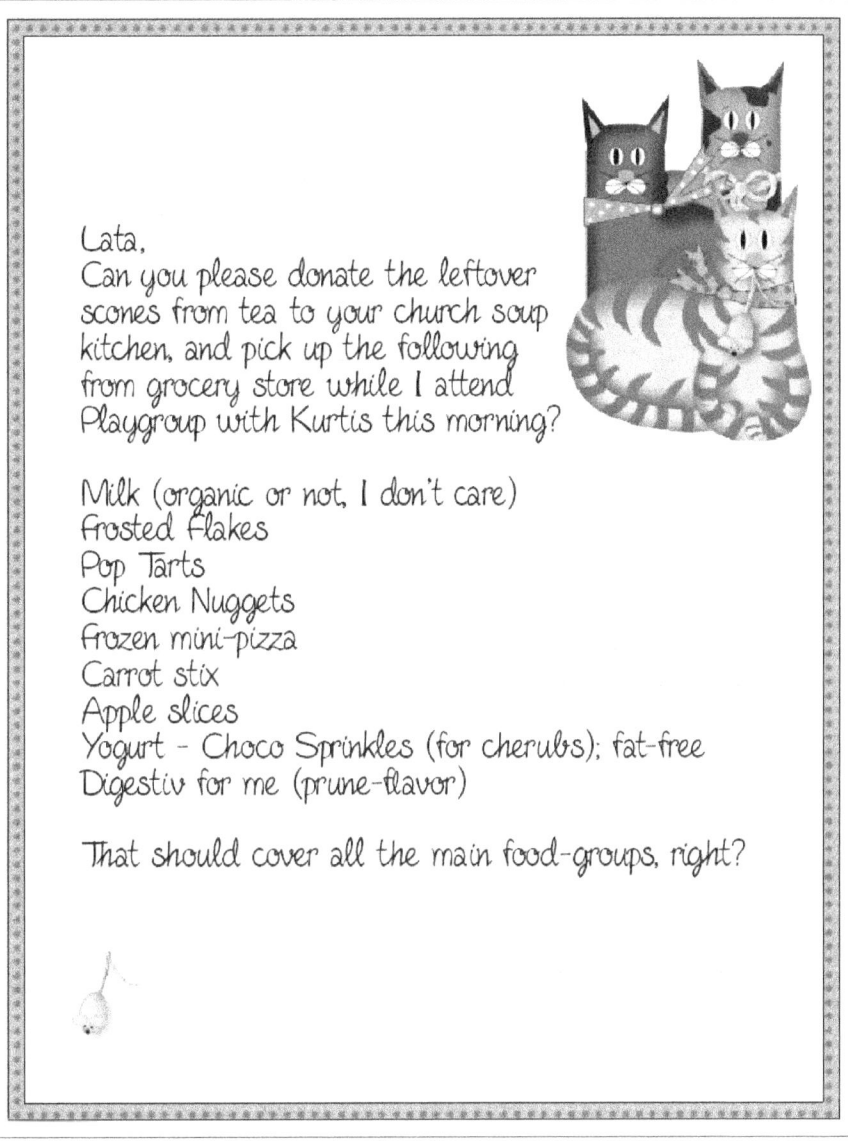

Lata,
Can you please donate the leftover scones from tea to your church soup kitchen, and pick up the following from grocery store while I attend Playgroup with Kurtis this morning?

Milk (organic or not, I don't care)
Frosted Flakes
Pop Tarts
Chicken Nuggets
Frozen mini-pizza
Carrot stix
Apple slices
Yogurt - Choco Sprinkles (for cherubs); fat-free
Digestiv for me (prune-flavor)

That should cover all the main food-groups, right?

Thursday, January 10

From: crystalmomof4exlaw@yahoo.com
To: gwalker@plunderhogg.com
What do you mean you need to go to the Bahamas? I may not be working, but I start my volunteer work in Karson's pre-K classroom soon and was relying on your support.

I get that our future depends on your ability to schmooze, but it's a little hard to swallow when I really need you here right now. Trust me when I say I understand income producing is a priority but you don't have to dismiss my room parent status with so audible a sigh. Believe it or not, there are some things Lata can't do, and being a husband and father is one of them!

From: crystalmomof4exlaw@yahoo.com
To: gwalker@plunderhogg.com
Fine. Just don't expect to have sex after you get back. At least not with me.

Friday, January 11

From: crystalmomof4exlaw@yahoo.com
To: phoebegb@channel8news.com
George is determined to go on a week-long trip to the Bahamas, with or without me. He claims it's strictly business, but I happen to know he'll be playing in a charity golf tournament, and he just ordered a new fly fishing rod online.

The way I feel about him right now, it's probably better he leaves. I know in theory I'm supposed to be able to handle things on the home front, especially now that I have Lata, and I'm not technically 'working'. But clearly, the man has no idea just how much is involved in managing the cherubs' after-school activities in this city, let alone play dates, medical/dental/therapy appointments and the multiple school functions we are supposed to attend (frequently on the same night) just to show we are involved parents.

That's just the routine stuff. I also need to start figuring out summer camps, spring break and what they plan to bring to their class Valentine's parties next month – not to mention how I can volunteer in three different classrooms at once. Meanwhile, I get a call from the health room or principal's office about one or other of the cherubs almost every day. Kevin just had his 3rd detention in as many weeks (for peeing in some kid's locker), and Kimberly seems to be rapidly developing into the kind of mean girl I aspired to be while still in elementary school. Can't help thinking their behavioral problems are due to the move from KC, and the fact that they almost never see their father these days, but I dare say society will find a way to blame it all on me.

And yes, in between all this, I'm focusing upon my breath. Or trying to, at least.

From: crystalmomof4exlaw@yahoo.com
To: phoebegb@channel8news.com
Forgot your mom's ban on electronic communication. Touch base tomorrow, after your parents leave!

Skye Chat
phoebethompson
Snuck laptop into loo while mother finishes breakfast.

You are not out of line. I have to mastermind absolutely everything, from whether or not girls have brushed their teeth, to what they are taking for lunch at VPS (at CRAC, the girls were served lunch by waiters from Designer

Cuisine). My mother thinks I'm a complete slave-driver, of course, but she doesn't understand that someone has to oversee what needs to happen when.

Meanwhile, believe it or not, Brad claims his recent experience as a stay at home father (all 4 days of it) has stimulated his desire to have another child. He's actually suggested I stop using the pill, which he knows I need for my skin, in order to make one final attempt to pop out a sprog before I turn 39 (again) this summer! As if I could afford the maternity leave at this stage in my career!

crystalwalker
Convinced most men are happy to keep spreading their seed, then walk away from the consequences, which is precisely why they must be stopped. Permanently.

Hilary was at least sympathetic when I called to tell her the latest. She has insisted on staying over to help with cherubs while George is gone next week. Touched by her kind offer, but also a little freaked out at having to make sure cherubs and I are on our best behavior while she's sleeping over. You'll have to teach me some pillow-fighting skills in case she wants to pretend she's back in boarding school.

phoebethompson
It's quite simple really. Aim for the head, and never pick a fight with the quiet girl. They almost always turn out to be the most FIERCE.

crystalwalker
Will keep in mind, thanks.

Monday, January 14

From: phoebegb@channel8news.com
To: crystalmomof4exlaw@yahoo.com
Don't think I've ever been so pleased to see my parents leave. Thought I would feel sad to be back at work after spending so much time with the family, but it's actually incredibly liberating to be in my own space. Are you quite sure you did the right thing by quitting?

From: crystalmomof4exlaw@yahoo.com
To: phoebegb@channel8news.com
Not sure how I ever found time to think, let alone be gainfully employed, before now, but being home with the cherubs these past couple of weeks has shown me how much I was missing. Kurtis now actually prefers me to Lata! This morning, she wouldn't let me put her down, so George was forced to pack for his trip by himself. As a result, he appears to have departed for 6 nights in the Bahamas sans underwear, mask, snorkel, flippers and favorite Penguin swimming trunks. Also without the usual precautionary round of conjugal relations that generally precedes all his trips, to preempt any urge

to stray while away from hearth and home.

He did ask if I had changed my mind about joining him at the last minute, until I proceeded to inform him of the obstacles in my way – thank you notes to everyone who wrote a letter of recommendation to Seton for the cherubs (expect yours soon); 6 month check-up appointment for Baby; and first meeting with Perky, who appears to have revived her interior design business because of the economic downtown in her husband's real estate development biz. (Perky wants to talk about upgrading our furniture from a style she described as 'not so much Midwest as Wild West' to the latest in Seat of Power Chic. So long as it helps with our application to the Village Club, I'm in.)

Needless to say, by the time I was finished, George was long gone, cheerfully waving 'See you Sunday!' from the beige calfskin seat of his all too familiar Town Car.

Hilary and I are planning a girly evening of manis, pedis, and Lata's signature massages tonight after the cherubs are in bed. Any chance you can join?

C.

From: phoebegb@channel8news.com
To: crystalmomof4exlaw@yahoo.com
Would love to, but working late on a story about what was on the White House menu for FDR's Inauguration, for viewers who lived through the Great Depression, as opposed to the current one we are in. Enjoy!

Thursday, January 17

From: crystalmomof4exlaw@yahoo.com
To: phoebegb@channel8news.com
Did you know that in addition to her Phd in Astrophysics and Gold Medal at the World Triathlon Games in Berlin, Hilary is something of a gourmet chef? The Baby Thrush En Gelee she cooked for us two nights ago were quite extraordinary, although the cherubs did not appreciate them. Thank God for the dog's habit of begging under the table, or I might as well have torn up their Seton applications up then and there.

Once you had removed the beak, feet and tongue, however, they were really quite tasty.

From: phoebegb@channel8news.com
To: crystalmomof4exlaw@yahoo.com
I'll take your word for it.

Posting on Village listserv
From: Tinklepaw4ever@aol.com
Does anyone know where I can find venison for sale? Tinklepaw II has been diagnosed with Irritable Bowel Syndrome, and the veterinarian is advising

me not to give her anything else.

From: ebraun@ivyleagueorbust.com
My pet Rottweiler, Snuggles developed the same problem last year. PetsRUs sells frozen venison meat in the freezer section right next to the doggy diaper and weight loss aisle. Alternatively, my husband, Fred would be happy to provide you with enough deer to last through the winter, for a small fee. His hunting license is up to date.

From: Tinklepaw4ever@aol.com
It pains me to have to feed my precious baby actual flesh, especially since I have raised her to be vegan since birth. But she wouldn't touch any of the leftover tofurkey I gave her from the dinner for the homeless at the Village Yurt, so I dare say, organic, locally-sourced venison is better than anything at the store. Please let me know the best way to get in touch with your husband and commission a kill.

Saturday, January 19

Posting on Village Listserv
From: pookiegranger@hotmail.com
I know this sounds crazy, but I think I just spotted a young man with an older guy in some kind of camouflage gear, armed with a bow and arrow apiece and stalking one of the deers on the Club golf course this morning. Does anyone know anything about this?

Posting from Village Police Center
Man and boy have been apprehended and are currently in custody, pending questioning. Deer is currently in the walk-in freezer at the Village Hall.

Update:
The persons recently apprehended on the Village Golf Course were a local resident in possession of a full and current hunting license, and a neighbor's son. The man in question swore under oath that he felled the deer in question with one arrow to the heart. We have therefore released the body into his custody. No further action will be taken in this matter.

Update:
A proposal to ban hunting from all Village Property has been posted outside the Village Office. You can read it by clicking on the link below. A vote on this proposal is scheduled for the February monthly meeting.

Text from Phoebe to Crystal
Was that Vira I just saw chained to the fence outside the Village Hall, protesting the senseless slaughter of innocent animals?

Text from Crystal to Phoebe
Wait till she finds out Fred = responsible. Have sneaking suspicion there's more to their relationship than meets eye.

From: crystalmomof4exlaw@yahoo.com
To: ishop4snobs@perkybydesign.com
Thanks so much for the consultation today.

Kimberly is thrilled with idea of getting the Crockery Barn Pink Princess bedroom of her dreams, and Kevin loves idea of the double shower head and white shag rug for his bachelor pad in the basement. Karson would probably be content in a monastic cell, as would George, but I dare say they will both derive some pleasure from the airplane hanger/legal library ideas you propose for them. When and if I do get to convert Kurtis' nursery into my home office, please let it be soundproof and sealed off from everywhere else in the house, so no one knows where to find me.

Your idea of ordering 2 blood-red, kidney shaped sofas for the 'great room' (aka the den) is interesting, but I need to run them by George first – both on aesthetic grounds, and b/c of the price. Will let you know asap.

FW: To George, with email attachment
What do you think of these sofas? They cost $8k apiece, but Perky says they will make the right kind of statement when we invite our new, soon-to-be friends from Seton and the Village Club round for dinner.

Reply:
That's just what good sofas cost these days. You may not think it's important what kind of statement we make, but trust me, DC is all about status. BTW, your 'out of the office' response is far too vague: 'I am out of the country with little, if any, access to email and voicemail. I will respond to your concerns when I return to the office.'

At least make it sound like you're working!

Text from Crystal to Perky Sparks
Any chance sofas can be delivered before George gets back? Much harder for him to return, if he's not here!

Text from Crystal to Kevin
Congratulations on your first kill! Too bad it wasn't with Dad, but Fred probably better shot anyway. No need to bring any offerings home after you're done dressing the beast – don't want to give Hilary any ideas.

Text from C to George with picture attachment of Kevin next to dead deer
Is this bigger than fish you just caught? How about teaching your own son how to hunt and gather, rather than relying on our neighbors to parent in your place?

From: Tinklepaw4ever@aol.com
For sale: 400lbs of fresh, organic venison meat, which is currently hanging in my garage to cure, $3/lb. My supplier assures me it is 100% Grade A, organic meat. 'Perfect for roasting, grilling or even eating raw,' or so he says, although I wouldn't know, not having eaten meat the past 50 years.

Skye Chat
phoebethompson
Have you heard anything from George recently? Brad is pining for his VBox partner. I suspect the two of them may be better matched than either of us with our respective other halves.

crystalwalker
George to come back tomorrow, and has made a good faith attempt to call each evening, but Hilary has become quite demanding about sitting down to eat sharply at 6, so I really don't have time to chat. A little concerned that there was no answer in his room when I tried to call him back during Baby's midnight feed last night, but there could be a million plausible explanations for this, including the fact that he might simply have switched his phone off. Still, lovely as it is to have Hilary's company – especially since she seems to like nothing better than to give me a foot rub after dinner!

phoebethompson
Might be time to remind hubby of his family obligations. You know the old saying, out of sight, out of mind.

From: crystalmomof4exlaw@yahoo.com
To: gwalker@plunderhogg.com
Subject: Attachment: Baby's first tooth!
See what you've been missing? Doctor says Kurtis is in 96% percentile for height, but only 25% for weight, so I think we have a budding supermodel on our hands. Esp. since she's so adept at spitting up. Please call or email to let me know what time your flight gets in this evening. If it's not too late, cherubs and I might even be able to pick you up.

Witter Posting from femilawyermom
Hubby back from his travels, looking very tanned. Hmm. So much for him telling me it was purely a business trip.

orangeglowlova is now following femilawyermom

Sunday, January 20

Text from Crystal to George
Taking cherubs to Mall to buy Karson jacket and tie for his cello recital at 10. I've set alarm for 9.30 a.m., so you can meet me there. CU soon. xc

Text from Crystal to George
How can u poss. be late to son's first cello recital?

Text from Crystal to George
I don't care if you were on work call. Your son is devastated you missed him. And what do u mean, u r leaving again on Wednesday?

Text from Crystal to George
Teacher giving me evil eye. TB Cont'd.

Skye Chat
crystalwalker
As the inauguration is upon us, hubby and I are expected to make an appearance at 6 balls. How to decide which to attend?

phoebethompson
all of them are probably fun, but the one that comes with a personal invitation from the White House is the only one that counts.

crystalwalker
George is insisting we go to them all and has hired a limo for the occasion. Guess we need to do our bit to show our firm's support for the party in power and pay for the new sofas we just ordered.

Monday, January 21

Album Posting from Crystal on MeBook
Our 44th President in person! George and I bundled up the cherubs and metro-ed down to the Mall for this historic occasion. Here's a picture of us all in front of the Washington Monument. Not sure you will recognize us under all the layers, but underneath the balaclavas, we are smiling.

Message from Phoebe
Still can't believe you actually went.

Reply
Nor can I. Cherubs bitched and moaned about the cold the entire way there and back. Guess they must be forgetting their midwestern roots. Thank God pictures tell a thousand words, most of them lies. Fortunately, George was also too traumatized by the experience to contemplate attending any of the inaugural parties this evening. Would you and Brad care to join us for a drink instead?

Reply
We'd love to. B there in 5.

Tuesday, January 22

Text from Phoebe to Crystal

Cecily and Emily expressing reluctance to be seen with their father at the bus-stop in the morning. Not sure if it's because he's the only Dad not wearing a suit, or the fact that he's refusing to shave until he gets a contract for his P-NIS. Think I should be concerned?

Text from Crystal to Phoebe

Have you considered introducing him as your new manny? I'm quite sure no one will recognize him beneath the new caveman beard he's sporting these days.

Text from Phoebe to Crystal

Alas, Brad not in impressive enough physical condition for me to pass him off as such. I've told Emily and Cecily to stand far away and pretend don't know him for now.

From: phoebegb@channel8news.com
To: crystalmomof4exlaw@yahoo.com

Can't tell you what a turnoff it is to come home from a hard day's work to find Brad dressed in his Hugglet and demanding sexual favors in return for having done the dishes. Tried pointing out that when I was a SAHM, doing the dishes was simply considered yet another one of my invisible duties, performed without comment, with the prospect of NOT having to have sex as a reward. Needless to say, Brad did not understand, although he looked a little hurt at my suggestion that we swap outfits so that I could at least stay clean while fulfilling my marital duty.

Doesn't help that today is technically our tenth wedding anniversary. At this rate, I'm not sure how many more we'll have.

From: crystalmomof4exlaw@yahoo.com
To: phoebegb@channel8news.com

Happy anniversary – I think. No grown man should ever be seen wearing a blanket with sleeves, I agree. At least the twins seem to be thriving at VPS. I hear the bullying issue has been resolved, right?

From: phoebegb@channel8news.com
To: crystalmomof4exlaw@yahoo.com

Apparently, they haven't laid a finger on another third grade boy since their first week. But I'm less happy about their preferred choice of companions. They seem to have latched onto the daughters of a couple of housekeepers in the Village, in a way that I find to be quite defiant.

From: crystalmomof4exlaw@yahoo.com
To: phoebegb@channel8news.com

I think it shows an admirable open-mindedness when it comes to making friends.

From: phoebegb@channel8news.com
To: crystalmomof4exlaw@yahoo.com
It would – except it makes things very awkward when the twins go for a play date with one of their new friends in the basement of a house belonging to one of their former classmates from CRAC.

Mind you, it's not as if any of their old friends have exactly bothered to stay in touch. I was hoping for an invitation from one of them to a ski chalet or fully staffed yacht over the holidays, but we haven't heard a peep. Maybe they assume I'm just too busy with the new job to take any time off, but I can't help feeling a little hurt.

Wednesday, January 23

From: crystalmomof4exlaw@yahoo.com
To: phoebegb@channel8news.com
Not sure I'm the one to offer marital advice, given that George has just jetted off on another junket today, but has it occurred to you that perhaps the tensions in your marriage are having an effect on your girls? You've all been through an awful lot of upheaval lately, between Brad losing his consulting job, you going back to work and the twins changing schools.

From: phoebegb@channel8news.com
To: crystalmomof4exlaw@yahoo.com
I was hoping to cut back on therapy bills altogether, especially now the twins seem to be all right at school. But it's true they are not used to having to make their needs known before they are met, let alone the necessity of waiting their turn or raising their hands in class. I'll make sure Brad mentions your concerns at their next appointment, and just pray all the recent upheaval hasn't damaged their young psyches too much.

Thursday, January 24

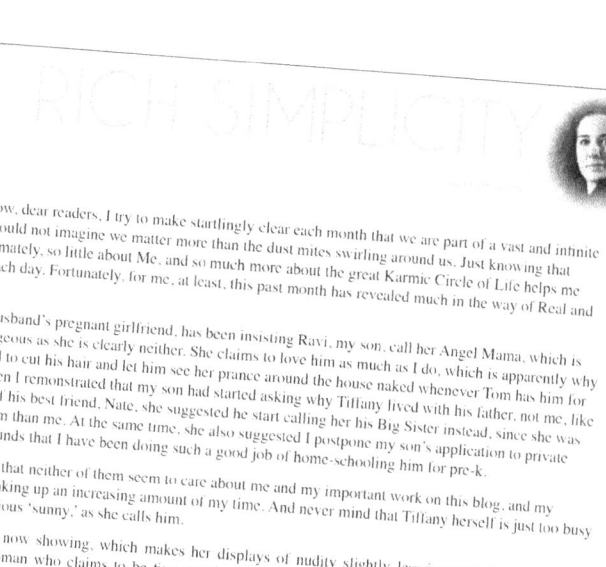

From: Rich Simplicity
To: phoebegb@sahmsrule.net

Rich Simplicity: A monthly newsletter bringing you a life of ultimate simplicity, no matter how much money I have.

Volume 04, Issue 01

Blessings,

As you well-know, dear readers, I try to make startlingly clear each month that we are part of a vast and infinite universe, and should not imagine we matter more than the dust mites swirling around us. Just knowing that existence is, ultimately, so little about Me, and so much more about the great Karmic Circle of Life helps me move forward each day. Fortunately, for me, at least, this past month has revealed much in the way of Real and Tangible Truth.

Tiffany, my ex-husband's pregnant girlfriend, has been insisting Ravi, my son, call her Angel Mama, which is objectively outrageous as she is clearly neither. She claims to love him as much as I do, which is apparently why she feels qualified to cut his hair and let him see her prance around the house naked whenever Tom has him for the weekend. When I remonstrated that my son had started asking why Tiffany lived with his father, not me, like the two mothers of his best friend, Nate, she suggested he start calling her his Big Sister instead, since she was closer in age to him than me. At the same time, she also suggested I postpone my son's application to private school, on the grounds that I have been doing such a good job of home-schooling him for pre-k.

It's amazing to me that neither of them seem to care about me and my important work on this blog, and my books, which are taking up an increasing amount of my time. And never mind that Tiffany herself is just too busy to educate her precious 'sunny,' as she calls him.

At least Tiffany is now showing, which makes her displays of nudity slightly less inappropriate than before, although how a woman who claims to be five months along can still fit into skinny jeans is beyond me. Just when I was beginning to despair of ever being able to make a True Connection' with the woman, however, Ravi did report back that Tiffany was complaining about some wiggly lines that were developing across her hips and belly. I'm hoping that a batch of my personal, homemade FatMama pregnancy poultice, made from a combination of cayenne pepper, crushed raw garlic and rancid ghee, will improve relations. I trust it will also remind Tiffany that she is about to join the great world tribe of women whose bodies have been indelibly marked (some would say scarred) by childbirth. And of course I hope that she will soon get to experience the True Blessings of Motherhood', which include letting go of your preconceptions and personal vanity, and embracing the joy that comes from the trials, tribulations and yes, the personal sacrifice that comes with it.

Text from Crystal to Phoebe
Think I've figured out why Vira, Pookie and Perky all look so good, in spite of P & P quitting tennis, and Vira boycotting yoga with Gunther for the time being. I knew it wasn't just breathwork giving her those six pack abs! Will email you the skinny – literally – soon.

From: crystalmomof4exlaw@yahoo.com
To: phoebegb@channel8news.com
Happened to spot Vira, Pookie and Perky hanging by their arms from some kind of furry stirrups bolted to Vira's in-home yoga studio ceiling, when I dropped Karson off for a playdate with Ravi just now. They were all doing some truly fierce-looking tricep extensions while taking orders from an attractive young Asian woman called Daphne, who may just be the fittest human being I've ever seen.

The door wasn't locked, so naturally I barged my way in and confronted the group. At first, Vira tried to claim they were practicing a modified version of tree pose using props, but the atmosphere in the room was far too sweaty for me to believe that.

After much prodding and probing, Vira finally 'fessed that for the past six months, she has been working out on sadomasochistic equipment personally designed and developed by a German fitness instructor, who was obsessed with making women suffer. Horribly. But their bodies, well, the bodies. Let's just say, all three women had abs that could repel bullets.

Vira begged me not to say anything to Gunther, so naturally I extracted a promise that we could join said group in return for our silence.

Skye Chat
phoebethompson
Do we really need to add this strange new ritual to our daily lives? I barely make it to yoga as it is.

crystalwalker
Vira said she only did yoga until she hit a critical age (not revealed), when only extreme measures will apparently keep all the body parts in their place. Especially when you want to attract a potential new mate.

phoebethompson
Do you know if she's seeing anyone these days?

crystalwalker
She mentioned the need to get toned for a special someone but wasn't "ready" to divulge who this person is. You know I have my suspicions about her designs on your husband.

phoebethompson
Brad hasn't shaved in weeks. I find it impossible to believe he's the object of anyone's affections.

crystalwalker
I'm not sure you've noticed, but your husband has become quite the darling of the stay-at-home moms in the 'hood. I think it's his genuinely sweet manner with all the neighborhood kids. Several of them, including Bitsy have even taken to wearing makeup to the bus stop in the mornings, and I don't think they are just following your example.

BTW, have you seen the size of George's tummy lately? They don't call it pork barrel politics for nothing, I guess.

phoebethompson
Meanwhile, you and I are expected to look as good at 50 as they did at 30 just to stay married, forget about to get a date. Speaking of which, I assume you have put Daphne's class on the Goggle calendar for us both. When do we start?

crystalwalker
Tomorrow @ 7am. See you then!

Friday, January 25

Text from Crystal to Phoebe
Question: when is a middle-aged woman not exercising?

Text from Phoebe to Crystal
Answer: when she's dead.

Text from Crystal to Phoebe
Same time tomorrow?

Text from Phoebe to Crystal
CU then.

Monday, January 28

Posting on Village Listserv, along with email attachment
From: ishop4snobs@perkybydesign.com:
If anyone recognizes the man in this photograph, please contact me asap. He is a conman who has committed a major fraud against me and my family, and must be apprehended.

From: phoebegb@channel8news.com
To: crystalmomof4exlaw@yahoo.com
FW: Just when you think you are the only ones in the Village with money problems

Heard on the grapevine that Perky and her husband are having money problems, so they rented their house to some phony British diplomat for the Inauguration, and agreed to cater a huge party for him. Naturally, the check bounced, and they have no way to track him down. Apparently, what hurts Perky the most, aside from the unfortunate threat of foreclosure, is that she agreed to dress up as a French maid and wait on his guests.

Guess this is why she has gone back to interior decorating, while Mummy and Daddy look for a new house for her to live in, and also possibly a new mate.

From: crystalmomof4exlaw@yahoo.com
To: phoebegb@channel8news.com
Re: Just when you think you are the only ones in the Village with money problems

I heard the Brown family from Boston also just skipped town, leaving the $4m house they just bought in foreclosure, and all their furniture on the street. You might have noticed the villagers swarming over there for the impromptu yard sale being hosted by the bank.

Naturally, I feel sorry for them, but my thrifty mid-Western head tells me we must go. How soon can you knock-off work?

Text from Phoebe to Crystal
On my way.

Wednesday, January 30

From: phoebegb@channel8news.com
To: crystalmomof4exlaw@yahoo.com
Any chance you're awake? It's just that I came home from work early today and discovered Vira sitting on my living room sofa with Brad, drinking a bottle of wine together. At 3 o'clock in the afternoon! Judging by Vira's puffy face and the mascara streaks on Brad's freshly laundered and pressed white shirt (did I mention he's become an expert at ironing?), she had been sobbing, and my husband had provided the requisite manly shoulder to cry on.

When Vira saw the look on my face, she immediately blurted out that she couldn't bear the idea that Tom was about to have another baby, while time was running out for her. And that you, dear C, just had too many children to be available to meet her emotional needs on a midweek afternoon. Needless to say, Brad just sat there like the proverbial deer in headlights, although I did notice that he had removed the Hugglet and shaved. But I could tell from the doe-like expression in his eyes that he would just love to provide Vira with the solution to all her problems, if given half the chance.

Not sure what I would have done, if the twins hadn't walked in just then, complaining loudly that their father had forgotten to pick them up at the bus-stop and provide them with the customary snack to sustain them on the ten yard walk home. As it was, I summoned my last remaining ounce of self-control to inquire if Vira would like to stay for tea with me and the girls (pointedly leaving out Brad). Of course, she couldn't get out of there fast enough, claiming she had some kind of womb-centering appointment downtown. But judging by the way Brad and the twins also scattered, I think I got the point across.

I can't believe Brad would contemplate cheating on me when I am so busy working to keep a roof over our heads. Too upset to talk to him about it right now, and he's skulking in the family room playing Vbox, anyway. I know it's late, but is there any chance you could join me for a drink down at the Village Lounge, so we can discuss?

Text from Crystal to Phoebe
Hilary sleeping over again while George out of town (again), so will wear coat over PJs to avoid waking her up. Can you pick me up in 5?

Text from Phoebe to Crystal
Thank you. Btw, didn't realize you and HM were sharing a bed these days.

Text from Crystal to Phoebe
With 4 cherubs at home, guest room = not an option. See u soon.

DC Diary

The Walkers Take on the Nation's Capital

1st month as a stay-at-home mom, retaining my sanity

Well, it's been another historic month here in DC - and not just because of the Inauguration. :) I have just finished my first month as a stay-at-home mom, and believe it or not, I am beginning to like it. Between shuttling the kids to their various after-school activities and appointments, working on their private school applications, and embarking on an exciting room by room renovation of our house, I frankly don't know how I ever had time to work.

Room by room we will get there!

The kitchen is getting close to done.

I'm hoping things will calm down soon, and that I can start to carve something for me, but in the meantime, I'm focusing on getting the kids into a good school, our family into the Village Country Club, and retaining my sanity at the end of the day. Wonder if the First Lady ever feels the same way? :)

Comment as: Select profile ...

Publish   Preview

Thursday, January 31

DC Diary
1st month as a stay-at-home mom, retaining my sanity

Well, it's been another historic month here in DC - and not just because of the Inauguration. :) I have just finished my first month as a stay-at-home mom, and believe it or not, I am beginning to like it. Between shuttling the kids to their various after-school activities and appointments, working on their private school applications, and embarking on an exciting room by room renovation of our house, I frankly don't know how I ever had time to work.

I'm hoping things will calm down soon, and that I can start to carve something for me, but in the meantime, I'm focusing on getting the kids into a good school, our family into the Village Country Club, and retaining my sanity at the end of the day. Wonder if the First Lady ever feels the same way? ;)

Chapter 7

February, 2013 Vol. 42, Issue 2
Always FREE, but donations appreciated

Please direct submissions and inquiries to:
whining@villagepress.com
P.O. Box 357 Village Town, MD

VILLAGE WHINER

Your trusty monthly newsletter of
the "Most Livable Village," 1989
Village Times Magazine

Update on Village Speed Bumps

The Board of Managers will be hosting an emergency monthly meeting starting at 7pm on Thursday, February 5th to vote on installing additional speed bumps on Lasham and Church Streets.

Residents are asked to refrain from the kind of name-calling and accusations that have characterized such discussions in the past. (Please see Miss Gertrude's Guide to Mannerly Meetings below as a reference). The meeting will adjourn promptly at 11pm, whether or not everyone attending has had a chance to speak.

The Board of Village Managers will also vote on a proposal to pay for another police officer to join the Village Police force, in addition to the three elite officers on Special Ops. Several residents have questioned the need for an extra officer, given that only one crime was reported in the Village over the past twelve months. The Board feels strongly that this outstanding record owes a great deal to the number of officers we already have on hand, as well as our zero tolerance policy towards loitering. A vote by show of hands on this proposal will take place at the end of the evening. Please note: all current Village officers will be in attendance.

CAUTION SPEED BUMP

Village Tennis Team

With the new USTA tennis season starting up, we'd like to welcome the two newest members of the Ladies Tennis Team.

Phoebe Thompson and Bitsy Bottomley already knocked off our number one pair, Perky Sparks and Pookie Granger in a nail biter of a match back in December. According to eye-witness accounts, Bitsy appeared to demonstrate particular focus in dispatching her former partner, slamming the ball into Pookie at the net in a way that looked, at times, almost personal. In what coach Xavier later described at "two grueling hours of airball," Bitsy and Phoebe eked out a third set tiebreak, winning against our intrepid number one pair, winning the match 5-7, 7-5, 1-0, and claiming their slot on the team, at least until challenge season next year.

The Gentlemen's Tennis team also managed to schedule and play its first match against Forest Hill Country Club in Glenbrook. Unfortunately, our men's team vastly overestimated its prowess in ranking themselves as 5.0 players, which meant they found themselves pitted against some of the strongest hitters on the senior circuit, including at least one former Wimbledon champion. The results below are not pretty, but we trust this will teach them to acquire some much needed humility before they step out on the court again. Who knows, they might even bother to practice!

Gentlemen's First Pair: 0-6, Retired due to ankle injury
Gentlemen's Second Pair: 0-6 Retired due to fatigue
Gentlemen's Third Pair: Retired as soon as they saw opponents

Miss Gertrude

Miss Gertrude has been frankly shocked and appalled at the behavior of some Village residents at a number of recent monthly board meetings. Since when has it become acceptable to heckle a speaker before their even open their mouth? Or, like a fellow resident as a "vicious old bat who is obsessed with destroying everyone else's fun?" Such blatant infringement of meeting etiquette suggests a review of Miss Gertrude's Rules for Mannerly Meetings is long overdue. See below:

1. No interrupting—unless the speaker has droned on for more than 5 minutes without pause.
2. No name-calling, hair-pulling, spitting, hitting or biting. Ever.
3. No re-arranging the furniture to suit your own aesthetic agenda. One's off-spring should also not engage in boorish behavior in a bid to have everyone riled to a most amusing frenzy, simply because one accidentally started a small house fire, albeit one requiring the assistance of the Village firefighters and those of two surrounding communities. Miss Gertrude would like to remind all her readers, especially those near and dear to her, to treat one's elders with respect—or face having them endow the Special Bumps for Canine Friends Fund with one's future inheritance.
4. No heavy sighing.
5. No tears.

Above all, there should be no criticism of the chair. Your years of experience as ambassador to Diplomats, or chief negotiator for the 1963 nuclear test ban treaty may indeed mean that you know how to run a meeting better than this day, but please keep this information to yourself.

Also, in case Miss Manners did not make it clear, these rules should apply to all discussions, whether in the domestic and public sphere...

Village Diversity Group

The Village Diversity Group will be conducting a survey to assess the needs of our senior citizens this month. The survey is designed to explore ways in which we can all pitch, gather as a community to help our older neighbors "age in place" at home, rather than a nursing home, where all of us stand to lose out on the benefit of their wisdom and guidance. Help can be as simple as replacing a most occasional doctor visit or grocery run, or volunteering to read a book to a neighbor whose sight is failing. Or, as the image to the left depicts, helping our seniors learn self-defense techniques for use on the potentially mean streets of the Village (one never knows!).

If you would like to be part of the 'Village Elders' steering committee, please email info@handofcranks.com

Local Business News

The Village's first and very own cup cakery opens this month! The Village Cake Shoppe will offer a selection of handmade cupcakes, painstakingly baked and decorated by our very own Pookie Granger and Perky Sparks. Their cupcakes will be bigger, better and more beautiful than anyone else's—and use a silicone mold in sight (at least when it comes to the cakes). Regular cupcakes $5 each. Custom designs and extra frosting are available for an extra fee. For more information, please email fantgsterymeadofcupcakesalready@gmail.com.

Update on Village Speed Humps

The Board of Managers will be hosting an emergency monthly meeting starting at 7pm on Thursday, February 5th to vote on installing additional speed humps on Eastham and Church Streets.

Residents are asked to refrain from the kind of name-calling and accusations that have characterized such discussions in the past. (Please see Miss Gertrude's Guide to Mannerly Meetings below as a reference). The meeting will adjourn promptly at 11pm, whether or not everyone attending has had a chance to speak.

The Board of Village Managers will also vote on a proposal to pay for another police officer to join the Village Police force, in addition to the three elite officers in Special Ops. Several residents have questioned the need for an extra officer, given that only one crime was reported in the Village over the past twelve months. The Board feels strongly that this outstanding record owes a great deal to the number of officers we already have on hand, as well as our zero tolerance policy towards loitering. A vote by show of hands on this proposal will take place at the end of the evening. Please note: all current Village officers will be in attendance.

Miss Gertrude

Miss Gertrude has been frankly shocked and appalled at the behavior of some Village residents at a number of recent monthly board meetings. Since when has it become acceptable to heckle a speaker before they even open their mouth? Or describe a fellow resident as a 'vicious old bat who is obsessed with destroying everyone else's fun'? Such blatant infringement of meeting etiquette suggests a review of Miss Gertrude's Rules for Mannerly Meetings is long overdue. They are as follows:

1. No interrupting - unless the speaker has droned on for more than 5 minutes without pause
2. No name calling, hair pulling, spitting, hitting or biting. Ever.
3. No rearranging the furniture to suit your own aesthetic
4. No heavy sighing
5. No tears

Above all, there should be no criticism of the chair. Your years of experience as ambassador to Djibouti, or chief negotiator for the 1963 nuclear test ban treaty may indeed mean that you know how to run a meeting better than they do, but please keep this information to yourself.

Also, in case Miss Manners did not make it clear, these rules should apply to all discussions, whether in the domestic and public sphere. One's offspring should also not engage in boorish behavior in a bid to have one removed to a nursing home, simply because one accidentally started a small house fire - albeit one requiring the assistance of the Village firefighters and those of two surrounding communities to extinguish. Miss Gertrude would like to remind all her readers, especially those near and dear to her, to treat one's elders with respect - or face having them endow the Speed Humps for Canine Friends' Fund with one's future inheritance.

Village Tennis Team

With the new USTF tennis season starting up, we'd like to welcome the two newest members of the Ladies' Tennis Team.

Phoebe Thompson and Bitsy Bottinger valiantly knocked off our number one pair, Perky Sparks and Pookie Granger in a nail biter of a match back in December. According to eye-witness accounts, Bitsy appeared to demonstrate particular focus in dispatching her former partner, slamming the ball into Pookie at the net in a way that looked, at times, almost personal. In what coach Xavier later described at 'two grueling hours of airball', Bitsy and Phoebe eked out a third set tie break win against our intrepid number one pair, winning the match 5-7, 7-5, 1-0, and claiming their slot on the team - at least until challenge season next year.

The Gentlemen's Tennis Team also managed to schedule and play its first match against Forest Hill Country Club in Glenbrook. Unfortunately, our men's team vastly overestimated its prowess in ranking themselves as 7.0 players, which meant they found themselves pitted against some of the strongest hitters on the senior circuit, including at least one former Wimbledon champion. The results below are not pretty, but we trust this will teach them to acquire some much-needed humility before they step out on the court again. Who knows, they might even bother to practice?

Gentlemen's First Pair: 0-6, Retired due to ankle injury
Gentlemen's Second Pair: 0-6 Retired due to fatigue
Gentlemen's Third Pair: Retired as soon as they saw opponents

Village Diversity Group

The Village Diversity Group will be conducting a survey to assess the needs of our senior citizens this month. The survey is designed to explore ways in which we can all pull together as a community to help our older neighbors age in place at home, rather than a nursing home, where all of us stand to lose out on the benefit of their wisdom and guidance. Help can be as simple as replacing a twist door knob with a lever (easier on arthritic hands); creating a phone tree to provide rides for the occasional doctor visit or grocery run; or volunteering to read a book to a neighbor whose sight is failing. Or, as the image below depicts, helping our seniors learn self-defense techniques for use on the potentially mean streets of the Village (one never knows!).

If you would like to be part of the 'Village Elders' steering committee, please email: **info@bandofcranks.com**.

Local Business News

The Village's first and very own cup cakery, opens this month! The Village Cake Shoppe will offer a selection of handmade cupcakes, painstakingly baked and decorated by our very own Pookie Granger and Perky Sparks. Their cupcakes will be bigger, better and more beautiful than anyone else's - and not a silicone mold in sight (at least when it comes to the cakes). Regular cupcakes $5 each. Custom designs and extra frosting are available for an extra fee. For more information, please email: **isnteveryonesickofcupcakesalready@gmail.com**.

Unlock the Secrets
of the Universe

Steamy Yoga
200 hour yoga teacher certification training
Enrollment opens March 1st

For more information,
visit ohgodhowineedinnerpeace@yahoo.com

From: phoebegb@channel8news.com
To: crystalmomof4exlaw@yahoo.com

Thanks so much for answering my cri de coeur last night. It meant a lot to know I could rely on you in an emergency, although I still had a sleepless night, tossing and turning about all the possible what-ifs.

What if it does turn out that Brad has inappropriate feelings for Vira? And what if she reciprocates? What then? Am I prepared to have my life, and the twins' turned upside down because of a foolish indiscretion on the part of a man experiencing a mid-life crisis?

I know I could NEVER forgive him, no matter how much I might be able to rationalize his behavior, so maybe it's better not to know, given that finding out might mean the end of everything. Let's face it, a divorced woman in her forties has about as much chance of being invited to your average dinner party in the Village as she has of ever fitting back into her favorite pair of pre-pregnancy jeans.

How do you think I should proceed?

Senior Affairs Reporter
Channel 8 Local News
Relentlessly local, round the clock

From: crystalmomof4exlaw@yahoo.com
To: phoebegb@channel8news.com

I'm sure a good marriage counselor would help you get to the bottom of what's really going on, but I like to keep the contact info. for DC's best divorce lawyer on hand, just in case. Forwarding below.

Fiona P. Forsythe (rumor has it, the middle initial is for 'Pitbull')
Balding + Gray, LLC
1701 Eye Street, NW
Washington DC 2005
www.webehaveunreasonablysoyoudonthaveto.com

According to Washingtonienne magazine, she's consistently voted one of DC's most likely to wear down her opponent. Good luck!

PTA Room Parent, Village Public School

From: phoebegb@channel8news.com
To: crystalmomof4exlaw@yahoo.com

Fiona has advised me to compile a list of Brad's income and our assets (Hugglet, anyone?), and let slip a couple of indiscreet details about the Browns' recent split over the phone. I can already tell that I like the woman. She's also advised me to contact a marriage counselor by the name of Pandora Chase, to demonstrate my willingness to work on the marriage. Supposedly, Pandora is the best, although I do wish she had a less ominous-sounding first name.

Senior Affairs Reporter
Channel 8 Local News
Relentlessly local, round the clock

From: crystalmomof4exlaw@yahoo.com
To: phoebegb@channel8news.com
Sounds like a good idea. Even if nothing inappropriate whatsoever has transpired between Brad and Vira, you guys have been through a lot of financial hardship together as a couple these past few months, so I'm sure there are issues that need to be addressed. Brad's refusal to shave for the past few weeks alone is alarming enough, and may start to attract the attention of Special Ops on the lookout for potential terrorists in the Village, if he's not careful.

Having said that, you might want to greet Brad at the end of a long work day with something other than, "So how's the P-NIS today darling?" I am sure your intentions are good, but I wonder how productive it is to reference a man's anatomy in the same breath you are disparaging his lack of success in selling a product named after same?

I realize all this must sound a little patronizing coming from someone whose own marriage is hardly in a much better state. I am finding it increasingly difficult not to resent George for not being here for me and the cherubs, even if I am lucky enough to have paid help. It's hard to be nice to the guy after he waltzes in from another all-expenses paid trip, while you've been up all night dealing with two cherubs who've just decided to projectile vomit in unison.

PTA Room Parent, Village Public School

From: phoebegb@channel8news.com
To: crystalmomof4exlaw@yahoo.com
Here I am going on about my own problems, and forgetting to ask about yours. Sorry. Please let me know if there's anything I can do to help.

Senior Affairs Reporter
Channel 8 Local News
Relentlessly local, round the clock

From: crystalmomof4exlaw@yahoo.com
To: phoebegb@channel8news.com
Nothing, nothing, except to please remind me that Kevin did not mean to miss the toilet when he threw up after his friend, Jason's birthday party last night, and to keep my mouth shut and not be such a b@*#$ to George all the time. No wonder he's never home!

BTW, I'm thinking of taking the yoga teacher training being offered by Gunther at Steamy Yoga next month. Hoping it will bring me the inner peace I need to deal with George and the cherubs, not to mention carve out a little corner of the world just for me. Can't say I will be thrilled to share time and space with Nina and the other likely near teen somethings prancing in their Prana pants for same, but I can't help thinking I could bring a wisdom and humility to teaching that youngsters lack.

Six months ago, if you had told me about any other stay-at-home mom contemplating such a path, I'd have judged her mercilessly. Karmic justice, perhaps?

PTA Room Parent, Village Public School

From: phoebegb@channel8news.com
To: crystalmomof4exlaw@yahoo.com
Steamy Yoga would be lucky to have you. And really, what is adult life about, if not the sobering revelation that everyone you know is full of it, including oneself?

Senior Affairs Reporter
Channel 8 Local News
Relentlessly local, round the clock

Monday February 4

Text from Phoebe to Crystal
Brad has agreed to see counselor. First emergency session tonight!

Text from Crystal to Phoebe
Have you asked if Pandora has children, or is even married herself? Thinking of making appt. for George and me, altho' taking relationship advice from someone who lacks either qualification = bit like getting military training from someone who's never been to war.

Text from Phoebe to Crystal
No idea, but will find out!

From: crystalmomof4exlaw@yahoo.com
To: jsmith@plunderhogg.com
Can you please remind my husband that he has an appointment with the urologist this afternoon at 3? I would put it on the Goggle Calendar, but I know it's harder for him to pretend he never got the reminder if it comes in the form of a physical prod from you.

PTA Room Parent, Village Public School

From: crystalmomof4exlaw@yahoo.com
To: jsmith@plunderhogg.com
That's OK. Thanks for trying. Hopefully your note under the door will do the trick, although I can't believe he is claiming to have an all day conference call and cannot by disturbed!

PTA Room Parent, Village Public School

Tuesday, February 5

From: crystalmomof4exlaw@yahoo.com
To: phoebegb@channel8news.com
Dare I ask how first session went?

PTA Room Parent, Village Public School

From: phoebegb@channel8news.com
To: crystalmomof4exlaw@yahoo.com
As well as can be expected, given that Brad spent the entire 50 mins. with his arms folded across his chest and not saying a word, leaving me to to do all the talking. It's an old trick he uses to make himself look smart, while I sound insufferable. Trust me, I do understand that other people have bigger financial problems than we do right now, even if we do seem to be the only people in the Village whose checking account is in the single digits before the end of each month.

At least Pandora thinks our problems are serious enough that we have a follow-up session later tonight.

Senior Affairs Reporter
Channel 8 Local News
Relentlessly local, round the clock

From: crystalmomof4exlaw@yahoo.com
To: phoebegb@channel8news.com
Let me know how it goes. Thinking of making a solo appointment to discuss how to get George to the urologist for his vasectomy consultation, which he missed today. There's no way I'm risking letting him breed with another woman, when we already have four cherubs of our own to raise!

PTA Room Parent, Village Public School

From: phoebegb@channel8news.com
To: crystalmomof4exlaw@yahoo.com
Tell me about it. Tried broaching the subject with Pandora, but Brad is adamant about holding onto what he likes to call his manhood. Beginning to wonder if he wants to preserve his virility for Vira. Didn't she say something about being desperate for another child?

Thank God I at least have work to distract me, although even there I do notice the difference a few years makes in terms of getting people's attention. What happened to the days when just a smile got me whatever I wanted – at least from men? These days, I'm viewed as a cranky complainer, even when I'm just pointing out issues like the lack of paper towels in the Ladies' locker room in what I think of as a helpful manner.

At least I'm discovering a new-found source of satisfaction in the exercise of power, which may be one of the few compensations for getting older. Only this morning, I sent my (male) assistant to drop the twins' urine samples off at Evelyn's lab. And to think, middle-aged men have been enjoying perks like these for millennia!

Can't imagine why you were ready to give all that up, especially as we enter the invisible years.

Senior Affairs Reporter
Channel 8 Local News
Relentlessly local, round the clock

Text from Crystal to Kevin
Y are u bothering me when Lata is here? I'm upstairs trying to book Jamaican family vacay for spring break.

Text from Crystal to Kevin
No, you can't borrow Dad's golf clubs. He has them at work. Should have thought about that b/f throwing Kim's bra on roof.

Text from Crystal to Lata
Was that Special Ops at door? Tell them we will remove underwear asap, if they agree not to fine us.

Text from Crystal to Lata
P.S. Tell Kevin to use broom handle. Also that he is grounded. Indefinitely.

From: crystalmomof4exlaw@yahoo.com
To: phoebegb@channel8news.com
Hate to bother you at work with this stuff, but do you have any recommendations for summer camps? Had no idea it was necessary to book this early, but according to Pookie at playgroup this morning, I may already be too late.

Took me FAR longer to book our flights to Jamaica than it would have done at work just now, b/c cherubs kept interrupting. At least I didn't have to keep pretending I was working at the same time.

PTA Room Parent, Village Public School

From: phoebegb@channel8news.com
To: crystalmomof4exlaw@yahoo.com
Camp Ridewell in Maine is where politicos and media types send their kids. They offer the usual – horseback riding, messing around in boats, and plenty of self-discovery in the cabins after lights out. Helps to be a legacy to get in, but Kate Kay managed it somehow (no doubt being a celebrity helps). You can check it out at www.sixweeksofhomesicknesswillbecomeyourfondestmemories. com

Senior Affairs Reporter
Channel 8 Local News
Relentlessly local, round the clock

Text from Crystal to Phoebe
Thx 4 camp recs. U do seem a tad fixated on Kate Kay these days. No worries, we can work on that in yoga.

Wednesday, February 6

Calendar Reminder from Phoebe to Brad
9am Put out trash.

Calendar Reminder from Phoebe to Brad
9.15 am Did you put out trash?

Calendar Reminder from Phoebe to Brad
9.30am Too late. Start thinking of excuse.

Posting on Village Listserv
From: ishopforsnobs@perkybydesign.com
my child was almost killed the other day by a driver who flew over the hill leading to our house, forcing my three year old's Barbie Jeep Wrangler off the road this kind of close call is an all-too-common occurrence on our block, which is why i strongly urge the Village to install speed humps on park street it's not fair that other people have them and we don't!

FIVE children live on our block, and all of them have little or no yard to play in because of all the additions we all put on during the property boom it's only a matter of time before one of our precious offspring is killed by a speeding or distracted driver, so i urge the Village to take action before it's too LATE.

From: crystalmomof4exlaw@yahoo.com
To: phoebegb@channel8news.com
FW:
doesn't perky only have one child, and isn't he a boy and hasn't she heard of punctuation or at least capital letters and isn't park st a cul-de-sac

PTA Room Parent, Village Public School

From: phoebegb@channel8news.com
To: crystalmomof4exlaw@yahoo.com
Yes, yes, no and yes. Understand the Barbie Jeep is a source of considerable tension between the parents. Husband was basically born and raised in a country club, so I don't think he has ever encountered an alternative lifestyle – at least not knowingly. God Bless Perky for sticking up for her son's predilection for all things pink.

Senior Affairs Reporter
Channel 8 Local News
Relentlessly local, round the clock

From: pookiegranger@hotmail.com
I would like to propose that parking on all Village streets be restricted to residents and members of their household staff or visitors only. And also, maybe limit the age of vehicles that can park there too?

It's all very well for non-residents to complain they sometimes need to park on our streets in order to access the Village Shoppes, but where are those of us who actually live there supposed to leave our second or third cars? And what about our service providers? It's incredibly selfish to ask a nanny with two or three children in her care to park round the corner, just so that someone who doesn't even live there can hog the space for a couple of hours.

From: chuckpalmer@aol.com
I have lived in the Village for over thirty years, and raised six kids in the one remaining house on Park Street that has not tripled in size.

This used to be a mainly Catholic community, which is why, when my kids were young, there were 147 children living on our block alone – all in houses that contained only one bathroom. All our kids played on the street, completely unsupervised, while we parents spent a great deal of time inside drinking. Yet somehow most of our children survived to adulthood more or less unscathed – at least physically. And please don't tell me times have changed. The most recent traffic study conducted by the Village in 2008 showed that out of 11,000 passing cars on Park St., not one was speeding.

I would also remind residents in question that county tax dollars were used to pay for Village road construction and maintenance, and that roads are a public good, not your personal private property. The parking space in front of your house does not belong to you! The fact that the average Village matron now requires an army of domestic staff and attendant vehicles to raise and transport her children is not our problem.

I urge the Board of Managers NOT to cave into this brand of 'squeaky wheel' politics, which has only become more shrill with the introduction of the Village listserv, and to oppose the motions described above. Nobody has the time or inclination to attend every monthly meeting in order to fend off every outrageous misappropriation of public property, but this does not mean the crazies should win.

From: perkysparks@perkybydesign.com
i find the tone of Mr. Palmer's remarks patronizing in the extreme in case he hasn't noticed, almost 3/4 of women with school-age children (including myself) now work, so they actually need the nanny and the housekeeper of which he so obviously disapproves the fact that stay at home moms also require help, in order to seek fulfillment through excessive exercising, shopping or affairs is IRRELEVANT just how many deaths would it take for you to recognize that times have changed there are far more cars on the road these days – not to mention motorists distracted by texting or email while they drive i ask you to look into my son's eyes and tell him he doesn't deserve to live long enough to drive the miniature backhoe we were planning on giving him for his next birthday just because you prefer to rely on mere statistics rather than doing what it takes to ensure the SURVIVAL of our youngest citizens

From: The Board of Managers
The Village Board of Managers has taken the precaution of shutting down the Village listserv to allow tempers to cool before tomorrow night's meeting.

Special Ops will be under strict instructions to summarily eject anyone who does not abide by Miss Gertrude's Guidelines for Mannerly Meetings, as outlined in the most recent Village newsletter.

Thursday, February 7

Goggle Calendar Reminder from Phoebe to Brad
2.15pm Leave to pick-up Cecily and Emily early from school for their quarterly check-up at the dentist. Remember, traffic on Connecticut Avenue is impossible after 3.15, so you should probably just stay for the duration.

Goggle Calendar Reminder from Phoebe to Brad
Drop Cecily and Emily at basketball practice.

Goggle Calendar Reminder from Phoebe to Brad
5.30pm Pick up Cecily and Emily and prepare dinner. I will be home by 7 tonight, but remember to feed twins no later than 6, so they are not tempted to snack beforehand. I've noticed a few extra dimples in their cheeks lately.

Goggle Calendar Reminder from Phoebe to Brad
7pm Speed Hump meeting at Village Hall. Don't forget, if Perky gets one, I want one too!

Goggle Calendar Reminder from Phoebe to Brad
7.30pm Oops. Forgot about appointment with Pandora. Guess speed hump will have to wait.

Skye chat
phoebethompson
Was that a Cake Shoppe cupcake I spotted in the girls' hands when they Skyped me at work just now? What did I remind you about no snacking b/f dinner? Those things have 400 calories each, not to mention 23grams of sugar!

phoebethompson
Oops, thought Dad was online. So glad you had fun at practice today, darlings. I'm sure the cupcakes were delicious, but remember what I told you about food pushers. Just because Mrs. Granger offers you a gigantic, delicious-looking sugary treat covered in sprinkles doesn't mean you have to take it. It's OK to say no, just like I expect you to when it comes to drugs or offers of money to lift up your shirt on spring break at college. Remember, I want you to grow up to be strong women, not girly people pleasers!

Text from Phoebe to Brad
Pookie trying to sabotage twins for Evelyn's food study. DON'T let twins eat her cupcakes in future. Bet her precious offspring didn't eat a thing.

Text from Phoebe to Brad
How convenient all 3 of her kids = allergic to wheat. I rest my case.

Friday, February 8

Posting on Village Listserv
The Village Board has voted unanimously to install speed humps on Eastham, Church and Park Streets, effective immediately, in spite of some spirited opposition from resident Charles Palmer. While Mr. Palmer certainly had statistics and fiscal prudence on his side, the organized lie-in by the toddlers from playgroup ultimately persuaded the board that we should not be gambling with our children's lives.

Special Ops is standing by to deal with any potential trouble-makers while construction is underway.

From: phoebegb@channel8news.com
To: crystalmomof4exlaw@yahoo.com
Do you think Pandora was right to say I should stop nagging Brad so much at our appointment last night?

She specifically recommended I NOT expect him to have the house clean, the twins bathed and a nutritious dinner on the table by the time I arrive home from work – even though that is precisely what men have enjoyed since the invention of the housewife. Her exact words were: "He's working too," as if the hours he spends surfing the web while they are at school could be called that!

Meanwhile, I'm expected to hold down a full-time job, spend quality time with my children, manage all family and household needs, exercise and engage in the kind of extreme grooming required to look decent on screen and somehow miraculously halt the relentless march of time – while Brad gets to relax on the sofa eating ice-cream. How is that fair?

I know my mother would tell me to bite my tongue and play nice, or risk pushing him further into Vira's arms, but I fear I am temperamentally unable to keep my mouth shut.

Senior Affairs Reporter
Channel 8 Local News
Relentlessly local, round the clock

From: crystalmomof4exlaw@yahoo.com
To: phoebegb@channel8news.com
Tell me about it.

George has put on almost 20lbs since moving to DC – most of it from expense account lunches and dinners. I realize this must be an occupational hazard for a lobbyist, but it's hard for me not to comment when he pops another button on his pants while I'm working my ass off to lose the baby weight and somehow look like a 22 year old after 4 kids and 12 years of marriage.

If it's any comfort, however, you do realize that all men are the same? So unless you plan to remain celibate, or turn lesbian, there is no point in trading. I also know from experience that divorce sucks, no matter whether or not you arrived there on principle.

PTA Room Parent, Village Public School

From: phoebegb@channel8news.com
To: crystalmomof4exlaw@yahoo.com
I dare say you are right. Remind me to work on coming back as a man in my next incarnation. I think it helps if I make it my intention in yoga class.

Senior Affairs Reporter
Channel 8 Local News
Relentlessly local, round the clock

Saturday, February 9

From: crystalmomof4exlaw@yahoo.com
To: phoebegb@channel8news.com
Hosting a little soiree to invite some ladies from the Club to show off my new sofas, which have FINALLY arrived, in the hopes of impressing Pookie et al with how far the Walker family has come in the world before the next prospective member cocktail party.

Also planning to use the occasion to give Hilary a discreet makeover at the same time. Think she could really look quite stunning, if only someone could tackle the hint of monobrow, and banish the sensible Danish sandals for a pair of decent heels, so I've hired an eyebrow specialist, who goes by the name of Flavi for the occasion. I used to think Pookie's permanently startled expression was the result of a mood disorder, but now gather it is Flavi's signature look. Pookie told me her husband continues to like an element of surprise in their marriage and the shape of her brows helps him nurture the thought that she is stunned by his physical presence each time he enters into her line of vision.

Fingers crossed Flavi will give Hils just the lift she needs to find that special someone, now that her divorce has come through.

Hope you can join!

PTA Room Parent, Village Public School

> Banish Those Post-Inauguration Blues Party
> Host: Crystal Walker
> Location: 5500 Park St.
> Date: Wednesday, February 13
> Time: 7pm
> Attire: Whatever you wore for the Inauguration
> Cocktails and Canapes Served
>
> Will you attend?

_ Yes

_ No

_ Maybe

Why Not? _____

From: phoebegb@channel8news.com
To: crystalmomof4exlaw.com
Wouldn't miss! How clever of you to secure Flavi for the evening. As a matter of fact, my slightly ironic arch is also her handiwork. She suggested I cultivate a slightly skeptical expression whenever I'm interviewing a politician, and I'm told the results have raised my credibility levels among the station's focus groups, although Brad claims I now remind him more than ever of my mother.

A word of warning, however: you do realize that obvious make-up and high fashion are frowned upon here in DC, where the average career woman dresses to be taken seriously, not to bed. This holds doubly true for the principals of private schools like Seton, who are considered only marginally less important than POTUS himself. Loathe as I am to follow these restrictions myself, I would strongly advise you to refrain from doing anything that might inadvertently destroy Hilary Manning's credibility, like turning her into a sex kitten.

Senior Affairs Reporter
Channel 8 Local News
Relentlessly local, round the clock

From: crystalmomof4exlaw.com
To: phoebegb@channel8news.com
Oops – too late. Hilary is thrilled by the idea, which just goes to support my theory that inside every judgmental DC matron, a frustrated beauty pageant contestant is just waiting to burst out.

PTA Room Parent, Village Public School

From: phoebegb@channel8news.com
To: crystalmomof4exlaw@yahoo.com
Fair enough, but my personal eyebrow design holds an inviolable trademark and it will be enforced. And I hate to mention it but I think Pookie's design may be enhanced by a little filler as her natural brow didn't have enough "body" to make the cut so to speak (not that I'm bragging about mine, of course—well, maybe just a touch).

Senior Affairs Reporter
Channel 8 Local News
Relentlessly local, round the clock

Sunday, February 10

From: phoebegb@channel8news.com
To: crystalmomof4exlaw@yahoo.com

Brad wants to up our sessions with Pandora to twice a week! That's 2 x $275, or almost one Trashy Couture dress a week, as I pointed out at our last session. Of course, that just led to an ugly discussion of my wardrobe choices. Do you know the woman actually had the temerity to claim that I dress inappropriately young for my age? So now I'm apparently supposed to take wardrobe advice from a woman whose idea of fashion is to wear a turtleneck under her homemade sweater. Hard to imagine she was able to snag one husband in that kind of attire, let alone four (she is currently going through her latest divorce).

I've told Brad to cancel his replacement crown at the dentist tomorrow in retaliation, as we just can't afford the extra $1k out of the monthly household budget right now. If necessary, he can claim British citizenship. Meanwhile, duty calls. My newsroom is about to attempt a reenactment of the explosive adult diaper failures that have local seniors literally knee deep in despair.

Senior Affairs Reporter
Channel 8 Local News
Relentlessly local, round the clock

Text from Crystal to George
Did you remember to complete all the Camp Ridewell health forms, like you promised? Deadline is today.

Witter from femilawyermom
What do you do with a husband who promised to fill out his children's medical forms, then conveniently forgets? Spank him? Schedule him for a colonoscopy? Or book him in for a vasectomy, but tell him it's just a consultation?

Spankme is now following femilawyermom
Getyourprobeon is now following femilawyermom
Banthesnipnow is now following femilawyermom

From: crystalmomof4exlaw@yahoo.com
To: phoebegb@channel8news.com
I know I should be grateful that George is gainfully employed these days, when so many others are out of work. But he's almost never home to help with anything, while it sometimes feels like my life is getting sucked away in all the petty details. I know someone has to do it, and G. doesn't have time, but will anyone ultimately remember that I was great at filling out camp forms and making sure the cherubs had all their check-ups after I am gone? Thank God I have Steamy Yoga!

PTA Room Parent, Village Public School

From: phoebegb@channel8news.com
To: crystalmomof4exlaw@yahoo.com
I suspect the only people who will ever recognize and appreciate what we did with our lives are our girlfriends, which is why we must always put them first.

Besides, husbands and children come and go, but I am counting on you to hit on all the young orderlies with me at the nursing home.

Senior Affairs Reporter
Channel 8 Local News
Relentlessly local, round the clock

From: crystalmomof4exlaw.com
To: phoebegb@channel8news.com
Count on it.

PTA Room Parent, Village Public School

Text from Phoebe to Brad
Can't make tonight's session with Pandora b/c of work, so you'll just have to go alone. Good luck!

Monday, February 11

Posting on the Village Listserv
The Village Public School will be closed today, due to the snow.

Please note, the Village snowplow is also currently under repair for damage incurred when it inadvertently hit the speed hump on Center Street early this morning. The late Tinkelpaw's remains were also disturbed during the incident in question. The Village has already agreed to underwrite the full cost of her reburial, including a replacement tutu for her to wear, and a new pink coffin. The repair to the snowplow may take several weeks, so residents are asked to refrain from calling the office in the interim, demanding to know why their street has not been cleared. We will let you know as soon as the snowplow is operational again.

Mebook Posting from Crystal
Walker family driveway appears to have become the designated sledding hill for the entire Village. It's a lot of fun – for about five minutes in 20 degree weather outside. Baby and I have now retired to the living room to make hot chocolate (for me) and warm breast milk (for her) by the fire. Rest of the cherubs and their friends now in the basement making s'mores. Parents welcome to collect anytime!

Text message from Crystal to Phoebe
Any idea how to remove melted marshmallow from sofa cushions, carpet and fake rocks in gas fire?

Text message from Phoebe to Crystal
Yikes. Suggest ask Lata.

Text message from Crystal to Phoebe
Lata threatening to quit unless all unrelated children leave NOW. Beginning to feel same way myself.

Text message from P mobile to Brad
Please pick up Cecily and Emily from C's ASAP. Sounds like may have outstayed welcome.

Text message from Crystal to Kevin and Kimberly
PLEASE REMOVE EVERY LAST TRACE OF MARSHMALLOW FROM BASEMENT BEFORE LATA LEAVES. OR I DO.

Text message from Crystal to Kevin and Kimberly
Gone to lie down in a dark room and do NOT want to be disturbed for next 20 mins. Did you really have to use Karson's toothbrush to tackle the hard to reach areas?

From: phoebegb@channel8news.com
To: crystalmomof4exlaw@yahoo.com
BTW, sorry I couldn't join you at yoga this morning. Pandora has insisted my wifely duty comes first, no matter what else has to happen that day – or what I would rather be doing. Finding it hard not to resent the additional imposition on my time, but her recommendation (whispered privately) is to check it off as a completed item on the to-do list, which helps. That, and making sure Brad and I practiced a vigorous flow sequence involving galloping pony pose.

See you bright and early for Daphne.

Senior Affairs Reporter
Channel 8 Local News
Relentlessly local, round the clock

Tuesday, February 12

Text from Phoebe to Brad
Please don't let Cecily and Emily leave the house with wet hair this morning. As a matter of fact, I really think you should drive them to school. It is 22 degrees and icy outside right now.

Text from Crystal to Phoebe
No idea how u functioned at work today. I can baRely move my arms to typE.

Text from Phoebe to Crystal
Took a little snooze in the loo at lunch. Btw, please don't mention Daphne's

class to Brad. Wd prefer him to think I'm getting an early start at the office.

Text from Crystal to Phoebe
My lips are sealed. The woman is clearly a sadist under that perfect body and winning smile. Same time next week?

Text from Phoebe to Crystal
Wouldn't miss.

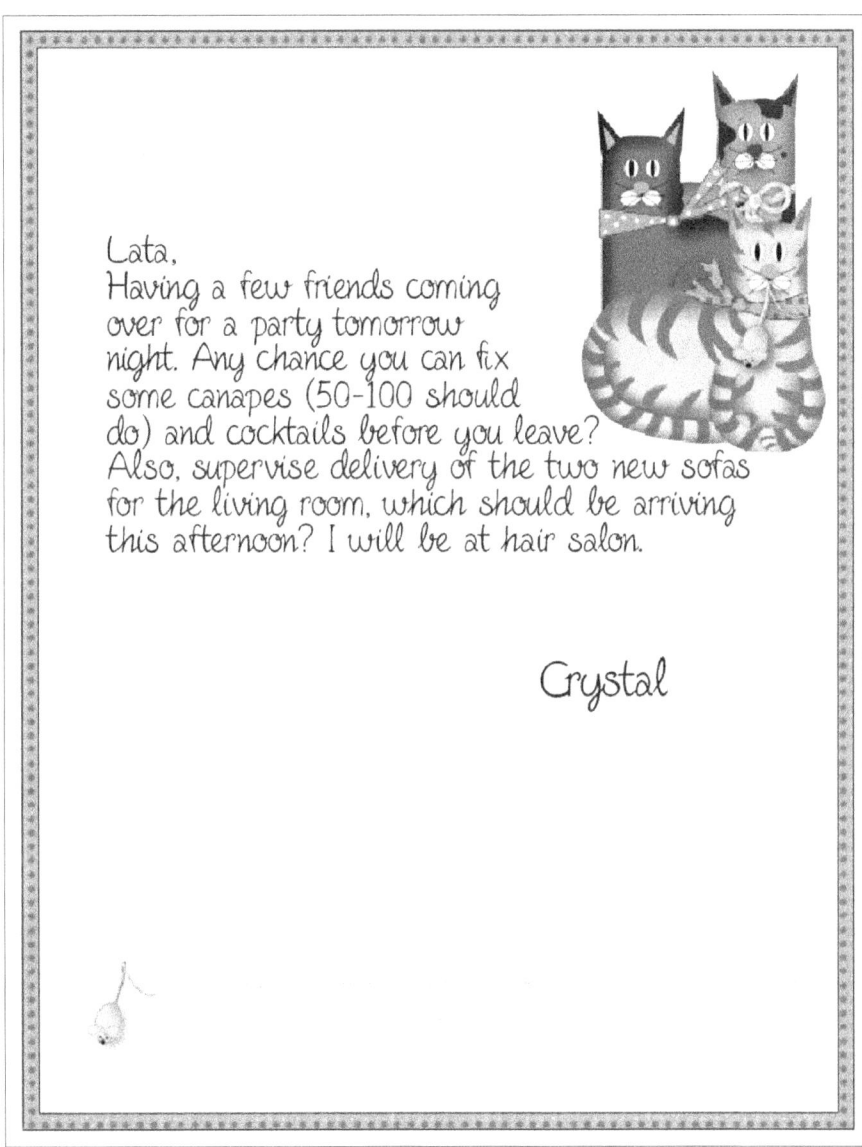

Lata,
Having a few friends coming over for a party tomorrow night. Any chance you can fix some canapes (50-100 should do) and cocktails before you leave? Also, supervise delivery of the two new sofas for the living room, which should be arriving this afternoon? I will be at hair salon.

Crystal

Text from Crystal to Lata
Of course you may have Monday morning off for your dr.'s appointment. Thanks for help with party. You are a godsend!

Wednesday, February 13

Text from Crystal to Phoebe
At hospital with Karson after he slipped on ice in driveway this morning. Pls thank Brad for making sure Kev and Kim made it onto bus.

Text from Phoebe to Crystal
Everything OK?

Text from Crystal to Phoebe
No concussion, thankfully. Hilary joined me at ER and insisted on plastic surgeon for Karson's stitches, to avoid a scar. Think I may be in love with the woman.

Text from Phoebe to Crystal
Sorry I couldn't B there 4U, but work = crazy. Where is George?

Text from Crystal to Phoebe
Good question. Didn't occur to me to call, since he's never available anyway. Is that wrong?

Thursday, February 14

From: phoebegb@channel8news.com
To: crystalmomof4exlaw@yahoo.com
Thank you for such a fun evening yesterday.

Your new sofas are quite literally stunning! And such an unusual shape. My mother's steak and kidney pie will never taste quite the same ever again.

Vira looked fabulous even without a trace of makeup, but I barely recognized either Evelyn or Hilary after Flavi was done shaping their brows. Hilary seemed particularly thrilled with the results, judging by the way she planted that lipstick smudge on your cheek.

Pookie also cleans up surprisingly well. Don't think I've ever seen her outside of her tennis clothes. I already knew she had good legs, but that micro mini really showed them off to great effect. Of course, she did have to point out that it belonged to her 13 year old daughter, and that she would never normally be caught dead wearing anything so trashy – even though both your dress and mine were shorter still. I fear there's really nothing to be done except embrace our inner teen.

Happy Valentine's Day, if we don't see each other later today. Not sure why I persist in testing Brad to see if he remembers, which he never does, but at this point, it's a habit. At least I know now to book an emergency mani-pedi for the afternoon to cope with the inevitable let-down.

Senior Affairs Reporter
Channel 8 Local News
Relentlessly local, round the clock

From: crystalmomof4exlaw@yahoo.com
To: phoebegb@channel8news.com

Glad you like the sofas, but George is apoplectic. Says it's impossible to stretch out and watch the game on a piece of furniture that lacks arms and curves in the middle. Naturally, Perky was horrified at the thought of him kicking back with a beer, since she claims these sofas are objets d'art, not objets de lounging. Good thing I didn't tell him about the cost, since George simply has no idea what it takes to keep up appearances round here. I don't need to hear him drone on and on about how each one of the sofas is more expensive than his first car.

Valentine's Day happens to be our wedding anniversary, but George has a dinner tonight, so we plan to celebrate tomorrow. We always try and keep it low key anyway – don't want Kevin to do the math and figure out that we've only been married for 12 of the 13 years he's been alive.

PTA Room Parent, Village Public School

PLEASE JOIN US IN SUPPORT OF

The 2010 Shambleton Expedition

TUESDAY, FEBRUARY 26TH 6:30 – 8:00 P.M.

Cocktails and light hors d'oeuvres will be served
Jackets and ties for gentlemen; cocktail dresses for Ladies. No miniskirts, please!

The pleasure of your company is requested to meet my second cousin, Kurt Shambleton, Explorer, Harvard Professor of Heroic Failures and one of the most extraordinary people I know. Kurt plans to re-create our great grandfather's epic journey across the Arctic - a journey that is celebrated for the way Grandpapa was able to save the men, dogs and pet cockatoo on his expedition from near starvation, even if they ultimately never made it to the North Pole.* Kurt has been voted one of the World's Most Beautiful Narcissists, by US magazine, but insists his expeditions are not about raising money to finance his own personal pipe dreams, but about raising awareness of environmental issues across the globe. The 2010 Anniversary Shambleton Expedition team will use a replica of Shambleton's original boat, the Albatross, along with a team of golden retrievers, a compass and a whistle.

"They soldiered on in sandals but my god, they refused to give up, even as others sled past them"

R.S.V.P.
Pookie Granger
301-555-5555
pookiegranger@hotmail.com
Journey's End, Park Street, The Village

*NOBODY REMEMBERS THE NAME OF THE NORWEGIAN EXPLORER WHO ULTIMATELY CONQUERED THE POLE AND MADE IT HOME IN TIME FOR PICKLED HERRING

Text from Crystal to Phoebe
Trust you got Pookie's invitation – hand-delivered just now. Think it's meant to send a message? Some parties are worthier than others?

Text from Phoebe to Crystal
Maybe, but definitely won't be as fun.

Roses are Red
Violets are Blue
Just go for the Snip,
And I'll sleep with you

Happy Anniversary,
Darling!

Can you believe
it's been 12 years?

Love, Crystal

Friday, February 15

Skye Chat
phoebethompson
Happy Belated Anniversary! How are you guys celebrating?

crystalwalker
George has gone golfing, of course, so I'm home alone with all 4 cherubs, icing cupcakes for all their class parties. Hold on, someone's at the door..

phoebethompson
Everything OK?

crystalwalker
Yes. It was just the florist delivering the biggest bunch of roses I've ever seen. Very excited. Can't believe George actually……oh wait, they are from Hilary! Sent her a small bouquet earlier, in case she was feeling lonely on her first Valentine's Day as a divorcee, but this is WAY over the top.

phoebethompson
If I were you, I would lose the card and claim they are from a secret admirer. It's always good for husbands to see their wives are still considered desirable.

From: crystalmomof4exlaw@yahoo.com
To: gwalker@plunderhogg.com
Darling, I'm so touched! These are the most beautiful flowers I've ever seen. I'll consider an exception to my new no snip, no sex policy, so long as you make dinner reservations for our belated anniversary/Valentine's Day celebration. xc

Text from Crystal to George
Centrale sounds perfect. I'll make a reservation for 7. xc

Text from Crystal to George
Where ru? I've been here for 1/2 an hour now, and the maitre d' is starting to give me dirty looks.

Text from Crystal to George
What do you mean you can't make it? How can a meeting with Senator from Arkansas about preserving tax breaks be more important??

Text from Crystal to Phoebe
My husband is dead to me. Any chance you might be willing to be my dinner date instead?

Text from Phoebe to Crystal
Would love to, but MIL just invited me to dinner. Seems Brad's father forgot VD also.

Text from Crystal to Phoebe

No prob. Hilary has agreed to come. At least we can count on the women in our lives. Bon Appetit!

Saturday, February 16

From: crystalmomof4exlaw@yahoo.com
To: phoebegb@channel8news.com
Help!

In a bit of a dilemma and wonder if I might ask for your good judgment and utmost discretion in the matter. Had the most delightful evening with Hilary last night, but think she may have the wrong idea about our relationship. I know I come across as friendly and approachable, which is one of the things I like to think we just do better in the midwest. But this time, it looks like I may have gotten myself in deeper than I intended.

Just as I was touching up her new lip liner in the powder room last night after dinner, Hilary took the opportunity to kiss me. And I don't mean the usual European "mwah, mwah" cheek to cheek air kiss I've learned to master since meeting you, dear P. It was full on the lips and try for a little tongue — an action in which I was a surprised but not entirely unhappy participant. Soon afterwards, I made my excuses and hurried home on the pretext of saying good night to the cherubs.

I confess that I came away feeling guilty —but also intrigued. Kissing Hilary simply didn't feel inappropriate the way, say, kissing Brad clearly would. I also know that George would probably find the idea of me making lip contact with another woman quite exciting and might even want to join in. But I need to know what you think. First, is it really possible that Hilary is a lesbian? She was married for more than a decade, but I guess that doesn't necessarily mean anything. I'm also pretty sure I'm not attracted to women – at least not physically. But frankly, George has been so distant both physically and emotionally of late, I'm beginning to wonder if I wouldn't be happier with someone who seems to be there for me, in every sense of the word.

Hard to think straight, with all four cherubs off school in honor of President's Day weekend, and no sign of George, who seems to be in full crisis mode, trying to prevent any changes to his clients' precious tax loopholes. But as someone who has surely encountered some of these same feelings during your time at boarding school, I would appreciate your advice. Am I just experiencing the first pangs of a passing fancy brought on by my current situation, or could it be that I have completely misjudged my life's path?

PTA Room Parent, Village Public School

From: phoebegb@channel8news.com
To: crystalmomof4exlaw@yahoo.com
I am out of the office for President's Day and will return on Tuesday, February 19th.

Sunday, February 17

From: phoebegb@channel8news.com
To: crystalmomof4exlaw@yahoo.com
Re: Help!

So sorry for not responding sooner. Took twins skiing for the day at Ski Mountainview in PA, where there was no mePhone reception, then too exhausted to check email after I got back. Somehow, skiing was so much simpler in Aspen.

Just read your email from yesterday and can only hope your relationship with Hilary has NOT progressed in the interim. Given everything that's happening between me and Brad right now, I find it hard to believe you actually want my advice about breaking your marriage vows. Whether or not you are a lesbian, dear C, is surely irrelevant at this point in your life. Might I remind you that you somehow managed to make four cherubs with George – the last one still a babe in arms?

I would also remind you that ALL of us had dreams of the way things would be once we were adults, and all of us wonder at times how the choices we made have somehow added up to a life we never wanted in the first place. But why can't we all just suck it up and accept that this is the way things are? I think our generation still has a lot of growing up to do, and it's NOT because we are still young.

Monday, February 18

From: crystalmomof4exlaw@yahoo.com
To: phoebegb@channel8news.com

I can see it was completely insensitive of me to burden you with my own marital difficulties at a time when you have your own. But I appreciate the fact that our friendship allows for such honesty. Rest assured, I have NOT pursued the relationship with Hilary in the interim, not least because I do not want to do ANYTHING to jeopardize the cherubs' chances of getting into Seton.

Still, I can't deny that the prospect of having a life partner who is sensitive to my needs and actually involved with my children is attractive. The other day, Hilary even came with me to the doctor's for Kurtis' six month check-up! Meanwhile, George probably still thinks the pediatrician is my foot doctor.

Hilary is also unfailingly attentive to my needs, in a way that no one else in my life is (you excepted, of course). Frankly, it feels damn nice to be taken care of, after spending all day looking after the needs of others.

Having said that, I am not ready to upset the apple cart over a physical relationship I'm not sure I want. Fortunately, Hilary is away for the rest of the week, attending an educational conference in Boston, but I know she will want to take the relationship a stage further soon.

PTA Room Parent, Village Public School

RICH SIMPLICITY

The last month has truly been an enriching one, full of soul-searching and dawning self-awareness. I am learning that the True Blessings of Motherhood need not be limited to our own children, but can be extended to anyone's offspring, as I discovered just the other day when I hosted a clothing drive for pregnant, innercity teen moms.. The girls in question were so touched by the outpouring of support hose, they were Truly Grateful™, even if they were horrified at the idea of having to wear a shirt with flaps for nursing.

Puzzlingly, Tiffany does not seem to be nearly so receptive, even though she seemed to have no problem claiming Ravi as her own. When I gently pointed out the danger to our unborn fetus from her continuing to drink caffeinated green tea each morning, and offered her one of my ran straight to the bathroom to throw up - without even taking a sip! instead, she

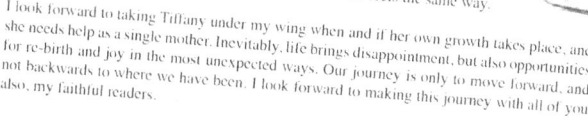

Then, I suggested a soothing belly rub using some of the FatMama poultice I happened to have with me to help her feel better, to which she finally acquiesced, albeit while muttering something under her breath about feeling too ill to argue. Unfortunately, the smell from the poultice seemed to make her only feel worse, so I have reluctantly agreed to leave her alone for a few days, or risk a restraining order.

While my own growth in this matter has been rapid and marked, I now recognize that others may not be so quick to embrace our co-parenting arrangement. Rest assured, however, I shall not give up. As Tiffany is still quite young, she understandably fails to realize that she will ultimately outgrow her much older lover, just as I did Gunther, who seems to have a new young protegee by the name of Nina in his life. Let's see how long it takes before she feels the same way.

I look forward to taking Tiffany under my wing when and if her own growth takes place, and she needs help as a single mother. Inevitably, life brings disappointment, but also opportunities for re-birth and joy in the most unexpected ways. Our journey is only to move forward, and not backwards to where we have been. I look forward to making this journey with all of you also, my faithful readers.

If you believe you are moving backwards, pause to look at my life and reflect upon the idea that thinking of others in ways they may not expect or want can change your direction in a delightful way. Don't discount that making yourself feel better, if not others, is often an unintended benefit.

To subscribe to Blessed Moments, Vira's monthly magazine, Special Offer: Subscribe for 24 months at only $3 an issue, and save 60% off the cover price!

To order a signed copy of The Blessings of Motherhood for only $24.99.

To order a batch of FatMama pregnancy poultice (only $39.99 for 8oz).

To sign-up to receive Vira's weekly newsletter via email (only $19.99 a year).

For Vira's signature Beetroot, rice milk and frozen juiuberry smoothie recipe, click here.

Thank you for visiting Rich Simplicity. We hope to see you again soon.

From: Rich Simplicity
To: phoebegb@sahmsrule.net

Rich Simplicity: A monthly newsletter bringing you a life of ultimate simplicity, no matter how much money I have.

Volume 04 Issue 02

Blessings, The last month has truly been an enriching one, full of soul-searching and dawning self-awareness. I am learning that the True Blessings of Motherhood need not be limited to our own children, but can be extended to anyone's offspring, as I discovered just the other day when I hosted a clothing drive for pregnant, inner-city teen moms.. The girls in question were so touched by the outpouring of support hose, they were Truly Grateful™, even if they were horrified at the idea of having to wear a shirt with flaps for nursing.

Puzzlingly, Tiffany does not seem to be nearly so receptive, even though she seemed to have no problem claiming Ravi as her own. When I gently pointed out the danger to our unborn fetus from her continuing to drink caffeinated green tea each morning, and offered her one of my signature beetroot, rice milk and frozen jujuberry smoothies instead, she ran straight to the bathroom to throw up - without even taking a sip!

Then, I suggested a soothing belly rub using some of the FatMama poultice I happened to have with me to help her feel better, to which she finally acquiesced, albeit while muttering something under her breath about feeling too ill to argue. Unfortunately, the smell from the poultice seemed to make her only feel worse, so I have reluctantly agreed to leave her alone for a few days, or risk a restraining order.

While my own growth in this matter has been rapid and marked, I now recognize that others may not be so quick to embrace our co-parenting arrangement. Rest assured, however, I shall not give up. As Tiffany is still quite young, she understandably fails to realize that she will ultimately outgrow her much older lover, just as I did Gunther, who seems to have a new young protegee by the name of Nina in his life. Let's see how long it takes before she feels the same way.

I look forward to taking Tiffany under my wing when and if her own growth takes place, and she needs help as a single mother. Inevitably, life brings disappointment, but also opportunities for rebirth and joy in the most unexpected ways. Our journey is only to move forward, and not backwards to where we have been. I look forward to making this journey with all of you also, my faithful readers.

Wednesday, February 20

From: crystalmomof4exlaw@yahoo.com
To: phoebegb@channel8news.com
Just got back from impromptu lunch with Vira – one of the perks of not having to head off to the office, although I did have to pretend to Lata that I had a very important meeting to attend.

You'll be glad to hear that Vira revealed that she is not interested in having a relationship right now, even though she is desperate to have another child before it's too late (rumor has it she turns forty-TWO next September). But now for the hard part. The reason Vira doesn't want to meet anyone is because she is apparently struggling with some confusing and possibly inappropriate feelings towards someone we both know. I pressed her to tell me who, dear P, but she would not reveal. But she did say that she would never act on those feelings because the person in question is married.

I THINK this means that even if Brad and Vira are engaged in some kind of emotional affair, dear P, you can rest assured that Vira, at least, has no intention of acting on it. While I do believe she means this, you might want to pay more attention to what's going on at home while you're at work, just in case.

PTA Room Parent, Village Public School

From: phoebegb@channel8news.com
To: crystalmomof4exlaw@yahoo.com
Do you really think I can trust Vira not to act on her feelings? I know I should be asking this question of Brad, but right now, I feel like I no longer understand the man. This morning, he came downstairs dressed in nothing but his stupid Hugglet, then proceeded to vacuum the entire ground floor in a way that I can only describe as passive-aggressive.

Senior Affairs Reporter
Channel 8 Local News
Relentlessly local, round the clock

From: crystalmomof4exlaw@yahoo.com
To: phoebegb@channel8news.com
That does sound disturbing. Have you discussed with Pandora?

PTA Room Parent, Village Public School

From: phoebegb@channel8news.com
To: crystalmomof4exlaw@yahoo.com
Yes, but she keeps telling me just to count my blessings. May have something to do with fact that Brad gave her some pesto at our meeting last night.

Senior Affairs Reporter
Channel 8 Local News
Relentlessly local, round the clock

Thursday, February 21

From: phoebegb@channel8news.com
To: crystalmomof4exlaw@yahoo.com
I've decided to take matters into my own hands and exchanged the set of talking scales Brad gave me by way of a belated Valentine's Day present (who needs their weight announced in four languages?) for a motion-activated security camera niftily disguised behind the façade of a bedside alarm clock.

I'm also reactivating the teddy bear cam we bought when Lata started with us in the living room. Must confess to feeling a little weird about spying on Brad while he is oblivious, and more than a little nervous about what I might find. Almost prefer not to know, to be honest.

Forgot to ask Fiona Forsythe if it would be legal to plant a camera at Vira's house, in case they decide to meet there. I know you are not a divorce lawyer, but any chance you can advise?

Senior Affairs Reporter
Channel 8 Local News

From: crystal@momof4exlaw@yahoo.com
To: phoebegb@channel8news.com
Yes, it would be illegal, not to mention unethical to spy on our friend in her house without her knowledge, but I have it on good authority that it was part of the pre-nup Vira signed with Tom that she would on no account bring a male into the house for recreational or romantic purposes while her son is still living at home. If she does, she automatically forfeits the house and all the fabulous artwork currently hanging from its walls. And judging by hints Vira has dropped on the subject, she takes holding onto those very seriously, no matter what she preaches about the Importance of Letting Go®.

PTA Room Parent, Village Public School

From: phoebegb@channel8news.com
To: crystalmomof4exlaw@yahoo.com
Alright, you have convinced me. The camera is programmed to record between the hours of nine and three, while I am out of the house and the twins are at school. Not sure I can bear to watch the results. If I send you the account name and password, would you mind vetting them for me first?

Senior Affairs Reporter
Channel 8 Local News
Relentlessly local, round the clock

From: crystalmomof4exlaw@yahoo.com
To: phoebegb@channel8news.com
Of course. In any other circumstances, I would agree out of prurient interest, but in this case, I sincerely hope I don't find anything interesting to watch.

PTA Room Parent, Village Public School

Friday, February 22

Mephone voicemail transcript from Phoebe to Crystal
Just wanted to let you snow, Operation Nanny Cam is a go-go. I've stationed the teddy bare cam on the sofa in the living womb, and the alarm cockadoodle doo cam next to my side of the bed upstairs. I will email you the abuser name and pass wad, so you can monitor the foot age. Thanks for doing this while I'm at wok. I apologize in advance for any shots of me in my udders. I will try and remember to turn the cameras off while Brad and I are undressing.

Transcribed using Yap® app technology.

From: crystalmomof4exlaw@yahoo.com
To: phoebegb@channel8news.com
FW: MePhone yap app
Got your voicemail – I think. Checking footage now.

PTA Room Parent, Village Public School

Text from Crystal to Phoebe
Happy to report Brad exploring inner reaches of his right nostril right now while reading in bed.

Text from Phoebe to Crystal
Thanks. Sorry you had to witness that.

From: crystalmomof4exlaw@yahoo.com
To: phoebegb@channel8news.com
Nothing of interest to report so far today, although I do see what you mean about the Hugglet. While it's encouraging to see a man actually doing some housework, it's a little disturbing to see his naked backside when he bends down to vacuum under the coffee table. What does Pandora have to say about it?

PTA Room Parent, Village Public School

From: phoebegb@channel8news.com
To: crystalmomof4exlaw@yahoo.com
According to her, wearing a Hugglet is a legitimate form of self-soothing, and very popular among the great and the good here in DC. W/O naming names, she implied that the former director of Homeland Security has been known to wear one in the privacy of his office. I personally think the occasional use of women's underwear would positively be titillating compared with having to face the sight of Brad in what is essentially a full length fleecy hospital gown and a pair of Rubbermaid's.

I've tried repeatedly telling him what a turn-off the thing is, but he says he feels the same way about me trying to tell him what to do the whole time. Pandora is threatening to resolve this impasse by conducting our next session in our marital bedroom. But surely there are some things that should be sacred in a marriage, even (or perhaps, especially) from one's therapist?

Senior Affairs Reporter
Channel 8 Local News
Relentlessly local, round the clock

From: crystalmomof4exlaw@yahoo.com
To: phoebegb@channel8news.com
You don't mind if George watches on the night in question, do you? Might be just the thing to get him off his addiction to Mischievous Meter Maids on Sho-all-time, which seems to have intensified considerably, since my sex strike.

PTA Room Parent, Village Public School

Saturday, February 23

From: crystalmomof4exlaw@yahoo.com
To: phoebegb@channel8news.com

Just studied the footage from yesterday afternoon, and stumbled across your joint bedroom session with Pandora. I see what you mean. Granted, she was positioned between you and Brad in bed, and her notebook must have been a distraction, but no one seemed to be having a good time.

I think you can trust Vira not to initiate an affair with your husband, but I can't vouch for what she might do if Brad were to press her. Judging from your experience with the Hugglet, it sounds like he can be pretty persistent when he sets his mind to something.

Besides, spending all my spare time watching various rooms in your house is making me question our new sofas, which George is insisting on returning. Remind me who your designer is again? Perky has been crossed off my list.

P.S. Just signed up for Steamy Yoga teacher training. Let's hope getting a little more zen in my life means I will be less likely to shout epithets at George even while I sleep.

PTA Room Parent, Village Public School

From: phoebegb@channel8news@yahoo.com
To: crystalmomof4exlaw@yahoo.com
Decoratrix accepts new clients only from the CRAC parent list and requires the household have no more than two children, because she believes strongly that the Feng Shui of any single family structure is ruined by more than four inhabitants – an approach that clearly won't work chez vous (even if you have since come to share her point of view). She is also unable to function unless all her specific requirements are met, including having a freshly chilled bottle of Evian at her disposal each time she enters your home. Oh, and she doesn't appreciate having a child swig from it first – as Cecily found out.

Hurrah on the yoga training front. Do know I will be there to support you emotionally in every manner possible and will endeavor to have a cocktail ready to soothe those sore muscles at a moment's notice.

Senior Affairs Reporter
Channel 8 Local News
Relentlessly local, round the clock

Monday, February 25

Posting on Village Listserv
For Sale:
Two brand new Dolce Vita Rene sofas, only used once. Original price: $16,000. Any reasonable offer considered. Contact crystalmomof4exlaw@ yahoo.com to view or for more information.

Skye Chat
crystalwalker
Help! Hilary is planning to attend the Granger's party tomorrow. Had no idea

she and Pookie were even friends. Would appreciate your advice on how to handle. You are completely right about not jeopardizing my marriage, and the cherubs' happiness for the sake of a relationship that I'm not even sure I really want. Guess I am just suffering from a huge loss of self-esteem after putting my career on hold, so I will try to do what you suggest and seek less drastic forms of fulfillment before doing anything I might regret.

phoebethompson
I promise to remain glued to your side all evening, if that would help.

crystalwalker
I would appreciate it, thanks. Naturally, George will be AWOL once again.

Tuesday, February 26

Text from Crystal to Phoebe
I've never left a cocktail party so famished. Or sober. How could she possibly think it was OK not to serve alcohol?

Text from Phoebe to Crystal
Pooks was apparently trying to recreate expedition rations with her buffet fare, but personally, I refuse to believe an Englishman would depart on exploration w/o lashings of both tea and gin.

Text from Crystal to Phoebe
Just as well Vira and Hilary were both no shows, claiming last minute work conflicts – yet another reason I'm beginning to regret giving up my high-powered career. CU bright and early for yoga.

Text from Phoebe to Crystal
CU then.

Wednesday, February 27

From: crystalmomof4exlaw@yahoo.com
To: phoebegb@channel8news.com
Don't want to sound the alarm, esp. while you are working, but just noticed something on the nanny cam that I fear you may find unsettling, or a relief – I'm not sure which.

Vira rang your front doorbell just now, and Brad handed her a small ziploc baggie much like the one that holds his pesto, only the contents were not the usual brilliant green. I had never seen this sauce before, but I have to confess, it did not look like one of your husband's best efforts, as it closely resembled a small, anemic-looking bag of my expressed breast milk. But maybe that's just me. For her part, Vira appeared genuinely delighted with the contents – enough to give Brad a big hug and smack on the lips, which seemed to make him equally happy.

I know Brad is still anxious to prove himself as an entrepreneur, so is it possible he's developing new pasta sauces behind your back?

PTA Room Parent, Village Public School

From: phoebegb@channel8news.com
To: crystalmomof4exlaw@yahoo.com
Doesn't sound like any pasta sauce I recognize, that's for sure. When can we meet to discuss?

Senior Affairs Reporter
Channel 8 Local News
Relentlessly local, round the clock

From: crystalmomof4exlaw@yahoo.com
To: phoebegb@channel8news.com
I'm afraid it's well past my bedtime already, so hope you don't mind if we speak in the morning. I'm sure there is an innocent explanation, so please don't worry.

Sleep tight.

PTA Room Parent, Village Public School

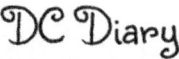

DC Diary

The Walkers Take on the Nation's Capital

First Tooth, Stitches, Yoga Training

It's been a busy few weeks, cooking, ferrying the cherubs to and from their various after-school activities, booking our spring break vacation and generally tending to the many and various needs of family and friends. But then, what's new, right? Sadly the diary is getting shorter, as I am finding much less time in front of the computer than previously.

Kurtis got her first tooth this month, which makes her look even more like a toothless old man than she did before.

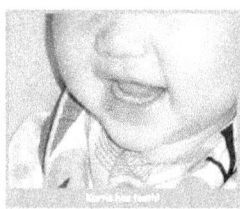

Kurtis first tooth

The rest of the cherubs are doing well, although Karson had a nasty fall on the ice requiring stitches the other day. Thanks to the quick intervention of my friend, Hilary, it looks like he won't even have a scar, but it could have been so much worse. Sometimes, especially during stressful economic times like now, it just helps to be reminded of what (and who)'s really important, right?

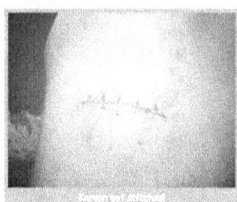

Karson got stitched

I have decided to sign up for yoga teacher training (no hoots from the peanut gallery please) next month, in the hopes of channeling a little inner peace among the day to day chaos of our lives. I will keep you guys updated about my progress. I figure someone needs to be centered in our household, and it may as well begin with me. Namaste to all!

Namaste to all my friends and family

Post a Comment

Comment as: Select profile

(Publish) (Preview)

BLOG ARCHIVE

First Tooth, Stitches, Yoga Training

1st month and a day of twins mom, including my own...

George's First Year at Home (first...

Kurtis Christening, Sister Traveling, Diary Memories...

Return to UK, Fraternal Morris (or, 2 MDBabies)...

Struggles, County Club and Maternity Leave

Baby Kurtis, Ethanol Fever and Missing Parents or...

DC Diary
First Tooth, Stitches, Yoga Training

It's been a busy few weeks, cooking, ferrying the cherubs to and from their various after-school activities, booking our spring break vacation and generally tending to the many and various needs of family and friends. But then, what's new, right? Sadly the diary is getting shorter, as I am finding much less time in front of the computer than previously.

Kurtis got her first tooth this month, which makes her look even more like a toothless old man than she did before.

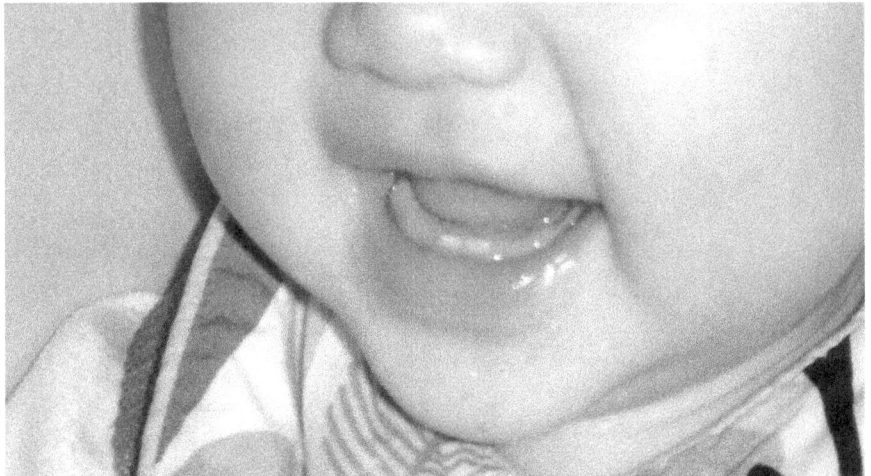

The rest of the cherubs are doing well, although Karson had a nasty fall on the ice requiring stitches the other day. Thanks to the quick intervention of my friend, Hilary, it looks like he won't even have a scar, but it could have been so much worse. Sometimes, especially during stressful economic times like now, it just helps to be reminded of what (and who)'s really important, right?

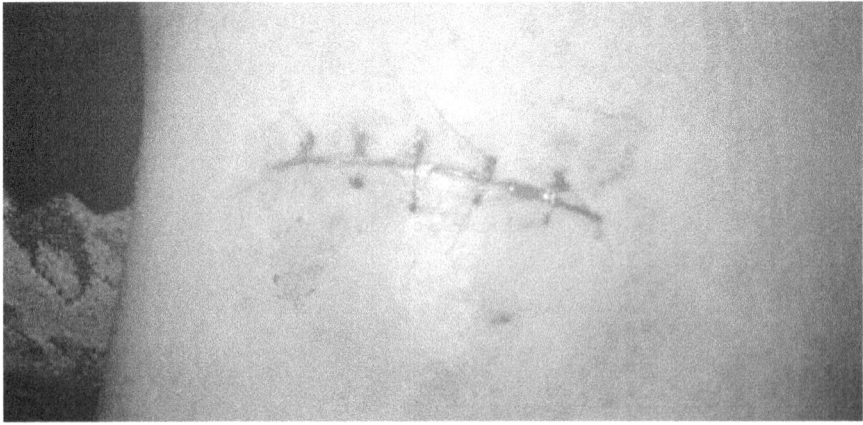

I have decided to sign up for yoga teacher training (no hoots from the peanut gallery please) next month, in the hopes of channeling a little inner peace among the day to day chaos of our lives. I will keep you guys updated about my progress. I figure someone needs to be centered in our household, and it may as well begin with me. Namaste to all!

Chapter 8

March, 2013 Vol. 42, Issue 3
Always FREE, but donations appreciated

Please direct submissions and inquiries to:
whining@village-press.com
P.O. Box 357 Village Town, MD

VILLAGE WHINER

Your trusty monthly newsletter of
the "Most Livable Village," 1989
Village Times Magazine

Board Meeting to Assess Fines for Unauthorized Tree Removal

The Village Board of Managers will convene a special town hall meeting at 7pm on Monday, March 9 to discuss the illegal removal of several oak trees from Mr. Palmer's property on Park Street. Residents are reminded that removal of ANY trees, regardless of whether they were intentionally planted or not, is illegal according to Article 389576 of the Village By-laws, and will result in the stiffest sanctions, including but not limited to the imposition of fines, imprisonment, and, in the most egregious of circumstances, ostracism at Village functions. Residents should note that they signed up to abide by all Village by-laws when they bought property here, and that these sanctions exist to preserve the unique character of our quaint and lovely hamlet. Anyone with questions or comments about this issue is requested NOT to post their thoughts on the Village listserv, but instead to attend next Monday's meeting. We look forward to seeing you there.

Village Tennis Team

The Ladies' First Team has won its penultimate match in the Ladies' Winter Day League, putting it on a par with Team Spank from Beech Hill Country Club, whom we are scheduled to play in the finals on March 11.

Captain Amanda Spank is known to try and cajole and undersize players on a critical play to maintain their position as the number 1 team in the League. So we need to engage in some rigorous physical and mental training to be ready for this challenge. To this end, Xavier will be conducting mandatory early morning training sessions from 5am each day, consisting of a 10K run followed by wind-sprints, weight lifting, and psychological warfare training with Dr. Jack Watson, Pentagon consultant, decorated Iraqi war veteran and author of the book *101 Ways to Kill The Enemy and Leave No Trace*. (Please note: for security reasons, Dr. Watson's name and identity have been changed). It's time to man up, Ladies (pun intended). Anyone who claims this is just a game should leave the team NOW.

The Gentlemen's Tennis team has been suspended for two months by the league for attempting to dress and pass themselves off as women. They will resume play in the Senior 2.5 circuit in May.

Captain Amanda Spank

Village Diversity Group

The Diversity Group will convene on Sunday, March 8 at 5pm to mourn recent wanton and senseless slaughter of innocent Village foliage. We have invited Sister Taylor Makelove, ordained Universalist minister, lawyer and environmental lobbyist with Plunder & Hogg Public Affairs to lead a humanist service of atonement for this atrocity in Mr. Palmer's yard, followed by a group hug-in around the remaining trees on Mr. Palmer's yard.

In other news, the Village Diversity Group has been underwhelmed by the complete lack of response from our survey to explore ways our community can pull together to help our Village Elders age in place. We are all extremely busy and important people, but surely we can all spare 15 minutes out of our day to help a senior. We have extended the survey another month in the hopes that we can guilt some of you into responding. The fact that many of these elders have more than sufficient resources to hire their own help should not influence your decision. It is clearly their right to believe they can't afford it and, perhaps, make senseless contributions to televangelists instead. Remember, you will be there soon enough, so it behooves us all to treat our elders as we would like to be treated ourselves. We look forward to hearing from you soon.

Miss Gertrude

It has come to Miss Gertrude's attention that there is a movement afoot among some of the Village Elders to age in place. Indeed, Miss Gertrude wanted to do this herself until her son encouraged some would say forced her to move to the Beautiful Swans Senior Community on the outskirts of our community. But to her own great surprise, Miss Gertrude has found that she has never been happier since the move.

Before you object, please consider that checking in on an elderly relative to make sure they have eaten, taken their meds and gone jarbed, not fallen, requires help from a small army of relatives, caregivers, neighbors and friends around the clock. And yet, given the advanced age of most first-time parents these days, many caregivers still have young children at home, not to mention careers and/or rigorous exercise schedules that take almost as much of their time as a full year law associate bills in hours. Miss Gertrude understands the sacrifices the older generation has made for family and country, but please consider how much more is expected of parents today. How many times did you go to your child's pre-school to volunteer in class, run a school auction or build a set for the school play? How about shuttling your child to four or five activities each week? How many hours did you spend at night and on weekends answering work emails? Of course you don't remember, because it never happened! Even fathers don't get off the hook the way they once did as any dad who tried to pull the old "I've been working hard all week, so I get to play golf all weekend" ruse would probably be laughed all the way to the emergency room.

In case you are wondering, gentle reader, I do not own stock in Beautiful Swan - just my own little piece of nirvana. Your son can have yours. I assure you it is far more dignified than the uncomfortable "I've accidentally baked the cat" call I was forced to make before my son was able to convince me it was time. (I certainly, I fully recovered loudly enough to startle, although that will teach her to jump into a warm oven to take a nap next time.)

Let my experience guide you when I say that feline life should be preserved at all cost. And if you wonder if it's too late - it just may be. Make the call now. I'd love to be your neighbor.

Take a senior jogging: they're cute they put on the campaign trails.

Board Meeting to Assess Fines for Unauthorized Tree Removal

The Village Board of Managers will convene a special town hall meeting at 7pm on Monday March 9 to discuss the illegal removal of several oak trees from Mr. Palmer's property on Park Street. Residents are reminded that removal of ANY trees, regardless of whether they were intentionally planted or not, is illegal according to Article 389576 of the Village By-laws, and will result in the stiffest sanctions, including but not limited to the imposition of fines, imprisonment, and, in the most egregious of circumstances, ostracism at Village functions. Residents should note that they signed up to abide by all Village by-laws when they bought property here, and that these sanctions exist to preserve the unique character of our quaint and lovely hamlet. Anyone with questions or comments about this issue is requested NOT to post their thoughts on the Village listserv, but instead to attend next Monday's meeting. We look forward to seeing you there.

Village Tennis Team

The Ladies' First Team has won its penultimate match in the Ladies' Winter Day league, putting it on a par with Team Spank from Beech Hill Country Club, whom we are scheduled to play in the finals on March 14.

Captain Amanda Spank is known to recruit college and underage players in a cynical ploy to maintain their position as the number 1 team in the league, so we need to engage in some rigorous physical and mental training to be ready for this challenge. To this end, Xavier will be conducting mandatory early morning training sessions from 5am each day, consisting of a 10K run followed by wind sprints, weight lifting, and psychological warfare training with Dr. Jack Warrior, Pentagon consultant, decorated Iraq war veteran and author of the book, '101 Ways to Kill The Enemy and Leave No Trace.' (Please note, for security reasons, Dr. Warrior's name and identity have been changed). It's time to man up, Ladies (pun intended). Anyone who claims this is just a game should leave the team NOW.

The Gentlemen's Tennis team has been suspended for two months by the league for attempting to dress and pass themselves off as women. They will resume play in the Senior 2.5 circuit in May.

Captain Amanda Spank

Village Diversity Group

The Diversity Group will convene on Sunday, March 8 at 5pm to mourn the recent wanton and senseless slaughter of innocent Village foliage. We have invited Sister Taylor Makelove, ordained Universalist minister, lawyer and environmental lobbyist with Plunder & Hogg Public Affairs to lead a humanist service of atonement for this atrocity in the Village Yurt, followed by a group hug-in around the remaining trees in Mr. Palmer's yard.

In other news, the Village Diversity Group has been underwhelmed by the complete lack of response from our survey to explore ways our community can pull together to help our Village Elders age in place. We are all extremely busy and important people, but surely we can all spare 15 minutes out of our day to help a senior. We have extended the survey another month, in the hopes that we can guilt some of you into responding. The fact that many of these elders have more than sufficient resources to hire their own help should not influence your decision. It is clearly their right to believe they can't afford it and, perhaps, make senseless contributions to televangelists instead. Remember, you will be there soon enough, so it behooves us all to treat our elders as we would like to be treated ourselves. We look forward to hearing from you soon.

Miss Gertrude

It has come to Miss Gertrude's attention that there is a movement afoot among some of the Village Elders to age in place. Indeed, Miss Gertrude wanted to do this herself, until her son encouraged -some would say, forced- her to move to the Beautiful Swans Senior Community on the outskirts of our community. But to her own great surprise, Miss Gertrude has found that she has never been happier since the move.

Before you object, please consider that checking on an elderly relative to make sure they have eaten, taken their meds and god forbid, not fallen, requires help from a small army of relatives, caregivers, neighbors and friends around the clock. And yet, given the advanced age of most first-time parents these days, many caregivers still have young children at home, not to mention careers and/or rigorous exercise schedules that take almost as much of their time as a a first year law associate bills in hours. Miss Gertrude understands the sacrifices the older generation has made for family and country, but please consider how much more is expected of parents today. How many times did you go to your child's pre-school to volunteer in class, run a school auction, or build a set for the school play? How about shuttling your child to four or five activities each week? How many hours did you spend at night and on weekends answering work emails? Of course you don't remember, because it never happened! Even fathers don't get off the hook the way they once did, as any dad who tried to pull the old 'I've been working hard all week, so I get to play golf all weekend' ruse would probably be laughed all the way to the emergency room.

In case you are wondering, gentle reader, I do not own stock in Beautiful Swan - just my own little piece of nirvana. You too can have yours. I assure you it is far more dignified than the uncomfortable "I've accidentally baked the cat" call I was forced to make before my son was able to convince me it was time. (Fortunately, Fluffy meowed loudly enough to survive, although that will teach her to jump into a warm open oven to take a nap next time).

Let my experience guide you when I say that feline life should be preserved at all cost. And if you wonder if it is too late, it just may be. Make the call now. I'd love to be your neighbor.

Take a senior fishing, but be sure they put on the emergency brake.

From: phoebegb@channel8news.com
To: crystalmomof4exlaw@yahoo.com

Finally had a chance to review the webcam after long day at work. The footage is a little grainy, but you are right, it does look like a new sauce. I knew we had been having some issues communicating, but I had no idea he would go behind my back like this.

Now the problem is how to figure out a way to let Brad know I know what he's up to, without revealing that I've been spying on him. As outraged as I am at his behavior, I know he would be more so at the idea that I have been secretly recording his most private moments. I simply can't afford to cede the moral high ground. Let me know how you would advise handling.

Senior Affairs Reporter
Channel 8 Local News
Relentlessly local, round the clock

From: crystalmomof4exlaw@yahoo.com
To: phoebegb@channel8news.com

Would it help if I had a little chat with Vira? I can let her know that you somehow witnessed the exchange and are understandably concerned. Alternatively, I am quite willing to put the head of Kurtis's beloved stuffed monkey in V's bed for you, if you prefer. Just say the word.

PTA Room Parent, Village Public School

From phoebegb@channel8news.com
To: crystalmomof4exlaw@yahoo.com

No need to go that far. A word or two about the extraordinarily fattening properties of Brad's sauces should suffice. I still haven't figured out a way to confront him directly about what's going on, but he does claim to have had some kind of 'breakthrough' in his private sessions with Pandora, which means he has started shaving again – at least for now.

Senior Affairs Reporter
Channel 8 Local News
Relentlessly local, round the clock

From: crystalmomof4exlaw@yahoo.com
To: phoebegb@channel8news.com

Got it. And would you mind if I cease watching any further footage for now? It's starting to make me feel like a peeping Tom.

PTA Room Parent, Village Public School

From phoebegb@channel8news.com
To: crystalmomof4exlaw@yahoo.com

Of course. And thank you for being such a good friend.

Senior Affairs Reporter
Channel 8 Local News
Relentlessly local, round the clock

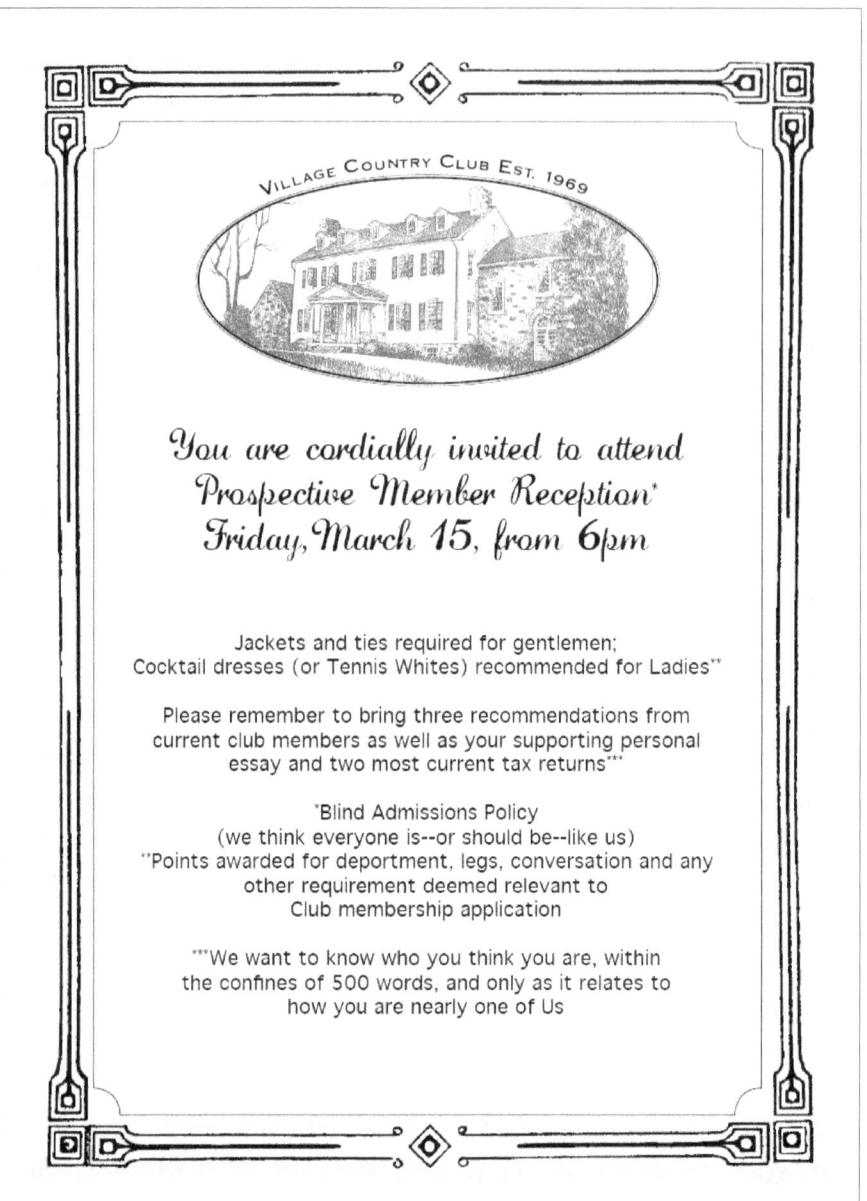

VILLAGE COUNTRY CLUB EST. 1969

You are cordially invited to attend
Prospective Member Reception*
Friday, March 15, from 6pm

Jackets and ties required for gentlemen;
Cocktail dresses (or Tennis Whites) recommended for Ladies**

Please remember to bring three recommendations from
current club members as well as your supporting personal
essay and two most current tax returns***

*Blind Admissions Policy
(we think everyone is--or should be--like us)
**Points awarded for deportment, legs, conversation and any
other requirement deemed relevant to
Club membership application

***We want to know who you think you are, within
the confines of 500 words, and only as it relates to
how you are nearly one of Us

RICH SIMPLICITY

Breathe in, Breathe Out. No matter what we face, whether it's the vice-like contractions of labor, the terrifying journey down the narrow birth canal, or an argument about custody arrangements with an ex-spouse, all we need do is remember to breathe, and everything will be just fine.

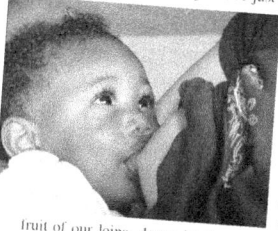

I try and demonstrate dragon breathing as I sit in Lamaze class with Tiffany, pressing my ear to her distended belly to listen to my future son ('stepson' is such an ugly word, even though Tom has unkindly pointed out he will not even technically be that) dancing to his precious womb music. As I remind Tiff constantly, she may be about to go through the most agonizing, long, drawn out physical pain she will ever experience, but so have billions of other women in the world, and they have for the most part survived.

Tiffany is still a little resistant to the idea of letting me breastfeed, but she does recognize the concept of mothers and fathers retaining exclusive rights over their children as a patriarchal construct that needs to be broken down. Only when we surrender the concept of 'ownership' over everything, including the fruit of our loins, do we begin to reap the True Blessings of Oneness*. So while she has yet to agree to let me proffer up my bosoms in offering to this new Life (once again, validation for the fact that I continue to breastfeed Ravi to this day), Tiff has at least agreed to keep meditating on the subject. In the meantime, I will continue to share my abundance with my dear sweet Ravi, although now mostly in his bpa free sippy cup.

I hope, dear readers, that you will continue to reflect on the Blessings of Sharing* this month also. With the world economy in crisis, and my own paid readership down from a year ago, now is the time for all those who are Blessed with True Wealth* in all its forms - spiritual enlightenment, rewarding work or a family trust fund - to share their good fortune with those who have less. For it is only in sharing our material and spiritual Blessings that we learn to appreciate what we have.

I will be away until March 22, attending a Complete Rest & Rejuvenation Retreat on the island of Mustique, so will not be able to answer any emails. I look forward to returning, refreshed, in April.

May you prosper inwardly,
Vira.

Want an easy homemade and environmental solution to disposable diapers? Shred some old newspapers and turn them into pulp with a mixture of water and potato starch, then wrap in cotton or sackcloth and hey presto you have a diaper that is both absorbant biodegradeable and stylish.

Thank you for visiting Rich Simplicity. We hope to see you again soon.

To subscribe to Blessed Moments, Vira's monthly magazine, *Special Offer: Subscribe for 24 months at only $3 an issue, and save 60% off the cover price!

To order a signed copy of The Blessings of Motherhood for only $24.99,

To order a batch of FatMama pregnancy poultice (only $39.99 for 8oz),

To sign-up to receive Vira's weekly newsletter via email (only $19.99 a year).

From: Rich Simplicity
To: phoebegb@sahmsrule.net

Rich Simplicity: A monthly newsletter bringing you a life of ultimate simplicity, no matter how much money I have.

Volume 04, Issue 03

Blessings,
Breathe in, Breathe Out. No matter what we face, whether it's the vice-like contractions of labor, the terrifying journey down the narrow birth canal, or an argument about custody arrangements with an ex-spouse, all we need do is

remember to breathe, and everything will be just fine.

I try and demonstrate dragon breathing as I sit in Lamaze class with Tiffany, pressing my ear to her distended belly to listen to my future son ('stepson' is such an ugly word, even though Tom has unkindly pointed out he will not even technically be that) dancing to his precious womb music. As I remind Tiff constantly, she may be about to go through the most agonizing, long, drawn out physical pain she will ever experience, but so have billions of other women in the world, and they have for the most part survived.

Tiffany is still a little resistant to the idea of letting me breastfeed, but she does recognize the concept of mothers and fathers retaining exclusive rights over their children as a patriarchal construct that needs to be broken down. Only when we surrender the concept of ownership over everything, including the fruit of our loins, do we begin to reap the True Blessings of Oneness'. So while she has yet to agree to let me proffer up my bosoms in offering to this new Life (once again, validation for the fact that I continue to breastfeed Ravi to this day), Tiff has at least agreed to keep meditating on the subject. In the meantime, I will continue to share my abundance with my dear sweet Ravi, although now mostly in his bpa free sippy cup.

I hope, dear readers, that you will continue to reflect on the Blessings of Sharing' this month also. With the world economy in crisis, and my own paid readership down from a year ago, now is the time for all those who are Blessed with True Wealth' in all its forms - spiritual enlightenment, rewarding work or a family trust fund - to share their good fortune with those who have less. For it is only in sharing our material and spiritual Blessings that we learn to appreciate what we have.

I will be away until March 22, attending a Complete Rest & Rejuvenation Retreat on the island of Martinique, so will not be able to answer any emails. I look forward to returning, refreshed, in April.

May you prosper inwardly,
Vira.

From: phoebegb@channel8news.com
To: crystalmomof4exlaw@yahoo.com
FW: Rich Simplicity
Looks like Vira is out of town for next 3 weeks. Damn. Guess I will just have to wheedle the truth out of Brad myself.

Senior Affairs Reporter
Channel 8 Local News
Relentlessly local, round the clock

Monday, March 4

Skye chat between Phoebe and Brad
phoebethompson
Leaving studio now, but too tired to think about dinner. How about whipping up one of those new pasta sauces I saw lurking at the back of the fridge?

phoebethompson
Glad your sauces are in such high demand, but it would be nice if you would spare some for your family.

phoebethompson
Hadn't considered the option of eating out midweek. Do we really want to go through the hassle of getting a sitter?

phoebethompson
OK, I'm troubled. What kind of 'news' is it, and why do we have to go to restaurant to discuss?

phoebethompson
Fine, but you know I don't like surprises. I will see if Lata is free and ask PA to book the Palm D'Or, although we're unlikely to get a reservation.

phoebethompson
I forgot about the economic collapse. Crystal has agreed to spare Lata and PA has booked us a table for 7. CU then. xp

From: phoebegb@channel8news.com
To: fforsythe@baldinggray.com
Re: Urgent question
Brad claims to have a new investor for his P-NIS. Only $15K, but surely he wouldn't tell me this information if he were thinking of ditching me for a newer model?

Senior Affairs Reporter
Channel 8 Local News
Relentlessly local, round the clock

From: phoebegb@channel8news.com
To: fforsythe@baldinggray.com
Re: Urgent question
OK. Will document anything I can find, just to be safe.

Senior Affairs Reporter
Channel 8 Local News
Relentlessly local, round the clock

Tuesday, March 5

Skye Chat Between Phoebe and Brad
phoebethompson
Sorry I had to go back to work after dinner. It was delicious, btw, but why r u being so nice to me all of a sudden?

phoebethompson
No, I like it. And I'm glad someone is excited enough about your hardware

solution to cough up some cold, hard cash. Just wondering if there's anything you need to tell me.

phoebethompson
Are you sure?

phoebethompson
No, I really don't have time to sneak home from work in the middle of the day to 'celebrate' the good news. Not sure what is inspiring this renewed friskiness, but if it's another child you want, now is most certainly NOT the time to throw caution to the wind. The last thing I need right now is to swell up to the size of the Walkers' inflatable Santa, as I did with the twins. And given that I've been on the job fewer than six months, any maternity leave they gave me would be so short, I might end up offering our viewers a whole new interpretation of 'Live on the Scene.'

Text from Phoebe to Pandora
Planning to attend tonight's session with Brad. Thanks for persuading him to give up the Hugglet and Rubbermaids, but need to make sure he promises to wear another kind of rubber going forward.

Friday, March 8

Text from Crystal to George
My dad is in the hospital, after falling at home, so just booked 5.10pm flight from DC for baby and me. Lata will cover till you get home tonight, but you will have to cancel whitewater rafting, as you are on your own with 3 elders until we get back on Sunday.

Text from Phoebe to Crystal
Sorry to hear about your Dad. Is he OK?

Text from Crystal to Phoebe
So far, he doesn't seem to have broken anything, but he needs more tests to determine cause. Have Kurtis w/me, but George can handle 3 eldest for weekend.

Text from Crystal to George
Don't forget, Karson has soccer game at 9, followed by Kevin's at noon. Karson also has b/day party at 2. Don't forget to buy gift!

Text from Crystal to Kevin
Yes, Stefan and Jeremy can come over tonite, but no girls! Don't trust Dad to supervise.

Text from Crystal to George
Don't forget to lock liquor cabinet!

Saturday, March 9

Text from Crystal to George
I TOLD u not to let Kevin watch a horror movie with Kimberly. Tell Kevin to hold his sister until she falls asleep, and that he is grounded until I get back.

Text from Crystal to George
Dad is doing better, btw, thank you for NOT asking. I know u are having tough weekend but so am I.

Text from Crystal to Kimberly
No, I will not order u cute cami from Forever Underage. Didn't Dad tell you you are grounded for rest of weekend too? Don't expect to leave house for anything except gym. U know better than to watch R rated movies.

Text from Crystal to Kimberly
Your pink leotard is in bottom drawer of dresser, where Lata ALWAYS puts it. BTW, may have escaped your notice, but I am actually out of town, dealing with Grandpa. How about thinking of someone else for a change?

Text from Crystal to George
Hospital tests all negative, so looks like they are releasing Dad from hospital this pm. Baby and I should be able to make our flight. Can u be at airport to pick us up?

Monday, March 11

From: crystalmomof4exlaw@yahoo.com
To: gwalker@plunderhogg.com
Thank you for picking me up last night, but what do you mean you have a pick-up game with POTUS tonight? What happened to Family Fun Night?

PTA Room Parent, Village Public School

From: crystalmomof4exlaw@yahoo.com
To: exrev@hotmail.com
Glad you had a good night, Dad, but I have too many children to be able to keep jumping on a plane at a moment's notice, so I'm researching some very nice assisted living places right here in DC. Check these out and let me know what you think.

www.beautifulswans.com
www.amnesiahouse.com
www.thefallsresidentialhome.com
www.elysianfields.com

x C

PTA Room Parent, Village Public School

Goggle Calendar Reminder

      What: Whiffawhats A Capella choral concert

      Where: Seton

      When: 7pm

      Are you attending?

            __ Yes

            __ No

      Why not? _____

Text from Crystal to Hilary

Wish I could join you at concert, but feel migraine coming on. Best if I just lie down in dark room. Sorry.

Tuesday, March 12

Karson,
I know I sent you to bed early because of the way you behaved after you found out Family Fun Night was cancelled, but Hilary has offered to take you to a very special concert at Seton tonight instead. Isn't that fun?

Love,
Mom

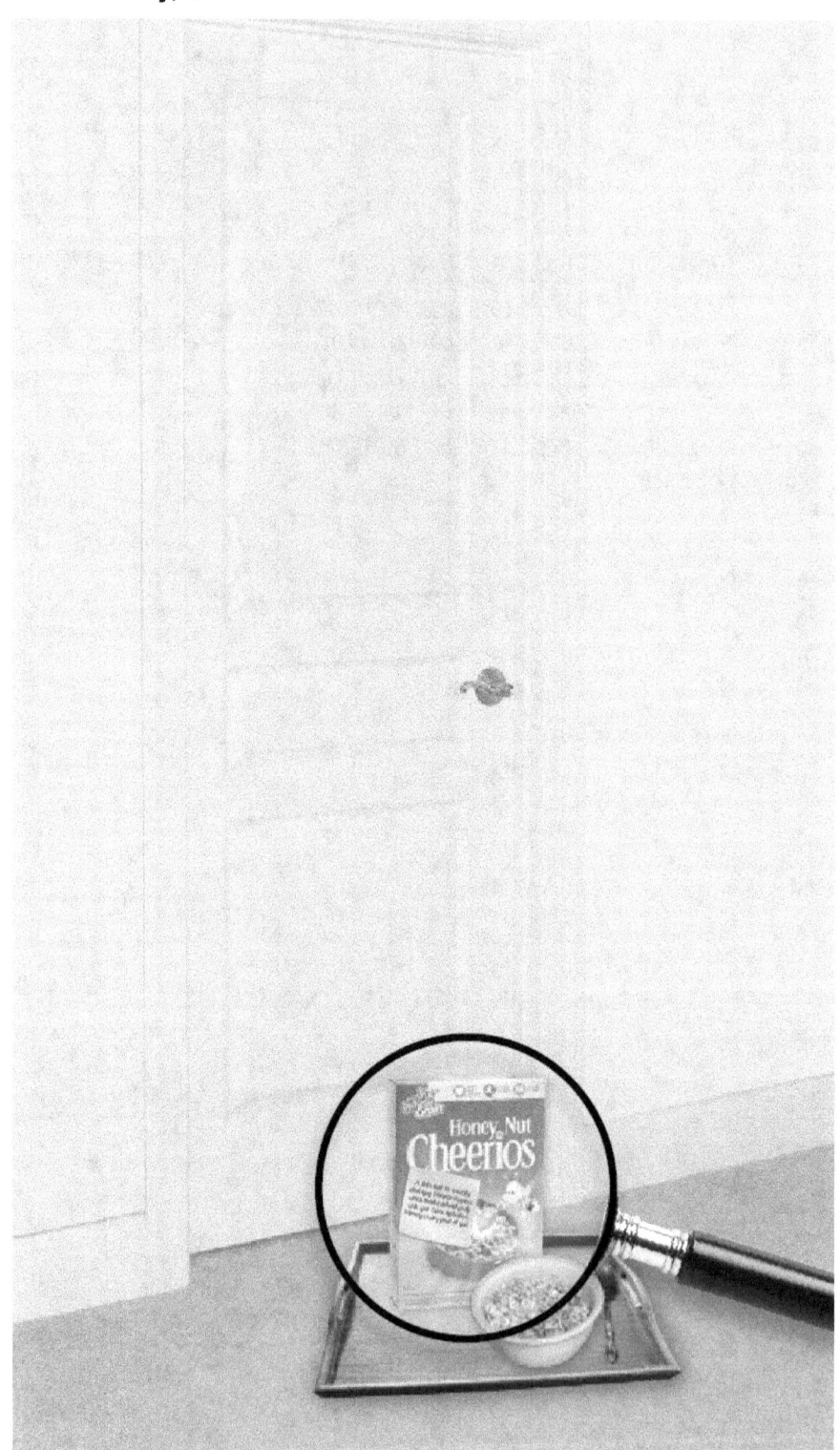

A little treat for correctly identifying Mozart's Requiem, which should definitely help with your Seton application. Mommy is very proud of you!

Text from Crystal to Kevin
Yes, u can visit Smithsonian with your friend, James. Thrilled u r taking advantage of what DC has to offer. Does this mean u r starting to like it?:)

Text from Crystal to Kevin
Remember to send pix. Don't want to discover u were really in James' basement enjoying kegger, not culture.

Text from Crystal to George
Kevin just texted me this photo from the Smithsonian. Who knew we were raising such a sophisticated young man?!

Text from C to George
I think the term u r looking for is 'metrosexual.' Just because u played college football and have never had an eyebrow wax does not make u an authority on all things hetero.

Thursday, March 14

From: crystalmomof4exlaw@yahoo.com
To: dcparentskilltokissmybutt@seton.edu
Dear Hilary,
I would LOVE to attend the Seton Annual Gala for LGBT Families (may I gently suggest a "Q" btw for those questioning their preferences?), but it's actually my birthday, so George is taking me to Toast, the new champagne and raw food bar on 7th and M. Guess the name is intended to be ironic.

By the way, I know letters from Seton about the cherubs' applications are about to go out, but is there any way you can give us a hint about what to expect? I'm finding it hard to focus on anything else until I know their future is settled.

Yours warmly,
Crystal

PTA Room Parent, Village Public School

From: crystalmomof4exlaw@yahoo.com
To: dcparentskilltokissmybutt@seton.edu
I understand the need to maintain the proper channels of communication, but just know that it would mean the world to the cherubs if they are lucky enough to get in. Guess we will just have to wait until the acceptance letters are mailed later this week.
Crystal

PTA Room Parent, Village Public School

From: phoebegb@channel8news.com
To: crystalmomof4exlaw@yahoo.com
A little birdie (actually, Mebook) informed me that you are celebrating your 36th birthday. Let me know if I can take you to lunch or dinner, by way of a celebration.

Senior Affairs Reporter
Channel 8 Local News
Relentlessly local, round the clock

From: crystalmomof4exlaw@yahoo.com
To: phoebegb@channel8news.com
Already have plans with George, but thanks anyway! Speaking of birthdays, I hear you have a big one coming up this year. Remind me of the date again?

PTA PRESIDENT, Village Public School

From: phoebegb@channel8news.com
To: crystalmomof4exlaw@yahoo.com
My birthday is July 29, although I would prefer if you could keep it hush hush. My advanced age not exactly a secret, but I don't need to advertise the fact to my employers, who are threatening to start broadcasting in HD any day now.

Senior Affairs Reporter
Channel 8 Local News
Relentlessly local, round the clock

From: crystalmomof4exlaw@yahoo.com
To: phoebegb@channel8news.com
My lips are sealed, but am also confident that you will look just fine with every pore magnified.

PTA PRESIDENT, Village Public School

From: phoebegb@channel8news.com
To: crystalmomof4exlaw@yahoo.com
Thanks. BTW, congrats on the promotion to PTA president! You are certainly one busy lady these days!

Senior Affairs Reporter
Channel 8 Local News
Relentlessly local, round the clock

From: crystalmomof4exlaw@yahoo.com
To: phoebegb@channel8news.com
More like a glutton for punishment. But I thought it might help for Hilary to know that I am willing to volunteer, a lot, in case it helps sway Seton's decision when it comes to the cherubs.

PTA PRESIDENT, Village Public School

Text from Crystal to Kevin
Thank you for the WONDERFUL tee from Forever Underage. Who knew my eldest son was such a fashionista? Yes, u can borrow my Chanel sunglasses, but you do realize they are women's, right?

Text from Crystal to Kevin
BTW, u do know it's ABSOLUTELY FINE if u r gay. Mommy and Daddy will love u just the same. Maybe more, in my case. Always good to be the woman u love most.

Text from Crystal to Kevin
P.S. This conversation can wait until u get back from school, of course, but might just be easier to say via text.

Text from Crystal to Kevin
P.S. Glad to hear you like girls. OK, glad not right word. OK, I'll stop now.

From: crystalmomof4exlaw@yahoo.com
To: jsmith@plunderhogg.com
Could you please ask my husband what he means when he asked you if we could move MY birthday dinner to tomorrow, so he can go for drinks with the Senate Majority leader instead?

Please remind him that our nanny's amateur wrestling group meets every week this time, and she has informed us that it's the only thing that allows her to release the stress she accumulates taking care of our cherubs the rest of the week. I'm not sure it's a good idea to mess with her right now, as she's promised to take Karson. Hoping that wrestling may be just the kind of sport, like squash, that's niche enough to ensure admission to the Ivy League.

And besides, Lata might hurt us if we don't let her go.

PTA PRESIDENT, Village Public School

From: crystalmomof4exlaw@yahoo.com
To: jsmith@plunderhogg.com
Glad to hear my husband has seen the light.

BTW, please remind him not to assume that taking me to dinner gets him out of having to buy me a present. Our first born managed to get me a very lovely, thoughtful gift, and his brain is completely addled by hormones.

PTA PRESIDENT, Village Public School

Text from Crystal to George
WTH are you? It's almost 8pm, and maitre d' is looking at his watch.

Text from Crystal to George
First Valentine's Day, now my birthday? Is this some kind of running joke? P on her way to take your place, so don't bother coming now. In fact, don't bother coming home at all, since you are NEVER actually there when we need you.

Friday, March 15

From: crystalmomof4exlaw@yahoo.com
To: phoebegb@channel8news.com
Thank you for saving the evening and making my 36th bday feel less like a tragedy, and more like a sign of personal growth.

I'm thinking of moving on from vasectomy straight to castration (the mechanical kind), after last night.

PTA PRESIDENT, Village Public School

Saturday, March 16

Text from Crystal to Phoebe
Cherubs on wait-list for Seton. Assume this means the school likes them, right, and will take them when and if their number comes up?

Text from Phoebe to Crystal
Wait-listing is Seton's way of giving you the brush-off. Sorry. Wish I could be more positive, but that's the way it is at all the private schools.

Text from Crystal to Phoebe
But I don't understand. The cherubs aced all their tests, and I thought Hilary and I had some kind of special relationship!

Text from Phoebe to Crystal
Seton always = hardest school to get into, and having First daughters there just makes competition for spaces 10x worse.

Text from Crystal to Phoebe
Was it the fact we are from midwest? Pookie is going to have a field day when she finds out.

Text from Phoebe to Crystal
Frankly, I'm not sure what it would take to get into Seton right now, short of a hotline to the Oval Office.

From: crystalmomof4exlaw@yahoo.com
To: dcparentskilltokissmybutt@seton.edu
Dearest Hilary,

I was touched to receive the beautiful diamond earrings, but I simply can't accept such a generous birthday gift.

I have to confess, George and I were devastated to hear the news that all three of the cherubs have been wait-listed for Seton, so I am in no mood to celebrate my birthday this year.

Frankly, I thought my background in Women's Studies, and George's, in environmental lobbying, meant we were exactly the kind of family Seton was looking for – not to mention the fact that you and I have become such good friends. Then there's the small matter of Kevin, Kimberly and Karson scoring well above average on all twelve of their entrance tests, without needing extra time, special lighting or a bouncy ball to sit on in order to help with their nerves.

It would mean the world for us to have our children attend such a wonderful school, so if there is anything we can do to move them up the waitlist – and I mean anything – please let me know.

Warmly,
C.

PTA PRESIDENT, Village Public School

Text from Crystal to Phoebe
Just returned from first session of teacher training at Steamy Yoga. Would email if my fingers worked. Managed drink w/ Hilary after, but that is all. More later.

Sunday, March 17

From: crystalmomof4exlaw@yahoo.com
To: phoebegb@channel8news.com
Happened to be having a drink with Hilary at the Village Lounge last night, when who should walk in but Vira, looking tanned and fresh from her trip to Martinique. Since you'll never guess who she was with, I'll just tell you: Fred Manly!

Vira looked more than a little embarrassed to be seen with him, and mumbled something about being there to ask Fred to mentor Ravi, the way he mentored Kevin. But could Fred actually be the married man Vira has feelings for, and not Brad after all? The only other creature I've seen him gaze so adoringly at is Snuggles.

By the way, the training yesterday reminded me that I am a full generation older than most of the other students. My Sitting Bull pose was, I fear, more like a nesting duck covered by an oil slick (you've seen the commercials). I've applied the arnica and am heading back for day two. Only wish I could have fully submerged my whole body in ointment. But, challenges are what life is really all about, right? Who knows what past life karma finds me competing with 19 year olds? Or maybe it's just the foolish choices I've made in this life? Either way, as an only child I was taught that I was truly special and could accomplish anything. I only hope this blind self-esteem is not a march to my complete physical demise.

PTA PRESIDENT, Village Public School

From: phoebegb@channel8news.com
To: crystalmomof4exlaw@yahoo.com
I do know you will not only survive but thrive in this teacher training. So glad to have the pleasure of only WATCHING you do it, but please know that I am with you in spirit! Oh, and Lata did have an amazing poultice for sore muscles. Must ask her to prepare for you asap.

In the meantime, can you find out more details about Fred and Vira? You have such a talent for getting people to divulge their deepest, darkest secrets. I'll never forget the time you persuaded the President of the Village Board to discuss his occasional bed-wetting.

Senior Affairs Reporter
Channel 8 Local News
Relentlessly local, round the clock

From: crystalmomof4exlaw@yahoo.com
To: phoebegb@channel8news.com
How do you think I got permission to take down five trees to put in a hot tub next summer? I'll see what I can do.

PTA PRESIDENT, Village Public School

Monday, March 18

From: crystalmomof4exlaw@yahoo.com
To: dcparentskilltokissmybutt@seton.edu
Dear Hil,

I know you would like us to see more of each other, with a view to exploring a potential relationship, but to be honest, I am still not ready. George and I have our issues, but even though we are not speaking right now, I happen to know he is under an awful lot of stress at work.

Frankly, I'm also struggling with the adjustment to being a stay-at-home mom as it is also a full-time job – only without the status or benefits. It's hard to go from being partner in a law firm, where you are validated by billable hours, to a life where no one seems to notice or appreciate anything you do in a day. Right now, I'm trying to remember that marriage, like life, is sometimes about sticking it out. I don't want to end up like my parents, who always seemed to think there was someone better out there for them, when in fact they should have known that all marriages have irreconcilable differences.

Still, I owe it to our children for George and I to figure out if our relationship is worth saving, before I can contemplate anything else. It would help if we actually had time to sit down and have a conversation, but as he is traveling again all next week, that discussion will just have to wait.

Of course, I'm sure I would be able to sort through my feelings faster if the cherubs' future were secure, since it would give me one less thing to worry about. I can't believe the application board admitted Ravi Bliss, who

314

isn't even fully potty-trained, and yet waitlisted Karson, who was walking, talking and wiping his own behind well before his second birthday.

But, as I'm learning through my yoga training, the universe is giving us exactly what we need right now (even if it makes me feel like a toddler ready to throw a tantrum).

Warmly,
Crystal
PTA PRESIDENT, Village Public School

Tuesday, March 19

Posting on Village Listserv
Results of Village Board meeting to discuss tree removal

The Village Board has voted unanimously to impose a $10,000 fine on Charles Palmer for the recent unauthorized and illegal removal of trees from his property, and ordered him to plant replacement trees within the next 30 days, or face being shunned at Village functions for the next three months.

Have you helped a Senior today?

Wednesday, March 20

From: phoebegb@channel8news.com
To: crystalmomof4exlaw@yahoo.com
Just had the most surreal encounter.

I left the office early to go for my annual appointment with the Ob/Gyn, when who should I run into but Vira! Turns out, we share the same doctor. She proceeded to give me a hug and thank me quite emotionally for making her future happiness possible. Naturally, I was taken aback, but did not want to reveal my ignorance in these matters, for fear it might encourage even more sneaking around behind my back. Instead, I merely murmured something about how I knew she and Brad had been working very hard on this joint venture for some time, and that I hoped they would milk it for all it was worth, as I was tired of doing all the heavy lifting myself.

Vira looked a little surprised, but managed to stammer something about how she couldn't believe how understanding I was, given the circumstances. She also offered me the chance to get involved as much, or as little as I liked. When she added that Brad had already committed to offering her two deliveries a week, however, I finally snapped.

I told Vira in no uncertain terms that it was bad enough that she and Brad were cooking up a plan to go into the pasta sauce business without consulting me. But even worse was the fact they hadn't let me sample a single batch first!

The expression on Vira's face turned from happiness to horror faster than

315

traffic light turns from green to red. Before I had a chance to find out why, however, she quickly back-tracked and claimed she had to run, then quite literally sprinted off in her oh-so-tight yoga pants, leaving me once again wondering if there is more to the story than meets the eye.

From: crystalmomof4exlaw@yahoo.com
To: phoebegb@channel8news.com
I have my suspicions, but I think it's time to confront Brad once and for all and find out what's really going on.

PTA PRESIDENT, Village Public School

From: phoebegb@channel8news.com
To: crystalmomof4exlaw@yahoo.com
Steeling myself to talk to him after I get home from work.

Thursday, March 21

Skye Chat between Crystal and Phoebe
crystalwalker
Everything OK? Missed you at yoga this morning.

phoebethompson
Still in shock from last night.

crystalwalker
What happened?

phoebethompson
You know that pasta sauce we have been talking about? Turns out it wasn't pasta sauce at all.

crystalwalker
What on earth was it then?

phoebethompson
Let's just say, rather than being a culinary creation of Brad and Vira, it was a bodily fluid involved in the actual act of creation.

crystalwalker
OMFG

phoebethompson
Quite.

crystalwalker
WTH was he doing giving a bag of it to Vira?

phoebethompson
Think hard enough and I'm sure you can guess.

crystalwalker
OMG.

phoebethompson
Brad has been talking about having another child ever since he became the primary caregiver to the twins, but I just haven't been receptive. Then he and Vira started hanging out, and she came round sobbing that Tom was having another baby with Tiffany, and she was desperate for another child before it was too late……So, to cut a long story short, Brad decided to take matters into his own hands. Literally. Vira paid him $15k for the results, which I guess solves the mystery of the angel investor in P-NIS.

crystalwalker
And he did all this without consulting you?!

phoebethompson
Fortunately, the plan had not proceeded so far that the contents of the baggie had been used, but it was a very close call. Vira has a follow-up appointment with the fertility clinic tomorrow. When I called her to demand that she cancel, she immediately launched into a long explanation of how she thought Brad had told me, and that she would never have agreed to do something like that behind my back, had she known I didn't know.

crystalwalker
At least you know they weren't having an affair.

phoebethompson
I'm not sure what to believe right now. What on earth was the man THINKING?!

crystalwalker
I think the real question is not WHAT was he thinking, so much as what part of his body was he thinking WITH?

phoebethompson
Point taken. At least one good thing appears to have come out of this little episode. Brad has agreed to go for a snip at the earliest possible opportunity, and I will be accompanying him to make sure it's done in the humane, but not necessarily painless way.

Saturday, March 30

Index · More ▼ Next Blog»

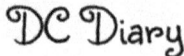

DC Diary

The Walkers Take on the Nation's Capital

Wait-listed, Obama Girls, Jamaica, Happy Easter

Well, life continues to be nothing, if not eventful here in the nation's capital. First: the good news: Kevin, Kimberly and Karson achieved high scores across the board on their Seton entrance tests! Now the not-so good news: because of the unprecedented number of applications this year, all three have nevertheless been wait-listed.

According to the head mistress at Seton, who has become a dear friend, the competition for spaces has been tougher than ever this year, in spite of the recession. She attributes this to the presence of the President's daughters, and an unusually high percentage of applications from children who are both gifted, talented AND special needs ('specially gifted', for short), who are exactly the kind of students Seton prizes. Just the other day, one of Karson's fellow applicants couldn't figure out how to pour his own cereal after he stayed for a sleepover - this in spite of the fact he has the IQ of Einstein. Naturally, he was admitted without question.

Sasha and Malia getting dropped off at Seton.

Meanwhile, George has been busy lobbying for fiscal cliff tax breaks for his clients on the Hill. Fingers crossed he can join us in Jamaica for spring break, although it won't be very relaxing if he's on his Blackberry the whole time. It doesn't help when Sister Taylor tells George and I that we would feel less anxious if we cut back on our extravagant lifestyle. She loves to remind us how much stress other people have just trying to keep a roof over their heads and food in their children's bellies, I know she's right, but it's hard not to get caught up in the insanity around here. I'm coping with all that by committing to the yoga teacher training course I mentioned last month which, while very physically and emotionally taxing, helps me believe the universe has good intentions for all of us, if we can just listen.

Happy Easter everyone. We miss you!

No comments:

Post a Comment

Comment as: Select profile... ▼

Publish   Preview

DC Diary
Wait-listed, Obama Girls, Jamaica, Happy Easter

Well, life continues to be nothing, if not eventful here in the nation's capital. First: the good news: Kevin, Kimberly and Karson achieved high scores across the board on their Seton entrance tests! Now the not-so good news: because of the unprecedented number of applications this year, all three have nevertheless been wait-listed.

According to the head mistress at Seton, who has become a dear friend, the competition for spaces has been tougher than ever this year, in spite of the recession. She attributes this to the presence of the President's daughters, and an unusually high percentage of applications from children who are both gifted, talented AND special needs ('specially gifted', for short), who are exactly the kind of students Seton prizes. Just the other day, one of Karson's fellow applicants couldn't figure out how to pour his own cereal after he stayed for a sleepover - this in spite of the fact he has the IQ of Einstein. Naturally, he was admitted without question.

Meanwhile, George has been busy lobbying for fiscal cliff tax breaks for his clients on the Hill. Fingers crossed he can join us in Jamaica for spring break, although it won't be very relaxing if he's on his Blackberry the whole time. It doesn't help when Sister Taylor tells George and I that we would feel less anxious if we cut back on our extravagant lifestyle. She loves to remind us how much stress other people have just trying to keep a roof over their heads and food in their children's bellies. I know she's right, but it's hard not to get caught up in the insanity around here. I'm coping with all that by committing to the yoga teacher training course I mentioned last month which, while very physically and emotionally taxing, helps me believe the universe has good intentions for all of us, if we can just listen.

Chapter 9

April, 2013 Vol. 42, Issue 4
Always FREE, but donations appreciated

Please direct submissions and inquiries to:
whining@villagepress.com
P.O. Box 357 Village Town, MD

VILLAGE WHINER

Your trusty monthly newsletter of
the "Most Livable Village," 1989
Village Times Magazine

Holier Than Thou Foods To Open This Month

We are happy to report that the final touches to the new Holier Than Thou store complete with custom counter and organic fair trade juice bar have now been completed, and the highly anticipated store opening will take place on April 1. Residents are strongly advised to flock there on the first day. Experts to avoid a mass stampede. Please note parking has purposely been restricted to encourage walking.

Please remember, most of the checkers are village grads who have worked hard for their expensive degrees in sustainable agriculture, so you are also expected to tip if they help you so your cart even if they just stand there watching while you wrestle with your purchases. New customers who request a bag, rather than bringing a reusable one from home, will be charged $5. Finally, if the Village finds a cart wheeled from the store to a resident's home, as has been known to happen with other Village Shoppes, you will be fined $100. The neighborhood security cameras Special Ops has just installed should help discourage residents from leaving a cart in a neighbor's yard.

Diversity Group

The Village Diversity Group is currently revising its corporate and environmental practices, as a result of a lively exchange between two of its longtime members, Pookie Granger and Perky Sparks at our most recent meeting. Pookie brought up the fact that Pookie's selfless devotion to worthy causes was somewhat at odds with her husband's work at the law firm of Keepem Down and Now, which is currently profiting from many of the evictions and foreclosures in the area - including, as it happens, on Perky's house. Pookie responded that it wasn't her fault that Perky's husband couldn't keep a job, which didn't go down well. Fortunately, Special Ops were upwards on hand to separate the two women and dispel the crowd of onlookers before things turned too physical.

Pookie was ultimately persuaded not to resign from the group, and to encourage her husband to turn in such a generous donation to the local homeless shelter, while Perky has been banned from the next two meetings, since she started the argument. In addition, Pookie will have to pay for Perky's eyebrow re-sleeping next month in order to cover the gap left by the unfortunate facial hair pulling incident.

The Village Diversity Group recognizes that our outreach programs are often undermined by corporations whose interests may conflict with the views of individual members. We would like to stress, however, that the quest for social, corporate and political justice is never an excuse for violence.

Perky Sparks foreclosed home

Elder Care Angels

Overwhelmed by the responsibilities of work family and aging parents? I know I was, with triplets and two parents with dementia to care for. Five years later, my children are now in kindergarten, and my parents have moved into higher education in the sky, which is why I have decided to turn the skills I learned taking care of their affairs into my vocation. For only $20 an hour month Elder Care Angels will drive, run errands, and schedule medical, dental, legal and personal grooming appointments for your loved ones and remind them to take their medication. For an additional $20 an month, we will shop for your loved one, pay bills, argue with Medicare and insurance companies, and listen to them repeat stories or talk about their health to the exclusion of anything else.

Note: We do NOT provide cleaning, laundering, bathing or pediatric services. For more information please email busybodymary@yahoo.com.

Miss Gertrude

Miss Gertrude is saddened to report a very nasty incident at the nursing home the other day, when she was attacked by a beautiful but ghostly creature by the name of Flo.

Flo is a swan who apparently led a difficult life before coming to Beautiful Swans, following an abusive relationship with a goose. In Flo's case, this only exaggerated her naturally aggressive temperament, which has led to a habit of chasing elderly residents on a regular basis. The problem arises as the residents in question exit a vehicle and proceed to the front door - hard enough to do with a walker at the best of times, let alone while tending off a 150lb assailant with webbed feet.

Whenever complaints about Flo's behavior are brought to the attention of management, however, the Beautiful Swans charter is cited, because the home's founder, Mr. Charles Palmer, donated the land on condition that it features a sanctuary for this demon in disguise. Apparently, he believes his dead wife's soul has been incorporated in Flo's body - a fact I have no trouble believing, knowing Flossie as I did.

As soon as the bruises have gone, and I recover the use of my left arm, I vow to continue the fight to have Flo removed - permanently. A lady knows when to stand up and fight, even if one's opponent has a stronger beak and far nastier temper. In the meantime, Miss Gertrude would like to remind her gentle readers of the following rules for responsible pet-ownership:

- Do not assume that just because you find your pet's drooling, knee-humping or begging adorable, others feel likewise.

- Do not assume that just because you say your pet is friendly, well-behaved, that he/she actually is, or that others believe you.

- Do not assume that when your pet goes bounding (or hissing) up to the border of your property, other people know you have an electric fence.

- Do not assume others are happy to be mauled to death by your poorly trained, out of control animal, just because you would be.

On a more positive note, Miss Gertrude is again pleased to open her spring Manners and Mores class to all Village children here, for the ages of 8 and 15 every first and third Friday of the month starting on your son, the opportunity to dance, hand in glove. Spaces for girls are filling rapidly, but boys are still very much in demand. Please offer (Miss Gertrude does make concessions to some modern mores, after all). Tuxedos (for boys or girls) and long dresses (for girls) are required.

Village Tennis Team

Congratulations to our Ladies team for their victory over Team Spark, facilitated in large measure by the Jack Worten's vigorous morning workouts which left our players spent but ultimately much better for it. On Court Four number 1 pair, Bites and Phoebe, pounded their opposition into ignominy, crushing them in a display of sustained focus and determination that was sometimes scary to behold. Our two champions were as gracious in victory as they would have been in defeat, comforting their sobbing teenage opponents with hugs and tissues, and ignoring one young lady's unfortunate comment as to the effect that Team 4 believes we lost to these old biddies. On court 2, Nancy and Gertrude fared even better, dispatching their opponents with a 6-0, 6-0 victory that saw everyone tucked in bed by 8. On court 3, Ethel and Mary glided to victory 6-2, 6-1 pairing only to admit their dentures. The glorious victory was a reminder, if we ever needed one, that consistency and ball placement can still trump youthful agility and power.

The victory means the Village Country Club Ladies Team are now officially League champions, and will have their names etched onto a small plaque in the Ladies' powder room.

The Gentlemen's team also enjoyed their first win this month in the 2.5 event, dominating courts two and three 6-4, 7-5 and 6-1, 6-3 respectively, although court 1 complained bitterly about being docked two games in the first set after one of their players arrived 10 minutes late. Welcome to the USTA boys, where it's ALL about the rules.

The Gentlemen's win will result in a notation on the gold plaque in the Gentlemen's Grill. Members of the Ladies team who complained they are asked to achieve far more to merit a mere mention in the Whiner should remember it is their former teammates (long dead and buried) who established the rule that women should be modest in dress and comportment at all times on Club premises which precludes a plaque listing their achievement. Ladies hoping to challenge this rule are encouraged to show up in person at our annual meeting next month, but must remember that 100% of members in attendance must agree to the change. We suggest you start lobbying now.

Holier Than Thou Foods
To Open This Month

We are happy to report that the final touches to the new Holier Than Thou store complete with caviar counter and organic, fair trade juice bar have now been completed, and the highly anticipated store opening will take place on April 1. Residents are strongly advised not to flock there on the first day it opens, to avoid a mass stampede. Please note: parking has purposely been restricted to encourage walking.

Remember that most of the checkers are college grads who have worked hard for their expensive degrees in sustainable agriculture, so you are also expected to tip if they help you to your car, even if they just stand there watching while you wrestle with your purchases. Also, customers who request a bag, rather than bringing a reusable one from home, will be charged $5. Finally, if the Village finds a cart wheeled from the store to a resident's home, as has been known to happen with other Village Shoppes, you will be fined $100. The neighborhood security cameras Special Ops has just installed should help discourage residents from leaving a cart in a neighbor's yard.

Elder Care Angels

Overwhelmed by the responsibilities of work, family and ailing parents? I know I was, with triplets and two parents with dementia to care for. Five years later, my children are now in kindergarten, and my parents have moved onto higher education in the sky, which is why I have decided to turn the skills I learned taking care of their affairs into my vocation. For only $3000/month, Elder Care Angels will drive, run errands, and schedule medical, dental, legal and personal grooming appointments for your loved ones, and remind them to take their medication. For an additional $2000/month, we will shop for your loved one, pay bills, argue with Medicare and insurance companies, and listen to them repeat stories or talk about their health to the exclusion of anything else.

Note: we do NOT provide cleaning, laundering, bathing or podiatric services. For more information, please email bitsybottinger@yahoo.com.

Miss Gertrude

Miss Gertrude is saddened to report a very nasty incident at the nursing home the other day, when she was attacked by a beautiful but ghastly creature by the name of Flo.

Flo is a swan who apparently led a difficult life before coming to Beautiful Swans, following an abusive relationship with a goose. In Flo's case, this only exaggerated her naturally aggressive temperament, which has led to a habit of chasing elderly residents on a regular basis. The problem arises as the residents in question exit a vehicle and proceed to the front door - hard enough to do with a walker at the best of times, let alone while fending off a 150lb assailant with webbed feet.

Whenever complaints about Flo's behavior are brought to the attention of management, however, the Beautiful Swans charter is cited, because the home's founder, Mr. Charles Palmer, donated the land on condition that it features a sanctuary for this demon in disguise. Apparently, he believes his dead wife's soul has been incorporated in Flo's body - a fact I have no trouble believing, knowing Flossie as I did.

As soon as the bruises have gone, and I recover the use of my left arm, I vow to continue the fight to have Flo removed - permanently. A lady knows when to stand up and fight, even if one's opponent has a stronger beak and far nastier temper. In the meantime, Miss Gertrude would like to remind her gentle readers of the following rules for responsible pet-ownership:

- Do not assume that just because you find your pet's drooling, knee humping or begging adorable, others feel likewise;

- Do not assume that just because you say your pet is friendly/well-behaved, that he/she actually is - or that others believe you;

- Do not assume that when your pet goes bounding (or hissing) up to the border of your property, other people know you have an electric fence;

- Do not assume others are happy to be mauled to death by your poorly trained, out of control animal, just because you would be

On a more positive note, Miss Gertrude is again pleased to open her spring Manners and More class to all Village children between the ages of 8 and 15 every first and third Friday of the month, starting on Friday, April 3. Spaces for girls are filling rapidly, but boys are still very much in demand. Please offer your sons the opportunity to dance, hand in gloved hand, with other Village children - girls and boys. (Miss Gertrude does make concessions to some modern mores, after all). Tuxedos (for boys or girls) and long dresses (ditto) are required.

Village Tennis Team

Congratulations to our Ladies' team for their victory over Team Spank, facilitated in large measure by Dr. Jack Warrior's rigorous morning workouts, which left our players spent, but ultimately much better for it. On Court 1, our number 1 pair, Bitsy and Phoebe, pounded their opposition into ignominy, crushing them in a display of sustained focus and determination that was sometimes scary to behold. Our two champions were as gracious in victory as they would have been in defeat, comforting their sobbing teenage opponents with hugs and tissues, and ignoring one young lady's unfortunate comment to the effect that 'I can't believe we lost to those old biddies.' On court 2, Nancy and Gertrude fared even better, dispatching their opponents with a 6-0, 6-0 victory that saw everyone tucked in bed by 8. On court 3, Ethel and Mary glided to victory 6-2, 6-1, pausing only to adjust their dentures. This glorious victory was a reminder, if we ever needed one, that consistency and ball placement can still trump youthful agility and power.

The victory means the Village Country Club Ladies' Team are now officially League champions, and will have their names etched onto a small plaque in the Ladies' powder room.

The Gentlemen's team also scored their first win this month in the 2.5 circuit, dominating courts two and three 6-4, 7-5 and 6-1, 6-3 respectively, although court 1 complained bitterly about being docked two games in the first set, after one of their players arrived 10 minutes late. Welcome to the USTF, boys, where it's ALL about the rules.

The Gentlemen's win will result in a notation on the giant plaque in the Gentlemen's Grill. Members of the Ladies' Team who complained they are asked to achieve far more to merit a mere mention in the Whiner should remember it is their former teammates (long dead and buried), who established the rule that women should be modest in dress and comportment at all times on Club premises. This rule clearly precludes a plaque listing their achievement. Ladies hoping to challenge this rule are encouraged to do so in person at our annual meeting next month, but must remember that 100% of members in attendance must agree to the change. We suggest you start lobbying now.

2013 COUNTRY CLUB
TENNIS LEAGUE CHAMPIONS
BITSY BOTTINGER
PHOEBE THOMPSON
GERTRUDE MARTINET
NANCY DANVERS
ETHEL MAY & MARY BLY

Diversity Group

The Village Diversity Group is currently revising its corporate and environmental practices, as a result of a lively exchange between two of its longtime members, Pookie Granger and Perky Sparks, at our most recent meeting. Perky brought up the fact that Pookie's selfless devotion to worthy causes was somewhat at odds with her husband's work at the law firm of Keepem Down and Now, which is currently profiting from many of the evictions and foreclosures in the area - including, as it happens, on Perky's house. Pookie responded that it wasn't her fault that Perky's husband couldn't keep a job, which didn't go down well. Fortunately, Special Ops were quickly on hand to separate the two women and dispel the crowd of onlookers before things turned too physical.

Pookie was ultimately persuaded not to resign from the group, and to encourage her husband's firm to make a generous donation to the local homeless shelter, while Perky has been banned from the next two meetings, since she started the argument. In addition, Pookie will have to pay for Perky's eyebrow re-shaping next month in order to cover the gap left by the unfortunate facial hair pulling incident.

The Village Diversity Group recognizes that our outreach programs are often underwritten by corporations whose interests may conflict the with the views of individual members. We would like to stress, however, that the quest for social, economic and political justice is never an excuse for violence.

From: pookiegranger@hotmail.com

My housekeeper has just returned from her first visit to the brand new Holier Than Thou Foods. While she reported they did offer a wide selection of organic, locally sourced and humanely harvested fruits and vegetables, their product labeling does apparently leave something to be desired. I had asked Maria to return with organic quail eggs to substitute for regular ones in my daughter's Easy Fake oven recipes, so imagine my surprise when I later found her taking a hammer and chisel to one of the dozen ostrich eggs she had mistakenly purchased in their place. Never mind that each dinosaur-sized egg cost upwards of $100, or that she had cracked 4 of them, per the recipe's instructions, before I happened upon the scene. Do the store's suppliers not realize that while their customers may be familiar with such exotica, very often the people doing the weekly grocery run on their behalf are not? I trust the Board of Villager Managers will bring this lapse to HTT's attention IMMEDIATELY, so that other Villagers are not inconvenienced the same way.

On a separate note, if anyone would like some eggs for an extremely large omelet, please contact me.

From: ishop4snobs@perkybydesign.com

Can the Village PLEASE also request HTT stock organic milk in glass bottles i literally can't stand the taste of the irradiated stuff they sell in those disgusting cartons which are no doubt also coated in PCP

From: cpalmer@aol.com

I think you mean BPA, not PCP, which would make for an interesting drinking experience. Either way, you should know that irradiated milk is perfectly safe to drink, and most people cannot tell the difference between that and the regular kind.

From: ishop4snobs@perkybydesign.com

Really? Personally I think there is a HUGE difference which is why I only drink grass-fed non-irradiated non-homogenized lactose-free fat-free organic milk sold in calfskin pouches

From: vbliss@richsimplicity.com

Personally, I only drink goat's milk straight from the udder, which is why I keep one tethered in my back yard.

From: barbivanhouzen@aol.com

How would you like it if I tethered YOU in my backyard? I can't BELIEVE you would do that to a poor, defenseless animal. I have requested Village Special Ops pay you a visit shortly.

From: pookiegranger@hotmail.com

Could Village Special Ops please pay a visit to my neighbor who just started keeping chickens? The stench coming from their backyard coop is overpowering. Surely it must be against Village by-laws to keep farm animals on residential property?

From: susielongsuffering@village.org
Residents should note that it is not within the authority of the Village Managers' office to attend to every resident's personal shopping preferences, nor is it a requirement that Holier Than Thou Foods stock food only Village people enjoy. It may have escaped some residents' notice, but they do have other customers!

Also, residents should note that according to Village By-law no. 86949, they are permitted to keep up to 8 domestic animals not exceeding 4" in height or 10" in length, and generating no more than 1 cubic foot of solid waste per week. These guidelines were instituted by the Village Diversity Group, which lobbied hard for residents to be permitted to engage in activities that increase energy and food security. While the Village stopped short of allocating funds for the collection, drying and distribution of animal dung for fuel, we do permit the pasturing of said animals, so long as these are confined to resident yards and not on public property.

From: cpalmer@aol.com
Anyone else see the same beautiful red fox I caught sight of outside my kitchen window this morning? I'm concerned it might be after my chickens.

Friday, April 5

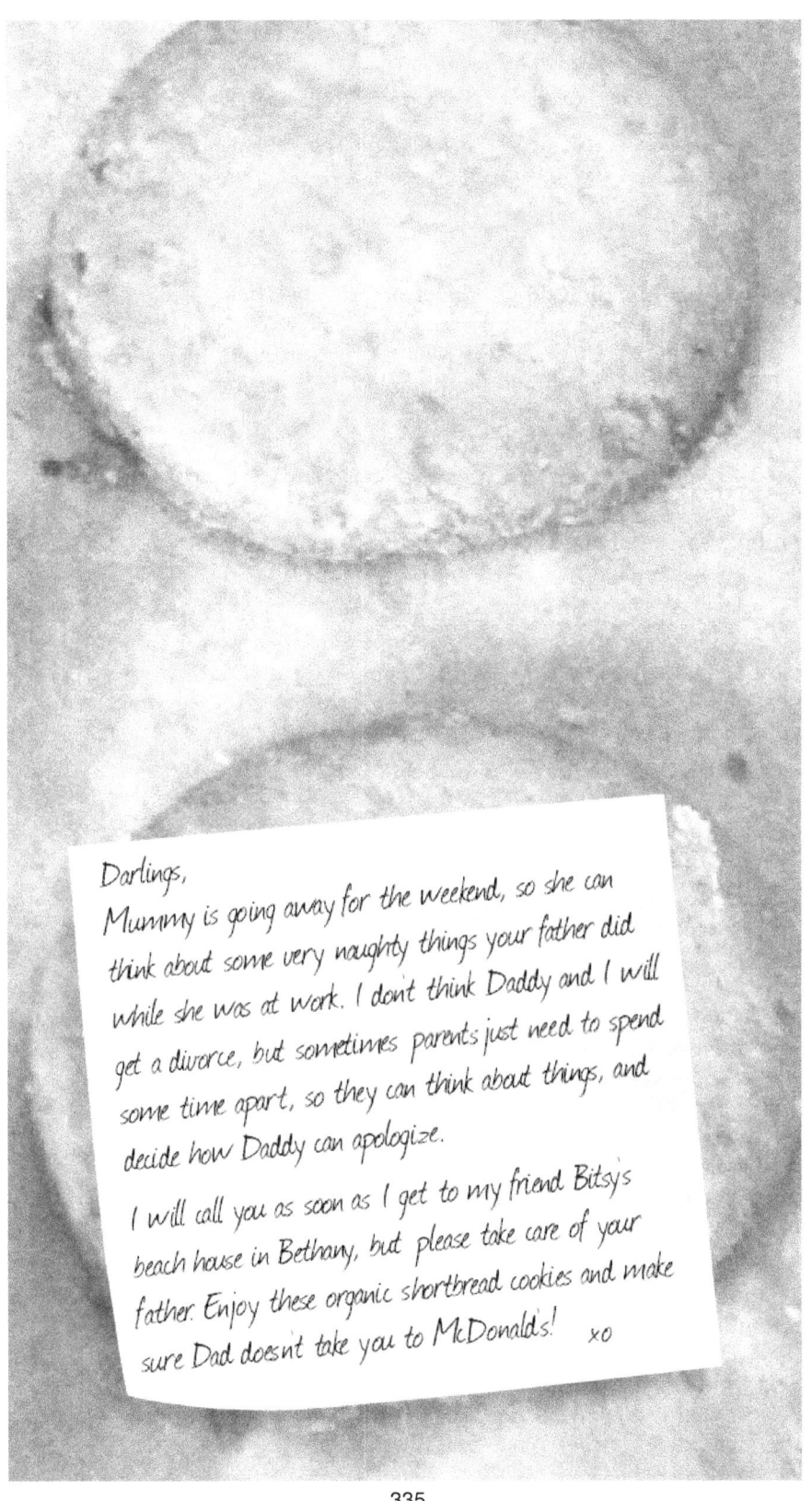

Darlings,

Mummy is going away for the weekend, so she can think about some very naughty things your father did while she was at work. I don't think Daddy and I will get a divorce, but sometimes parents just need to spend some time apart, so they can think about things, and decide how Daddy can apologize.

I will call you as soon as I get to my friend Bitsy's beach house in Bethany, but please take care of your father. Enjoy these organic shortbread cookies and make sure Dad doesn't take you to McDonald's!   xo

Text from Phoebe to Brad
Still can't believe you DIDN'T have an affair with V, but selling your DNA bad enough. Suggest you make appt. with Pandora for Monday, so we can talk.

Saturday, April 6

From: crystalmomof4exlaw@yahoo.com
To: bthompson@pnisventures.com
I would be honored to organize P's 40th surprise birthday party this summer, but are you sure you should be thinking about this now? I know you and Phoebe have been having some issues of late, so you may want to resolve those first.
PTA PRESIDENT, Village Public School

From: crystalmomof4exlaw@yahoo.com
To: phoebegb@channel8news.com
How is the beach?

Have you spoken to Brad since you arrived? He seems very eager to please, judging by the interaction I had with him on the matter of your impending birthday. I've been sworn to secrecy, but suffice to say, I will make sure you get EVERYTHING your heart desires.
PTA PRESIDENT, Village Public School

From: phoebegb@channel8news.com
To: crystalmomof4exlaw@yahoo.com
Brad and I have agreed not to speak until Monday. Frankly, I find his eagerness to please highly suspicious, given that he generally doesn't even remember my birthday. In my experience, men only buy their wives gifts when they are feeling guilty about something.

Bitsy's marriage is in an equally fraught state right now, following the revelation that her husband has been sleeping with their housekeeper. He claims she never had time for him between Botox appointments, Pilates and tennis matches at the Club. Can you imagine? I mean, it's one thing for a husband to betray his wife, quite another for him to do so with someone who is at least 20lbs heavier and looks like she doesn't have time to workout. Then again, Bitsy is looking a little sinewy these days, so maybe a little extra padding feels good?
Senior Affairs Reporter
Channel 8 Local News
Relentlessly local, round the clock

Text from Crystal to Lata
So sorry to hear about earthquake in Peru. Rounding up supplies for you to take to Lima tomorrow. What time is your flight?

Witter posting from femilawyermom
SOS. Babysitter leaving me to deal with crisis in Peru, and hubby about to leave town for a week. How will I survive?

concernedcitizenoftheworld is now following femilawyermom
howcanwehelpthepeopleofperu is now following femilawyermom

Text from Crystal to George
Kurtis just came down with fever and we are out of Tylenol. Can you PLEASE come home now, and pick some up on your way?

Text from Crystal to George
Surely your daughter's health more important than another pick-up game of basketball with the Prez?

Text from Crystal to George
Apparently not. Guess I won't see you before you leave for trip to Bahamas, as I have to take Kimberly to her gym practice at 2. Have safe trip.

Sunday, April 7

Voicemail transcript from Crystal to her father
Dad – why don't you ever pick up your phone? I need to know you are OK. Did you remember to take your medicinal marijuana? I have tutu much else going on to worry about you too. I know you don't want to leave KFC, but frankly, it will make MY life easier if you are here, so I'm going to look at some assisted dying places this afternoon. If you don't want to move, then you are just going to have to find another trouble and strife to take care of you. CALL me.

Transcribed using Yap app voicemail technology

From: crystalmomof4exlaw@yahoo.com
To: marygoodall@aol.com
Thank you so much for checking on my Dad just now. I was worried when I couldn't get hold of him, so I'm glad to learn he has good neighbors, who can be relied on to check on him. Sorry you caught him in bed. I know he still likes to sleep naked, but I don't see why he can't keep a bathrobe close at hand.

I am planning to move him to DC, where I can keep a close eye on him, but in the meantime, I will notify his doctor that he seems to be having another one of his spells.

PTA PRESIDENT, Village Public School

Text from Crystal to Kevin
Can you sign card for Lata, and forge sibs' signatures 2? Know you think u have FAR better things to do w/ time, but she has done LOT for u, and not sure when we will see her again.

Text from Crystal to Kevin

Yes, you can borrow Dad's Brooks Bros. socks, but only if you sign card first. Wouldn't want me to post pix of Lata giving u that neck massage on MeBook, would u?

Good Luck Card from Crystal to Lata, containing check and attached to suitcase full of supplies

Just a small token of gratitude for everything that you have done for us these past few months. I have no idea how we will manage without you, but I guess we will survive! Let me know if there is anything we can do to help while you are gone.

P.S. Thank you for re-grouting the bathroom before you left.

Witter posting from femilawyermom

OK, panic over. I can do this. I am stay at home mother, after all, so how bad can it be? Maybe if life weren't so crazy here in DC, I wouldn't need so much help.

milfwatcher is now following femilawyermom

Text from Crystal to Kevin

STOP torturing your little brother RIGHT NOW or I will come downstairs and SPANK you. I expect u to be on best behavior while Lata and Dad are gone, or you will NOT be going to Jamaica for spring brk.

Monday, April 8

From: crystalmomof4exlaw@yahoo.com
To: bitsybottinger@yahoo.com
Dear Bitsy,

I am responding to your ad for Elder Care Angels in the Village newsletter. I have a 62 year old father who will soon need to relocate to the DC area, as he is divorced and has some health issues. I am also an only child. (Why do I get the feeling our generation is paying for all the fun our boomer parents had?)

Your monthly rate sounds a little steep for what I think my father needs, plus I am home and can help with a lot of the doctor runs, etc., but I would love to meet with you, and work out a compromise package, if you are amenable.

Please let me know what works.
Crystal

PTA PRESIDENT, Village Public School

Text from Crystal to her father

Sorry you are locked out, but don't have time to fly to KC to sort out. Saw

GR8 1 bed apt this pm. Will complete paperwork, but suggest you suck it up in meantime and call mom, as she has spare key.

From: crystalmomof4exlaw@yahoo.com
To: bitsybottinger@yahoo.com
On second thought, I would be happy to pay the full monthly stipend for your services when it comes to taking care of my dad. How soon can we meet?

By the way, do you really think we need to throw yet another class party to mark the end of the marking period, and the start of spring break?

Maybe I'm jaded because Karson is my third child, but I don't think I can bear to sit through another hi-octane sugarfest so soon after Valentine's Day.

Count me in for paper goods and juice boxes, but I draw the line at the chocolate fountain.

Crystal
PTA PRESIDENT, Village Public School

Tuesday, April 9

From: crystalmomof4exlaw@yahoo.com
To: phoebegb@channel8news.com
Sorry for not checking in sooner, but I'm sans George AND Lata this coming week. Leave you to guess whom I miss more. :0

How did last night's session with Pandora go?

PTA PRESIDENT, Village Public School

From: phoebegb@channel8news.com
To: crystalmomof4exlaw@yahoo.com
Suffice to say, it was cathartic to be able to scream at him in a neutral space, but I'm not sure it was helpful.

No doubt, Pandora is right about Brad having many fine qualities as a husband and father, along with exceptionally poor judgment about appropriate ways to raise capital. And you have taught me better than anyone that there is no perfect partner out there. We would just be exchanging one set of issues for another, if we were to seek out another mate. Besides, the chances of a woman in her forties getting another date seem pretty slim, given the abundance of young women like Nina, who seem foolish enough to settle for one they will soon have to visit in the nursing home.

But no matter how much I try to rationalize his behavior, I am still incredibly hurt that he would think so little of our family unit as to consider introducing half-siblings into the mix. And I'm not ready to resume marital relations, which is why Brad is sleeping in the guest room for now.

Sorry to hear you are alone with the cherubs this week. I have been so distracted by my own problems of late, I'm afraid I haven't been able to focus on anyone else's. What's going on?

Senior Affairs Reporter
Channel 8 Local News
Relentlessly local, round the clock

From: crystalmomof4exlaw@yahoo.com
To: phoebegb@channel8news.com
Normally, I would agree with you about exchanging one set of problems for another, but I am beginning to think the cherubs and I might actually be better off with a shared custody arrangement, whereby George is forced to spend time with his kids, and I could be guaranteed some time off.

Did I mention that Lata left for Lima on Sunday?

PTA PRESIDENT, Village Public School

From: phoebegb@channel8news.com
To: crystalmomof4exlaw@yahoo.com
You did – several times. Sorry to hear things with George are so rough. Please don't do anything hasty, especially with Lata gone.

Senior Affairs Reporter
Channel 8 Local News
Relentlessly local, round the clock

Wednesday, April 10

Text from Crystal to Nina
Can u drive Kimberly to school this morning? Lata out of town, and Baby just fell asleep after being up all night with fever. Sorry for short notice, but I'm desperate!

Text from Crystal to Nina
Didn't mean to wake you – sorry. She needs to be there in 10 or will miss bus for school field trip. Can you be ready in 5?

Text from Crystal to Nina
Fact that kids bike to school from age 2 in Germany = impressive, but I don't see anyone doing it here.

Text from Crystal to Nina
OK, biking it is. I'm desperate.

Thursday, April 11

Skye Chat

phoebethompson

rang doorbell on my way to Pilates this morning, but no response. Everything OK? You haven't been answering your home/cellphone, so I was getting concerned.

crystalwalker

recovering from 8 hour ordeal behind bars in the Village Jail yesterday, after I was arrested for allowing Kimberly to bike the 5 blocks to school on her own. I suspected it was against Village bylaws, but she IS ten, and I was out of options. To cut a long story short, she bumped into Tinklepaw II as Barbi Van Houzen was walking her on Park St., which doesn't have a sidewalk. The dog is fine, but naturally, Barbi called Special Ops, claiming Kimberly had assaulted her pooch with a deadly weapon. Of course, I lost my temper with Officers Cuffim and Runn for waking Kurtis up when they rang the doorbell, and found myself pointing out the fact that I rode my bike solo to school from the age of eight. Before you know it, they had whipped out the plasticuffs and marched me off to the Village Jail, where I was charged with reckless child endangerment.

phoebethompson

OMG! That's TERRIBLE. So sorry I wasn't available to help. Did you try asking Brad?

crystalwalker

Felt weird asking him, given everything that's going on between the two of you, but now, of course, I wish I had. Fortunately, Hilary came to my aid and posted the $5k bond they demanded before the authorities would release me. She also took care of the three older cherubs in my absence after they got home from VPS.

I have a hearing date at the beginning of next month.

phoebethompson

Do you have a lawyer?

crystalwalker

I've chosen to represent myself, although frankly, I'm so disgusted with the whole system of over-protective parenting around here, I'm not sure I trust myself not to say something I might regret. Just how many stay-at-home parents, nannies and back-up caregivers does it take in DC to raise a child?

phoebethompson

where was George in all this?

crystalwalker

Deep sea fishing in the Bahamas with a potential investor in the lobbying firm. To be honest, I didn't even think of calling him, which says a lot about the state of our marriage. Pookie and Perky are going to have a FIELD day about this once word gets out.

From: crystalmomof4exlaw@yahoo.com
To: jsmith@plunderhogg.com
Please make alternative accommodation arrangements for my husband when he returns from his trip tomorrow. I will pack up enough clothes for him to last a couple of weeks, and arrange for them to be delivered to the address you supply.

Thank you.
PTA PRESIDENT, Village Public School

Text from Crystal to George
MANY reasons I'm not speaking to you, but yesterday's incident with Special Ops was just final, incontrovertible proof I needed that you are NEVER around when I need you. I've canceled your ticket to Jamaica next week. Pls ask Jane to arrange to have rest of your things picked up after u get back.

Text from Crystal to Kimberly
No need to lock yourself in room. I know u didn't mean to run over Tinklepaw II, or her owner. Special Ops (and mommy) = just over-reacting. I promise everything will be OK.

Friday, April 12

Posting on Village listserv
It has come to the Village Board of Managers' attention that a minor child was given permission by her mother to cycle unaccompanied to the Village Public School recently. While technically not against federal or state law, this practice could set a dangerous precedent, given how busy the Village streets are, which is why Special Ops has decided to prosecute the mother for reckless child endangerment.

The parent, who has not been named to protect her family's privacy, and particularly her children's ability to secure playdates, has been released upon her own recognizance, following the payment of a $5000 bond.

From: ishop4snobs@perkybydesign.com
i can't believe anyone would be so irresponsible if this woman was too busy working or couldn't be bothered to drive her kid to school after the kid missed the bus perhaps she should have considered hiring a nanny.

From: pookiegranger@hotmail.com
I hear the Walker kid knocked down an old lady and almost killed her, is that right?

From: ishop4snobs@perkybydesign.com
i heard she wasn't even wearing a helmet

From: tinklepaw4ever@aol.com

I was the old lady in question, and while I can't remember if the young lady who hit me was wearing a helmet, I can attest that she was cycling at speed, with complete disregard to where she was going. I can only imagine what kind of home she must come from to have learned such lack of respect.

From: chuckpalmer@aol.com
In my day, our children all rode our bikes to school as soon as they took the training wheels off, and aside from one single involuntary amputation of a pinky toe on the spoke of a back wheel, they were fine. How are kids today ever going to hold down a job, raise a family or God Forbid fight a war without mommy or daddy on hand to wipe their a@$?

From: pookiegranger@hotmail.com
Oh, shut up!

From: crystalmomof4exlaw@yahoo.com
For the record, my daughter WAS wearing a helmet, and I AM a stay at home mom with a husband out of town and a full-time nanny, who happened to be in her home country, tending to her countryfolk who lost EVERYTHING in the recent earthquake. Sometimes things happen, no matter how many contingencies you plan for. And frankly, I agree with Chuck. I'm sick and tired of judgmental DC types who won't let their kids so much as pick their own nose without an adult's supervision, and yet can't tear themselves away from their precious career or Country Club to actually spend time with them. Why do you all care so much what I do with mine?

PTA PRESIDENT, Village Public School

From: phoebegb@channel8news.com
To: crystalmomof4exlaw@yahoo.com
URGENT

I can certainly understand why you might be upset with all the listserv comments, but you might not want to respond so publicly. I know the Post has got wind of the story, and the local Gazette is writing a piece for their front page. Besides, don't you still have an application to the Village Country Club, not to mention a court case, pending?

Senior Affairs Reporter
Channel 8 Local News
Relentlessly local, round the clock

From: crystalmomof4exlaw@yahoo.com
To: phoebegb@channel8news.com
At this point, I can't even remember why I wanted to join the Village Country Club, especially if it involves hanging out with such insufferable b@#$%es. What was I thinking?

Plus, when I see my village listserv posting and remember that I'm currently training to be a yoga teacher, it's hard to believe the same person is involved in both. Maybe this is why so many who pursue true spiritual enlightenment decide to lead a monastic life?

PTA PRESIDENT, Village Public School

From: phoebegb@channel8news.com
To: crystalmomof4exlaw@yahoo.com
Point taken, but remember, what happens on the listserv stays on the listserv, so in future, you might want to try toning down your responses. FYI, this story is ALL over the wires now, not to mention Witter, so you need to be extra careful about what you say.

But this gives me an idea. How about we set up an interview with Channel 8 news and I interview you, to get your side of the story? For now, let's leave your yoga journey out of the picture. Shocking as it may be to you and me, some ill-informed people still think of it as the preserve of hippies and flakes.

Senior Affairs Reporter
Channel 8 Local News
Relentlessly local, round the clock

From: crystalmomof4exlaw@yahoo.com
To: phoebegb@channel8news.com
Normally, I would be wary of giving an interview that might prejudice my case, but in this situation, I can't believe it wouldn't help. I mean, does anyone SERIOUSLY think 10 is too young to be allowed to bike unaccompanied to school?

PTA PRESIDENT, Village Public School

From: phoebegb@channel8news.com
To: crystalmomof4exlaw@yahoo.com
You'd be surprised. Around here, a lot of children Kim's age still have full-time nannies.

I promise to present your side of the story as sympathetically as possible, and not ask any hard questions. If you're amenable, I'll be round with a camera crew in 40 mins.

Senior Affairs Reporter
Channel 8 Local News
Relentlessly local, round the clock

From: crystalmomof4exlaw@yahoo.com
To: phoebegb@channel8news.com
Yikes - I have nothing to wear and no time to shop. Can you lend me something?

PTA PRESIDENT, Village Public School

From: phoebegb@channel8news.com
To: crystalmomof4exlaw@yahoo.com
Mi closet is su closet. Brad will let you in. Just remember to wear something that makes you look like a devoted soccer mom. And no black!

Senior Affairs Reporter

Channel 8 Local News
Relentlessly local, round the clock

From: phoebegb@channel8news.com
To: crystalmomof4exlaw@yahoo.com
Congratulations! You were wonderful.

The Lily Pulitzer shift dress you found at the back of my closet made you look like a card-carrying member of the Village Country Club (albeit with a subversive sexiness under that demure Jackie O exterior), while your lawyer training helped you talk with articulate, controlled passion about about how out of control parenting has become in in this town – and probably elsewhere.

I was particularly impressed with the figures you provided on accident and crime rates involving children. Had no idea they were actually higher in the seventies than they are now, but as we know from the fracas over speed humps, irrational fear trumps facts on the ground every time.

The station has asked me to continue tracking your case, and interview you again after your court appearance. On a personal note, I can't thank you enough for the opportunity to work on a story that involves a genuine miscarriage of justice, as opposed to softball pieces with titles like 'When Swans Attack'. It's stories like yours that make my job worthwhile (and not just because they enhance my career).

Senior Affairs Reporter
Channel 8 Local News
Relentlessly local, round the clock

From: crystalmomof4exlaw@yahoo.com
To: phoebegb@channel8news.com
Thank you for the reinforcement about the interview. You could not have been kinder with your questions, and, and the swift kick you gave me every time I was tempted to look at the red light on the camera was helpful, if painful.

Hoping your piece will correct some of the outrageous rumors out there in the Wittersphere, about me leaving my children home alone to go bar hopping at the Village Lounge, etc. I may have made my share of mothering mistakes, but I'm not a monster.

PTA PRESIDENT, Village Public School

Text from Phoebe to Crystal
Just re-posted interview on U-tube, and we're up to 3,000 hits already. You are also trending higher than the First Lady on Goggle!

Text from Crystal to George
Yes, that was me and Kevin you spotted on CNN. Didn't answer phone just now b/c there is nothing to discuss. You are simply never there for me when I need you, and I've had enough. Watch video and you'll see what I mean. www.utube\whengoodmomsgobad\

Bitsy - Might have known you would be a no show for the pre-k Spring Fling class party yesterday afternoon, leaving me and Ms. Banderburg to deal with hoards of crazed five year olds around the chocolate fountain - not to mention, clean up the mess. How convenient that you would turn out to have an urgent tennis match on the day in question.

FYI, Ms. B. was NOT happy about having her dry-clean only dress completely destroyed by 25 pairs of sticky brown hand-prints, but I made it abundantly clear that the fountain was YOUR idea, and that I was resigning as room parent, effective immediately.

Good luck putting on the class play at the end of the year. I hear they are doing Jungle Book, and that you are expected to sew 25 fur costumes single-handedly, then deal with complaints from parents about why their precious son/daughter got assigned the part of the coconut.

Break a leg.

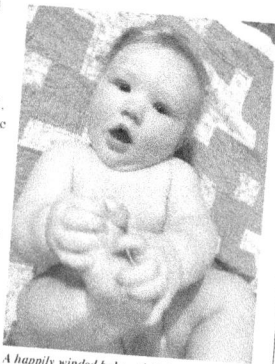

RICH SIMPLICITY

Facing the challenge of an expanding family to include my ex's new girlfriend, Tiffany, and their unborn child has been more complicated than I anticipated. And though my own growth has been rapid and marked, I now recognize the fragility of the human ego. Tiffany seems threatened by the idea of including me in her intimacy circle, which would explain why she neglected to invite me to her baby shower last week. But really, when you think about it, how can Ravi and I be anything less than full-on participants in Tom and Tiffany's future family life? Tom and Tiff already sleep in a cot bed on my master bedroom floor twice a week, because Ravi insists on sleeping in my bed on the nights they have custody. And Ravi is already looking forward to having a captive audience in his new brother or sister for his impromptu piano recitals - performances for which, alas, I so seldom myself have time.

I am also looking forward to passing on mothering tips and insights gleaned over five years of devoted nurturing, which I describe in my tome, The Blessings of Motherhood (available to order online by clicking on the link below.) Indeed, the patented technique I taught Tom to wind an infant, involving bending baby's legs over their head until they either toot, burp or groan, is surely something Tiff will surely thank me for. As I have often said, one of the True Blessings" of marrying someone with prior marital experience is that you get the benefit of all the previous spouse's corrective training, which is invaluable, even if it probably contributed to the divorce.

The good news is we still have a couple of months before the child arrives to work on this stuff, so I am confident that Tom and Tiff will open their bodies, hearts and minds to me by then. As Tiffany is still quite young, I know she has much to learn, including the fact that she will probably soon outgrow having a much older man for a life partner, just like I did Gunther, after I realized he seemed to be more interested in having a nursemaid rather than a vibrant, sexual partner. Maybe then Tiffany will really learn to appreciate the True Blessing" of having an Ex for your Ex.

May you shed old skins and walk towards the light,

Vira

A happily winded baby...ahhh!

Learn how to spin your own wool and crochet a blanket for your baby in 108 easy steps! Click on the link to see a UTube video of Vira crocheting one for the new baby in her life using wool from the pet goats she rescued from the Taliban.

To subscribe to Blessed Moments, Vira's monthly magazine, Special Offer: Subscribe for 24 months at only $3 an issue, and save 60% off the cover price!

To order a signed copy of The Blessings of Motherhood for only $24.99,

To order a batch of FatMama pregnancy poultice (only $39.99 for 8oz.),

To sign-up to receive Vira's weekly newsletter via email (only $19.99 a year),

Thank you for visiting Rich Simplicity. We hope to see you again soon.

From: Rich Simplicity
To: phoebegb@sahmsrule.net

Rich Simplicity: A monthly newsletter bringing you a life of ultimate simplicity, no matter how much money I have.

Volume 04, Issue 03

Blessings,

Facing the challenge of an expanding family to include my ex's new girlfriend, Tiffany, and their unborn child has been more complicated than I anticipated. And though my own growth has been rapid and marked, I now recognize that others may be on a slower trajectory. While meditating about this very issue yesterday, I was reminded again of the fragility of the human ego. Tiffany seems threatened by the idea of including me in her intimacy circle, which would explain why she neglected to invite me to her baby shower last week. But really, when you think about it, how can Ravi and I be anything less than full-on participants in Tom and Tiffany's future family life? Tom and Tiff already sleep in a cot bed on my master bedroom floor twice a week, because Ravi insists on sleeping in my bed on the nights they have custody. And Ravi is already looking forward to having a captive audience in his new brother or sister for his impromptu piano recitals - performances for which, alas, I so seldom myself have time. I am also looking forward to passing on mothering tips and insights gleaned over five years of devoted nurturing, which I describe in my tome, The Blessings of Motherhood (available to order online by clicking on the link below). Indeed, the patented technique I taught Tom to wind an infant, involving bending baby's legs over their head until they either toot, burp or groan, is surely something Tiff will thank me for. As I have often said, one of the True Blessings' of marrying someone with prior marital experience is that you get the benefit of all the previous spouse's corrective training, which is invaluable, even if it probably contributed to the divorce.

The good news is we still have a couple of months before the child arrives to work on this stuff, so I am confident that Tom and Tiff will open their bodies, hearts and minds to me by then. As Tiffany is still quite young, I know she has much to learn, including the fact that she will probably soon outgrow having a much older man for a life partner, just like I did Gunther, after I realized he seemed to be more interested in having a nursemaid rather than a vibrant, sexual partner. Maybe then Tiffany will really learn to appreciate the True Blessing' of having an Ex for your Ex. May you shed old skins and walk towards the light,
Vira

Tuesday, April 16

From: phoebegb@channel8news.com
To: gwalker@plunderhogg.com
Dear George,

Thanks for your email. Crystal is fine, just not returning your emails and calls right now. Not sure what you can do to change the situation, short of getting Crystal off the hook with the magistrate next month, but if I do think of anything, I'll let you know.

Phoebe

Senior Affairs Reporter
Channel 8 Local News
Relentlessly local, round the clock

From: phoebegb@channel8news.com
To: crystalmomof4exlaw@yahoo.com
FW:
Sorry to hear things with George are still dicey, but trust you approve of my response.

Pandora has suggested Brad and I take a vacation together (our first in five years), without the twins, to see if we can work on our relationship without distraction.

I've nixed her idea of her accompanying us, but managed to outsource the girls to my in-laws. We're looking at five days on a private island in the Turks and Caicos, which sounds fancy, but it's not, which is why we can (just about) afford it.

Apparently, the island is so remote, you have to take two planes and an inner tube just to get there, but once you do, you utterly relax, because there's no internet, no phones, no spa and nothing to do. Have you heard of it? www.bydaytwoyoullbebeggingtogetoff.com.

Senior Affairs Reporter
Channel 8 Local News
Relentlessly local, round the clock

From: crystalmomof4exlaw@yahoo.com
To: phoebegb@channel8news.com
A vacation sounds like just what you guys need.

Coincidentally, the Village magistrate has agreed to let me travel next week before my hearing, which means I can go to Jamaica, provided I travel with a responsible adult who promises to stay with me and the cherubs at all times. Normally, I wouldn't think of leaving town with the court case still pending, not to mention me and Geroge, but the bank of TV vans and reporters camped permanently outside our house ever since my arrest is proving more than a little disruptive to the cherubs. Kimberly in particular seems to like the attention a little too much – especially when a photographer from US News and Foreign Report showed up and asked her to pose for the front cover.

I know you already have plans for spring break, so am thinking of asking Hilary, to thank her for posting bail the other day.

PTA PRESIDENT, Village Public School

From: phoebegb@channel8news.com
To: crystalmomof4exlaw@yahoo.com
Do you think that would be wise? You know she has feelings for you.

Senior Affairs Reporter
Channel 8 Local News
Relentlessly local, round the clock

From: crystalmomof4exlaw@yahoo.com
To: phoebegb@channel8news.com
I know, but to be honest, she has been there for me in a way George hasn't, so I'm beginning to think I should be more open to exploring a possible relationship.

Besides, we are traveling with all four cherubs, so unlikely to get more than a moment to ourselves.

PTA PRESIDENT, Village Public School

Wednesday, April 17

Dear Hilary,

I can't thank you enough for coming to my aid the other day, and rescuing me from the Village jail. I had no idea the Village even had a cell until I became its sole occupant. If I'd known that's where all our hard-earned tax dollars were going, I might have been tempted to vote Republican.

I am writing now to ask whether you would do me the honor of being our guest in Jamaica next week for spring break? George won't be able to come after all, but the cherubs and I can't imagine a more helpful, not to mention stimulating companion for our trip. Let me know if you can join.

Fondly,
C.

Thursday, April 18

From: crystalmomof4exlaw@yahoo.com
To: dcparentskilltokissmybutt@seton.edu
So glad you can come!

I am attaching the proposed itinerary. Feel free to embellish with any educational side trips you might enjoy. I hear the masseuse at the resort is to die-for. Looking forward to spending time together soon.

xc

PTA PRESIDENT, Village Public School

GIGANTIC
World Travel Inc.
"WE'LL GET YOU THERE SOMEHOW"

If names of passengers must be changed...just text us!   Agency Record Locator: RMQP02

Passengers: Walker; George, Crystal, Kimberly, Kevin

ITINERARY / INVOICE 034829839   Hilary
AIR TICKET 7387534741 WALKER, GEORGE   (stepchild
AIR TICKET 7387534742 WALKER, CRYSTAL + LAP   (Karson

Electronic Billed to AMEX 8344 $2,739.11
SUB TOTAL $1,739.11
NET BILLING $1,739.11
TOTAL AMOUNT DUE: 0.00

AIR	Day 01

SouthBest Airlines
from: Washington, DC (IAD)
To: Montego Bay, CO (MBJ)
Stops: 0
Seats 06A, 06B
Equipment: Boeing 767 Jet

Flight Number:099
Depart: 07:03am
Arrive: 10:25am
Duration: 03hrs 22 min.
STATUS: CONFIRMED
MEAL: brown bag avail for purchase

- 2.5 hour bus trip following immigration to resort.
- Drop bags at reception and relax (often teeny tiny wait for suite to be ready, usually only a couple of hours)
- Settle kids into rooms--Kurtis will bunk w/ us in the master, so Kimberly has tween girl privacy. Kevin and Karson will fight it out in the room w/ twin beds.
- Cocktails served all day long at the bar. Think you'll find one helpful immediately upon arrival to settle in. Buffet dinner with an "all red" theme (be prepared for color of the day!)
- Post-dinner sing-a-long for all talented cherubs (Walker clan included). Again, cocktails helpful.

ACTIVITY   Day 02

- Bus trip to Dunn's River Falls with teen group. Agreed we'd chaperone, which means Karson and Kurtis too.
- Return to resort for lunch and afternoon fashion show, giving resort gift shop opportunity to exhibit their best wares on the children. Kimberly LIVES for it but hopes that tween vixen blond from Montana won't return and demand all the best western-themed clothing.
- Afternoon siesta, followed by ten and under waterslide extravaganza. One parent required but b/c Kurtis is so young, I'll need it to be you. Thanks in advance b/c the slide can be a little nausea-inducing.
- Buffet dinner with a "Jamaican flag" theme. Really, any garment with a combination of yellow, green and black will do.

ACTIVITY   Day 03

- Teen scuba adventure and boat ride for adults. Be sure to bring Dramamine!
- Afternoon shopping bus trip to Ochos Rios. They require 1 adult per 2 kids, so we'll need to divide and conquer.
- Queen's tea: hat and gloves required. A lingering British formality, but one taken quite seriously. Happy to pack you a fascinator if you aren't used to travelling with one.
- Adult dinner off-property: Usually try to hit a fabulous Indian place in a small town near the resort, but nervous to leave all cherubs behind without at least one adult - esp. this year. You should feel free to go, but I'm also happy to have your company at the Jamaican night buffet.

ACTIVITY   Day 04

- Junior Olympics, Jamaican style, mon. Goat races (adult companion required), basket weaving and jewelry making. The cherubs love this part of the vacay and I must admit to enjoying it too. Dinner buffet tonight, = always British food, so you may want to feast at lunch on the Jamaican peas and rice, as the evening's canned offerings can be rather bland.

Don't have the remaining three days firmly in place yet, but I think you get the gist. Please let me know if any special outings you'd like too [illegible] that can accommodate the cherubs of course! B/c you are so very generous to accompany us. I forget what people without four children might do on vacation, but I'm totally happy to add anything to our agenda that might appeal!   C

Friday, April 19

Text from Crystal to George
Hilary coming to Jamaica in your place. Thought u should know.

Text from Crystal to George
BTW, made an appointment with Phoebe's lawyer, Fiona Forsythe, to meet with your lawyer after we get back. I'm sad that it has come to this, but not sure how else to get through to you.

Text from Crystal to George
Yes, that was picture of me and Kim on front page of the Post. Op ed by

Charles Krabbhammer inside a little strident, but at least he's supportive. Unlike some.

Text from Crystal to Phoebe
Bon Voyage for the Turks! Know you are still mad at me for inviting Hilary to Jamaica, but I need to see if a relationship with another woman could work. Parents' divorce taught me never to judge anyone else until I've walked a mile in their shoes, so hope you will do same 4 me.

Text from Phoebe to Crystal
After what just happened between me and Brad, I can't believe you would even THINK about engaging in an extra-marital relationship. Has everyone gone mad?

Saturday, April 20

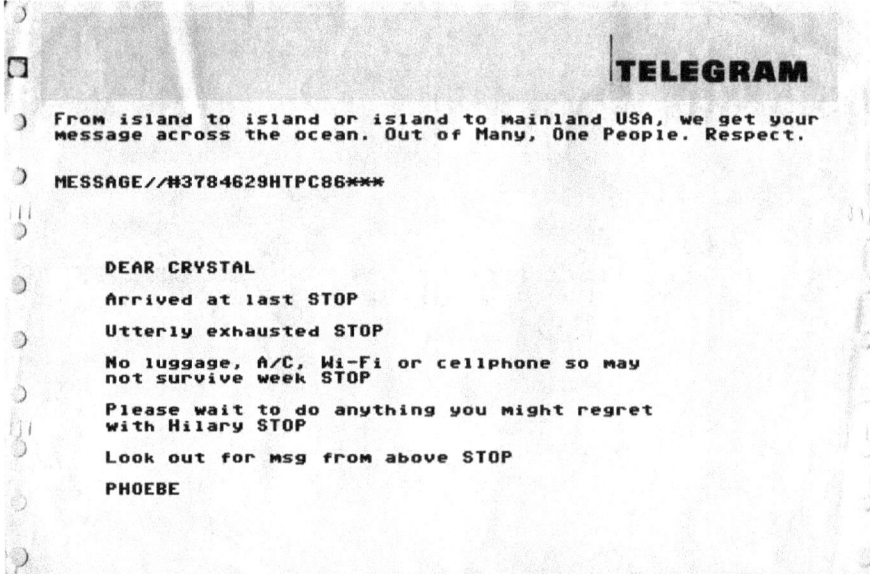

TELEGRAM

From island to island or island to mainland USA, we get your message across the ocean. Out of Many, One People. Respect.

MESSAGE//#3784629HTPC86***

DEAR CRYSTAL

Arrived at last STOP

Utterly exhausted STOP

No luggage, A/C, Wi-Fi or cellphone so may not survive week STOP

Please wait to do anything you might regret with Hilary STOP

Look out for msg from above STOP

PHOEBE

Dear Crystal,

Hope this letter actually reaches you before you leave for Montego Bay. The island postman assures me that Pete the Pigeon's sense of direction is better than any sat-nav, but I'm not so sure. Whatever happens, please don't shoot the messenger, as I've already forked over a $300 deposit for the little bugger.

The island we are staying on is every bit as beautiful as I had been expecting, but not sure it was worth the 48-hour ordeal just to get here. I am also less than enamored of the other three British couples staying with us in rather uncomfortably close quarters, as they appear to have been coming here for the past twenty years and don't want anything to change. This means we are leading a pre-historic existence without running water, electricity, any form of modern communication or even goddamn ice for our drinks (what is it w/ Europeans on this point?!?), so I fully expect rather fewer of us to return. As a matter of fact, if Sara from Woking suggests one more round of charades before dinner, I may just have to start the culling myself.

Brad and I are still not talking, which would make things awkward with the other couples on the island, if Sara from Woking didn't fill the void so eloquently. We are also not touching, so at least I'm catching up on 10+ years of lost sleep. I'm still not sure whether I am most angry at Brad, for attempting something so foolish, in order to get us out of the financial mess in which we find ourselves, or at myself, for letting it happen in the first place.

I am really writing to plead with you not to put your marriage in jeopardy by sleeping with Hilary. Brad and I have been pretty close to the brink these past few weeks, so I've been forced to contemplate life after divorce, and believe me, the prospect is terrifying. Two burned out British music producers from the sixties showed up on the island last night with their very young trophy wives, and even younger families, and you should see the shameless lusting on the part of the menfolk still on their first marriage. So it's clear to me that I would not merit so much as a second glance from the same men, were I ever to divorce and find myself on the singles scene. The only comfort is perhaps the fact that the wrinkled old codgers who get to enjoy such young, nubile flesh can expect to spend their dotage going to Back to School nights and being mistaken for their own child's grandfather (or worse).

Suffice to say, please don't do anything you might regret.

xo, Phoebe

Monday, April 22

MeBook Posting from Crystal

Thank you to everyone who posted kind words of support for my current legal predicament. This experience has been a great way to learn who my true friends are, both on MeBook and the real world. To those who posted critical comments, I'd love to say some choice words, except I've already de-Friended you.

With everything that just happened, I feel truly grateful for the opportunity to get away from DC and especially from the Village for a week. Fortunately my friend and bail sponsor, Hilary, was able to accompany me and the cherubs on vacation to Montego Bay, while George is otherwise engaged. It is such a relief to go somewhere I'm not recognized, and not have to think about the court case for a week. People outside DC can't believe what I did could even be considered a crime, while those in DC can't believe they haven't already just locked me up and thrown away the key.

Here' a shot of Hilary and I enjoying some partner yoga on the beach, while Kimberly and Karson water-ski, and Kurtis plays with her very own resort nanny. (Yes, that is the HM of Seton Academy in a tankini, in case you were wondering.) Haven't seen Kevin since he went for a walk on the beach, but he seems to be quite happy chilling in his room most of the time, which is I guess just what teenagers do, right?

Next, Hills and I are off for a cut and blow dry at the resort salon. Always fancied getting a bob, and this seems like the perfect place to go for it, since it's so hot here anyway. Who needs a husband, when you have help and a friend who actually WANTS to do girly stuff with you?

Dear Phoebe,

My cherubs would be flummoxed by your novel method of communication, but I like to be prepared for any eventuality. Thank God I still vaguely remember how to use a pen.

The Scandals resort we are staying in is fine, but I suspect the Swedish owners would fit right at home with your fellow Brits, given that the order of the day seems to be all about joining in. Please don't worry about me and Hilary. Having to share a bed with both her and Karson is an inhibiting factor, and besides, I don't think Hills really enjoys all the aforementioned activities, as I overheard her muttering under her breath something about the fact she didn't get a PhD just to dance around in a grass skirt.

Having said that, it's nice to spend time with someone who actually likes to talk about their feelings. And the cherubs seem to be having a good time, even if they do occasionally ask when Ms. Manning is leaving, and Dad is coming to replace her - fortunately mostly out of earshot. Must be something to do with the way she keeps trying to lecture them about the oppression of the Jamaican peoples, right after they've ordered up another fruity drink round the pool and changed it to our suite.

As for you and Brad, have you considered just sleeping with the man as a way to overcome your marital impasse? I know this probably sounds hollow, coming from someone who can't even face vacationing with her husband, but in my experience, engaging in physical relations, no matter how angry you feel, is often the first step to re-establishing real emotional intimacy. Your body sometimes tricks you into thinking you might actually have warm feelings towards this person, even if your mind tells you that you loathe them with every ounce of your being.

xc

P.S. Did I mention how much I love my new short hair? People keep mistaking me and Hilary for twins, although I like to think it's partly because she's started borrowing some of my clothes.

"Just when you thought love couldn't get more confusing..."

1-888-SCANDALS

355

Scandals

Dear Hilary,

Sorry you felt obliged to sleep on the pullout sofa in the suite living room last night, but Karson is a restless sleeper, plus I think he's missing his father, which is perhaps why he keeps clambering between us and kicking you in the head (involuntarily) in the middle of the night.

While I enjoyed our (surprise) encounter in the steam room yesterday, I haven't told the cherubs that George and I are attempting a trial separation yet, so I would appreciate if you wouldn't attempt to snuggle or in any way touch me in front of the cherubs. I realize this is frustrating, since you have clearly embraced your new sexual orientation with the gusto of a convert, but neither the cherubs, nor I, are quite there yet, and hence the need for discretion.

As an educator who prides herself on putting the needs of children first, I'm sure you understand.

Crystal

"Just when you thought love couldn't get more confusing..."
1-888-SCANDALS

Dear Phoebe,

Wow - signed, sealed and delivered in less than a day. That must be some kind of record.

To answer your question about Hilary, we did have an encounter in the resort steam room the other day, and while it was certainly enjoyable, it also felt like I was crossing a Rubicon in my relationship with George, and I'm not sure I am ready to do that yet.

Besides, just between you and me, being in Hilary's company 24/7 is turning out to be a teensy bit oppressive. The woman doesn't leave me alone for a second. It would be one thing, if she were good company, but all she seems to do is complain about the fact that we have to do stuff with the kids the whole time. What was she expecting? And if she makes one more comment about the fact that her boobs are bigger than mine, I may just have to point out that her butt is also at least 7 times larger, which might explain why she keeps busting out of my bikini - at both ends.

XC

P.S. Have you slept with Brad yet?

"Just when you thought love couldn't get more confusing..."

1-888-SCANDALS

Dearest Crystal,

I can't believe you would betray George like that, especially after everything I just went through with Brad. And to answer your question, no, he and I have not resumed marital relations. I'm not sure what it will take.

Phoebe

Mom,

I think this was for you?

-Kevin

Dear Phoebe,

Trust me, I regret it myself. If I have to hear one more time about her having dinner with the President and First Lady, I may have to tape her mouth shut. She seems to think they want her brilliant advice on reforming the public education system, rather than to suck up to her as the minion in charge of their children's college applications (not that they need to worry, mind you. The President's daughters could probably burn Seton down and still get into whatever Ivy League they wanted). When I ventured a comment about how hard it must be to understand the challenges of raising and educating children when she hasn't had any of her own, she actually responded that not having children made it easier for her to spot the mistakes others were so clearly making with theirs (with a pointed look at cherubs as she spoke). She also had the gall to point out that she still has a full-on career while I seem to have 'retired' - to which I naturally had to respond that the situation was indeed rather ironic, given that she is at least ten years older than me.

It doesn't help that Hilary gets quite jealous whenever she sees me using my mePhone, and has taken to sticking it down her (ample) cleavage, whenever she sees me surreptitiously trying to send a text under the table at lunch. Find myself wanting to yell at her that she is not my mother, except I fear it would set a bad example in front of Kimberly, who of course is just lapping up all this tension.

Two more days of this, then we'll be back in DC and I can figure out what to do about the gigantic life mess I seem to have got myself into.

Crystal

Sunday, April 28

Text from Phoebe to Crystal
Back in the 'hood. How 'bout you?

Text from Crystal to Phoebe
In taxi on way from Dulles.

Text from Phoebe to Crystal
Can't believe I'm coming home more shattered than I left. Private islands = over-rated, if this is how hard it is to get to them.

Text from Crystal to Phoebe
Don't think I've come back refreshed from vacay since having cherubs. This time particularly bad, since I couldn't even nag Hilary for not helping, like I could w/ George. Just praying to God Lata's back.

Dear Lata,

Thank you for your letter, which was waiting on the doormat for us when we returned from Jamaica over the weekend. I'm sorry to hear communications have been so disrupted by the quake in Lima, but between you, Phoebe and a week without Wi-Fi, I'm getting used to putting pen to paper.

I'm also sorry to hear about the Flores' family losing their house, but glad to hear Catholic Charities has offered to re-locate them temporarily in the US, while their homes are re-built. Of course they can stay with us for a few weeks until they get a new home - especially if it means you will be coming back to us sooner, rather than later.

Their presence may also help my case with the Village magistrate next week. How incredible that you heard the news about my arrest on Univision. I'm hoping she lets me off with probation and some court-ordered visitation from Child Protective Services, but anything I can do to persuade the authorities that I am a person of good character would help.

When can we expect the Flores family to arrive?

Crystal

From: crystalmomof4exlaw@yahoo.com
To: phoebegb@channel8news.com
I haven't heard a peep from Hilary since our trip, and am agonizing over how to tell her I am not interested in pursuing the relationship with her further, for fear of how it might impact the cherubs' position on the Seton waiting list. Trust me, I have frequently wished I were in a lesbian relationship over the years, as it always seemed to be so much easier to have someone who could serve as your best friend, bedmate and free wardrobe all rolled into one. But I fear I'm just too competitive to share my life with another woman.

The cherubs are also increasingly asking after their father, and when they can expect to see him again. While I'm certainly not ready to let George back into my life, I am feeling increasingly guilty about depriving them of their Dad, so I've texted George to see if he can take them this weekend, while I'm preparing for the hearing next week.

I'm sure there's some kind of life lesson to be gleaned from all the misery I've caused myself and others these past few weeks, but if so, I'm having trouble appreciating it. If you have any insight, I'd appreciate it.

PTA PRESIDENT, Village Public School

From: phoebegb@channel8news.com
To: crystalmomof4exlaw@yahoo.com
I think I may have just hit upon a glorious way to cement your break-up with Hilary, with no hard feelings on her part. Just tell her you are, in fact, ready to move in with her together WITH all four of your cherubs.

I'm sure there's nothing quite like looking forward to spending the evening with a houseful of boisterous children at the end of a long day running a school filled with same. Oh, and you're sure she won't mind also taking the cat, the lizard, the hermit crabs and of course, the dog-who-shall-not-be-named? If that isn't enough to send Hilary running for the hills, she may be a keeper, after all.

Senior Affairs Reporter
Channel 8 Local News
Relentlessly local, round the clock

From: crystalmomof4exlaw@yahoo.com
To: phoebegb@channel8news.com
Did as you suggested and worked like a charm. Hilary just texted me to say she doesn't have room for more than one mate in her new bachelorette pad (1 bedroom penthouse on Capitol Hill) and that besides, she knows I am not a 'real' lesbian, after all. She claims I can probably only be happy with a man, however difficult I make that for myself. Now how did she make that sound like a curse?

PTA PRESIDENT, Village Public School

Tuesday, April 30

Posting on Village Listserv
From: cpalmer@aol.com
On behalf of all the oldtimers here in the Village, let me be the first to welcome the Walker family back from their much needed break, and to wish Crystal the best in her court case next week. We continue to be outraged that you have been singled out and persecuted for something that should not be a crime in the first place. What would our wonderful Republican candidate for Vice President (sadly let down by her running mate) have done in the same circumstances?

I urge everyone who is not a crazy, overprotective parent in the Village to write to Congressman Dutch Holland about this egregious miscarriage of justice, and let kids, and parents, regain some of their freedom!

From: crystalmomof4exlaw@yahoo.com
To: phoebegb@channel8news.com
FW: Village Listserv Posting
WTF? Appealing to Vice Prez candidate's supporters is definitely not going to help my case around here. On the other hand, Chuck did send me $10, to help with my legal costs. I guess I should be grateful, right?

PTA PRESIDENT, Village Public School

From: phoebegb@channel8news.com
To: crystalmomof4exlaw@yahoo.com
Too bad he didn't quote the First Lady. Hasn't she started a campaign to get kids back on bikes, as a way tackle childhood obesity? Which gives me an idea. What if we try and enlist the support of the First Lady for your cause? Not sure how we would do this yet, but if we can pull it off, it might solve your problems with the Village and the board of Seton in one go.

What do you think?

Senior Affairs Reporter
Channel 8 Local News
Relentlessly local, round the clock

From: crystalmomof4exlaw@yahoo.com
To: phoebegb@channel8news.com
It's a great idea, but short of asking George, who plays a pick-up game of basketball with the President most Sundays, I'm not sure how you could pull this off. And I'd rather do time than ask him for that kind of favor. I don't want to let him think his job has been anything but a destructive force in our marriage.

PTA PRESIDENT, Village Public School

Text from Crystal to Kevin and Kimberly
Flores family arriving from Lima on Friday. Expect you to welcome them into our home, and clear space in your closet for Luiz and Yolanda. Remember,

they have lost everything, while you guys are just going through some family/legal stuff. Might help to have some perspective.

Text from Crystal to Kevin and Kimberly
Yes, you can spend the night with your father, but tell him to pick u up. Karson also.

DC Diary

The Walkers Take on the Nation's Capital

BLOG ARCHIVE

My Arrest, My Hearing, My Support From All of You

I know many of you have seen the footage of me on U-tube or CNN being arrested on the grounds of reckless child endangerment for letting Kimberly ride her bike by herself to school. It was traumatic, to say the least, to find myself in the Village Jail for something I had no idea was even illegal (it's not). Even worse was the realization that George was unwilling, or unable, to help me during my time of need.

Kimberly happily riding her bike

My hearing date is set for early next month. I am planning to plead guilty to this ridiculous charge, on the grounds that I wouldn't change a thing about what I did. While the authorities are unlikely to impose a custodial sentence, I will likely face probation and follow-up visits from Child Protective Services for sometime to come. All this is very trying for both me and Kimberly, who has done absolutely nothing wrong, but I am at least grateful for the opportunity to gain some clarity into what has and has NOT been working in my marriage, and my life as a stay-at-home mom.

In the meantime, I truly appreciate the support from my friends and family in Kansas City, as well as the outpouring of support from friends, neighbors and even complete strangers here in DC, not to mention the world beyond. If it weren't for my friends, or for my yoga training, I would not have survived these past few weeks.

No comments:

Post a Comment

Comment as: Select profile

Publish   Preview

DC Diary
My Arrest, My Hearing, My Support From All of You

I know many of you have seen the footage of me on U-tube or CNN being arrested on the grounds of reckless child endangerment for letting Kimberly ride her bike by herself to school. It was traumatic, to say the least, to find myself in the Village Jail for something I had no idea was even illegal (it's not). Even worse was the realization that George was unwilling, or unable, to help me during my time of need.

My hearing date is set for early next month. I am planning to plead guilty to this ridiculous charge, on the grounds that I wouldn't change a thing about what I did. While the authorities are unlikely to impose a custodial sentence, I will likely face probation and follow-up visits from Child Protective Services for sometime to come. All this is very trying for both me and Kimberly, who has done absolutely nothing wrong, but I am at least grateful for the opportunity to gain some clarity into what has and has NOT been working in my marriage, and my life as a stay-at-home mom.

In the meantime, I truly appreciate the support from my friends and family in Kansas City, as well as the outpouring of support from friends, neighbors and even complete strangers here in DC, not to mention the world beyond. If it weren't for my friends, or for my yoga training, I would not have survived these past few weeks.

Chapter 10

May, 2013 Vol. 42, Issue 5
Always FREE, but donations appreciated

Please direct submissions and inquiries to:
whining@villagepress.com
P.O. Box 357 Village Town, MD

VILLAGE WHINER

Your trusty monthly newsletter of
the "Most Livable Village," 1989
Village Times Magazine

Village Board of Managers Meeting

The Village Board of Managers is aware of the controversy about the arrest of a Village resident last month on reckless child endangerment charges, after she let her ten year old daughter bike unaided to school. Unfortunately, we are unable to comment further, while the case is ongoing, but we will be reviewing our by-laws on the matter at our board meeting next month.

In other news, The Board of Managers continues to work on guidelines for keeping live animals on Village property, following a number of complaints about Chuck Palmer's new rooster, which awakens the entire Village each day punctually at 4 a.m. The Board has given Mr. Palmer ten days to figure out a solution to this problem, or evacuate the bird to the nearest farm animal rescue facility.

Vira Bliss has also been granted permission to keep the two goats she just had down in specially from Afghanistan to begin production of fine cashmere sweaters for exclusive sale to Village residents and subscribers to her newsletter, but on no account are said goats permitted to breed. She must also relocate the male and female ostriches on her property as there have been too many complaints from parents of small children about the female's proclivity to lean its head over the fence and steal balls from them on the Village Green. Apparently the female also does not take kindly to anyone attempting to retrieve said objects from under her bottom while she is nesting. Aside from the exceptions above, no resident may acquire a new animal for the production of food, shelter or clothing until the Board is able to have a full airing of the issues involved at its June meeting. While it is commendable that residents are choosing to live off the land it is also true that many of the agricultural products being produced in Village backyards are available for sale at Hillet than Thoid Foods - often at lower cost, once you factor in the hourly rates for the landscaping crews and migrant workers many residents are using to tend to their crops and livestock.

Miss Gertrude

Miss Gertrude is saddened to announce the death of Flo, the grand old dame of swans living at the Beautiful Swan Retirement Village, after a tussle with a resident over a string of priceless pearls. Flo managed to swallow them all but the damages in question, only to choke to death while trying to re-adjust the strands around her own neck (allegedly). Residents will be glad to hear that Flo will be interred as part of the Village speed bump program and that Miss Gertrude will be thinking of her every time she visits her son and damages her suspension in the process.

Several Village teens have written to me to bemoan the demise of the practice of young men "meeting the parents" before taking a girl on a date. Teens these days would apparently rather send a text to inform said date that they are waiting outside, and think it's completely lame of parents to insist on such old-fashioned niceties. While it's not clear to Miss G. that anyone actually even dates anymore, given that most teens like to go out in feral packs, pairing off for vague assignations charmingly known as "hook-ups," she urges teens to consider how much more likely they are to get lucky "as the saying goes, if they are prepared to stand out from the crowd by charming the cuisties first. Miss G. would be curious to hear from Village teens how this approach works. Feel free to let her know in writing, via email or by text if necessary. :)

Village Tennis Team

It has come to the Village Country Club's attention that several players on the Ladies' tennis team have been taking prescription medication to improve their performance. This practice came to light after Bitsy Bollinger was caught stealing a vial of Ritalin from Pookie Granger's purse at a playground the other day. When confronted about the theft, which was captured by CCTV cameras on the Village Green, Bitsy responded by screaming at Pookie that it wasn't fair her son was prescribed performance enhancing drugs by the Granger's family concierge family physician, while Bitsy's triplets were critically tested by the Village Public School and pronounced "normal." Labels that Bitsy claims will haunt their educational prospects forever on up.

When pressed further, however, Bitsy ultimately confessed to stealing the pills to her own personal use during her upcoming match with Phoebe Thompson against the Belleville Country Club in Potomac next week. According to Bitsy, the women on the Belleville team are used to popping the pills like Tic-Tacs right before a match so Bitsy felt obliged to level the playing field. As a result of these allegations, the entire Ladies' Tennis intra-club league has been suspended for the rest of the month pending further investigation, and the league will institute random testing once play resumes.

The Gentleman's Tennis team has issued a statement deploring the use of any chemical or artificial stimulants on recreational tennis, but has petitioned the league to exclude Cialis and Viagra from its list of performance enhancing drugs. A number of their wives have filed objections to this exception.

Diversity Group

The latest round of complaints to our Village Board make clear there is a growing divide in our lovely burb between those inclined to live in harmony with the earth and those who believe the industrial revolution happened for a reason. The lack of civil discourse between the two viewpoints has resulted in a growing inability to appreciate valid arguments on both sides. If we aren't talking at each other, we aren't understanding each other either. Therefore, at the suggestion of Country Club member and Village resident Molly Mills and her neighbor, Bob "the plant fanatic" Lieberman, the VDG will host an Earth Summit on Sunday, May 10th, in the Gentleman's Lounge of the Village Country Club to promote a better understanding of each others' beliefs. As a temporary measure, the Club is willing to lift its "no denim" rule in order to accommodate those who claim to possess no other fabric in their wardrobe.

We look forward to seeing you there.

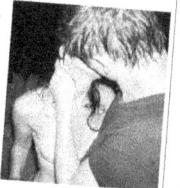

Bob Lieberman in denim, moments before digging a hole

Village Board of Managers Meeting

The Village Board of Managers is aware of the controversy about the arrest of a Village resident last month on reckless child endangerment charges, after she let her ten year old daughter bike unaided to school. Unfortunately, we are unable to comment further, while the case is ongoing, but we will be reviewing our by-laws on the matter at our board meeting next month.

In other news, The Board of Managers continues to work on guidelines for keeping live animals on Village property, following a number of complaints about Chuck Palmer's new rooster, which awakens the entire Village each day punctually at 4 a.m. The Board has given Mr. Palmer ten days to figure out a solution to this problem, or evacuate the bird to the nearest farm animal rescue facility.

Vira Bliss has also been granted permission to keep the two goats she just had flown in specially from Afghanistan to begin production of fine cashmere sweaters for exclusive sale to Village residents and subscribers to her newsletter, but on no account are said goats permitted to breed. She must also relocate the male and female ostriches on her property as there have been too many complaints from parents of small children about the female's proclivity to lean its head over the fence and steal balls from them on the Village Green.

Apparently, the female also does not take kindly to anyone attempting to retrieve said objects from under her bottom while she is nesting. Aside from the exceptions above, no resident may acquire a new animal for the production of food, shelter or clothing until the Board is able to have a full airing of the issues involved at its June meeting. While it is commendable that residents are choosing to live off the land, it is also true that many of the agricultural products being produced in Village backyards are available for sale at Holier than Thou Foods - often at lower cost, once you factor in the hourly rates for the landscaping crews and migrant workers many residents are using to tend to their crops and livestock.

Miss Gertrude

Miss Gertrude is saddened to announce the death of Flo, the grand old dame of swans living at the Beautiful Swan Retirement Village, after a tussle with a resident over a string of priceless pearls. Flo managed to wrestle them off the dowager in question, only to choke to death while trying to re-adjust the strands around her own neck (allegedly). Residents will be glad to hear that Flo will be interred as part of the Village speed hump program, and that Miss Gertrude will be thinking of her every time she visits her son and damages her suspension in the process.

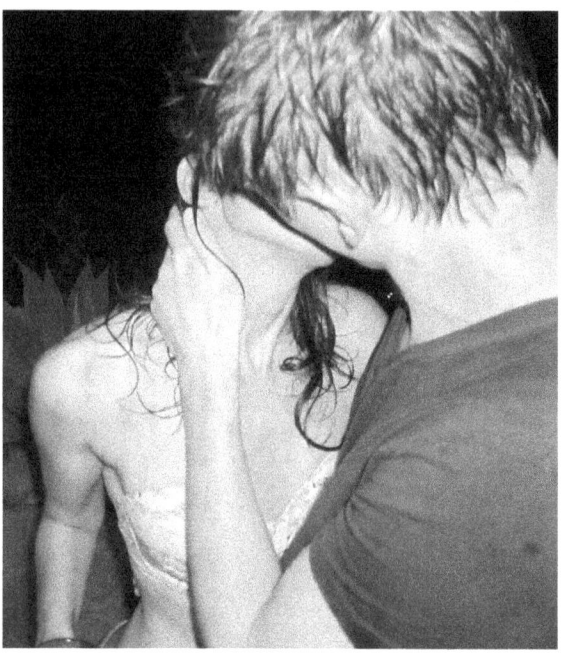

Several Village teens have written to me to bemoan the demise of the practice of young men 'meeting the parents' before taking a girl on a date. Teens these days would apparently rather send a text to inform said date that they are waiting outside, and think it's completely lame of parents to insist on such old-fashioned niceties. While it's not clear to Miss G. that anyone actually even dates anymore, given that most teens like to go out in feral packs, pairing off for vague assignations charmingly known as 'hook-ups,' she urges teens to consider how much more likely they are to 'get lucky,' as the saying goes, if they are prepared to stand out from the crowd by charming the crusties first. Miss G. would be curious to hear from Village teens how this approach works. Feel free to let her know in writing, via email, or by text, if necessary. :)

Diversity Group

The latest round of complaints to our Village Board make clear there is a growing divide in our lovely burb between those inclined to live in harmony with the earth and those who believe the industrial revolution happened for a reason. The lack of civil discourse between the two viewpoints has resulted in a growing inability to appreciate valid arguments on both sides. If we aren't talking at each other, we aren't understanding each other either. Therefore, at the suggestion of Country Club member and Village resident Muffy Mills and her neighbor, Bob "the plant fanatic" Lieberman, the VDG will host an Earth Summit on Sunday, May 10th, in the Gentlemen's Lounge of the Village Country Club, to promote a better understanding of each others' beliefs. As a temporary measure, the Club is willing to lift its 'no denim' rule in order to accommodate those who claim to possess no other fabric in their wardrobe.

We look forward to seeing you there.

Bob Lieberman in denim, moments before digging a hole

Village Tennis Team

It has come to the Village Country Club's attention that several players on the Ladies' tennis team have been taking prescription medication to improve their performance. This practice came to light after Bitsy Bottinger was caught stealing a vial of Ritalin from Pookie Granger's purse at playgroup the other day. When confronted about the theft, which was captured by CCTV cameras in the Village Yurt, Bitsy responded by screaming at Pookie that it wasn't fair her son was prescribed performance enhancing drugs by the Granger's fancy concierge family physician, while Bitsy's triplets were officially tested by the Village Public School and pronounced 'normal' - a label that Bitsy claims will haunt their educational prospects from now on.

When pressed further, however, Bitsy ultimately confessed to stealing the pills for her own personal use during her upcoming match with Phoebe Thompson against the Belleville Country Club in Potomac next week. According to Bitsy, the women on the Belleville team are used to popping the pills like Tic-Tacs right before a match, so Bitsy felt obliged to level the playing field. As a result of these allegations, the entire Ladies' Tennis interclub league has been suspended for the rest of the month pending further investigation, and the league will institute random testing once play resumes.

The Gentlemen's Tennis team has issued a statement deploring the use of any chemical or artificial stimulants in recreational tennis, but has petitioned the league to exclude Cialis and Viagra from its list of performance-enhancing drugs. A number of their wives have filed objections to this exception.

FOR SALE

Cashmere sweaters! These exclusive sweaters are hand-knitted and spun from wool gathered from goats who are hand-reared on the private estate of Vira Bliss.

Sizes available: xxsmall, xsmall, small and petite. Only $500 each.

Please note: all sweaters are dyed using vegetable coloring, so they must be carefully hand-washed in cold water, unless you absolutely love the color of beetroot. For best results, send to organic dry cleaners.

Thursday, May 2

From: phoebegb@channel8news.com
To: crystalmomof4exlaw@yahoo.com

Pandora thinks a Relationship Rebirthing session might help Brad and I break through our relationship impasse and resume physical relations. Apparently, it's a symbolic way to work through the pain, heal wounds and emerge, hopefully with a new, stronger bond born out of the ashes of the past.

I have no illusions that it will succeed, but don't know what else to try, so I'm leaving work early in order to prepare. Any chance you might have a wading pool we can borrow?

Senior Affairs Reporter
Channel 8 Local News
Relentlessly local, round the clock

From: crystalmomof4exlaw@yahoo.com
To: phoebegb@channel8news.com

I do have a wading pool, and only wish our hot tub was ready for you to use in its place. I truly admire the lengths you will go to return to a state of marital bliss or, at least, the state of detente that generally exists after the ten year mark.

The pool is very large and unwieldy, so I'm sending Kev down with it now. I'm encouraging him to step up as the man of the house in George's absence, so please feel free to ask him to inflate it. Might take a while before the palm trees get fully erect and the water fountain starts working, but I think you'll enjoy the effect once it does.

Good luck!

PTA PRESIDENT, Village Public School

Friday, May 3

From: phoebegb@channel8news.com
To: crystalmomof4exlaw@yahoo.com

Thanks for lending us the wading pool. It was a lot of fun once it was fully inflated, which took a couple of hours and only one call to the out of hours doctor when Brad accidentally hyperventilated. Since we have no intention of going through the ordeal of attempting to deflate it before returning, I have asked Brad to sluice the pool down with bleach before driving it over on the roof rack of our minivan this morning, while I'm at work.

The re-birthing session itself turned out to involve a ritual reenactment of actual labor, complete with simulated water-breaking, and several pints of pigs' blood. Thank God it's Brad's responsibility to scrub whatever Pandora used to simulate amniotic fluid off the floor tiles in the bathroom, and to wash all the towels.

Blood, guts and tears aside, the process did elicit from Brad just how badly he wants more children, which was apparently a big motivating factor in his decision to sell his seed to Vira (the other factor being to raise seed money to set up a manufacturing facility for his new pesto business – pun intended). And while the session did have the effect of forcing Brad and I to bond over our mutual humiliation at having to simulate labor while squatting naked and knee-deep in a pseudo birthing pool (albeit one with exotic palm trees that squirted one in interesting places), I'm not sure I can be persuaded of the wisdom of having another child, especially with someone who has just demonstrated such poor judgment.

At least the events of the past few weeks have made me appreciate having a job to escape to, as well as an independent income, if it turns out I can't move beyond what transpired between him and Vira. I'm increasingly coming round to the view that a woman simply can no longer indulge in the luxury of not working, no matter her economic circumstances. Quite apart from the risk of ending up divorced or widowed, being subject to the hair-brained business ideas and general incompetence of another human being is a risk no one, be they husband or wife, can afford to take.

Besides, the story of your arrest is continuing to raise my visibility at the station in the way that makes me think I might actually have a chance of making anchor one of these days. Is it wrong that I am also enjoying throwing my new found weight around with the young know-nothings in the production room, who have learned to fear, if not respect me, every time I call them into my office to correct them on their use of the English language?

Of course, I'm also aware that my good fortune comes at the expense of your suffering. Perhaps now is a good time to tell you that against your wishes I did ask George to see whether the First Lady could help in any way. It seems so clear to me that you could benefit from her intervention. George fell all over himself assuring me he was "on it," but this doesn't mean his efforts will necessarily pay off. I don't want to offer you false hope, but I can't let you walk into the Village kangaroo court without knowing that your husband is at least trying his best to make things right.

All the best, and know that come what may on Monday, I will be there with my camera man to record it!

Senior Affairs Reporter
Channel 8 Local News
Relentlessly local, round the clock

From: crystalmomof4exlaw@yahoo.com
To: phoebegb@channel8news.com
I'm not convinced George cares enough about anything aside from work to help me or the cherubs right now, although I am encouraged to know that seeing his wife get arrested does at least seem to have gotten his attention. But I'm determined to tell the truth and let the chips fall where they may, whether or not the First Lady deigns to intervene. And since yoga has taught me that I can't control the universe, only my intention, I'm going to focus on framing what I have to say in the calmest, most direct possible way.

By the way, I think having another child is an excellent idea, if only because you will be beleaguered in much the same way I am now. Nice, huh? Seriously, I wonder how I ever managed to create the time to have the cherubs, and why now I can't find a moment to spend with them.

I blame the Steamy Yoga training, which initially seemed an excellent way to find more zen – something my family suggests I need desperately – and now seems like just another time suck.

Just yesterday, I found myself mortified that my Drooping Butterfly pose contained so much more sag than Nina's. Of course, it did, because I'm a full seventeen years older than her! Why in the world did I need to set myself up for this ridiculous competition? I'm afraid, dear Phoebe, that I may be my own worst enemy after all.

Thanks for wishing me luck on Monday. I have a feeling the Village Hall will be mobbed with those determined to see me burned at the stake near the Village Yurt.

PTA PRESIDENT, Village Public School

Text from Crystal to Kevin
I don't care if Luis used your laptop w/o permission last night. While Flores family are guests in our home, I expect u to share your belongings w/o complaint. Btw, have I told u how much I love you?

Text from Crystal to Kimberly
Yes, you do need to sit with Maria at lunch tomorrow. Her English may not be perfect, but it's definitely way better than your Spanish. :0 Btw, mommy loves u oh so very much. And it is NOT your fault I'm going to court 2morrow, no matter what Pookie's daughter says.

So sorry Mommy over-reacted tonight when you punched me on the arm for wrestling the VBox console out of your hands so you could come to dinner. I know you are missing Daddy very much right now, but that doesn't mean you get to take out your feelings on me. Mommy needs to focus on her hearing tomorrow, but I promise to talk to Dad and figure out a way for us all to get along once that is over.

xo, Mom

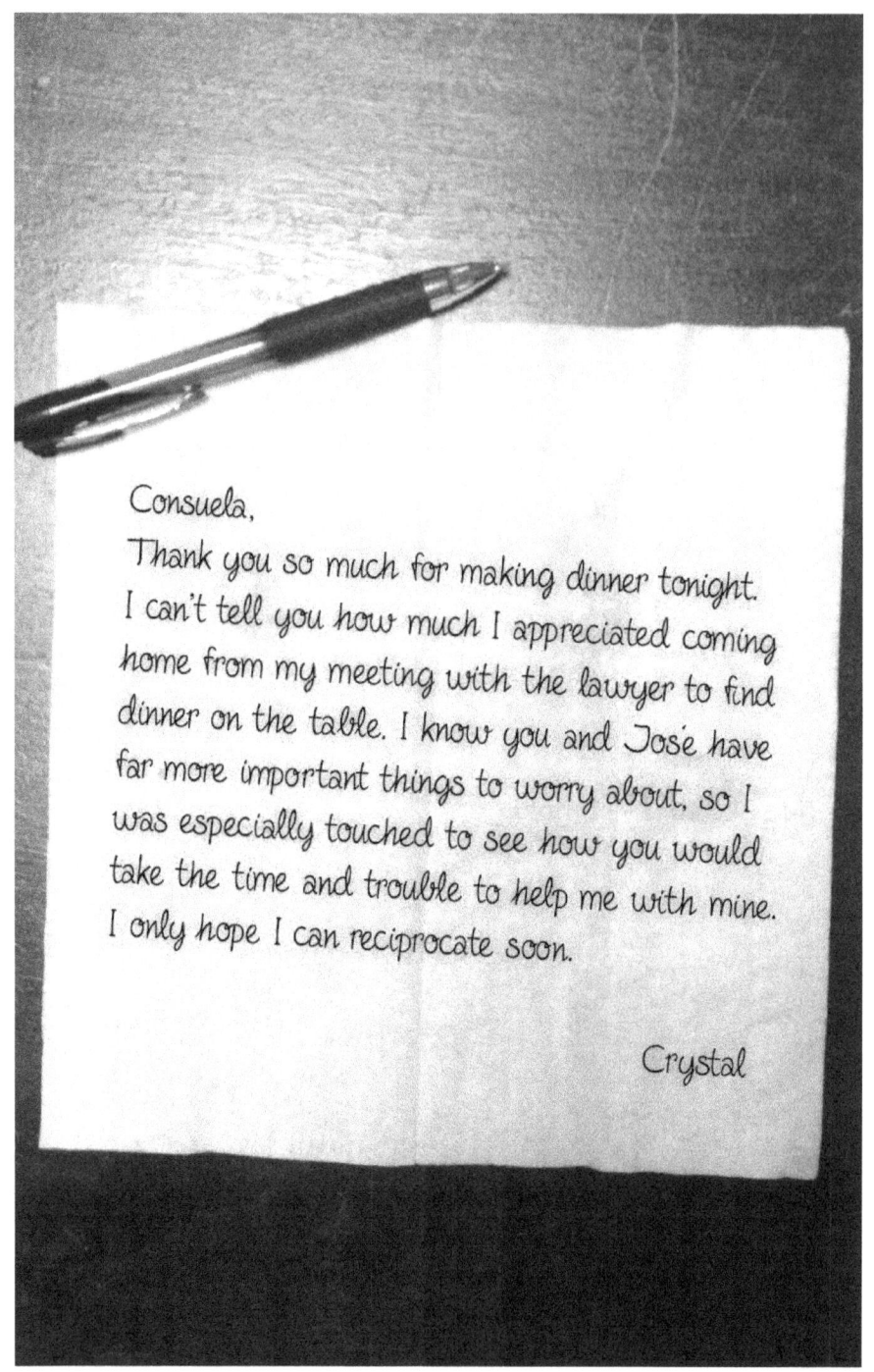

Consuela,

Thank you so much for making dinner tonight. I can't tell you how much I appreciated coming home from my meeting with the lawyer to find dinner on the table. I know you and José have far more important things to worry about, so I was especially touched to see how you would take the time and trouble to help me with mine. I only hope I can reciprocate soon.

Crystal

Monday, May 6

Text from Phoebe to George
No sign of FLOTUS in the hearing room so far. Any idea if she will show?

Text from Phoebe to George
I guess it was too much to hope that she would take time out of her busy schedule for rich people problems.

Posting on Village Listserv:
From: pookiegranger@hotmail.com
In case you are wondering why there's a helicopter hovering over my house and Special Ops are out in force, I'm delighted to report that I've just spotted "Renaissance" (secret service name for our very own First Lady) sitting in the back of an armored limo making its way through our peaceful 'hood. Assume she's headed to the ladies' luncheon I'm hosting at Club today, even though you'd think she would have bothered to tell her social secretary to RSVP in the normal way. Note to self: use the good china! Too bad for those who opted not to come today, in favor of attending the hearing......

From: crystalmomof4exlaw@yahoo.com
To: phoebegb@channel8news.com
I'm still in a state of shock and awe that the First Lady actually showed up at my hearing! Her testimony about the obesity rate of children in this country and the need to get them moving again clearly made an impact on the magistrate. And the look on Pookie's face as she watched the motorcade scream past the luncheon tent at the Club was almost worth getting arrested for in the first place, as was Barbi's reaction when the magistrate threw the case out. Almost.

I'm also encouraged that the Village Board of Managers is considering adopting a formal endorsement of children ages 8 and above being given permission to ride bikes unaccompanied (with proper helmets, flashing lights and fluorescent armbands at all times) at their next monthly meeting, even if this means increased patrols by Special Ops. Is it possible that good intentions and confidence in the universe actually can make the right thing happen?

Taking the Flores family and cherubs out for dinner to celebrate. Any chance you guys can join?

PTA PRESIDENT, Village Public School

From: phoebegb@channel8news.com
To: crystalmomof4exlaw@yahoo.com
Need to wrap up your story back at the studio, but enjoy!

Senior Affairs Reporter
Channel 8 Local News
Relentlessly local, round the clock

Text from Crystal to George
Thank you for sending FLOTUS to my defense today. It really made a difference. When can we talk?

From: crystalmomof4exlaw@yahoo.com
To: phoebegb@channel8news.com
Found myself drunk texting George in a moment of elation after we got back from dinner last night to thank him for putting my case on the First Lady's radar.

He didn't respond, so I left a voicemail saying I was touched to see that he would call in such a big political behavior on my behalf, and asking him to call so we could talk.

The message on his voicemail suggested he was out of the country until yesterday, so I contacted his office just now, but he isn't there – even though they were expecting him. He had been in the Bahamas, apparently, meeting with a big new Plunder & Hogg client and was supposed to report back at their monthly Board meeting this morning, but he didn't show up.

I'm not surprised about his change of plans, but it is weird that he would miss work without reporting in. Think I should be concerned?

PTA PRESIDENT, Village Public School

From: phoebegb@channel8news.com
To: crystalmomof4exlaw@yahoo.com
First, let me just say what a privilege it was to have been the one reporter to arrive early enough to capture the First Lady's on-record comments about your case. My first ever exclusive! I could get used to this.

I will refrain from commenting upon Pookie's listserv posting about her luncheon, as it's surely bad karma to gloat at another's public misunderstandings, but surely this was one of those signs from the universe you are always going on about since you started yoga teacher training?

As for George, I can absolutely assure you he is desperate to make amends for his many absences these past few months. I can't imagine he would promise the First Lady's staff to intentionally lose at basketball for the next six months, just so that the Prez wouldn't mope on Sunday nights, then promptly jeopardize any goodwill he earned with you by neglecting to call.

Pretty sure there must be some innocent explanation, like his cellphone and laptop batteries have both died, but you might want to contact the Bahamian authorities, just in case.

Senior Affairs Reporter
Channel 8 Local News
Relentlessly local, round the clock

Wednesday, May 8

From: crystalmomof4exlaw@yahoo.com
To: reservations@royalbahamianhotel.com

To whom it may concern:

I am trying to trace the whereabouts of my husband, George Walker, who was booked to stay in your hotel until last Sunday, May 5. The confirmation for his booking number is ezylife41.

I believe he checked out earlier today, but he did not return home on his originally scheduled flight, and he is also not returning my calls, or responding to email or texts.

I would appreciate if you can provide any insight into where he might have gone, as I am getting concerned.

Yours Faithfully,
Crystal Walker
PTA PRESIDENT, Village Public School

From: crystalmomof4exlaw@yahoo.com
To: reservations@royalbahamianhotel.com

I am glad to hear my husband apparently extended his stay at your hotel, even though neither your staff nor any of the guests report seeing him for the past couple of days. Would you mind checking the resort one more time to make sure he hasn't run off with one of the mermaids from your Aquarium, as I know from experience he finds them mesmerizing?

PTA PRESIDENT, Village Public School

From: crystalmomof4exlaw@yahoo.com
To: phoebegb@channel8news.com

George is STILL not responding to the repeated texts and voicemail messages I have left. The hotel in Nassau said their records indicate he checked out this morning, as scheduled, but the airline says there's no record of him on the flight back to DC. No one in his office, Sister T included, seems to have any idea where he is either.

I am getting very concerned, although I can't say it's the first time he's been hard to track down. Guess I must still care about the man after all. What do you think I should do?

PTA PRESIDENT, Village Public School

From: phoebegb@channel8news.com
To: crystalmomof4exlaw@yahoo.com

Have you checked the other airlines to see if he caught another flight?

Senior Affairs Reporter
Channel 8 Local News
Relentlessly local, round the clock

From: crystalmomof4exlaw@yahoo.com
To: phoebegb@channel8news.com
Did that just now, but there's no record of a passenger with his name on any of them. I'm in the process of filing a missing persons report with the Bahamian police, but from the sound of it, middle-aged men go AWOL down there all the time, only to re-emerge sober and chastened, and usually without their wallet or ID several days later.

PTA PRESIDENT, Village Public School

From: phoebegb@channel8news.com
To: crystalmomof4exlaw@yahoo.com
If only Lata were here, I'm sure she could track him down in a jiffy. But as it is, I'm not sure what to suggest.

Senior Affairs Reporter
Channel 8 Local News
Relentlessly local, round the clock

Thursday, May 9

From: crystalmomof4exlaw@yahoo.com
To: phoebegb@channel8news.com
I found a business proposal on George's home computer last night, which makes me think things are more serious than I originally suspected.

I know he had talked of commuting weekly between DC and Nassau to develop a relationship with their new client, Shell Holdings. Shell wants P&H to lobby to stop the new administration from preventing US corporations from avoiding taxes by incorporating overseas. George should know by now commuting like that would basically spell the end of our marriage, and would hope he would agree not to go ahead. But maybe our separation these past few weeks have convinced him there's nothing for him here in DC? The proposal certainly looks like it's a done deal – all that's missing is George's signature.

Naturally, I'm devastated that George would even consider something like this, but as Consuela keeps pointing out, I was the one to kick him out, even though he's basically been a good husband and father, as well as a great provider, for so many years. (For the record, she may be right about this, but that doesn't mean she needs to tell me all the time).

The Bahamian police have finally agreed to file a missing person's report, but in the meantime, I'm booking myself on the noon flight out of DC tomorrow, and asked Jose and Consuela to look after the cherubs in my absence.

May I take the liberty of giving the Flores's your numbers in case of emergency? I know how busy you guys are, but I have found that only Brad is able to calm your goddaughter in moments of distress with a swaddling maneuver using his apron that not even Lata has mastered.

God Bless the liberated man!

PTA PRESIDENT, Village Public School

From: phoebegb@channel8news.com
To: crystalmomof4exlaw@yahoo.com
OF COURSE. Please let me know if there is anything else I can do. And I mean, ANYTHING.

Senior Affairs Reporter
Channel 8 Local News
Relentlessly local, round the clock

Friday, May 10

Text from Crystal to Phoebe
Any chance you and Brad can watch Kurtis while I am out of town? She appears to have come down with croup, and neither Jose nor Consuela understand instructions for her nebulizer.

Text from Phoebe to Crystal
More than happy to keep our goddaughter for the duration, so long as it doesn't give Brad any ideas. Assume you will supply emergency contact information and everything she needs?

Text from Crystal to Phoebe
Absolutely. Will drop K. off with suitcase, insurance card, emergency contact information and medical waiver as soon as I finish packing. This only confirms why George and I chose you and Brad as godparents! Will drop off her daily schedule asap.

Kurtis' Daily Schedule

Wake-up: Usually between 5:30 and 6:00am, but with an early morning feed, you should be able to keep her down another hour

Breakfast: Still no solids (waiting 1 year before now recommended, according to pediatrician), so ideally more breastmilk ingested through nursing bra. I really hope this isn't too inconvenient for Brad!!!

Developmentally appropriate tummy time: Right after breakfast can be risky as I've more than once been forced to shower after a spontaneous eruption, but if Brad needs to take her out, I prefer she get her practice crawling early in the day.

Nap: Generally by 10am. Best if she can be in her crib, but a car seat is fine if Brad is making house calls at that hour

Lunch: Kurtis loves her lunch time bonding. Would appreciate if you could gently discourage Brad from playing video games or watching TV while feeding her. Too much neck strain as she tries to engage can be detrimental to her sight & neuro-motor development. Again, breast bags will keep her in the nursing habit!

Playgroup: Brad should have a great time w/ the Village gals (or their nannies) from 12:30-2. He is free to take my Starbucks mug full of any special beverage he chooses, which I find always makes conversation flow more easily.

Afternoon Nap: Kurtis will be exhausted after playgroup as she already seems to have developed some competitive tendencies with Shyla, a six month old who lives on the east side of the Village. Kurtis seems to be slightly ahead in her milestones, so even though Shyla is officially 'specially gifted', and has a private session with an occupational therapist to keep her this way each week, I think you'll find she's no real threat.

Early Evening Developmental Play: I religiously carve out these sessions twice a day, b/c I know otherwise how quickly Kurtis's needs can be overlooked. I'm leaving her Baby Geniuses are Fun! book in her diaper bag, so don't hesitate to take a peek for some enrichment activities the whole family can play.

Dinner: I hesitate to ask Brad to strap on the feed bags one more time, but he should know how indebted I am.

Bath Time: Another opportunity for stimulation (but not too much) before bedtime.

Bedtime: A final feeding and stories in a dimly lit room should do the trick.

Please remind her that mama loves her!

Text from Crystal to Phoebe

Landed safely. Off to find Hubby hard at work, and hopefully fully clothed. Kiss Kurtis for me, pls!

Saturday, May 11

From: crystalmomof4exlaw@yahoo.com
To: phoebegb@channel8news.com

Just called the boat company in Nassau, which was his last point of contact, according to his cellphone records. They confirmed that George rented a mid-price speedboat with accommodations for 2 for three nights this week and that he loaded it up with supplies before he left. They are assuming he was planning to dock it on one of the many deserted islands dotted around the Bahamas overnight. When he returned the boat yesterday morning, apparently, he was looking disheveled and asked to borrow a razor and use the company's outdoor shower, before changing into a suit and departing with the remainder of his belongings on foot.

All very troubling. I'm hoping the fact that he was wearing a suit means he was going for another business meeting, so I've asked George's assistant, Jane, to give me the name and address of Shell Holdings, to see if they know his whereabouts. Will let you know what I hear back.

Sent from my mePhone

From: phoebegb@channel8news.com
To: crystalmomof4exlaw@yahoo.com
You'll be glad to hear that Kurtis slept through the night last night – at least, as far as I know.

Brad got up several times during the wee hours to check on her, but she never screamed loud enough to wake me, and he didn't feel obliged to involve me in her care, which was a welcome change from the days when he used to thump me awake to nurse the twins. Now, of course, he thinks he's a bloody childcare expert, and actually believes the twins are thriving under his 'supervision', if you can call the hours he continues to spend playing video games with them involved parenting. I dare say he's teaching them how to survive a military ambush – at least in a virtual world.

Senior Affairs Reporter
Channel 8 Local News
Relentlessly local, round the clock

From: crystalmomof4exlaw@yahoo.com
To: phoebegb@channel8news.com
You are a lifesaver!

Promise to repay you with a girlfriend trip out of town next month, by way of a thank you, and early celebration of the big B-day. One long weekend at the R. Kardashian yoga retreat center in South Beach Gunther recommended, and I guarantee you the anchor job at Channel 8 News will be yours.

Sent from my mePhone

Sunday, May 12

From: crystalmomof4exlaw@yahoo.com
To: phoebegb@channel8news.com
Still no sign of George. I've scoured all the beaches for any sight of his slightly tubby white body, but no luck. Keep worrying I fill find him in the arms of some other woman, which would serve me right, of course, but might also result in the kind of scene out of which bad eighties movies were made. Rest

assured I will let him know in no uncertain terms that he will be living with all four cherubs and no Lata, if that is the case.

Sent from my mePhone

Text from Phoebe to Crystal
Any news?

From: crystalmomof4exlaw@yahoo.com
To: phoebegb@channel8news.com
Finally discovered George at the home of Shell Holdings' founder, Catherine Douglas when I insisted upon pushing my way inside – after being told by the butler (yes, BUTLER) that his mistress, whom we shall call Miss Bahamas 1987, was in her study, and had asked not to be disturbed.

Naturally, I proceeded to march into the house, down the hallway and throw open the doors of her vast office to find a distressingly attractive woman in her mid-forties watching George wave his magic pointer over a Powerpoint presentation projected onto a pull down screen from his laptop. Following a heated exchange between myself and George in front of Ms. Douglas, during which I somehow found myself wrapped around him, swinging from his tie and screaming like a banshee, George eventually managed to explain that it was all a misunderstanding. Ms. Douglas, though certainly beautiful, was not the whorish she-devil I was describing. Yes, she did want to engage in an alliance with Plunder & Hogg and take advantage of the leverage the firm could bring to her US interests, having been impressed with the strength and reach of George's contacts when she visited DC last January. But no, she wasn't interested in George personally, as she is in fact the richest person in Nassau, besides being happily married to a movie star almost ten years her junior.

According to George, he spent the last few days alone on a deserted island, debating whether to go ahead with the potentially lucrative deal, or put his family first. At some point, his cellphone battery died, as you suspected, so he couldn't call to tell us where he was, or what he had decided – not that there would have been any network reception on the island, anyway.

George claimed he was here today to tell Ms. Douglas the deal between her company and Plunder & Hogg had fallen through, since he was not prepared to leave me and the cherubs for four days each week in order to commute to Nassau. He said the absolute solitude of the island, which he had always dreamed of escaping to after a weekend at home in DC with the cherubs, turned out to be the loneliest experience of his life. Believe it or not, he actually 'fessed up to missing the cherubs, my honey-do lists, having to walk the dog and even me. Imagine that!

Frankly, it was a huge relief to learn the truth. When we had all calmed down, Ms. Douglas ordered the butler to fetch us some drinks and we shared a civilized moment discussing the stunning view of Lyford Cay (and her husband, sunning himself around her pool) from her verandah. She was actually quite impressed with my yoga teacher training and asked me to spend some time meditating with her before we left. She mentioned, not pointedly I hope, that this kind of practice works wonders when one is prone to hysteria. I naturally insisted we do a fluid Ruined Temple pose together and hope her thighs feel the burn tomorrow.

In the cab back to the hotel afterwards, George explained how he was initially dazzled by the prospect of landing such a huge business deal, but after almost a week of fun in the sun, he had came to realize that he was missing me and all the cherubs too much, and was determined to figure out a way to reconcile.

He seemed pleased that I felt strongly enough about him to physically fly out to try and find him, and promised that things would be different from now on.

I blurted out everything that happened between me and Hilary, and how I really only longed for him to be more available to me and the cherubs, even if I did manage to express that longing mostly in the form of regular tirades about all the ways he was failing us.

He asked for far more details about the sleeping arrangements with Hilary in Jamaica than I expected, but said that a relationship between two women, even if one was married, could only be considered a beautiful thing, especially if we could demonstrate with pictures. He even likes my new haircut!

So I guess all's well that ends well. In fact, George and I have just enjoyed the most amazing evening together in years (despite the inevitable spurt of breast milk). Even better, he has promised to take a few days off to watch the cherubs while we are on retreat at Steamy Yoga next month. Of course, I neglected to mention that Lata might not be there to help him (must ease the man back in gently, after all), but I'm hoping this is the start of a brand new domestic regime.

Since we have already missed the last flight of the day home back to DC, I am taking advantage of my child free state to order room service, watch a movie straight through without interruption, and fall sleep beneath 800 thread count sheets. I can't thank you and Brad enough for taking Baby these past few days and helping to save my marriage in the process, dear P. You and Brad really are the best!

George and I will be on the first flight back to DC in the morning.

Sent from my mePhone

Monday, May 13

From: phoebegb@channel8news.com
To: crystalmomof4exlaw@yahoo.com
So glad to hear you and George have resolved your differences and are back on the road to marital harmony – at least for now. Good to see you both looking so tanned and happy together when you picked up Kurtis earlier.

Did I mention how much time and attention Brad devoted to the memo regarding Kurtis' care while you were gone? Can't imagine how Lata managed to accomplish all this in a single day for one cherub, let alone all four. Or did you require her to focus her attention solely on your youngest?

Come to think of it, I did see Lata following Kurtis with a sippy cup at all times in a way that reminds me of our Queen and her beloved Nanny, back in the day.

Senior Affairs Reporter
Channel 8 Local News
Relentlessly local, round the clock

Tuesday, May 14

From: crystalmomof4exlaw@yahoo.com
To: phoebegb@channel8news.com
It is good to be back, although I was immediately assaulted by Kevin and Kimberly with a litany of complaints about the many perceived infractions that occurred while I was out of the country – most involving Luis and Maria taking too long in the bathroom.

I've also just received a letter from Seton, informing me the school made a mistake in saying Kevin and Kimberly were wait-listed, and that all three of my cherubs are officially not welcome at the school. Guess this is a result of the interview I gave to you at Channel 8 about the plague of over-parenting in this town. I know this conflicts with Seton's core mission statement, which explicitly requires parents to give up their own lives in order to tend to their child's every single thought, need and deed, but I also know the cherubs' wholesale rejection is really Hilary's doing.

The strange thing is, I really don't care. This past week looking for George, worrying that he was dead – or worse, had left me for someone younger and more glamorous – showed me that giving up my career and working my a$$ off to get my kids into an exclusive private school just to show a bunch of stuck-up country club snobs like Pookie I can do it is just CRAZY, especially when the kids are perfectly happy where they are, at VPS.

Is this what they mean by enlightenment?

PTA PRESIDENT, Village Public School

Wednesday, May 15

From: phoebegb@channel8news.com
To: crystalmomof4exlaw@yahoo.com
I've been getting hundreds of hits a day on my Witter account about the interview you gave after the hearing, in which you spoke about opting out of the craziness of life in DC, and the importance of adopting a more relaxed family schedule, as well as a more old-fashioned, hands-off approach to parenting.

Your speech was inspired, and I think you've really touched on a hot button issue for parents everywhere, which is why I have pitched our producer with the idea of doing a series of follow-up interviews on parenting in the slow lane, and the importance in particular of family dinners, household chores and God forbid downtime.

The First Lady is also apparently a big fan what you had to say, and re-posted your words on her own Witter account, along with a url link to your full speech.

Would you be open to the idea of having a camera crew in your house for a couple of days next week, to follow the cherubs around, capturing interactions between you and the Flores family, and contrasting parenting styles between here and Peru, etc.? I think it could be the basis for a great in depth report on the crisis levels of stress in this city, as well as helping raise awareness and funds to help the Flores family rebuild their house in Lima following the earthquake.

Senior Affairs Reporter
Channel 8 Local News
Relentlessly local, round the clock

From: crystalmomof4exlaw@yahoo.com
To: phoebegb@channel8news.com
It's a great idea! Besides, since Seton has already rejected the cherubs, what do I have to lose?

PTA PRESIDENT, Village Public School

From: phoebegb@channel8news.com
To: crystalmomof4exlaw@yahoo.com
Great! I will send a camera crew around bright and early tomorrow, so they can start filming the family's morning routine while we're at yoga – although they may want a shot or two of you engaged in Upward-facing Pelvis Thrust pose.

Senior Affairs Reporter
Channel 8 Local News
Relentlessly local, round the clock

Thursday, May 16

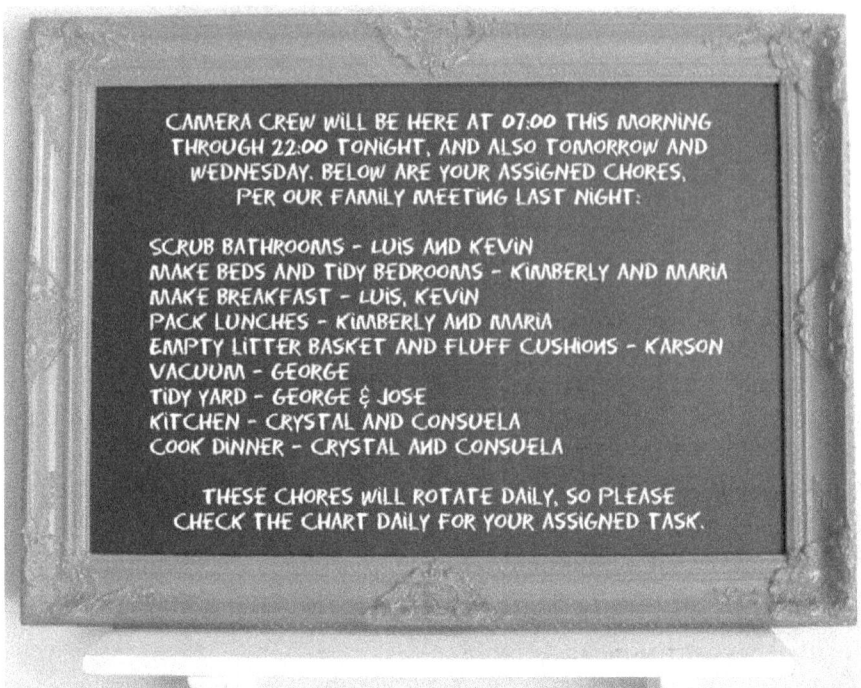

CAMERA CREW WILL BE HERE AT 07:00 THIS MORNING THROUGH 22:00 TONIGHT, AND ALSO TOMORROW AND WEDNESDAY. BELOW ARE YOUR ASSIGNED CHORES, PER OUR FAMILY MEETING LAST NIGHT:

SCRUB BATHROOMS - LUIS AND KEVIN
MAKE BEDS AND TIDY BEDROOMS - KIMBERLY AND MARIA
MAKE BREAKFAST - LUIS, KEVIN
PACK LUNCHES - KIMBERLY AND MARIA
EMPTY LITTER BASKET AND FLUFF CUSHIONS - KARSON
VACUUM - GEORGE
TIDY YARD - GEORGE & JOSE
KITCHEN - CRYSTAL AND CONSUELA
COOK DINNER - CRYSTAL AND CONSUELA

THESE CHORES WILL ROTATE DAILY, SO PLEASE CHECK THE CHART DAILY FOR YOUR ASSIGNED TASK.

Friday, May 17

Text from Crystal to Kevin
Sorry camera crew followed you into shower, but can't this wait? Trying to stay centered in upward-facing Frog pose. Hard to hold onto soles of feet and text at same time.

Text from Crystal to Kevin
P.S. They will pixelate relevant parts. If you are nice to them, they might even offer to enhance area first.

Witter posting from channel8breakingnews
Check out the pixels on this cutie, gals. http://bit.ly/kmFzy. Enough to make this reporter wish I were 20 years younger (OK, 25) and single!

fbiguy is now following channel8breakingnews

Monday, May 20

Witter posting from channel8breakingnews
You won't want to miss your favorite teen boys ironing their shirts today, girls. Helps that they're topless! http://bit.ly/omg.ht

cpssocialworker is now following channel8breakingnews

Tuesday, May 21

From: crystalmomof4exlaw@yahoo.com
To: gwalker@plunderhogg.com

Well, that seemed to go better than I expected, don't you think? Thanks for coming home early to give Kurtis her bath.

Did you see the part where Kimberly lent Maria her favorite new Forever Underage shirt, after Maria helped her with her Spanish homework? I would say she only did it because the camera crew was there, but she genuinely seemed to want Maria to have it.

PTA PRESIDENT, Village Public School

Wednesday, May 22

From: crystalmomof4exlaw@yahoo.com
To: exrev@hotmail.com
Email attachment containing UTube interview between Kevin and Luis
Dear Dad,

Glad you are doing well, and that Mary Goodall has proven to be such a great neighbor to you recently, as well as what sounds like a good friend. Is there anything else you want to tell me about the relationship?

We are all doing OK, after what has turned out to be a traumatic month, to say the least. I know you were aware of my court case, even if you somehow didn't have time to call, but suffice to say, the Village let me off, and George, the cherubs and I are getting back to normal – or rather, better than normal, as George has made a real commitment to cutting back on work.

Not sure if you were aware that in the midst of all the court case craziness, we've had a lovely family from Lima staying, after they were made temporarily homeless in the recent earthquake, and the cherubs seem to have really bonded, after a rocky start.

My English friend, Phoebe actually did a story about our two families for Channel 8 news, to help raise money to rebuild the Flores' family home. Check out the interview Kevin gave in the link below, talking about how he hated having to share a bedroom with Luis at first, but now he misses him whenever he or Luis gets invited to a friend's house for a sleepover.

Surely, George and I can't have done everything wrong as parents if our cherubs are willing to express sentiments like this on camera, when they know they're being watched by all of their friends.

And to think, Seton Academy rejected them! I think they're going to be just fine, don't you?

www.utube.youllwanttobarfitssotouching.com

Thursday, May 23

From: crystalmomof4exlaw@yahoo.com
To: Principal of VPS
CC: bitsybottinger@yahoo.com
My 8th grade son, Kevin Walker, would like to organize a fashion show and clothing drive at VPS this weekend as part of the annual Spring Fling, to raise funds to help the Flores family and others, whose homes were destroyed in the recent earthquake in Lima. I understand I need permission from the PTA and the school before proceeding. Do you guys have any objection?

PTA PRESIDENT, Village Public School

Reply
Great! OK if we add a bake sale? My daughter, Kimberly wants to help too. I will make it clear that the clothes on display must cover shoulders, chests and hips, and that none of the baked goods contain wheat, nuts, sugar or dairy, per MCPS regulations.

PTA PRESIDENT, Village Public School

Friday, May 24

From: crystalmomof4exlaw@yahoo.com
To: pookiegranger@hotmail.com, ishop4snobs@yahoo.com
Would the Cup Cakery be willing to donate some cupcakes to the Village Public School bake sale tomorrow, which is being featured on Channel 8 Local news, as part of the final installment of its feature on Parenting in the Slow Lane? Attaching the county's elementary school dietary regulations now.

I realize this is extremely short notice, but could be great exposure for your biz as well!

PTA PRESIDENT, Village Public School

Posting on Village Listserv

From: phoebegb@channel8news.com
Wanted: gently used, clean clothing for Lima earthquake drive at VPS Spring Fling tomorrow. We particularly need warm sweaters and coats, but anything is appreciated!

Senior Affairs Reporter
Channel 8 Local News
Relentlessly local, round the clock

Saturday, May 25

Text from Phoebe to Brad
Can u have Bitsy's triplets round for playdate this morning, so she can start carving ice-sculptures for Spring Fling this pm? Hard to memorialize Flo the swan accurately with a chain saw while 3 six year olds dance round one's feet.

Text from Phoebe to Brad
Oops. Forgot you were making pesto. Think of this as chance to pass on your secret recipe to younger generation. Whatever you do, don't let them help!

Sunday, May 26

Text from Crystal to Phoebe
Spring Fling was awesome. We had record turnout, and raised lots of $$ for the Flores family and other earthquake victims.

Text from Crystal to Phoebe
P.S. Remind me never to volunteer for anything ever again.

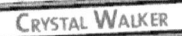

CRYSTAL WALKER

Dear Lata,

I am enclosing a check for $1897.03 to help victims of the earthquake in Lima today. George and Kevin are also planning a trip there after school lets out to help rebuild some of the destroyed houses.

I know your countrymen need you right now, but any idea when you might be coming back? The Flores family is wonderful in so many ways (although just between ourselves, I do wish Consuela wouldn't pass comment on how I choose to spend my time. She seems to consider yoga to be some kind of religious cult, and is always encouraging me to attend Mass with her instead).

We miss you!

Crystal

1115

PAY TO THE ORDER OF   Outreachu - Picchu $ $1897.03

One Thousand Eight Hundred and Ninety Seven Dollars and Three cents.   DOLLARS

MEMO   Miss you Lata!   Crystal Walker

⑆060077059⑆ ⑈50⑊20707584⑈

From: phoebegb@channel8news.com
To: crystalmomof4exlaw@yahoo.com

Wanted you to be the first to know: The station manager asked to see me this morning, and judging by the lemonlike expression on Production Assistant's face, I knew it was good news. I am now officially the anchor of Channel 8 news! I can hardly believe it. Brad just doesn't appreciate how much this means – particularly because I was chosen over a much younger woman – but I know you will understand.

Of course, I won't get home before 9 pm most days, which means I will never see the twins after school. Having said that, I don't have to start working until 11 each day, which means I can schedule lessons with Xavier again, and I will get a decent pay raise, so there are some upsides to the promotion.

Phoebe Thompson
News Anchor
Channel 8 News
Relentlessly Local, round the clock

From: crystalmomof4exlaw@yahoo.com
To: phoebegb@channel8news.com

Congratulations! I know you will miss seeing the twins, but they really do seem to be thriving under Brad's care and attention, if you can ignore the unmade beds, the pile of unwashed dishes in the sink, and the general aura of benign neglect that now seems to permeate your household. Trust me, it's a small price to pay for financial independence.

BTW, Hilary just sent an email asking if I can meet with her this afternoon. Weird thing is, she also wants to see George. How do you think I should respond?

PTA PRESIDENT, Village Public School

From: phoebegb@channel8news.com
To: crystalmomof4exlaw@yahoo.com

Any idea why she wants to see you?

Phoebe Thompson
News Anchor
Channel 8 News
Relentlessly Local, round the clock

From: crystalmomof4exlaw@yahoo.com
To: phoebegb@channel8news.com

None, unless it's about the comment Kevin made on camera the other day, saying he'd rather go to public school than a snooty, stuck-up place like Seton Academy, which refused to admit the Flores family on scholarship mid-way through the year.

Surely, Hilary can't be planning to re-hash our relationship in front of George?

PTA PRESIDENT, Village Public School

From: phoebegb@channel8news.com
To: crystalmomof4exlaw@yahoo.com
You guys didn't engage in sexting, did you?

Phoebe Thompson
News Anchor
Channel 8 News
Relentlessly Local, round the clock

From: crystalmomof4exlaw@yahoo.com
To: phoebegb@channel8news.com
Not that I'm aware of.

PTA PRESIDENT, Village Public School

From: phoebegb@channel8news.com
To: crystalmomof4exlaw@yahoo.com
Then I suggest just deny everything and go on the offensive, like the good lawyer you are, and you should be just fine.

Phoebe Thompson
News Anchor
Channel 8 News
Relentlessly Local, round the clock

From: crystalmomof4exlaw@yahoo.com
To: phoebegb@channel8news.com
Well, George and I marched into Hilary's office, and I was about to accuse her of engaging in an improper relationship with a parent of not one, not two but THREE potential students when I noticed the entire Seton Academy Selection Board sitting next to her round the conference table in her office.

Turns out, several of the Seton Board members had watched Kevin and Kimberly on TV, talking about how they felt depressed and worthless after getting rejected from Seton, only to have their spirits lifted by the arrival of the Flores family, who had just experienced a far more serious trauma in their own lives. One board member confessed to being moved to tears when she heard how Kimberly went from using the bee-ach word on Maria, for wearing Kimberly's new signature scent w/o permission, to inviting Maria to share her bed one night when she heard her quietly sobbing from homesickness in the pullout cot bed next to her.

I was expecting the board to go on to talk about issuing a writ against us for defaming the Academy several times during the course of the week's coverage, but instead they proffered a letter stating that after careful reflection, they had decided to re-consider the cherubs' applications, and would now like to offer a space to all three for next fall! They are also planning to offer full scholarships (including boarding fees) to Luis and Maria, if they decide they want to stay in the US.

George and I were naturally speechless at this turn of events, so we asked to sleep on the offer while we considered what's best for the cherubs. I've promised to let them know by the end of the week. It's certainly a tempting offer, but I can hardly go back on my publicly stated vow not to turn into one of those pushy DC parents who send their kids to elite private schools just to make themselves look good for having smart kids.

Or can I?

PTA PRESIDENT, Village Public School

From: phoebegb@channel8news.com
To: crystalmomof4exlaw@yahoo.com
Are you crazy? You would be remiss as a parent if you didn't leap at the chance to offer the cherubs an opportunity to make priceless social connections for later in life – not to mention, to develop a sense of entitlement that will enable them to waltz into any Ivy League school and the creative/worthy/lucrative career of their choice later on.

Just think, Kimberly may soon be having sleepovers at the White House! Pookie is going to die when she hears this!

Phoebe Thompson
News Anchor
Channel 8 News
Relentlessly Local, round the clock

DC Diary
First Lady, Reality TV, Seton Academy

As many of our friends in Kansas City already know, it's been a tumultuous month, starting with my trial and acquittal here in the Village, on charges of reckless child endangerment for letting Kimberly ride her bike to school unaided.

Fortunately I was lucky enough to have the First Lady of the United States come to my aid and provide dramatic testimony at the hearing about the correlation between childhood obesity, and the increase in the number of children being driven to school. Her testimony was enough for the magistrate to throw out the case against me for being without merit, after which I was inundated with offers of interviews and magazine articles from local and national media.

Then the Walker family was invited to star in our very own local TV reality series on Channel 8 local news, during which the camera crews followed us around 24/7, capturing footage of the interactions between the cherubs and the Flores family from Lima, who are staying with us temporarily after the earthquake in Lima destroyed their home. (Thanks, Mom and Dad, for helping to spread the word, but did you really think it was necessary to tell the mailman?)

Lata is busy building them a brand new house back in Lima as I write, and it looks like Kevin and George may even go down and help with the final construction after school lets out in June. Let's just hope George doesn't nail himself to any crossbeams, they way he did with the holiday lights this past Christmas! Finally, by way of icing on the cake, several members of the application board at Seton Academy watched the reality TV series, and were so moved by the way the cherubs and the Flores children all interacted, they completely reversed their decision and agreed to accept Kevin, Kimberly and Karson - which means they may end up going to school with the daughters of the First Family after all! Can't wait to tell my neighbor and nemesis, Pookie Granger that my daughter has been invited to a sleepover at the White House!

Chapter 11

June, 2013 Vol. 42, Issue 6
Always FREE, but donations appreciated

Please direct submissions and inquiries to:
whining@villagepress.com
P.O. Box 357 Village Town, MD

VILLAGE WHINER

Your trusty monthly newsletter of
the "Most Livable Village," 1989
Village Times Magazine

Village Board of Managers Meeting

The Village Board of Managers has voted unanimously to ease the restrictions on children over the age of eight who wish to walk, ride, or otherwise use non-motorized means to commute to school and around the neighborhood. Regrettably, Special Ops was compelled to forcibly remove Barb Van Houzen from the Village Hall premises, after she chained herself to the lectern in protest at this change in the Village by-laws, but her objections objections have been duly noted in our monthly meeting notes.

The Board has also voted to continue to permit the keeping of livestock by Village residents for the foreseeable future. However, please note the Village Green is NOT available for grazing cows, sheep or goats, despite the attempts of the various legal scholars around the neighborhood to assert this right. The term "Village Green" may technically refer to a public space for recreation and pasturage under English Common Law, but it has no such other legal status this side of the Atlantic. Residents who claim grazing their pets on the Green eliminates the need for mowing fail to realize that many residents object to frolicking among cow pats and poop droppings.

In related news, the Board of Village Managers is saddened to report the death of Chuck Palmer's rooster, which disappeared in a puff of feathers and a lone crow one morning last week. Mr. Palmer is at present unable to suspect the rooster was dispatched by a disgruntled resident tired of being woken up at 5 a.m. Special Ops has agreed to investigate the incident in question, but right now the main suspect appears to be the Village fox, whose red coat is looking sleeker and glossier every day.

Village fox, Paula

Village Diversity Group

Group therapy for the women's subcommittee, funded by fines from motorists caught going ballistic cameras the finger while going over the speed humps in the Village, will be offered in the Village Yard next Wednesday, from 10-11am.

Miss Gertrude

Miss Gertrude is generally loathe to pass judgment on modern parenting practices, in the belief that times change, and what passes for good parenting in one generation frequently looks like child endangerment to the next. However, she would like to share a few concerns about an incident the other day that gave her pause.

1. When in line at the supermarket, it is considered extremely bad form to unload your groceries onto the conveyor belt faster than the person standing in line in front of you can unload theirs. Believe it or not, your time is not more important!

2. Ditto when it comes to abandoning your purchases as they are being rung up in favor of picking up the three or four items you forgot;

3. The "ten items or less" rule applies to EVERYONE - even you, Ms. Bliss.

Village Tennis Team

Village Board of Managers Meeting

The Village Board of Managers has voted unanimously to ease the restrictions on children over the age of eight bicycling, walking or otherwise commuting to school and around the neighborhood unaccompanied. Regrettably, Special Ops was compelled to forcibly remove Barbi Van Houzen from the Village Hall premises, after she chained herself to the fence in protest at this change in the Village by-laws, but her strenuous objections have been duly noted in our monthly meeting notes.

The Board has also voted to continue to permit the keeping of livestock by Village residents for the foreseeable future. However, please note: the Village Green is NOT available for grazing cows, sheep or goats, despite the attempts of the various legal scholars around the neighborhood to assert this right. The term 'Village Green' may technically refer to a public space for recreation and pasturage under English Common Law, but it has no such official status this side of the Atlantic. Residents who claim grazing their pets on the Green eliminates the need for mowing fail to realize that many residents object to frolicking among cowpats and goat droppings.

Village fox, Paula

In related news, the Board of Village Managers is saddened to report the death of Chuck Palmer's rooster, which disappeared in a puff of feathers mid-crow one morning last week. Mr. Palmer is alleging fowl play(sic), but as of present, there is no reason to suspect the rooster was dispatched by a disgruntled resident tired of being woken up at 4 am. Special Ops has agreed to investigate the incident in question, but right now the main suspect appears to be the Village fox, whose red coat is looking sleeker and glossier every day.

Village Diversity Group

The Village Diversity group intended to spend the last several months figuring out ways to serve the homeless community without allowing them anywhere near our beautiful 'burb, but alas, the women's subcommittee has found itself embroiled in yet another distracting controversy regarding our chair, Simon Better (previously, Simone). The committee previously voted to retain Mr. Better, in spite of his gender realignment surgery several months ago, but a petition is now circulating to oust him from the subcommittee altogether.

According to several members, who spoke off the record, Mr. Better is engaging in atavistic male behavior at group meetings, with the result that other members of the subcommittee are getting tired of doing all the work, while he takes all the credit. 'He was such a lovely woman," one member, who prefers to remain anonymous, was quoted as saying, 'but the testosterone injections have rendered him virtually useless. If I want a man who plays online poker all day long while he's supposedly 'working', I can go home to my husband.'

Group therapy for the women's subcommittee, funded by fines from motorists caught giving traffic cameras the finger while going over the speed humps in the Village, will be offered in the Village Yurt next Wednesday, from 10-11am.

Miss Gertrude

Miss Gertrude is generally loathe to pass judgment on modern parenting practices, in the belief that times change, and what passes for good parenting in one generation frequently looks like child endangerment to the next. However, she would like to share a few concerns about an incident the other day that gave her pause.

Many grocery stores, including Holier Than Thou Foods, now provide adorable miniature grocery carts to amuse our little ones while their parents shop. Fun as these contraptions may be, Miss Gertrude would appreciate if parents would recognize their limitations. These carts are not an excuse for a parent to wander off, browsing the aisles for aged tofu or sprouted quinoa, leaving one's darling offspring alone to assault other shoppers with what is in effect a deadly weapon. Miss Gertrude was the victim of one such attack last Friday, and her ankle is as blue as the language she was involuntarily forced to utter as a result.

Miss G. has heard from several of her friends at Beautiful Swan who have been on the sharp end of several similar assaults, and knows how such confrontations can quickly turn ugly. Please remember that many elderly shoppers, including Miss G., are holding on to their shopping carts for dear life just to remain upright, so the sight of a wild-eyed infant charging full force down the aisle straight at them may be the tipping point, literally.

Miss Gertrude has noticed a couple of other unfortunate habits creeping into the shopping practices of DC residents, so she trusts that the reader will not object to a quick refresher course on the subject:

1. When in line at the supermarket, it is considered extremely bad form to unload your groceries onto the conveyor belt faster than the person standing in line in front of you can unload theirs. Believe it or not, your time is not more important!

2. Ditto when it comes to abandoning your purchases as they are being rung up in favor of picking up the three or four items you forgot;

3. The 'ten items or less' rule applies to EVERYONE - even you, Ms. Bliss.

As always, the most important rule in all etiquette matters is to show consideration for others. If shoppers only follow this rule, Holier Than Thou Foods will become a more civilized, and pleasant place, rather than the "my time is more valuable than yours" free for all it has become.

Village Tennis Team

The Ladies' Tennis Team captain has received several calls, emails and even insistent knocks on her front door from a reporter from The Post, who has apparently been assigned to write a story on the recent so-called 'doping scandal' in the Ladies' Inter-club League. Since she has no idea what the reporter in question is talking about, she has naturally refused to pass comment, and hopes that other members of the Ladies' Tennis Team will do the same (and also recycle their copies of last month's newsletter).

It has come to the captain's attention, however, that certain members of the Gentlemen's Tennis Team have not been so reticent. Indeed, one gentleman was quoted in last week's Suburbia section of the Post talking about the marked decline in performance among the Ladies' ever since the two players with 'specially gifted' school-age children quit the game. The Ladies' team captain vigorously refutes this outrageous charge, and challenges the Gentlemen's Team to a doubles tournament at the time and place of their choosing, to demonstrate just how wrong her male colleagues can be. We look forward to seeing them on the courts.

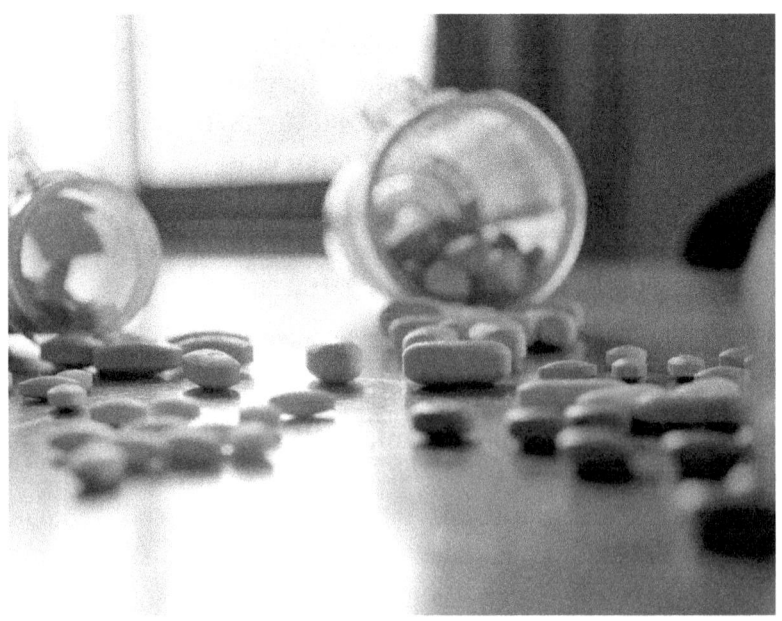

Text from Phoebe to Crystal
Are you coming to yoga this morning? Rang doorbell, but no response.

Text from Crystal to Phoebe
Just nodded off w/Kurtis after sleepless night. Sorry!

Text from Phoebe to Crystal
No prob. Everything OK?

Text from Crystal to Phoebe
Everything fine. Decision about Seton just weighing heavier than I thought.

Text from Phoebe to Crystal
I thought you had decided to send cherubs?

Text from Crystal to Phoebe
Did, but feeling uneasy ever since. Cherubs = so happy at VPS, and must say I'm enjoying my little corner of power on the PTA. George feeling ambivalent too, so he's actually leaving work early to discuss.

Text from Phoebe to Crystal
Good luck! Let me know what you decide.

From: phoebegb@channel8news.com
To: crystalmomof4exlaw@yahoo.com
How did your meeting with George go?

Phoebe Thompson
News Anchor
Channel 8 News
Relentlessly Local, round the clock

From: crystalmomof4exlaw@yahoo.com
To: phoebegb@channel8news.com
George got a call from the chairman of Plunder & Hogg just before he was leaving work, informing him the firm has received an acquisition offer from Shell Holdings they just can't refuse, and offering him a buyout if the deal goes through, which seems likely.

Apparently, George's refusal to spearhead the venture with Shell suggested to P&H that he is insufficiently aggressive about going after new business, so they would rather cut their losses than keep him at the firm. So I guess George was actually right about the need to give up your right to a family life, or indeed any life, outside work, or risk being sidelined. Then again, this approach is really no different from any law firm, so why should I be surprised?

PTA PRESIDENT, Village Public School

From: phoebegb@channel8news.com
To: crystalmomof4exlaw@yahoo.com

Yikes. I hope this doesn't mean you will be in a precarious financial situation, esp. now with the cherubs about to start private school.

Phoebe Thompson
News Anchor
Channel 8 News
Relentlessly Local, round the clock

From: crystalmomof4exlaw@yahoo.com
To: phoebegb@channel8news.com

Fortunately, the P&H offer is generous, so we should be OK for a while, although George will need to do something else, eventually – for my sake, as much as his. And besides, much to my own surprise, we've decided to decline Seton's offer of admission.

PTA PRESIDENT, Village Public School

From: phoebegb@channel8news.com
To: crystalmomof4exlaw@yahoo.com

OMG. Really? I'm speechless. I was counting on Kimberly to spill the beans about sleeping arrangements at the White House? Do you think they would notice if I sent the twins instead?

Phoebe Thompson
News Anchor
Channel 8 News
Relentlessly Local, round the clock

From: crystalmomof4exlaw@yahoo.com
To: phoebegb@channel8news.com

George and I actually feel really good about this decision. Seton feels like one more way we would increase our stress levels both at work and at home, and who needs that? We do live in an area where the public schools are actually excellent, so why should George and I kill ourselves working to drum up the additional 120k in post tax dollars just to give ourselves bragging rights with Pookie and Perky? Not to mention, there's a good chance we would destroy our marriage, and all chance of a happy family life, in the process.

PTA PRESIDENT, Village Public School

From: phoebegb@channel8news.com
To: crystalmomof4exlaw@yahoo.com

Wow. I admire your willingness to walk away. Is this the Steamy Yoga training talking? You were muttering something about it all being about the journey in Eat Crow pose the other day. Something along the lines of, there is no 'arriving', since nothing is permanent anyway.

I can certainly imagine how tempting it must be to show Pookie all that you have become in just the few short months since she dared to diss us.

Phoebe Thompson
News Anchor
Channel 8 News
Relentlessly Local, round the clock

From: crystalmomof4exlaw@yahoo.com
To: phoebegb@channel8news.com

That may well be true, but I should mention that I also got a call from the First Lady's office this morning, asking if I would agree to be a spokesperson for her 'On Your Bike' initiative. That should be enough to put Pookie in her place, don't you think? We are all still human, after all. And don't discount the small corner of power I've developed as PTA President at VPS. It may be a small pond, but it is all mine.

Speaking of yoga, are you still game for our retreat weekend in South Beach? Feeling a little guilty about leaving all four cherubs overnight with George and no paid help, but Gunther says the R. Kardashian Retreat & Spa has the best Ashtanga teacher outside of India, and it should help me overcome my fear of handstands before my final exam next week.

PTA PRESIDENT, Village Public School

From: phoebegb@channel8news.com
To: crystalmomof4exlaw@yahoo.com

I think we need to take a leaf out of Vira's book and start calling all our vacations 'retreats' from now on, don't you? Funny how enlightenment, for her, only seems to come during the course of a stay at a five star resort.

When did the notion that a woman should feel guilty about taking time out from child-rearing to have an interest of her own take hold?

Phoebe Thompson
News Anchor
Channel 8 News
Relentlessly Local, round the clock

From: crystalmomof4exlaw@yahoo.com
To: phoebegb@channel8news.com

Around the same time they started going back to work.

PTA PRESIDENT, Village Public School

With Great Pride and Solemnity
The Village Club Announces the Following:

Admissions Privileges to its Facilities and Hallowed Grounds
Beginning after Labor Day:

Professor and Mr. Lieberman

Mr. and Mrs. George Walker

~~Mr. and Mrs. Brown~~ (foreclosure on Village property forfeits opportunity)

The formal dance party and coronation ceremony (re-acknowledging the Club President and his contributions to Club life) will be held in the fall, and formal and engraved invitations will follow. In the interim, potential members may accompany their sponsors to the Club (remember the strict no denim rule!) and use the sponsors' Club number for all payments in the interim. This is a wonderful opportunity for sponsors to indoctrinate the potential new members into the ways of the Club and to be certain they are a good fit for its culture. Sponsors are wise to remember they are forevermore responsible for the behavior of members they have nominated, including any unpaid expenses incurred by them.

Sanctions

Mr. and Mrs. Theodore Sparks: membership suspended until dues made current **

Mr. Frank Manly: membership suspended until you offer a written apology to the Club President for questioning his masculinity b/c he was unable to repair the broken toilet in the Gentlemen's Grill

**Remember that your Club sponsors are liable for any past dues not paid and members are responsible for all dues until an official notice of resignation is sent by certified mail and acknowledged by the full Club Board. There is sometimes a lag of two months or more in this procedure but liability for same is assured under terms of the member contract. A member may not use the excuse of inebriation when said contract signed as a defense to its terms.

Thank
Y O U

Wednesday, June 5

Text from Phoebe to Crystal
Congrats on club admission. May want 2 rethink before hazing ceremony if any doubts.

Text from Crystal to Phoebe
OMG! Poor Perky. I assume her setback is temporary but the public humiliation is too much. More reason to assume some yoga needed there?

Text from Phoebe to Crystal
Little chance Club Prez will assume Gentle Turkey pose any time soon but his wife was on your side at the hearing, so I think she is flexible (pun intended).

Text from Crystal to Phoebe
Club decision comes same moment we are trying to assume a slower lane lifestyle, but seems such large part of Village life will be hard to turn down offer even if I should.

Monday, June 10

From: phoebegb@channel8news.com
To: crystalmomof4exlaw@yahoo.com
How can I ever possibly thank you for such a terrific yoga experience? I must admit, I was a little disturbed to learn of the strict no-caffeine, meat, alcohol or hanky panky rules at the retreat center, but I dare say the experience has done me good. Several people have even remarked that I look a good couple of decades younger today – at least from a distance. One even went so far as to say I seem to have become reacquainted with my inner child, judging by the renewed look of wonder on my face! No one has come right out and asked if I've had any work done, but I can see the thought crossing their minds, which is confirmation enough that the trip was worth every penny.

Phoebe Thompson
News Anchor
Channel 8 News
Relentlessly Local, round the clock

From: crystalmomof4exlaw@yahoo.com
To: phoebegb@channel8news.com
It was incredible for me to have the opportunity to interact with Swami Bruce, who seemed to the have magic touch when it came to spiraling my inner thighs, but the best part of the trip for me was George's reaction after I got back. The Flores family flew back to Lima the same day we left, so after 4 days alone with the cherubs, George finally understands the urgent need for population control. Believe it or not, he has actually agreed to getting the snip!

Naturally, I'm anxious to get the procedure done before he changes his mind. Does Brad have an appointment yet? Perhaps we could kill 2 birds with two sets of stones, as it were, and schedule them together?

PTA PRESIDENT, Village Public School

From: phoebegb@channel8news.com
To: crystalmomof4exlaw@yahoo.com
Brad does NOT have an appointment yet, as he's a bit squeamish about whoever performs the procedure, but he will be thrilled to have George's company for what seems like a fate worse than death (to him, anyway). I will put out a call for recommendations on the Village Listserv asap, before either changes their mind.

Phoebe Thompson
News Anchor
Channel 8 News
Relentlessly Local, round the clock

Posting on Village Listserv
From: phoebegb@channel8news.com
Can anyone recommend a good urologist to perform a delicate procedure on my husband?

Phoebe Thompson
News Anchor
Channel 8 News
Relentlessly Local, round the clock

From: bitsybottinger@yahoo.com
Dr. Frank Cutter on Nebraska Ave. is the BEST. He persuaded my Johnny to go under the knife, and I've been impressed with the results.

From: ishop4snobs@perkybydesign.com
My husband went to Dr. Cutter, but I was disappointed with the results. Those kind of operations don't work, no matter what all the spam emails tell you!

From: phoebegb@channel8news.com
To: crystalmomof4exlaw@yahoo.com
FW:
What do you think?

Phoebe Thompson
News Anchor
Channel 8 News
Relentlessly Local, round the clock

From: crystalmomof4exlaw@yahoo.com
To: phoebegb@channel8news.com
Why don't you ask Pookie? I hear she threw a party just to celebrate the occasion. Not sure her husband has ever quite recovered, either mentally or

physically from the ordeal, but he seems to have little interest in doing so, either – a fact for which Pookie also seems much relieved.

PTA PRESIDENT, Village Public School

From: phoebegb@channel8news.com
To: crystalmomof4exlaw@yahoo.com
Pookie recommends Dr. Cutter's partner, Dr. Jon Weiner. He actually encourages husbands to come in pairs, as he finds men who come on their own to be rather skittish. As a couple, however, they can reassure one another by holding hands and making promises to reaffirm their manhood with a post-procedure trip to Vegas, even though any kind of lap dance or other physical contact is out of the question, since patients must spend the first few days with a bag of frozen peas firmly attached to their groin.

I've scheduled the procedure for tomorrow. Will that work for George? Feel free to share the date I've synced onto your Mecalendar with him, although I can't imagine he will appreciate having someone else's wife tell him when he's losing his manhood.

Phoebe Thompson
News Anchor
Channel 8 News
Relentlessly Local, round the clock

From: crystalmomof4exlaw@yahoo.com
To: phoebegb@channel8news.com
Perfect.

PTA PRESIDENT, Village Public School

From: phoebegb@channel8news.com
To: crystalmomof4exlaw@yahoo.com
Planning to keep Brad in lock-down from now until the appointment, in case he gets any last minute ideas. May offer the old boy one last dose of real love to keep him busy. Can't do any harm, right?

Phoebe Thompson
News Anchor
Channel 8 News
Relentlessly Local, round the clock

Tuesday, June 11

From: crystalmomof4exlaw@yahoo.com
To: phoebegb@channel8news.com
I was touched to see George and Brad holding hands in the recovery room, but understand from the nurse that hubby reached for Brad's paw as soon as he saw the size of the needle required to anesthetize certain parts. Nice to know men aren't afraid to display emotion when push comes to shove (or snip, in this case).

PTA PRESIDENT, Village Public School

From: phoebegb@channel8news.com
To: crystalmomof4exlaw@yahoo.com
Brad is resting quietly at home in bed this morning, declining all offers of food and staring into space. You don't suppose we made a mistake, encouraging them to go for such a life altering procedure? Much as I like to complain about well, pretty much everything, I'd hate to think I had stripped my huband completely of the will to live.

How is George?

Phoebe Thompson
News Anchor
Channel 8 News
Relentlessly Local, round the clock

From: crystalmomof4exlaw@yahoo.com
To: phoebegb@channel8news.com
George = much the same, so I've suggested he shuffle down the street and keep Brad company, while you are at work.

God knows I can't stare at his hang dog face for a second longer. Went so far as to promise the boys they could play as much VBox as they liked today, and that I would bring them lunch. That seemed to cheer both of them up.

PTA PRESIDENT, Village Public School

Text from Crystal to George
At Holier Than Thou Foods. Do you guys need anything?

Text from Crystal to George
They don't sell beer. Or cinnabuns.

Text from Crystal to George
Fine. I will run to 7/Eleven. Anything else while I'm out?

Text from Crystal to George
No video games, and manager says they are fresh out of NY Times, altho' I think he was being sarcastic. And no, I'm not stopping anywhere else.

Text from Crystal to George
BTW, the op you guys had was technically a PROCEDURE, not death sentence. Nurse said should be fine for you and Brad to drive by now.

Wednesday, June 12

From: crystalmomof4exlaw@yahoo.com
To: phoebegb@channel8news.com
Was it my imagination, or did Gunther pay us more attention than usual

in class today, perhaps as a result of our recent retreat? Meanwhile, Vira didn't say a word. Have decided to take this as a sign she's jealous of our rejuvenated appearance, but could have more to do with the fact it's impossible to talk during Defecating Pigeon.

Speaking of Vira, how are things between the two of you these days?

PTA PRESIDENT, Village Public School

From: phoebegb@channel8news.com
To: crystalmomof4exlaw@yahoo.com
We are civil whenever we run into each other, but frankly, I'm not sure there is anything she could do to restore our friendship. Why do you ask?

Phoebe Thompson
News Anchor
Channel 8 News
Relentlessly Local, round the clock

From: crystalmomof4exlaw@yahoo.com
To: phoebegb@channel8news.com
It's just that I've arranged to meet her for lunch today at the little Thai place next to my former office, before she hops on a plane to Martinique for two weeks. Can you join?

PTA PRESIDENT, Village Public School

From: phoebegb@channel8news.com
To: crystalmomof4exlaw@yahoo.com
After everything that's happened, I'd rather eat my young, but I also can't wait to tell her that Brad's seed business has officially stopped operating. Please tell me what time and where, and I will be there!

Phoebe Thompson
News Anchor
Channel 8 News
Relentlessly Local, round the clock

RICH SIMPLICITY

My devoted followers, today I write from the balmy shores of Martinique, a truly charming island and former French colony located deep in the heart of the Caribbean. The French people are delightfully receptive to my yogic truths, although I was a little surprised to find many people here still practice the ancient art of step aerobics. Really.

My mastery of the French language is proceeding a little more slowly than I'd imagined, so our communication generally occurs via simple hand signals, most of them friendly. Eventually, I hope to wean the natives off their habit of holding a cigarette in one hand and a glass of wine in the other, but it is - as I say so often - a journey for all of us.

For those who doubt the Blessings of A Complete Physical and Mental Meltdown", I ask you how, in the space of less than a week, my relationship with my ex's new girlfriend could have gone from being challenging, to say the least, to being one of serene cooperation and mutual respect. It turns out, Tiffany was more surprised than most to discover that a baby is for life, not just for fun, and has been especially oppressed by the prospect of having to take care of her little darling 24/7, with no help from the father - even though I warned her repeatedly this would be the case. Sensing that all was not well chez mon ex, I invited Tiffany and Bhakti to accompany me down here on my private jet for a spiritual retreat. At first, Tiffany refused all offers of assistance, not realizing, silly thing, that the term 'retreat' has no meaning when traveling with infants, unless paid help is involved. Ditto with the notion of 'vacation.' Fortunately, it took only a single day of Bhakti wailing piteously for twelve hours straight for Tiffany to capitulate and let me hold her, and from then on, one thing then led to another, and soon it was yours truly waking the nurse up to give my spiritual daughter her nighttime feeds.

The upshot of our few days here together here is that Tiffany now feels so comfortable leaving me with Bhakti that she has decided to attend a three week retreat with my Guru in Goa after she gets back, to catch up on rest and consult Her about whether or not motherhood is in fact compatible with the practice of Buddhism.

Tiff has asked me to watch Bhakti while she embarks on this voyage of self-discovery, and Tom has no objection, so I feel very privileged indeed, although I do wish the artificial breastfeeding device my friend, Crystal, lent me didn't poke out from underneath my bikini top.

I feel almost as though I gave birth to Bhakti myself - and that our family has expanded in the most unexpected and yet wonderful way. I know Tom will soon feel the same way about having two mother wives, even if he has just embarked on a course of therapy to find out why he seems to be attracted to controlling women. I guess you could call this the Blessing of Being Left Holding the Baby.

In the meantime, you may be thrilled to learn I've developed a mad crush on the scuba instructor here at the resort - I mean, of course, retreat. Although he likes to flirt shamelessly with the teenage girls - endlessly creating underwater mepod headphones from seaweed in an attempt to make them laugh - he is quite attentive to his "yogi folle" as he has taken to calling me when none of them are nearby. I hope to understand more of what he means very soon.

En amour et serenite,

Vira

From: Rich Simplicity
To: phoebegb@sahmsrule.net

Rich Simplicity: A monthly newsletter bringing you a life of ultimate simplicity, no matter how much money I have.

Volume 04, Issue 06

Blessings,
My devoted followers, today I write from the balmy shores of Martinique, a truly charming island and former French colony located deep in the heart of the Caribbean. The French people are delightfully receptive to my yogic truths, although

I was a little surprised to find many people here still practice the ancient art of step aerobics. Really.

My mastery of the French language is proceeding a little more slowly than I'd imagined, so our communication generally occurs via simple hand signals, most of them friendly. Eventually, I hope to wean the natives off their habit of holding a cigarette in one hand and a glass of wine in the other, but it is - as I say so often - a journey for all of us.

For those who doubt the Blessings of A Complete Physical and Mental Meltdown', I ask you how, in the space of less than a week, my relationship with my ex's new girlfriend could have gone from being challenging, to say the least, to being one of serene cooperation and mutual respect. It turns out, Tiffany was more surprised than most to discover that a baby is for life, not just for fun, and has been especially oppressed by the prospect of having to take care of her little darling 24/7, with no help from the father - even though I warned her repeatedly this would be the case. Sensing that all was not well chez mon ex, I invited Tiffany and Bhakti to accompany me down here on my private jet for a spiritual retreat. At first, Tiffany refused all offers of assistance, not realizing, silly thing, that the term 'retreat' has no meaning when traveling with infants, unless paid help is involved. Ditto with the notion of 'vacation.' Fortunately, it took only a single day of Bhakti wailing piteously for twelve hours straight for Tiffany to capitulate and let me hold her, and from then on, one thing then led to another, and soon it was yours truly waking the nurse up to give my spiritual daughter her nighttime feeds.

The upshot of our few days here together here is that Tiffany now feels so comfortable leaving me with Bhakti that she has decided to attend a three week retreat with my Guru in Goa after she gets back, to catch up on rest and consult Her about whether or not motherhood is in fact compatible with the practice of Buddhism.

Tiff has asked me to watch Bhakti while she embarks on this voyage of self-discovery, and Tom has no objection, so I feel very privileged indeed, although I do wish the artificial breastfeeding device my friend, Crystal, lent me didn't poke out from underneath my bikini top.

I feel almost as though I gave birth to Bhakti myself - and that our family has expanded in the most unexpected and yet wonderful way. I know Tom will soon feel the same way about having two mother wives, even if he has just embarked on a course of therapy to find out why he seems to be attracted to controlling women. I guess you could call this the Blessing of Being Left Holding the Baby.'

In the meantime, you may be thrilled to learn I've developed a mad crush on the scuba instructor here at the resort - I mean, of course, retreat. Although he likes to flirt shamelessly with the teenage girls - endlessly creating underwater mepod headphones from seaweed in an attempt to make them laugh - he is quite attentive to his "yogi folle" as he has taken to calling me when none of them are nearby. I hope to understand more of what he means very soon.

En amour et serenite,
Vira

Friday, June 14

meCalendar Reminder: Last day of school, VPS (half day). School lets out at 12.35pm.

Text from Phoebe to Crystal

Hope you are enjoying last few moments of freedom b/f VPS lets out, and we face 2 1/2 months of quality time with our children. Gulp!

Text from Crystal to Phoebe

Thank God I enrolled boys in golfing lessons, and Kim in Quilting camp for first 2 weeks of summer. Hoping it will prepare them for Country Club life, but right now, looks like Kev may switch with Kim.

Text from Phoebe to Crystal

Twins have only been home 5 mins and already texting me to go to mall. I'm tempted, just 'cos newsroom = dead and I desperately need new clothes. For some reason, can't fit into any of my old summer dresses. Care to join?

Text from Crystal to Phoebe

Promised cherubs would take them to the public pool. Have fun!

Text from Phoebe to Crystal

I'm sure I've been doing yoga longer than you, and all I have is a Buddha belly to show for it. Please don't tell me it's karma. Hate to think my body is paying a price for something I did in a previous life and don't even remember doing, let alone enjoying.

Monday, June 17

George,

Here is the camp schedule for the Cherubs.

love,
C

8:00am Drop Kimberly at Smithsonian quilting

9:15am Drop Kevin at Young Titans Golf Acade﹏

10:00am Put Kurtis down for her morning nap in

10:45 Drop Karson at Daddy's Legacy Golf Aca﹏

11:30 Pick up Kevin at Young Titans Golf Academ﹏

11:45 Pick up Kimberly from Smithsonian (adult must enter facility to pick-up); on NO ACCOUNT LEAVE KURTIS ASLEEP IN CAR WHILE YOU ARE INSIDE. THIS IS ILLEGAL, NO MATTER WHAT OUR PARENTS DID WITH US BACK IN THE DAY

12:00 Lunch for kids

1:15pm Drop Kurtis at Little Captains of Industry Tennis Academy at Club

1:45pm Drop Kevin at Ruling with Class Tennis Academy at Club (early arrival not allowed)

2:00pm Take Kimberly to Krafty Kids workshop at Perky's house

2:15pm Pick up Kurtis at Little Captains of Industry Tennis Academy

3:00pm Put Kurtis down for afternoon nap in her car seat

3:45pm Pick up Kevin from Ruling with Class Tennis Academy at Club

4:15pm Pick up Kimberly from Perky's

5:00pm Dinner for kids

5:30pm Kurtis' bath and playtime

6:00pm Enforce summer reading with three elders

6:30pm Put Kurtis to bed in her car seat

6:45pm Drop Karson at the Little Senators tball batting practice at Club

8:00pm Pick up Karson

11:00pm Pick up Kevin from inevitable party or movie with friends

Tuesday, June 18

From: phoebegb@channel8news.com
To: crystalmomof4exlaw@yahoo.com

I don't believe it! In spite of not consuming a single drop of alcohol, ounce of sugar or grain of salt all weekend, I still can't fit into my bell weather pair of jeans – the ones that always leave tire marks across my stomach if I'm more than a few pounds off. If anything, they seem a little tighter than before our trip.

What's worse, viewers have been calling in to the station to complain they don't like my new expression, which they describe as 'wooden'. Apparently, they are accusing me of lacking empathy, and are beginning to question the station's judgment in appointing a 'cold, British b@#$%' in one reader's words to cover the upcoming July 4th celebrations. WTF??

Phoebe Thompson
News Anchor
Channel 8 News
Relentlessly Local, round the clock

From: crystalmomof4exlaw@yahoo.com
To: phoebegb@channel8news.com
Since when has a woman needed facial expressions to get ahead in this town? Just look at Pookie and Bitsy.

Come to think of it, they've probably had a few 'retreats' too many, which might explain why they never quite seem to be able to muster so much as an acknowledgment whenever I approach. Must remember to be more compassionate next time I'm tempted to dismiss them for being unfriendly. They may also just be as hungry as we were this weekend!

PTA PRESIDENT, Village Public School

Wednesday, June 19

Text from Phoebe to Crystal
Do you have time for lunch today? My treat. Have some exciting news would love to celebrate.

Text from Crystal to Phoebe
Alas, I need to take minivan in for servicing, then shop for your party. What's up?

Text from Phoebe to Crystal
Holier Than Thou wants to sell George's pesto!

Text from Crystal to Phoebe
Congrats! Does this mean you get to quit your job?

Text from Phoebe to Crystal
It's early days yet, and besides, not sure I want to. :0 Is that weird?

Text from Crystal to Phoebe
Not at all. That's called a good problem to have. Now if you'll excuse me, need to run to first tennis lesson w/ Xavier. If anyone asks, tell them I'm very, very busy juggling multiple balls in the air to keep everyone happy. Including me.

Dearest Lata,

I am delighted to hear that you are planning to return to our corner of the world after all, at the beginning of July.

However, much has happened in the time you've been gone, including the fact that George and I have decided to spend more time together as a family, and less time working, which means we no longer require the services of a full-time sitter. Having said that, Phoebe Thompson may be in the market for a nanny again, as it looks like Brad Thompson's pesto business is taking off. I am taking the liberty of suggesting a nanny share arrangement – hope that's OK.

You'll be glad to hear that you have inspired George and Kevin to brush up their handyman skills (under the tutelage of Frank Manly) and sign up for a Homes for Humanity trip to Lima at the end of July to help re-build some of the houses that were destroyed in the earthquake. Ironically, it looks like we may have several of your countrymen working on installing the hot tub in our backyard here in DC at the same time, but hopefully it will prove to be just the father-son bonding trip both of them need, after what has certainly been a rocky year for the Walker family, although things are hopefully improving now.

Look forward to seeing you soon.

With love,

Crystal

Sunday, June 30

DC Diary

The Walkers Take on the Nation's Capital

BLOG ARCHIVE

Public School, New Opportunities, Fanny Packs

At long last, the Walker clan seems to be finding its groove here in the nation's capitol. After a stressful couple of months, and much soul searching, we have decided to decline Seton Academy's offer of places for all the cherubs, and keep them in the local public school for now. This is partly because the cherubs seem happy there, and partly thanks to my commitment and George's to spend less time working and generally running ourselves ragged trying to keep up with the pace of life in DC.

In that spirit, George has decided to leave his lobbying firm for other opportunities, and I seem to be finding my bliss - at least for now - by teaching yoga. Oh, and did I mention that I was recently offered the opportunity to become the spokesperson for the First Lady's 'On Your Bike' movement? Naturally, I accepted, even though I'm not sure yet how it's all going to work out, especially with the cherubs home from school for the summer. But that's all part of the journey, right? In the meantime, I do hope you will consider paying us a visit. We're happy to give you a tour of the DC sights, sounds and celebrity hangouts of the city.

Just remember to leave your fanny packs at home if you want to be taken for a native (as Kevin learned the hard way)

No comments:

Post a Comment

Comment as: Select profile

Publish   Preview

DC Diary
Public School, New Opportunities, Fanny Packs

At long last, the Walker clan seems to be finding its groove here in the nation's capital. After a stressful couple of months, and much soul searching, we have decided to decline Seton Academy's offer of places for all the cherubs, and keep them in the local public school for now. This is partly because the cherubs seem happy there, and partly thanks to my commitment and George's to spend less time working and generally running ourselves ragged trying to keep up with the pace of life in DC.

In that spirit, George has decided to leave his lobbying firm for other opportunities, and I seem to be finding my bliss - at least for now - by teaching yoga. Oh, and did I mention that I was recently offered the opportunity to become the spokesperson for the First Lady's 'On Your Bike' movement? Naturally, I accepted, even though I'm not sure yet how it's all going to work out, especially with the cherubs home from school for the summer. But that's all part of the journey, right? In the meantime, I do hope you will consider paying us a visit. We're happy to give you a tour of the DC sights, sounds and celebrity hangouts of the city.

Just remember to leave your fanny packs at home if you want to be taken for a native (as Kevin learned the hard way).

Epilogue

July, 2013 Vol. 42, Issue 7
Always FREE, but donations appreciated

Please direct submissions and inquiries to:
whining@villagepress.com
P.O. Box 357 Village Town, MD

VILLAGE WHINER

*Your trusty monthly newsletter of
the "Most Livable Village," 1989*
Village Times Mirror, Inc

Village Board of Managers Meeting

The Village Board is delighted to announce the publication of another parenting guide by a Village resident, well-known local parenting guru, Evelyn Braun. Her latest tome, which goes by the catchy title, *Your Problem Teen is a Result of Your Poor Toddler Parenting*, is sure to be another bestseller. We look forward to the book launch, hosted by Pookie Granger and Perky Sparks, in the Village Yurt next Tuesday. Organic, locally sourced, gluten, sugar, fat and flavor free cupcakes will be served. Please note: We have been warned to expect a large and potentially hostile crowd of parents picketing this event, so Special Ops is on standby to deal with any trouble.

In more resident news, Pookie Granger and Bitsy Bobinger are about to become the Village's first reality TV celebrities, following the truly astonishing success of the Village Cup Cakery. Although there appears to be some jealousy among other would-be local entrepreneurs (see quotes such as "Cupcakes for God's sake? Are we all out of your olds now?" on the listserv), we encourage other Village entrepreneurs to continue with their endeavors and not despair that they too can make a fortune with an expensive, fattening food indulgence that nobody really needs. Speaking of which, rumor has it that our favorite pesto producer will soon be selling his sauces through Holier than Thou Foods, as soon as he is able to provide a detailed nutrition guide and demonstrate that his basil is truly local and organic, using aerial photography of his garden crop supposedly dusted from federal drug planes.

In other news, the Village speed bump on Center Street is scheduled for smoothing down following complaints from Barb Van Houten, who claims the noise of car axles being scraped along concrete was keeping her up at night. As the Village has also heard from a number of insurance carriers on the matter of repairs, it felt obliged to remedy the problem, although our legal team has advised us to note that the Village still assumes no liability in these matters. Residents are reminded that they waive all rights to pursue any such claims thanks to the homeowner's agreement they were forced to sign when they first moved into the Village. Moreover, if you drive within the posted speed limit of 10mph, your vehicle should avoid catastrophic damage.

Village Diversity Group

The Diversity Group is happy to report that Sutton Better, the Village women's subcommittee chair has agreed to work more cooperatively and proactively with its members in future. According to Mr. Better: "Doing anything cooperatively since my gender realignment surgery has been challenging, especially since I feel that my newly assertive male leadership has helped the committee achieve its goals. At the same time, having been a woman myself, I also recognize the vital importance of conciliation and teamwork, which is why I always make sure to pay a woman a compliment before asking them to do whatever needs to get done. Through therapy, I hope to move towards a more genuine model of appreciation, although it would help if the women's sub-committee were composed of some more attractive, younger members."

This month the Diversity Group will focus upon the emerging tension between those in the Village who wish to live off the grid and those who believe the best use of public land is a well-maintained (private) golf course, with a tennis court and pool to keep the rest of the family happy.

Miss Gertrude's Manners

Miss Gertrude has departed for her annual vacation to the south of France, and will resume writing her column in the fall. In the meantime, she encourages anyone who spots her sunbathing topless in Saint Tropez, per the local custom, to use their discretion and NOT take the opportunity to say hello. Updating her on Village gossip can wait until she returns.

Village Board of Managers Meeting

The Village Board is delighted to announce the publication of another parenting guide by a Village resident, well-known local parenting guru, Evelyn Braun. Her latest tome, which goes by the catchy title, *"Your Problem Teen is a Result of Your Poor Toddler Parenting"* is sure to be another bestseller. We look forward to the book launch, hosted by Pookie Granger and Perky Sparks, in the Village Yurt next Tuesday. Organic, locally-sourced, gluten, sugar, fat and flavor-free cupcakes will be served. Please note: We have been warned to expect a large and potentially hostile crowd of parents picketing this event, so Special Ops is on standby to deal with any trouble.

In more resident news, Perky and Pookie are about to become the Village's first reality TV celebrities, following the truly astonishing success of the Village Cup Cakery. Although there appears to be some jealousy among other would-be local entrepreneurs (see quotes such as, "Cupcakes for God's sake? Are we all four-year olds now?" on the listserv), we encourage other Village entrepreneurs to continue with their endeavors, and not despair that they too can make a fortune with an expensive, fattening food indulgence that nobody really needs. Speaking of which, rumor has it that our favorite pesto producer will soon be selling his sauces through Holier than Thou Foods, as soon as he is able to provide a detailed nutrition guide and demonstrate that his basil is truly local and organic, using aerial photography of his garden crop subpoenaed from federal drug planes.

In other news, the Village speed hump on Center Street is scheduled for smoothing down following complaints from Barbi Van Houzen, who claims the noise of car axles being scraped along concrete was keeping her up at night. As the Village has also heard from a number of insurance carriers on the matter of repairs, it felt obliged to remedy the problem, although our legal team has advised us to note that the Village still assumes no liability in these matters. Residents are reminded that they waive all rights to pursue any such claims thanks to the homeowner's agreement they were forced to sign when they first moved into the Village. Moreover, if you drive within the posted speed limit of 10mph, your vehicle should avoid catastrophic damage.

Village Tennis Team

After much delay, allegedly caused by the men's tennis team's repeated failure to calendar the date, the men's and women's village teams battled it out on the courts at the Club last week, despite some consternation about allowing Ladies to play on the courts after 3pm. The Club Board ultimately relented in the face of female club members who threatened to publicize the archaic and sexist club rules to the media immediately. A new committee on the Board has been formed to study the continuing fairness of such rules, considering the fact that most female club members now work and don't have the same opportunity to play early in the day as they once allegedly did.

A rain delay kept the final result elusive, since the club courts are now closed for re-surfacing and cannot be played upon. Suffice it to say, each team believes it is victorious, which may be the best result of all.

Village Diversity Group

The Diversity Group is happy to report that Simon Better, the Village women's subcommittee chair has agreed to work more cooperatively and proactively with its members in future. According to Mr. Better, "Doing anything cooperatively since my gender realignment surgery has been challenging, especially since I feel that my newly assertive male leadership has helped the committee achieve its goals. At the same time, having been a woman myself, I also recognize the vital

importance of conciliation and teamwork, which is why I always make sure to pay a woman a compliment before asking them to do whatever needs to get done. Through therapy, I hope to move towards to a more genuine model of appreciation, although it would help if the women's sub-committee were comprised of some more attractive, younger members."

This month, the Diversity Group will focus upon the emerging tension between those in the Village who wish to live off the grid and those who believe the best use of public land is a well-maintained (private) golf course, with a tennis court and pool to keep the rest of the family happy.

Miss Gertrude's Manners

Miss Gertrude has departed for her annual vacation to the south of France, and will resume writing her column in the fall. In the meantime, she encourages anyone who spots her sunbathing topless in Saint Tropez, per the local custom, to use their discretion and NOT take the opportunity to say hello. Updating her on Village gossip can wait until she returns.

PHOEBE IS TURNING 40!

Please join for a celebration of half a lifetime in the Village Yurt

 Saturday, July 13, 6:30 - 11pm

Dinner & Dancing
Pisco Sour Fountain Freely Flowing

We love your children, especially if you keep them at home on this special occasion

No gifts por favor

Wednesday, July 3

Posting on Village Listserv
Mr. Palmer has asked us to point out that technically, Pookie Granger and Perky Sparks will not be the Village's first TV celebrities, since the Village has in fact boasted several prominent news anchors and political commentators among its residents. To quote Mr. Palmer, 'just because Perky and Pookie happen to be more attractive than the rumpled old fogies who grace our screens on the PBS Newshour every evening does not automatically entitle them to be considered more prominent.' Our sincerest apologies.

From: crystalmomof4exlaw@yahoo.com
To: phoebegb@channel8news.com
Isn't it terrible about Gunther's catastrophic injury?

I'm glad the paramedics were able to transport him safely to ER for emergency surgery. He must have been terribly uncomfortable with his feet stuck around his ears like that. Still, if our over the hill but still enthusiastic yoga instructor can get stuck in Crow's Nest pose, requiring a team of surgeons to free him, then what hope is there for the rest of us?

It's particularly heart-rending that his injury occurred at my certification to teach ceremony, although I will never understand why he felt compelled to use the occasion to jump on stage and start a yoga throw-down against Nico, our 28 year old, very handsome instructor. I guess he needed to prove to the nubile young twenty somethings, including Nina, in my training that he still has the stuff. Personally, I view certification as a way to take it a bit easier.

Unfortunately, Nina appears to have hopped onto a plane just this morning, in order to put the wheels in motion to set up her own yoga studio in Munich this fall. I can't help thinking that the prospect of nursing a frail old man may have influenced her decision, although I dare say she's right that her countrymen will ultimately need her more.

Planning to visit Gunther in the hospital myself on Friday, and Vira's new houseboy is pureeing some homegrown, organic veggies for him as I write. Vira herself claims to be too sensitive to hospital disinfectant to visit, which is just what I would expect from the woman. Shall I pick you up on my way?

PTA PRESIDENT, Village Public School

From: phoebegb@channel8news.com
To: crystalmomof4exlaw@yahoo.com
That would be great, thank you. I worry that Gunther may have very few willing to tend to his many needs now that Nina is gone, and he is no longer capable of placing his magic hands on others' bodies. As sympathetic as we are, dear Crystal, I implore you NOT to consider filling that bill either. Surely, we both do enough care taking of others to take on the (considerable) needs of our guru, as well.

Friday, July 5

From: phoebegb@channel8news.com
To: crystalmomof4exlaw@yahoo.com

Hospital visit went as well as can be expected, don't you think?

Must admit to taking a little malicious pleasure in forcing Gunther to swallow the kind of salt, dairy and seasoning-free food he was always lecturing us to eat, but we never actually see him ingest. Good to see he's already flirting with the nurses. I think that's a positive sign, don't you? Once you lose the drive, there's really nothing left. Of course, it can't hurt that the Home for Aging, Injured and Retired Yogis only allows patients to attempt poses with the assistance of nubile young therapists. What better motivation is there, really, to get better?

You must be thrilled that Gunther has asked you to take over the studio while he 'recovers' (even though you and I both know he never will, fully). You would be GREAT, dear Crystal, although I fear you will never hear the end of it when Vira finds out.

Phoebe Thompson
News Anchor
Channel 8 News
Relentlessly Local, round the clock

From: crystalmomof4exlaw@yahoo.com
To: phoebegb@channel8news.com

I was surprised and honored by Gunther's request. I have to say, while I am excited by the opportunity, I am determined not to let work (no matter how satisfying) dominate my life, so I have approached the Village Country Club about offering Steamy Yoga classes at the Club and providing child care facilities for anyone who wants to attend (women and men). That way, I can minimize overhead and still provide a small royalty income to Gunther for his special brand of yoga touching. Loathe to march into the Club and start shaking things up before I am even a member, but I am also determined to change the culture there, so that happy hour doesn't always require a cocktail.

Only potential fly in this ointment is that George was so shattered from his "easy" day of shuttling the cherubs from camp to camp and back that he's already begun to consider his work options. So much for devotion to hearth and home. I don't blame the man, but why does he see childcare as optional?

BTW, how do you feel about changing the no gifts request on your evite to asking for donations to the Home for Aging, Injured and Retired Yogis (HAIRY)? Judging by the number of crippled and impoverished yogis we saw shuffling around when we visited Gunther, I think the need is great, don't you?

PTA PRESIDENT, Village Public School

From: phoebegb@channel8news.com
To: crystalmomof4exlaw@yahoo.com
Normally, I'm loathe to capitulate to the idea that every party needs a worthy cause, but I daresay that's the way things are done in DC, so why buck the trend now? About to run into a production meeting, but want you to know how much I appreciate you organizing all this!

Phoebe Thompson
News Anchor
Channel 8 News
Relentlessly Local, round the clock

From: crystalmomof4exlaw@yahoo.com
To: phoebegb@channel8news.com
I will make sure to decorate the Village Yurt with blow-up pictures of HAIRY residents, so that the guests are truly moved by the plight of someone who can no longer manage anything more strenuous than Rotting Corpse pose. Plus, the home has agreed to lend us their most nubile male assistant to lead a short practice of gratitude to mark the occasion.

My new Steamy Yoga responsibilities apparently involve assisting Vira with the last of the 8 week long Tantric Couples' workshop series she and Gunther originally taught next Friday. Dragging George along for the occasion, as his appetite for carnal relations actually appears to have increased since he had the snip, and frankly I'm exhausted. Hopefully, this course will teach him to slow down and enjoy the moment, rather than automatically gallop for the finish line to prove things are still functioning down there.

PTA PRESIDENT, Village Public School

From: phoebegb@channel8news.com
To: crystalmomof4exlaw@yahoo.com
You know Sting's wife curses the day he ever donned a pair of yoga pants, no matter what she claims in interviews about the joys of Eastern love. Why do you think I'm so happy to be back at work?

Phoebe Thompson
News Anchor
Channel 8 News
Relentlessly Local, round the clock

Monday, July 8

From: crystalmomof4exlaw@yahoo.com
To: phoebegb@channel8news.com
Missed you at yoga today. Everything OK?

BTW, I've discovered the upside of all the hi-jinks involved with tantric yoga is that George is amenable to any suggestion whispered in his ear before, during and afterwards. The yard and family minivan have never looked quite so spiffy. May be the most useful marital aid ever created. Suggest you try!

PTA PRESIDENT, Village Public School

From: phoebegb@channel8news.com
To: crystalmomof4exlaw@yahoo.com
Sorry – I simply don't have the energy right now. Maybe it's because I'm turning forty, but I really can't see the point of doing something that doesn't seem to help me lose weight, let alone find inner peace (the two are intimately connected – for me, at least).

Phoebe Thompson
News Anchor
Channel 8 News
Relentlessly Local, round the clock

From: crystalmomof4exlaw@yahoo.com
To: phoebegb@channel8news.com
I really think you should make a doctor's appointment and find out exactly what is going on with your health.

PTA PRESIDENT, Village Public School

From: phoebegb@channel8news.com
To: crystalmomof4exlaw@yahoo.com
Just made an appointment with my Ob/gyn. Hopefully, she should be able to get to the bottom of whatever is going on.

Phoebe Thompson
News Anchor
Channel 8 News
Relentlessly Local, round the clock

Tuesday, July 9

From: crystalmomof4exlaw@yahoo.com
To: phoebegb@channel8news.com
Brad has asked me to finalize last minute details for your party next week. Thank God he agreed not to make it a surprise, since I assume you prefer to be forewarned, not overheard speaking candidly about your husband,

parents and any of your friends as you enter the room where they have been hiding in preparation. The excuse that you have been hurt by their refusal to acknowledge your special day simply doesn't fly with anyone you have just described as a 'fat-ass, horse-face or dingbat.' Trust me.

Here's the deal. I've booked the DJ and tent, and Brad, of course will supply the food, but Pookie and Perky would like to know if you would like to make a grand entrance by jumping out of one of their giant signature cupcakes? It would definitely be a fun, if rather messy way to make your appearance, but if you prefer a more dignified entrance, let me know.

Oh, and since George now has more time at home these days, he's decided to create an itinerary of important events on the day of the party. Forgive him please (I may not) if his involvement seems a little overbearing and misplaced. He needs a sense of purpose, and so far, the many details involved in running a household don't seem to capture his interest on a regular basis. The only thing worse than having him follow me around, critiquing my every movement, is catching him staring into space while I'm running around like a headless chicken. Please don't trot out the old line that you should be careful what you ask for. I GET IT!!

PTA PRESIDENT, Village Public School

From: phoebegb@channel8news.com
To: crystalmomof4exlaw@yahoo.com
Welcome to the world of the 'work at home' husband. If George is anything like Brad, he will soon have a whiteboard posting of minute to minute activities for you and the cherubs. It may make you want to dash out his eyes, but it would be bad form not to acknowledge he is at least trying. Hopefully, he will eventually tire of micro-managing your life and find something else to do with his own.

What do you think about me leaping out of coffin at my party?

Phoebe Thompson
News Anchor
Channel 8 News
Relentlessly Local, round the clock

From: crystalmomof4exlaw@yahoo.com
To: phoebegb@channel8news.com
I think the coffin is a darling idea for your party, and not at all melodramatic. Forty IS the official end of youth as we know it, so what better way to mark that passing, symbolically, at least, before leaping out of the casket as your gorgeously rejuvenated, reincarnated self, and prove to everyone there is life after death after all?

I do so enjoy having a friend even slightly older than me, can't you tell?

PTA PRESIDENT, Village Public School

Wednesday, July 10

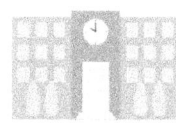 The Village Club

Admission Events for New Members (not optional):

Professor and Mr. Lieberman, Mr. and Mrs. George Walker

~~Mr. and Mrs. Brown~~ (foreclosure on Village property forfeits opportunity)
**All new male members shall meet at 06:00 sharp on Labor Day
to begin the day in the steam room (no clothes allowed)**

The all-male group steam will be closely followed by a brisk dip in the unheated indoor pool. Please note: the Club will be closed for the day to allow the men to move straight from the steam to pool without the need for swim trunks. Post-swim, the men will convene again in the Grill Room to nourish their new bonds as Club Brothers. It should be noted that "old boys" (current Club members) sometimes enjoy the childhood tradition of locker room towel snapping. All new Club members should be prepared to endure this behavior without complaint. Crying is strongly discouraged, although swearing is fine. Rest assured that any lingering red marks are impermanent and Club counsel advises that members forego any right to sue when they sign the liability waiver on the Club membership forms.

**All new female members shall gather at 09:00 on Labor Day (to allow time for
nannies and housekeepers to start work) in the Beatrice Knitter Memorial Room**

The ladies will greet the full Holiday Event Planning committee and begin strategizing for the Club Holiday Women's Luncheon. Although the luncheon is not 'till early December, it has become clear that early planning is necessary to combat a serious decline in Holiday Event Planning committee members (most by natural causes). Women members are no longer required to perform a full curtsy when meeting the existing committee members, but holiday sweaters are encouraged. In addition, please bring any home crafts or sewing/knitting/quilting you've done during the year, so they may be considered for one of the lovely display and/or sale tables. We regret to say that jewelry makers are no longer invited to contribute, as we have so very many of them in the Village.

After a full buffet lunch featuring shrimp cocktail and prime rib (what else?), new female members may return home to attend to family issues and to prepare for the return of possibly intoxicated new member husbands by early nightfall. Although some new female members might feel their skill set would better serve the Club community in another role, it is firm Club policy that new Ladies' members serve at least two full years on the Holiday Event Planning Committee before moving on to less aged pastures.

**The formal dance party and coronation ceremony
(re-acknowledging the Club President and his contributions to Club life)
will be held in the Stewart Fine Hall. Black Tie Attire.**

All new club members, male and female, are asked to return by 6pm sharp for cocktails, dinner and dancing (no children, please). A select group of existing Club Members will be on hand to give their final blessing to the new arrivals. Belligerent or boisterous behavior is highly discouraged, no matter how long you may have been imbibing, and no one should consider taking another dip in the indoor pool. As new members, you will be fully subject to Club sanctions for unbecoming behavior.

445

Thursday, July 11

Text from Crystal to George
Where r u? I thought I was the only one to get up at 5:30am.

Text from Crystal to George
You're at gym? But cherubs = still asleep and I have yoga class to teach in 15 min. Get your a$$ back here so I can make it in time!

Text from Crystal to George
FYI, just b/c u aren't working right now does not mean u can do what u want. Cherubs are YOUR responsibility also

From: phoebegb@channel8news.com
To: crystalmomof4exlaw@yahoo.com
So excited, I don't know where to begin. Looks like Brad and his partner have an offer to buy P-NIS!

Just as the world economy disappears in a puff of smoke, along comes an entrepreneur from China, and before you know it, Brad and his business partner are offered a lot of money for the whole shebang: patents, licensing rights, even the name, which apparently sounds very auspicious in Mandarin.

As if that weren't enough, Holier Than Thou Foods is planning a playful advertising campaign touting his pesto's addictive but healthful properties. If this keeps up, I may be able to quit my job by the end of the year – assuming I want to, that is.

Phoebe Thompson
News Anchor
Channel 8 News
Relentlessly Local, round the clock

From: crystalmomof4exlaw@yahoo.com
To: phoebegb@channel8news.com
Wonderful news about Brad, but I would counsel you not to do anything hasty on the job front. I know the money may sound great, but you and I both know how much it costs to live in this town. Besides, it sounds like Brad will still be 'working from home,' which I'm beginning to think means you need to spend as much time as possible outside of it.

George still seems to think his parenting responsibilities are optional, in spite of the fact he's between jobs, so our 'slowdown' hasn't created the state of marital give and take I was expecting. Meanwhile, my time is really filling up, between teaching yoga classes at the Club, my PTA responsibilities and oh, the little question of managing the cherubs' lives. I'm beginning to think the only answer may be another au pair. Putting out feelers to Au Pair International again, as I've decided I'd rather be happy than right.

PTA PRESIDENT, Village Public School

From: phoebegb@channel8news.com
To: crystalmomof4exlaw@yahoo.com

I'm definitely not as elated at the prospect of giving up work as I expected. As you know, NOT working doesn't guarantee uninterrupted bliss, or even the ability to meet kid needs, since all of us are so good at filling up our free time with stuff that's just not that important. But maybe that's OK? Why are we all so afraid to admit that? (Please don't tell Evelyn I said that).

Besides, I've only just been promoted to anchor, and so haven't really had a chance to enjoy the perks of this position. For one thing, I now have my own office and computer—one that will never get invaded by frisky husbands or sticky-fingered children looking to play a game. For another, I finally get Production Assistant to myself! Nothing to be sniffed at, even if she is completely incompetent.

Only today, I asked her to book the best table at Café Rustico's to celebrate Brad's software sale, and she somehow contrived to reserve us a corner booth, where we could neither see nor be seen. Thankfully, the maitre de recognized me from the 11 o'clock news and quickly rectified the situation, but I will clearly have to hire another, more competent PA to pick up the slack.

Phoebe Thompson
News Anchor
Channel 8 News
Relentlessly Local, round the clock

meCalendar Appointment Reminder
Annual Check-up with Dr. Feelit, 9a.m.
No food or alcohol after 9pm the night before

Friday, July 12

From: crystalmomof4exlaw@yahoo.com
To: phoebegb@channel8news.com

What did Dr. Feelit say? I'm imagining it was something along the lines of: 'I'm concerned you haven't been able to get rid of the bug you picked up in Miami, although if I didn't know you better, I'd say you had visited a surgery, rather than a yoga retreat while you were gone, since your boobs seem to have gone up several cup sizes. Are you sure there isn't something you want to tell me?'

PTA PRESIDENT, Village Public School

From: phoebegb@channel8news.com
To: crystalmomof4exlaw@yahoo.com

I wish that were the case, but as it is, the doctor examined me, took some blood and scheduled me for my first colonoscopy.

I hear that preparations for the latter are the only thing worse than the procedure itself, but I am hoping the three-day fasting will help me fit into my DVF LBD. Pookie tells me she lost 12lbs that way, and was able to fit back into her wedding dress so she and her husband could renew their vows.

But if annual mammograms and occasional invasive rectal procedures are all I have to look forward to in my dotage, I may not bother rising out of my coffin at the party.

Phoebe Thompson
News Anchor
Channel 8 News
Relentlessly Local, round the clock

From: crystalmomof4exlaw@yahoo.com
To: phoebegb@channel8news.com
Putting the final touches on your party decorations down at the Village Yurt, and you'll be glad to hear that Gunther shows up beautifully in the montage of photos we are displaying from HAIRY around the dance floor. One glance at his deeply pained expression and I predict the donations will come rolling in.

Let me know if you need any help getting ready. George has helpfully dropped off some detailed notes about the best schedule for you to follow as you bathe and prep for the occasion. Did you know it's better to do make-up before hair? I now do, as my darling husband so helpfully timed me the other day. Imagine, he can't believe I hadn't done the math myself before now!

PTA PRESIDENT, Village Public School

From: phoebegb@channel8news.com
To: crystalmomof4exlaw@yahoo.com
Feeling sick with nerves, but my party dress only continues to get tighter, in spite of the fact that I must have thrown up twice this morning.

About the only good news is that my boobs are filling out the bust nicely, even if I'm busting out at the seams everywhere else. Hope Brad and the other pall-bearers don't end up having to join Gunther and the other residents at HAIRY under the strain.

Phoebe Thompson
News Anchor
Channel 8 News
Relentlessly Local, round the clock

RICH SIMPLICITY

So much has happened these past few months, I hardly know where to begin. The first piece of news is that Tiffany has officially given me permission to adopt Bhakti (formerly, Britney Love), meaning that I may now call her my daughter in name, and not just in spirit. My ex-husband, Tom, seems perfectly happy with this development, since he likes the shared custody arrangement with our son, and will simply take Bhakti with him on the days he has Ravi.

I am also thrilled to announce that I am helping fund Tiffany's Buddhist meditation center, Om Sweet Om here in DC, as soon as she returns from seeing her guru in Goa. It is important to me that Bhakti comes to know Tiffany as the woman who made it possible for me to give what I call "virtual birth" to my second child.

As we approach another high summer, dear readers, and I embark upon a much-needed month long silent retreat on a horse ranch in Patagonia, while Ravi and Bhakti spend time with their father, I want you to recognize that in this, as in all things, light comes from darkness, just as darkness from light. I hope you have used my lessons and hard work to recognize what may be possible for you too. Doubtless, some of you will continue to persist in the notion that not everyone has the time or resources to pursue personal fulfillment. To which I would like to respond: 'Build the Yurt, and they will come.' Thankfully, my own Village continues to be flush with funds (thank you, speed cameras!), so I see a future in which more of our community needs can be met. On that note, I invite you to attend the next session of "The Blessings of a Blissful Life for All," sponsored in the Village Yurt this fall. Details to follow in my next newsletter, hopefully written from the Tibetan monastery where I began my Journey, and where I plan to spend August with my children and staff.

Till then,
Vira

Om Sweet Om

Special Offer:
Subscribe for 24 months
at only $3 an issue,
and save 60% off the
cover price!

To order a signed copy of The Blessings of Motherhood for only $24.99,
To order a batch of FatMama pregnancy poultice (only $39.99 for 8oz),
To sign-up to receive Vira's weekly newsletter via email (only $19.99 a year),
Thank you for visiting Rich Simplicity. We hope to see you again soon.

From: Rich Simplicity
To: phoebegb@sahmsrule.net

Rich Simplicity: A monthly newsletter bringing you a life of ultimate simplicity, no matter how much money I have.

Volume 04, Issue 07

Blessings,
So much has happened these past few months, I hardly know where to begin. The first piece of news is that Tiffany has officially given me permission to adopt Bhakti (formerly, Britney Love), meaning that I may now call her my daughter in

name, and not just in spirit. My ex-husband, Tom, seems perfectly happy with this development, since he likes the shared custody arrangement with our son, and will simply take Bhakti with him on the days he has Ravi.

I am also thrilled to announce that I am helping fund Tiffany's Buddhist meditation center, Om Sweet Om here in DC, as soon as she returns from seeing her guru in Goa. It is important to me that Bhakti comes to know Tiffany as the woman who made it possible for me to give what I call "virtual birth" to my second child.

As we approach another high summer, dear readers, and I embark upon a much-needed month long silent retreat on a horse ranch in Patagonia, while Ravi and Bhakti spend time with their father, I want you to recognize that in this, as in all things, light comes from darkness, just as darkness from light. I hope you have used my lessons and hard work to recognize what may be possible for you too. Doubtless, some of you will continue to persist in the notion that not everyone has the time or resources to pursue personal fulfillment. To which I would like to respond: 'Build the Yurt, and they will come.' Thankfully, my own Village continues to be flush with funds (thank you, speed cameras!), so I see a future in which more of our community needs can be met. On that note, I invite you to attend the next session of "The Blessings of a Blissful Life for All," sponsored in the Village Yurt this fall. Details to follow in my next newsletter, hopefully written from the Tibetan monastery where I began my Journey, and where I plan to spend August with my children and staff.

Till then,
Vira

Sunday, July 14

From: phoebegb@channel8news.com
To: crystalmomof4exlaw@yahoo.com
How can I ever thank you, dear C?

My party was AMAZING, from the New Orleans' marching band to the wake complete with gospel choir. I knew you had invited Hilary, but I was genuinely touched to see Pookie, Perky, Bitsy and Vira all looking FABULOUS dressed as black widows. Just for the record, I could have done without the large banner you had printed and positioned outside the entrance to the Village Yurt, announcing my age in bold letters, as I may have given Pookie and Bitsy the impression that I was younger than them sometime in the past. I daresay they will have relished learning that I am the first of our Village posse to cross over to the dark side. No real harm done, except that I hope the station doesn't find out.

As I retired to bed a little early with a bout of food poisoning, I'm counting on you for some good gossip!

Phoebe Thompson
News Anchor
Channel 8 News
Relentlessly Local, round the clock

From: crystalmomof4exlaw@yahoo.com
To: phoebegb@channel8news.com

I'm so glad you enjoyed the party, in spite of getting sick. Rest assured, I disabused Pookie et al of the notion that you might have over-indulged at the Pisco Sour Fountain, and that it was a rogue shrimp that laid you low, but who cares what they think, anyway?

In the meantime, did I mention that I caught Vira and Frank Manly making out like a couple of teenagers outside the Village Yurt?

PTA PRESIDENT, Village Public School

From: phoebegb@channel8news.com
To: crystalmomof4exlaw@yahoo.com

Yikes. Did Evelyn see? I know the woman lives on a higher plane, but even she must want to keep her eagle eyes on that husband of hers whenever Vira is around. What woman could be expected to resist a guy who's so handy with his tools?

Phoebe Thompson
News Anchor
Channel 8 News
Relentlessly Local, round the clock

From: crystalmomof4exlaw@yahoo.com
To: phoebegb@channel8news.com

There's a reason why Evelyn wasn't looking, and that's basically because she couldn't take her eyes off Hilary! I happened to see the two of them engaged in deep discussion all night, to the point where they completely ignored Pookie, Bitsy and basically everyone else's attempts to suck up to them. Based on what little snippets I managed to overhear, I think we have just witnessed the start of a beautiful friendship.

PTA PRESIDENT, Village Public School

From: phoebegb@channel8news.com
To: crystalmomof4exlaw@yahoo.com

But what about Evelyn and Frank's marriage? Are you telling me it was a sham?

Phoebe Thompson
News Anchor
Channel 8 News
Relentlessly Local, round the clock

From: crystalmomof4exlaw@yahoo.com
To: phoebegb@channel8news.com

I overheard Evelyn saying to Vira that she and Frank had a purely working relationship, based on an agreement whereby they pretended to be married to her so she wouldn't have to admit she was a lesbian. In return, Frank got to potter round the house while she made the money to support them. Evelyn apparently thought no-one would accept parenting advice from a childless lesbian, but now she feels times have changed, and who knows, she and Hilary might even choose to have some.

PTA PRESIDENT, Village Public School

From: phoebegb@channel8news.com
To: crystalmomof4exlaw@yahoo.com
Wow. Perhaps the fact that we complain endlessly about our husbands is actually a sign that we still care? It's a sobering thought, but no time to discuss now, as Brad, twins and I are about to hop on a plane to the Vineyard for the next two weeks. Perky's husband just got arrested for tax evasion, so we were able to rent her beach house at a knockdown price!

Phoebe Thompson
News Anchor
Channel 8 News
Relentlessly Local, round the clock

From: crystalmomof4exlaw@yahoo.com
To: phoebegb@channel8news.com
That explains all the kerfuffle with the taxi and your twelve suitcases just now.

Before you go, did I mention the rumor currently flying around the Village about Evelyn's latest parenting tome, which comes out next week? The entire Village is atwitter (literally) with speculation about whose offspring are included and why. I'm sure the twins will come off just fine, particularly since winning most improved award at VPS. Brad really does seem to have a knack for parenting through benign neglect. Dare I say it's in keeping with your movement to parent in the slow lane. You can assume my cherubs, on the other hand, will be held up as examples of the kind of offspring who should be rounded up by the Child Catcher in Chitty Chitty Bang Bang – particularly after Evelyn caught Karson peeing against her new cherry tree the other day. The fact that it's never looked healthier as a result is obviously beside the point.

What have you decided to do about work now that Brad seems to be doing so well?

PTA PRESIDENT, Village Public School

From: phoebegb@channel8news.com
To: crystalmomof4exlaw@yahoo.com
I've decided I will not be quitting the anchor job, no matter what happens with Brad's various ventures. Strange to think I was so adamantly against being a working mother when we first met, while you were so much the career woman, and lo and behold, less than a year later, our positions are completely reversed!

One other bit of good news: Production Assistant has left the news channel! Seems station manager's wife found a piece of bubble gum under the station manager's toupee. One glance at her blowing and snapping away in the newsroom the other day, and she was history.

Any chance Helen Wheels might be available to replace?

Phoebe Thompson
News Anchor
Channel 8 News
Relentlessly Local, round the clock

From: crystalmomof4exlaw@yahoo.com
To: phoebegb@channel8news.com

I will ask. For my part, not sure how I ever practiced law here, between chauffeuring the cherubs between summer camp, baseball and now tennis with Xavier at the Village Club. I used to think having a powerful career would force George to share equally on the home front and protect me from potential financial catastrophe if the marriage didn't work out. I've since realized, however, that for our marriage, at least, a team approach is a far more realistic perspective if we hope to have any semblance of a family life beyond children who long for more screen time. So for now, my commitment to teach Steamy Yoga's patented brand of yoga touching at the Club twice a week will be more than enough to keep me occupied, although I can't say it pays anything like my usual hourly rate as a lawyer.

Needless to say, I'm not happy about my economic dependence, but trust that a good education will at least, keep me ready to re-enter the paid work force when and if the need should arise. Of course, I'm fully prepared to make taking every dime from George my full-time career, if he ever decides to leave us.

BTW, the Home for Aging and Retired Yogis mentioned that I did such a great job at raising money for them at your party, that they would like me to chair their annual auction. Beginning to understand now why I may never have paid work again and yet still somehow manage a full-time career - as a volunteer. There may even be a day in the not too distant future when such necessary unpaid duties get the respect they deserve. Remind me to mention this initiative to the Prez's lovely wife when George and I have dinner at the White House next week. She seems like a gal who will understand.

P.S. Glad Lata is back in the bosom of your family, where she belongs. I've decided to try another au pair beginning next month, because I really do want to try and balance my various work/life/volunteer obligations without taking it out on George and the cherubs. I'm insisting the next au pair hail from a less privileged native land than Germany, so that he/she hopefully won't view her entire stay with us as a vacation tour of DC with the children as minor annoyances in her day.

PTA PRESIDENT, Village Public School

From: phoebegb@channel8news.com
To: crystalmomof4exlaw@yahoo.com

Can't tell you how thrilled I am to have Lata back, although she is threatening to brew up a special new elixir to treat me for the lingering effects of my food poisoning.

Determined to get back in shape after I get back from the Vineyard on Sunday. So sad to think Gunther may never teach again, although I suspect it's the touching that his students (and he) will miss most. I've heard Daphne is opening DC's first fitness spa, complete with Ballet Butt classes and a hot beeswax treatment room next week. Care to check it out?

Phoebe Thompson
News Anchor
Channel 8 News
Relentlessly Local, round the clock

From: crystalmomof4exlaw@yahoo.com
To: phoebegb@channel8news.com
I notice they have a 6am class on Mondays. See you there?

PTA PRESIDENT, Village Public School

From: phoebegb@channel8news.com
To: crystalmomof4exlaw@yahoo.com
See you there.

Phoebe Thompson
News Anchor
Channel 8 News
Relentlessly Local, round the clock

Wednesday, July 31

More ▾ | Next Blog»

DC Diary

The Walkers Take on the Nation's Capital

Phoebe's 3rd, New Neighbors, New Au Pair

It's been a (thankfully) quiet month for the Walker family, with the cherubs out of school, and George and I adjusting to a life of him working less, now that he's been bought out of Plunder & Hagg, and me working more, as a fully qualified yoga teacher at the Village Country Club, where we recently became members.

I am, however, thrilled to tell you that my dear British friend, Phoebe, is expecting her third child. Although I do recall a bit of judgment about the size of our family after our initial landing in our sweet Village, she now fully embraces her role as godmother to Kurtis (with reciprocal obligations forthcoming for her third, I hope!).

Who knew that George and Brad would also become kindred spirits? Between V-Box and the big V, they've become virtually inseparable, in spite of having little in common on the surface. A man who can barely stand to be undressed befriends a man who can barely bother to get dressed? Wonders never cease. But wait, who is the cute new guy with the three day stubble ringing my doorbell?

Turns out, his name is Jeff, and he just bought Miss Gertrude's house down the street. He and his equally adorable strawberry blond wife appear to have only one child, a rising kindergartener at VPS. According to Jeff, he's just negotiated the right to work from home with his parent company in Canada, and is excited about the prospect of entertaining his daughter every day from 1-6, while his wife pursues her career at Fannie Mayn't. Can't wait to find out how that works out for them. Taking a plate of Kimberly's home-baked brownies to them as soon as they come out of the oven.

Our new neighbor Jeff

Before I sign-off, I wanted to let my friends in KC know that we plan to welcome a new au pair this fall. We've Skyped with the lovely young woman from Estonia, and she seems eager to join our family. Some of you guys in the midwest might find it amazing that our family would still require so much paid help, since neither George nor I are pursuing full-time employment, but my yoga classes and volunteer activities are proving more demanding than I could ever have imagined. And George, while certainly independent much of the time, is somehow never available when I actually need him. Really, we're both just doing our best to give the cherubs what they need, while not forgetting that as parents, we have lives too.

Our new Au Pair, Tuuli

Don't forget to visit! Just heard what sounds suspiciously like my best lamp in the living room shattering, and Kurtis waking up in her crib. Wonder if I can steal a few moments first to practice Stinging Scorpion, Hidden Vertebrae pose?

No comments:

Post a Comment

DC Diary
Phoebe's 3rd, New Neighbors, New Au Pair

It's been a (thankfully) quiet month for the Walker family, with the cherubs out of school, and George and I adjusting to a life of him working less, now that he's been bought out of Plunder & Hogg, and me working more, as a fully qualified yoga teacher at the Village Country Club, where we recently became members. I am, however, thrilled to tell you that my dear British friend, Phoebe, is expecting her third child. Although I do recall a bit of judgment about the size of our family after our initial landing in our sweet Village, she now fully embraces her role as godmother to Kurtis (with reciprocal obligations forthcoming for her third, I hope!).

Who knew that George and Brad would also become kindred spirits? Between V-Box and the big V, they've become virtually inseparable, in spite of having little in common on the surface. A man who can barely stand to be undressed befriends a man who can barely bother to get dressed? Wonders never cease. But wait, who is the cute new guy with the three day stubble ringing my doorbell?

Turns out, his name is Jeff, and he just bought Miss Gertrude's house down the street. He and his equally adorable strawberry blond wife appear to have only one child, a rising kindergartner at VPS. According to Jeff, he's just negotiated the right to work from home with his parent company in Canada, and is excited about the prospect of entertaining his daughter every day from 1-6, while his wife pursues her career at Fannie Mayn't. Can't wait to find out how that works out for them. Taking a plate of Kimberly's home-baked brownies to them as soon as they come out of the oven.

Before I sign-off, I wanted to let my friends in KC know that we plan to welcome a new au pair this fall. We've Skyped with the lovely young woman from Estonia, and she seems eager to join our family. Some of you guys in the midwest might find it amazing that our family would still require so much paid help, since neither George nor I are pursuing full-time employment, but my yoga classes and volunteer activities are proving more demanding than I could ever have imagined. And George, while certainly underfoot much of the time, is somehow never available when I actually need him. Really, we're both just doing our best to give the cherubs what they need, while not forgetting that as parents, we have lives too.

Don't forget to visit! Just heard what sounds suspiciously like my best lamp in the living room shattering, and Kurtis waking up in her crib. Wonder if I can steal a few moments first to practice Stinging Scorpion, Hidden Vertebrae pose?

The End.

www.ingramcontent.com/pod-product-compliance
Lightning Source LLC
Chambersburg PA
CBHW071244250626
47163CB00002B/316